Awake

Gladys Hobson

Awakening Love

Gladys Hobson

Cover picture © Steven Hunziker
www.stevehunziker.com

ISBN 978-0-9548885-6-5
First Published Sept. 2007
Magpies Nest Publishing
awakening@magpiesnestpublishing.co.uk

Books for sale online at
www.magpiesnestpublishing.co.uk

To Diane

Note from the author

When I was young there were no such things as mobile phones or electronic games. We had few toys and life was full of simple pleasures. My friend, Brenda, lived across the road behind a high brick wall. She lived in a huge house, or so it seemed compared with our three-bedroom semi. At one time, the house was owned by people who had servants – the bell system was still in place. The huge garden once had a tennis court, pavilion, greenhouse, potting shed, root store, fruit and vegetable plots, flower borders, an orchard, and even a toilet tucked away in a corner. There was a courtyard, washhouse, tool shed, and a stable-carriage house with loft. The front garden was rich with mature trees. Like so many things, the house has gone and the whole area converted to flats. The factories where I worked as a designer are no more. Nottingham's industrial base seems to have given way to student and business accommodation: textile factories have become expensive apartments.

The setting of this novel is the Nottingham area as I knew it. The factory scenes and 'primitive' washday at the Armstrong's are authentic, as is much of the background to this story. Certain things were still on ration, coal was in short supply and petrol on coupons. My friend's home, although far from the luxury of Bloomfield, inspired part of the background, and certain activities at that house – dancing with my friend, sewing to earn money, making a ballet dress, playing tennis, and being kissed passionately by her much older brother – actually happened. A few years ago, when writing my illustrated book of childhood memories – When Phones Were Immobile and Lived in

Red Boxes – I recalled these happenings and pondered on 'What if?' My imagination took wings. My friend and her family became socially superior, and instead of my innocent secret kissing sessions petering out, they turned into a full-blown passionate love affair. Likewise, although I entered a factory to train in dress designing, there certainly was no sexy entrepreneur to assist me up a ladder of success! So it is true to say that all characters and events in this novel are purely fictitious and bear no resemblance to persons living or dead.

Prologue

Summer, 1949

'Oh, come on, June, give me a chance to prove we're a perfect team. You don't need anyone else for sex. Believe me, it doesn't come any better.'

She struggled to free herself. 'Let me go at once! I'm going home. You've no right to stop me.'

He gripped her arms and captivated her with his smouldering eyes. 'You're *nothing* without me. I've made you as a designer, now let me show you what else I can do for you.' He bent his head to kiss her again.

She turned her face away. 'No, Rob. Let me go!'

Still holding on to her arms, he pushed her a little way from him. A lecherous look crept over his face. His deep dimples became rugged clefts and his dark eyes glittered under their heavy brows. His smile twisted with lustful intent. When he spoke, his voice was deep and seductive. There was no mistaking the true meaning of his words: 'We have business to finish first.'

Excited by his compelling sexuality but fearful of what he might do, her heart raced inside her breast. 'I've had enough of your business for today.' Her voice quivered uncontrollably.

'We haven't done anything… yet!'

She was terrified by her inability to control the situation. 'Let me go! Let me go!'

But he pulled her to the carpeted floor and pinned her down.

'Come on, just relax,' he said calmly, as though talking to an overwrought child.

'Get off me! Get off!'

She pushed and thumped but knew she was powerless to move him. Under his weight, struggling was quite useless; she was just burning up energy. She waited for him to make a move so she could act: kick, scratch, knee him in the groin.

'Okay, you win,' he said suddenly, lifting himself up and turning away.

She closed her eyes and breathed a sigh of relief. But when she moved to get up she saw his belt unbuckled and his fly flapping open. He'd tricked her!

Quickly pinning her down again, he murmured softly, 'Don't struggle. Do you want me to hurt you?'

Fear gripped her heart. 'No! No! No! Don't touch me! Let me go!'

She continued to struggle, but he was too strong for her. While kissing her with lips wet with passion, his hand went up her skirt.

She pulled her lips away from his. 'Oh, please, Rob, don't do it. I don't want you to. I really don't.' Her whole body shook with fear.

'See, my sweetie, you're trembling for it. You want me just as much as I want you. Admit it. I know the signs. Playing hard to get turns you on. Okay, let's do it your way.'

He tore at the bodice of her dress, stripping off the buttons. He pulled the widened neck over her shoulders, trapping her arms and exposing her breasts. She was powerless to stop his wet mouth moving sensuously over her peaked nipples. Her body was on fire and she was filled with a potent mixture of dread and guilt. Dread of what was going to happen, and guilt because part of her wanted, desperately, to experience his torrid lovemaking.

Her juices were flowing. Soon, very soon, he would discover it for himself and play on it. He must not get that far. She renewed her efforts to free herself, screaming again and again. But Rob merely increased the fervour of his love-play.

'Leave me alone! You can't do this to me!' she yelled. 'I'm Arthur's. He'll *kill* you!'

'Stop struggling and enjoy it. We both know what you want all right. Old Arthur's no match for a real man. You won't want him near you after this.'

'Please, Rob. Please. Please. Oh, please don't–'

He kissed her mouth and silenced her.

Chapter One

Late summer, 1947

In a state of euphoric excitement, June slipped the veil of a dress over her bare shoulders and watched the white mist float about her. In triumph she pulled up the zip – perfect! Pleased with herself, she looked in the mirror and liked what she saw. True, the net skirt was a little skimpy, and the lace top barely covered her breasts, but she'd used up every inch of the scrap material she'd been given so it would have to do. And it would do nicely – very nicely indeed. Humming a ballet tune, she went up on her toes and did a few twirls.

'Lovely, lovely, lovely!' she squealed joyfully.

'It is indeed,' said a familiar rich voice from the doorway. 'You're a clever young lady.'

'Arthur!'

She was surprised to see him; apart from Mrs Craven, the domestic, she'd thought she was alone in the house. She felt horribly embarrassed. How long had he been standing there?

'I'm sorry, I know I shouldn't be in here but I wanted to look in the mirror,' she explained. 'I'd better go. I'm sorry. Really, really sorry. I should have asked.'

'It's quite all right, June. Carry on, I only came for a book I left in here.' His eyes were scanning her body appreciatively. 'Is that for the concert you're doing with Clare? It's very pretty.'

His approval pleased her. 'Yes, the *Swan Lake* bit. Do you really like it?'

'Yes, I really do,' he answered, picking up a heavy leather-bound book from the table and hurrying to the door.

She saw his jacket catch on the doorknob, tearing off a button. The book fell to the floor, its pages splayed. He picked up the weighty tome and examined the damage.

'Bloody hell!' He muttered under his breath, then looked towards her and quickly apologised. 'Sorry, bad habit. Please forgive me.'

'It's okay – you should hear my dad swear. He was a sergeant in the army. Oops!' She put a hand to her mouth. 'I'm sorry, I forgot; you were in the army too, Major Rogers.' She wanted to say something nice to cover up her blunder. 'Clare says you've got lots of medals.'

'A few maybe, but so have many others. Some didn't live to collect them.' He sounded bitter. Clutching his book, he picked up the button from his jacket and turned to leave. 'Enjoy your concert.'

She had seen the pain etched into his face, and felt guilty at stirring up tragic wartime memories. She wanted to make things better.

'If you give me your jacket, I'll soon stitch the button back on, Major Rogers.'

He smiled, turning the lines of pain into expressions of pleasure. 'Arthur will do, June. I'm not in the army now.' He took off his coat and gave it to her. 'Oh dear, looks as if the material has torn away.'

In a house full of highly-educated people, it made her feel good to be able to do something they couldn't. 'Give me your button. I'll soon mend the tear,' she said with childlike enthusiasm. 'I'm good at sewing.'

She felt his penetrating look as his eyes took in the ballet dress she was wearing.

He cleared his throat. 'I can see that. Well, I'd better leave you to it. Thanks, I'll come back for the jacket later.'

Book under arm, he quickly left the room, keeping well clear of the door.

She watched him go and then examined the jacket. It was going to need a bit of invisible sewing. Humming to herself, she set to work, enjoying the challenge. Her thoughts were on Arthur, and her mind went back to their first meeting. She relived the surprise of seeing him a few days after he had come home from the war and finding out who he was.

'Gosh, he looks old enough to be your dad,' she had remarked to her friend Clare, the major's younger sister.

'Well, Arthur is the eldest. He's twenty years older than I am. Anyway, you wouldn't look so young yourself if you'd been through what he has. He was lucky to be badly injured – most of his men were killed. You should see all his medals. Arthur's a war hero, you know.'

Arthur was quite unlike his tall, handsome, dark-haired younger brothers. His fair hair was tinged with grey and his face bore the lines of experience. He was five feet nine inches tall and his body seemed to be too thin for his broad shoulders. He may have looked more like Trevor Howard than her heartthrob Gregory Peck, but when he looked at her, his brilliant blue eyes fascinated her and made her feel all funny inside.

June brought her mind back to the present, imagining Arthur sitting alone by the fire with his book, the morning sunlight streaming through the windows tinting his hair with gold. He seemed to enjoy his own company away from the others.

She looked around her. The large room was furnished with rich mahogany furniture: intricately-carved sideboard, dining table to seat twelve, heavy but elegant cushioned chairs, a long serving table, magnificent display cabinet and a huge heavy mirror over the mantelpiece. Comfortable maroon leather armchairs were placed either side of the marble fireplace, the grate of which glowed with the remnants of a log fire. A thick, deep-blue carpet covered the floor and rich blue-and-silver brocade curtains hung each side of the two tall windows that overlooked the gardens. Awesome mouldings, just like the ones in the town's old library, framed and patterned the ceiling. It was the same richness all over the house, and so unlike her own home. Colonel and Mrs Rogers certainly wouldn't have any of their utility matchwood in their exquisite Bloomfield – not unless it was chopped up for firewood! Well, one day she would make it to the top and have nice things too – and she would get there through her own efforts.

Thinking about the day when she would be a celebrated designer with lovely clothes to wear and a beautiful home to live in, the time seemed to pass by quickly. She looked at her finished work. The tear was now quite invisible and the button stitched on to perfection.

'Good,' she muttered to herself, and was about to get changed when she decided to try out a few ballet steps to music. Colonel Rogers wasn't due back for ages, and Mrs Rogers wouldn't mind her playing her own record on their posh radiogram – too bad if she did! She giggled at her audacity, and went into the big front lounge with her *Swan Lake* record.

Sitting in his bedroom trying to read, Arthur was in a bit of a sweat. He'd entered the room just as the dress was veiling June's semi-naked body, and he'd been caught off guard by the vision of loveliness before his eyes. For some inexplicable reason he, Major Arthur Rogers, the mature, self-possessed, recently retired war veteran, was embarrassed by his aroused sexual feelings. It was quite ridiculous! The girl must only be sixteen – twenty years his junior and far too young for him to be experiencing such erotic feelings. And yet he'd had to make a hurried exit before he made a fool of himself. It shouldn't happen, and yet his body cried out to hold her, kiss her, and…. But he refused to acknowledge the full extent of his desires.

As he sat in his room trying to read his book, a year-old memory of the first time she had taken him by surprise flooded his mind. He was home on leave – yes, that was it, just before leaving the army. She had turned up at the house damp from the rain and was looking as sweet and fresh as a rosebud sparkling with dew. Her rich brown hair was twisting in damp curls and her pretty hazel eyes were shining with the vitality of youth. When she spoke, her voice was soft and innocent: completely different from the girls he'd met during the war.

He'd seen her around the house occasionally, but rarely to speak to. He knew she did a little mending and dressmaking for his mother, as well as making dance outfits for Clare. She was bright and cheerful and her girlish prettiness was always appealing, but he'd never been more distracted than by what he had just witnessed. What a sight! The skirt failed to hide those shapely thighs, the flimsy lace revealed her firm, rounded breasts, and her shoulders were completely bare and inviting. Her dark hair flowed over her face when she bent over, partly shrouding her deep cleavage – incredibly provocative. Had she any idea what she did to him?

There was no doubt about it: he was intrigued by that exquisite innocence that seemed to shroud her in an aura of sanctity. But beneath her outward timidity, did he detect a longing to experience something more? To explore her growing sexuality? He reproved himself; she was a mere child. To even ponder her sexuality was a violation of her girlhood virtue.

Finding it impossible to relax, he deliberately turned his mind back to the war years. Controlling one's emotions had been vital when courage and endurance were needed. He thought of his comrades and what they had all been through together: North Africa and the battles fought in desert heat, then Sicily, Italy, and finally the struggles within Europe for the hard-fought victory. So many lives lost; so much anguish and pain. Incredible suffering that did not distinguish between friend or foe, adult or child. And finally, the discovery of the death camps that made him fully realise what it was all about.

And then there was afterwards... coming home to find his fiancée had left him for a rich American colonel. The loss of his Barbara was a cruel blow. Would he ever trust a girl again? Certainly not an experienced gold-digging society woman: he wanted an innocent girl to love him for himself alone.

Through his open door, sounds of music drifted up from the ground floor. All the family were out, and he'd been surprised to find June in the dining room. Annie Craven certainly wouldn't be playing music in the main part of the house; she was busy in the kitchen anyway. Intrigued, he went down to see if June was having a little dancing practise.

He followed the sound to the lounge. Through the crack in the slightly open door he watched June moving in time to the music. How delightful! Her movements were graceful, and her body so lithe and beautiful. He pulled himself away reluctantly and went to the dining room to see if his jacket had been mended. It had; she'd done a fantastic job and he wanted to tell her so.

The music stopped and he heard a patter of feet. Flushed and happy, she arrived in the dining room carrying her record. She stopped abruptly when she saw him. She was obviously apprehensive.

'You didn't mind me playing my record, did you, Arthur?'

'Of course not.' There was a second or two of awkward silence, then he continued, 'I've seen your handiwork – the jacket, that is. An excellent job; you must let me pay you.'

'No, please, I wanted to do it for you. The button won't come off again.' She laughed a little nervously and dropped her eyes. 'If it does, I'll buy you a new jacket.'

He smiled at the thought of it. She had no idea of the cost of Savile Row tailoring. He took the coat from her hand. 'Thanks, but I won't hold you to it, the button might split and fall off.' On a sudden impulse, he kissed her lightly on her cheek. 'It's kind of you to do it for me. I really appreciate it.'

She lifted her head and gazed at him, her bright hazel eyes caught and held his own. 'No, not kind. It's my pleasure, Arthur,' she said softly.

Whenever she spoke his name, it connected with his inner longing for her. And now her eyes were enticing him to respond. He dropped his jacket and drew close to her, his hands on her shoulders and his lips ready to kiss. But she suddenly dropped her head and blushed deeply.

'Sorry… I'm so sorry. I've embarrassed you,' he murmured, dropping his hands to his sides and stepping back. 'I'd better go. Thanks again.'

'No, you didn't,' she said as he was about to pick up his jacket.

He hesitated. His acute sense of propriety held him back. She was just a child, for goodness sake, and he had a man's hunger for expressive love. But his body cried out for satisfaction: it had been over two years since he had kissed a woman with passion. Apparently she was willing, so why not?

He lightly touched her arms and lowered his lips to hers. But she pulled away and ran giggling towards the door. Was she playing games? No, surely she was just nervous. He pursued her like a lovesick youth and trapped her against the door with his arms. Standing still with her eyes closed, she didn't try to escape her cage. Her rosy lips were full and moist, held loosely together as though inviting his kisses. He wrapped his arms lovingly around her soft, warm body. There was no resistance. Oh, what bliss!

Gently but firmly he pulled her closer to him, bending his head slowly until their lips met. Wonderful exquisite feelings set his body alight. He gently pressed a little harder and she seemed to melt in his arms. Oh, the wonderful, exquisite agony of being in love.

He knew he had to release her soon; she was far too enticing. But it was hard to control his carnal desires and pull away. He struggled not to touch her insensitively and ruin the moment. It was enough that her lightly-veiled body felt so delectable held close to his. His heart was beating heavily in his breast. There was no denying it; the girl had captivated his soul. He knew it was no excuse for his headstrong behaviour, but it had been so long – so very long – since he'd last held a pretty girl in his arms.

He stroked his cheek against her soft flowing hair, thinking what to say to her. Words of love? But, suddenly, boisterous laughter and jolly voices sounded from the hall. His brothers, Charles and George, must have returned from their tennis match. The spell was now broken and he felt like a love-starved fool caught out in the act. Damn it! He was old enough to know better. What was he thinking of, kissing a girl of sixteen and allowing erotic sensations to control his body? A ridiculous aberration that must not be repeated. Love? Of course not. Simple lust. How could he have thought of it as anything else? He must be mad.

'June… forgive me… I was carried away… I…'

She was looking at him, with a puzzled expression. The voices in the hall grew nearer and he quickly stepped away. 'I'd better go. Sorry, very sorry.' What else could he say?

Passing his brothers with a cursory nod, he returned to his room to gain control over his mind and body. But his passion had to spill out before he could rest. This wouldn't do; it must *not* happen again. She was still a youngster, even if his body told him she was a highly desirable woman. That indeed was the problem. After tasting the delights of sweet innocence, he knew his desire for her would not go away.

Chapter Two

June sat down, trembling with emotion. Afraid of being caught out, she picked up her needle and tried to look busy. Soon she would take her clothes to the cloakroom and change there, but for the moment she needed to calm her nerves.

Her lips were still tingling and her cheeks felt flushed. She couldn't believe that a kiss could move her so deeply. Boys had kissed her before but they had been clumsy and awkward about it, leaving her feeling that kissing was extremely overrated. But this had been altogether different; gentle but passionate. She had felt the hunger of a man's desire in the pressure of his lips. Bewildered and excited, her emotions refused to settle. What was happening to her? She couldn't understand. Was this love or just sex?

'Hello, what's up with Arthur? He came out of here like a bat out of hell!' Dressed in his tennis whites, Charles – Arthur's tall, dark and handsome younger brother – had entered the room without her noticing.

'He was looking for something. A book I think,' June said, trying to sound normal but not entirely succeeding. She glanced up and saw him looking at her rather strangely. 'I think he was in a hurry to go somewhere,' she added, feeling a need to explain Arthur's speedy departure.

'I'm not surprised,' he said, his eyes sweeping admiringly over her thinly-clad body.

Sensitive to his savouring gaze, she felt embarrassed and deeply ashamed of her appearance. It was so inappropriate to be in a flimsy ballet dress in someone else's dining room. Next thing, George would be arriving. Or maybe the Colonel!

'I have to change,' she blurted out, getting up and grabbing her dress to hold in front of her. 'I'll be late home.'

'Pity, you really brighten the old place up,' he told her, smiling appreciatively.

She felt her cheeks colouring even more. 'Thank you, Charlie,' she muttered, stuffing her bits and pieces inside her quilted sewing bag. 'I really must hurry.'

Picking up the rest of her things, she rushed out of the room to change in the cloakroom. In her haste, she almost ran headlong into George, the Colonel's youngest son and a teenage version of Charles.

He stopped in his tracks to look at her. 'I say, you look pretty.'

She dashed by him, keeping her head down. 'Thanks, George. Can't stop,' she said, quickly closing the cloakroom door behind her.

Her heart was beating furiously, her mind was in a daze, and the whole of her flesh seemed to be sensitised. She caught sight of herself in the ornate mirror over the Victorian washbasin. Yes, she did look pretty. The deep pink of her flushed cheeks helped, but her eyes were shining brightly too. Heavens! Her family was bound to notice her face and her shakes. But she had to get out of the house before the rest of the family still living at Bloomfield – Clare, Kate, Colonel and Mrs Rogers – arrived home. Quickly changing, she rolled up her ballet dress and stuffed it into her bag, the white net frothing out like a large dose of liver salts in warm water. She waited until it was quiet in the hall and swiftly made her exit.

She took a shortcut through the courtyard, vegetable patch, orchard and the back garden, avoiding the tennis court where George and a friend were now hitting balls around. When she reached the door in the high wall, her heart sank – it was locked. Butterflies were now fluttering within her. She dodged back again and left by the front drive, breathing a sigh of relief when she finally reached the lane.

Arriving at her end-of-terrace home with its patch of garden, she crept quietly up the stairs to her small bedroom. She dropped her things on a bed already scattered with costumes and pieces of fabric, then cleared a space, sat down and took a deep breath. As she often did after visiting Bloomfield, she looked at her cheap old dressing table cluttered with sewing bits and bobs, her wardrobe with a door that wouldn't close, and the cardboard boxes pushed into corners that overflowed with an assortment of her little treasures. She sighed; one day she would live in a house that had space and modern comforts. But today she had better things to dream about, her emotions were still very much alive and she wanted to hold on to her luscious feelings.

Hearing voices downstairs, she made her way to the bathroom. It was the only place she could hide from her prying brothers and sisters. She locked the door and turned on the taps of the old, rusting bath. But her mother had obviously heard her running the water.

'If you're 'avin' a bath, my girl, don't use all the water,' she yelled up the stairs, 'your dad wants one later.'

June was now in a world where everything was predictable. She closed her eyes to the mean surroundings: dark green and cream painted walls, cracking linoleum, chipped washbasin, and the toilet with its newly-painted seat that stuck to your bottom if you sat on it too long. She lay in the warm water and thought over what had happened. Major Arthur Rogers had kissed her! It had been just like a movie. He'd looked at her with those piercing blue eyes, and butterflies had danced in her tummy. She'd wanted him to kiss her, but she didn't want him to think she was a tart. Men didn't respect girls who were too willing. But he'd come after her when she'd run away… so maybe it was all right to let him kiss her.

A thrill ran through her body as she relived that kiss over and over and over again. His lips had touched hers ever so gently… mm, yes, quite heavenly, really. Then he'd pressed harder and longer as though he couldn't help himself. Maybe he couldn't. His heart was thumping, thumping, thumping close to her own. She'd felt it. Did he love her?

She thought her way through a great variety of scenarios of what might happen next. No use telling herself that she was being stupid. He had kissed her. Surely that meant something? After all, he was an officer and a gentleman. Well, maybe he kissed lots of girls – but then again, maybe he didn't. She sighed deeply and went on with her dreaming.

From the hall, her mother's voice called out loud and strong, 'Get out of that bathroom, the rest of us need to use it.'

Reluctantly, June pulled herself up and out of the water. As she dried herself, she noticed that her nipples were unusually firm. She looked down at herself. Her breasts seemed to be getting so big. Embarrassed at her own womanhood, she pressed them down, trying to make them look smaller. As her hands came in contact with them, a slight pleasurable sensation ran through her body.

She felt confused, and a flush of shame attacked her face; nice girls and boys did not touch certain parts of their bodies. She'd been touched by dirty old men in crowds and in the cinema, and her mother had been furious when she'd told her about it.

'Don't let it happen again. I don't want folk callin' a daughter of mine a tart.'

It continued to happen, but she thought it must be her fault they were being dirty, so she didn't tell her mother. Now here she was, proving it by touching herself. It was only accidental but…

Her mother called again, this time telling her to come down and help with the ironing. She quickly dried herself, dressed, left the bathroom and went downstairs, heading for the kitchen.

Flushed with guilt, she looked in the hall mirror, just visible between the many coats hanging on too few hooks, to see if it noticed. She looked closer. Horror of horrors! Little bruises dappled her lips. Before anyone could see them, she ran to her sister's room, found her lipstick and put on a thick layer to cover the tell-tale marks of passionate kissing. *That should do it,* she said to herself, and made her way to the kitchen.

She stood back as her father, dressed in his old sergeant's shirt and trousers, passed her on his way to the bathroom. He stopped and looked at her face in utter disgust.

'Take that bloody muck off your face,' he said angrily, 'or I'll take it off for you.'

'But, Dad–'

'No buts, young lady. No daughter of mine is going out looking like a tart.' He pushed his thumb roughly across her lips, smearing the lipstick all over her face. 'Now get it washed off, and come straight back to me in the kitchen for inspection.'

June knew better than to stand and argue. Trying not to cry, she ran upstairs to the bathroom to do as she'd been ordered. She used the nailbrush to scrub her lips hard, hoping to make them deep red so the blue wouldn't show. Face washed, she went back downstairs for inspection.

She knew he'd be waiting impatiently in the kitchen. She was trembling and close to tears, fearful of what would happen if he saw the bruising.

'That's better,' he began. 'What's this?' He'd seen the tell-tale blue patches. 'Dear God! I'm sorry, love. I didn't mean to be so rough. Here, let me kiss you better.'

He kissed her on the top of her head and smoothed her hair. Her nerves were so tensed up that she didn't know whether to laugh or cry.

'I'm sorry, love. If anyone else had bruised my little girl like that, I would have put the blighter in bed for a week.'

'It's all right, Dad, it really is. It doesn't hurt a bit.'

She was feeling truly guilty now, not only because she'd deceived her dad, but because she'd enjoyed Arthur's bruising kiss. She went back to her bedroom, saying she would do the ironing after some sewing she wanted to finish. She flopped on her bed, oblivious to her ballet dress and sewing bits. Was she so wicked to want Arthur to kiss her again? Would he seek her out and be romantic, like in the films? But he had apologised. Surely that meant he would do no such thing. No – it had been a mistake on his part and he'd regretted doing it. After all, he was old enough to be her father.

She rarely saw him during the following week, and when she did he only gave her the briefest of smiles. She concluded that he had just used her. Even so, her imagination carried her into secret areas of her heart where she longed to experience again the pressure of his lean body against hers, and feel him kissing with lips that held her spellbound. He'd made her feel like a woman and she would never be the same again. It was so strange that in spite of her helpless position, she had felt a curious kind of power over him. And yet he didn't seem to want her anymore. It was awesome, but terribly confusing.

Months passed by: Arthur was never around. Clare told her that he was always working, often spending the night away, so she gave up on any hope of history repeating itself. What a fool she was to have such thoughts. 'Grow up,' she told herself, 'men like Arthur don't fall for girls like me.'

On a cold winter's evening, she was sitting alone in Bloomfield's opulent, thick-carpeted lounge, sewing for Mrs Rogers and thinking how lucky she was. Compared with her boring day job, sewing was more like play. Back home, the front room had linoleum and pegged rag rugs on the floor, and there was an old mock-leather suite to sit on. What bliss to be sitting by a flickering fire, enjoying the luxury of a feather-cushioned armchair, rather than the cold comfort of home with her brothers constantly hassling her. It was such a joy to be at Bloomfield that she would gladly have worked for nothing. Perhaps it was just as well Arthur didn't want her; Mrs Rogers might have sent her packing.

Feeling sleepy, she put down her needle to rest her eyes. Voices sounded in the hall. Arthur was home! Excited, she tried to look busy with her tacking as footsteps came her way. Arthur, cold from his long drive, walked into the room and headed for the fire. As soon as he saw her sitting there, a look of delight spread across his grey, pinched face, easing out the chiselled lines and warming his cheeks to a more pinkish hue. June's heart beat faster with joy and expectation. He was pleased to see her! He did care about her after all.

'Hello, Arthur,' she said shyly.

He spoke to her softly: 'Hello, June, it's a wild old night for you to be out.'

There was nothing waiting for her at home but hot Ovaltine and a cold bedroom. 'I don't mind,' she told him. 'I want to get this finished for your mother.'

Arthur stood with his back to the fire, warming his hands and legs. She looked up and caught him smiling at her. She smiled back and then went on with her sewing, feeling a kind of contentment.

When he spoke again, it was with concern. 'I really think you should be getting home. It was snowing again when I came in. It's quite thick, you know.'

His mother arrived with a tray for him. She put it down on a small table.

'Have a hot drink, Arthur, you must be frozen. There are a few sandwiches too – your favourite, Stilton with pickle.'

Mrs Rogers sat by the fire and picked up her knitting. She looked across at June. 'Don't you think you should be getting home, my dear?'

June didn't want to go. She wanted to be near Arthur. 'I'll just finish this first, Mrs Rogers.'

Arthur crouched over the fire and rubbed his arms. 'Jolly cold driving tonight. It's worse here than London way. Just as well I came home a day early.'

'I'm glad you did, Arthur. I hope your father has as much sense.' Mrs Rogers rose from her seat. 'Sit here by the fire. I'll get you some rum for your cocoa.'

June was alone again with Arthur. Excitement was tensing her nerves. She glanced up and saw him looking at her from the seat opposite. She quickly dropped her eyes.

'Nice fabric,' he said, getting up and moving towards her.

Her heart started beating even faster. 'Yes, it is rather lovely. I don't know where your mother gets it from. Friends in the trade, I suppose.' She was immediately sorry for speaking about something that was none of her business. She quickly added, 'Your mother has impeccable taste.'

'My mother can afford to have whatever taste she wants,' he answered, smiling. He sat down on a pouffe next to her. 'I haven't seen you for a while, are you well?'

She was elated that he was making conversation with her. She looked up from her tacking. 'Yes, thank you. Clare says you've been busy working.'

He was looking at her rather strangely. 'Well, that's certainly true,' he said. He frowned. 'June, I…' He seemed at a loss for words.

She didn't want the embarrassment of him making excuses. 'It's all right, Arthur. I understand.' She dropped her head and pretended to sew. 'You don't have to say anything.'

'I don't want you to think that… no, sorry, what else can you think? I'll let you get on.' He went back to his chair by the fire.

But she couldn't sew. Her mind was again pondering what had happened in the dining room three months earlier. She'd been out with Harry from the office since then. He was the chief clerk and thought a lot of himself. He'd been wanting to take her out since she was fourteen and just the tea girl, but, like all the boys, after a few dates he'd given her up and found a lass more obliging. All males were the same.

Her mind drifted to the ballet dress, the prettiest thing she had ever made for herself. One day she would make herself beautiful clothes to go out in… one day when she had money to spend on such things. She rethreaded her needle and went on sewing the dress for Mrs Rogers and dreaming her dreams. But Arthur kept popping into her consciousness. Every now and then she glanced in his direction but he was now sitting reading, apparently unconcerned at her presence.

Mrs Rogers returned with a bottle of brandy and a glass. 'It seems we are out of rum,' she told Arthur apologetically. 'Have this to go with your drink.'

June couldn't help but notice Arthur was his mother's favourite son. Perhaps it was because he went missing during the war when he was badly wounded. Or maybe she felt closer to him because he was the eldest child, and the only one to fully inherit her fair hair and facial features: clear blue eyes, straight nose, and lips that curled handsomely at the corners.

Mrs Rogers went over to the window and pulled aside a heavy, wine-coloured velvet curtain. 'We seem to have a bad snowstorm, June,' she said, turning to face her. 'You had better leave the sewing and go home before the weather gets even worse. Perhaps Arthur will take you to the end of the lane. I don't want you to have an accident.'

June's heart started to beat faster. 'Is that all right, Arthur? I'm quite happy to go by myself.'

'Arthur will be pleased to escort you,' Mrs Rogers said, speaking for her son. 'There's no one else in except Clare and Kate. I'd rather you not go home alone, I feel responsible for your safety. The pavement is being repaired halfway along the lane and it could be dangerous. You can't use the garden path, the gate will be blocked by drifting snow.'

Five minutes later, thrilled with expectation, June was waiting in the hall. Having swallowed down his warming drink, Arthur arrived, buttoned inside his heavy army coat with the collar turned up. He was smiling pleasantly. 'Ready to go?' he asked her, in his authoritative officer's voice that somehow went with the uniform.

Pulling an astrakhan hat over his hair and ears, Arthur led the way through the flurrying snow, down the tree-lined drive and into the lane beyond.

Just as they were turning the corner, June lost her balance on hidden ice formed by tyre tracks. She fell backwards. Arthur tried to catch her but lost his balance too and landed almost on top of her. Seeing the funny side of it, she giggled nervously and was pleased to find Arthur was laughing with her. He tried to get up and pull her up with him, but he slipped again and they rolled into a snowdrift. Before long, they were flicking snow at each other and laughing like children playing in a white wonderland.

Arthur stood up, dusted clumps of snow from his coat and hat, and helped her over to a sheltering nook in a wall. He carefully brushed the snow from her coat, and then removed his gloves to warm her cheeks with his hands. Lifting her chin, he bent to kiss her. She offered him her lips unreservedly. His ardent kissing aroused within her wonderful and strange feelings. When he murmured softly, 'You are adorable,' she could have wept for joy.

Eventually, he took her by the hand and led her home. Occasionally, he stopped to dust the snow from her face and woolly hat, cup her cheeks with his gentle hands and kiss her waiting lips. She was warmed by the heat of love, and didn't even notice the bitterly cold wind biting at her cheeks. For the rest of the way the snow continued to fall, giving a cloak of silent softness to hide his tender embraces. She had never felt so happy.

Away from the twinkling light of a street lamp, he held her close and whispered, 'June, my dearest, it's been wonderful; you have made me young again.' With just a brief peck on the cheek, he left her standing by her door.

'Goodnight, Arthur,' she whispered softly at his retreating figure. Without making a sound, she mouthed the words: 'Please, please, never stop wanting me.'

That night Arthur lay on his bed thinking over what had happened. He relived the thrill of warming her lips with his kisses and that brief moment on top of her body in the snow. He smiled to himself: if only that snow had been his bed. But he was instantly ashamed of his thoughts; she was far too young and vulnerable for him to allow such images to enter his mind.

But he couldn't stop his imagination working. How far could he go with a sixteen-year-old, and still remain within the bounds of decent behaviour? He realised he was being ridiculous, but in his heart he knew there could never be any other girl for him.

While the nights were dark, he would sometimes volunteer to escort June down the shadowy drive to the gate. There he would quickly, but passionately, kiss her, and with hardly a word see her down the lane. She seemed so happy and eager to be with him, if only for a short time. Surely it was better to get her alone for brief periods than to be completely starved of her presence? But his hunger for her was increasing.

One night, he walked her down the lane and wrapped his arms around her. With moonlight filtering through the trees above them, he looked at her lovely, eager face. She was flowering into a most attractive woman. He had awakened her passionate nature, and the experience had added to her radiant bloom. He knew it without doubt and didn't want to halt that progress to womanhood. She was part of his life now – part of him. He could never let her go.

Pulling her close to him, he found her lips and kissed her without restraint. He gently moved his lips over her face, kissing her eyes, her mouth and her throat. She threw her head back and sighed with the pleasure of it. His heart beat faster and his urges grew stronger.

He wanted to undo their coats and press his body hard against hers, but he resisted the urge. Restraint was agony. Had he already gone too far? He knew he was being ridiculous to carry on seeing her in such a secretive manner; his feelings were mounting and becoming more and more difficult to control. They should be walking out together, meeting people socially, enjoying theatre visits, dancing together and getting to know and love each other in everyday situations. A normal relationship couldn't possibly be built on sneaky kissing sessions. It wasn't fair on June and it was hellish agony for him.

But there was no choice but to wait until she was a little older, then he could propose marriage. She was almost seventeen. They could be engaged when she was eighteen, however much his parents might object. He'd waited years for Barbara – before the war, and when he was home on leave. They had gone no further than kissing and the lightest of petting, but their relationship, being open and shared by friends and family, was less intense. His love affair with June was between them alone and all the more powerful because of it. Apart from which, he absolutely adored her. Yes, he could – and would – wait.

Back at Bloomfield, he went upstairs to his room, changed into his pyjamas and sat on the bed. He tried to control his urges, but passion had already overtaken him. After showering, he put on a robe and walked down the stairs for an evening drink. His father came out of the games room, billiard cue in hand, and asked him to join him for a few minutes.

Putting chalk on the tip of his cue, the Colonel said casually, 'We are both army men, Arthur. I know what it's like to be without a woman for a long time, but June's much too young. Don't deny you fancy her, I've seen the way you look at her and I know what's happening. She's a pretty little thing but she's just a child; can't be seventeen yet.' He cleared his throat. 'I don't want to interfere in your life – heavens, you're an experienced officer – but I beg of you, find someone nearer your own age. This affair can only lead to unhappiness for both of you.'

'You may be right, Father, but I love her. Trust me to do the right thing.'

'Your mother has one or two lovely women lined up for you to meet. Do try and be home for her next dinner party. There's one lady in particular she would like you to get to know better.'

'That's kind of her, but I seem to remember I met Barbara at one of her special dinner parties.'

The Colonel cleared his throat more loudly. 'Shame what happened to that woman. She didn't deserve to be engaged to a son of mine. Going off with a damn Yank! You're better rid of her, Arthur – we all are.'

Keeping his emotions under firm control, Arthur left the room bidding his father, 'Goodnight, sir.'

Chapter Three

Arthur often stayed late at work with the excuse that reports had to be finished. Was he trying to avoid being alone with her, so as not to get in too deep? June would never ask him. She realised that everything had to be kept secret.

How would Colonel and Mrs Rogers react if they knew their eldest son was fond of Clare's friend, the sewing girl? Perhaps Mrs Rogers would stop giving her work to do, maybe even stop her going to the house to see Clare. No, although she longed to be with Arthur, she didn't want to drive him away by complaining. It was better to relish an occasional chat and secret kiss when he found her alone, and treasure the memories. Common sense told her to keep things open and plan her own life.

Tired of her boring clerk's job, she had decided to train for dress designing and was looking at a variety of college courses. It would mean having to study at night school to qualify for entry, but that could be fun. She knew that a future with Arthur was most unlikely, but she didn't want to end up tied to someone with no ambition, like so many of the girls she knew. Not for her a council house, masses of nappies to wash and mouths to feed, while a dissolute hubby spent every night in a pub with his mates. She wasn't interested in boys anyway; at least not the ones at work who were always trying to get her in the cupboard. They were all the same: inadequate, fumbling creeps. She was sick of their pimply faces rubbing up to hers while she was typing. No more would she have groping hands that reached for her knickers at office parties. It was all so dirty and squalid. She had tasted something far better. If she couldn't have Arthur, then she didn't want anyone else.

Despite being so busy, Arthur's thoughts often strayed to June. He was only sorry that he couldn't tell her how much he loved her. Would she hold on until she was a bit older? He prayed that she wouldn't find a serious boyfriend, yet he wanted to give her the freedom to do so.

Eventually, working late hours kept his mind too occupied to think about her during the day or to worry about what his body craved for at night. But he tried to manage an occasional brotherly chat with her about how she was getting on at work, and listen to her talk about her ambitions, of which he wholeheartedly approved. Such brief contacts were important to him, and could be enjoyed openly and without secrecy on the few occasions when he saw her around the house.

One day, he heard her singing in the morning room where she used the sewing machine. He popped his head around the door, hoping to find her alone.

'Hello, June, sewing for Mother again?'

She looked up from the sewing machine, her eyes bright and her lips curling into an eager smile.

'Yes, Arthur. Isn't it a nice colour?'

'A bit like your eyes… beautiful.'

She blushed most charmingly.

'Sewing's all right,' she told him, frowning a little, 'but I'm still determined to be a designer.'

'I'm sure you'll be anything you want to be.'

She dived into her handbag and pulled out some papers. 'I've got all the details about a night school course that will get me to college.'

He took the papers from her, thinking to himself how easy things had been for him and his brothers. What with private education and passage straight into Cambridge, their careers had been guaranteed. Whether the armed forces, Civil Service or business, his father had enough influence to get him anywhere he might choose. Of course, he had to work and show ability, but compared with the likes of June, his path was far smoother and easier to travel.

He quickly read the information and handed back the papers. 'If I can help you in any way, you will let me know won't you?'

A determined frown crossed her face as she stuffed the information back into her bag. 'Thank you, Arthur, but I can manage all right myself.' She looked up into his eyes and smiled. 'But it's really kind of you to want to help.'

He was about to pull her from her chair and kiss her when Charles came into the room. It seemed impossible to get her alone for long.

Charles grinned. 'Hello, June, you here again? I thought the sun was shining in this room. You must come more often.'

'Thank you, Charlie. Nice offer, but I have a full-time job as well.'

Knowing what his brother was like with women, Arthur didn't want to leave him alone with June.

'Come on, Charles, we'd better let June get on with her work. How about I beat you at billiards?'

'You wish!'

Just a couple of weeks later, Arthur arrived home from work to find Clare and June about to play tennis.

'Come on, Arthur, drag Charlie out and we can have a mixed doubles,' his young sister pleaded.

'Sounds great to me. I'll see what I can do.'

Charles didn't take much persuading, and within ten minutes they were both changed and running onto the court.

June was absolutely radiant. Her eyes were shining, her skin glowing, and her glossy hair bounced around her shoulders as she ran for the ball. Arthur couldn't keep his mind on the game. Her white flared shorts revealed her shapely legs and her white sleeveless blouse clung to her comely figure. His thoughts went back to when he had caught her in that white ballet dress. Would it still fit her? She was taller and slimmer now, but her breasts were fuller, pulling at the buttons of her blouse as though wanting release and freedom.

Both he and his brother were hitting the balls erratically, and far too hard for the girls to return. He didn't know what was wrong with Charles, but he knew why he couldn't concentrate. Balls were flying right over the netting and getting lost in tall bushes or the pond. He came to a decision. He gripped the handle of his racquet and hit the ball so hard that it went sailing over the high wall and into the lane beyond.

'Sorry, last ball. I'll go round and look for it,' he called out, already leaving the court.

After a while he shouted that he couldn't find the ball. He heard June volunteer to help him look – he knew she would come. He pulled her to the bushes by the wall and held her trembling body close to his. He kissed her willing lips and felt the urgency of her hunger to be loved. He moved his mouth softly over her face: eyes, nose, cheeks, ears and on to her throat, using lips and tongue to pleasure her and to satisfy his own burning need.

'Ahhhh,' she sighed. 'Oh Arthur, Arthur.'

He was burning up with love for her, carnal desire urging him onwards. He pulled himself away, fearful of where things were going.

'I've missed your kisses so much,' she whispered, pressing herself against his hot, damp body.

'I know, my sweet love. I've missed you too, you have no idea how much.'

The lightness of their clothing and the closeness of their bodies did more for him than she realised. She took the initiative and kissed him with renewed passionate longing. It was sweet agony for him. Had she no idea what she was doing to him? Being so close, it should be obvious. He wanted to grip her buttocks and pull her up to him, but he knew he must do no such thing. Sweat was soaking his clothes from the heat of her close presence. It had to stop before he lost all control.

He was about to push her away when he heard Clare calling.

'Come on, Arthur, we can't wait all day. Charlie's rescued two balls from the pond.'

'Be there in a minute,' he called back.

'All right, June? Ready to go back?'

She sighed and nodded.

He picked up the ball and ran back to the garden with June following behind.

'Found it,' Arthur shouted as he reached the lawn, sweaty and dishevelled.

Charles looked at him and grinned. 'I wonder what else you found behind the wall?'

'Tangled undergrowth,' was all that Arthur volunteered.

The summer was soon over but Arthur now made sure he saw June a little more often, usually when she was sewing and most of the family were out. But it wasn't easy. He would feign a headache or pressure of work as an excuse not to play golf with his father or go swimming with his brothers. When he did manage to get her alone, they would talk a little and indulge in nothing more than gentle kissing. He was determined to keep control of his powerful libido.

He was putting even more time into his job. The concentration and energy required kept his mind off June and released some of his inner tensions. His military experience was a vital asset to a firm with government contracts, and his valuable skills, including languages, were now earning him promotion to upper levels of management. He was in line for an important post, linking up the business with a French firm with European subsidiaries. But if he took the job it would mean living abroad for a while.

He didn't want to leave June behind, but being away for six months might be a good thing. When he returned, she would be eighteen and their relationship could come out into the open. A few trips home during that time should be enough to keep the flame of love alive. He was going to have to tell her about it soon, before she found out elsewhere, but he didn't want to worry her just yet. There was plenty of time before the event, and there was always the possibility that the project might be cancelled. Anyway, the intended merger was not yet public knowledge.

June appeared to be happy with the way things were going, especially once she started her evening classes. But how he would enjoy taking her to places of culture, and going walking, skating, swimming and dancing together. For now though, such pleasures would have to wait.

A few days before Christmas, he found her working on his mother's sewing machine in the morning room at the back of the house, and they kissed behind the screen his mother used for trying on her dresses. He had planned to tell her of his coming departure, but he hated to spoil the moment; they had so little time together. It could wait for another time.

Knowing that they would soon be parting, he longed to make love to her. Not to go all the way of course, as great as his need was, but enough to let her feel the pleasure of being adored.

He became aware that she was pressing something into his hand. It was a tiny parcel neatly wrapped in tissue paper. She held her lips up to his and he kissed her gently, savouring the pleasure of her offering. But the precious moment was violated, as so often happened, by the sounds of approaching footsteps. June quickly returned to her sewing.

Back in his room, he unwrapped the little package. Inside was a gold-plated lighter. On one side was an enamel eye, the iris of which was flecked with shades of gold. A tiny diamond added a touch of sparkling brilliance. Instantly, June's enchanting eyes were brought to mind. He looked at the little lighter and thought of all the care with which it had been chosen. For someone in her situation, it was a royal gift indeed. The next time he saw her, he would let her know just how much it pleased him.

Chapter Four

Mrs Rogers wanted her dress finished in time for Christmas, so June was round at Bloomfield the following day. It was mid-morning when she arrived and most of the family had gone to church. Charles let her in; Mrs Rogers had said he would be at home. She was pleased to see him; he was always nice to her and could be quite funny. Dressed in his soft white roll-neck jumper and slim grey slacks, he looked quite stunning, the clothes emphasising his powerful physique and handsome appearance. But the attraction was no more than that. She knew he was a 'bit of a lad' as her father had once called him, and she had no intention of adding to his tally of conquests – not that she would ever get the chance!

He followed her into the sewing room. It was hot in the room, Mrs Rogers having left the electric fire on, so after taking off her coat she pulled off her cardigan too. Charles stood behind her and began straightening the collar of her red jumper.

'Red suits you. And the white collar is a nice touch. You look quite radiant,' he said, putting his hands on her shoulders and turning her to face him.

She lowered her head shyly and pulled herself away. 'I didn't know you cared,' she said jokingly, trying to cover up her embarrassment.

She moved towards the sewing machine but Charles went after her and stood behind her chair.

'Of course I care. I care very much. Don't you like me just a little bit?' he said, teasingly.

'I like you a lot. You're handsome and quite charming. Everything a girl could want – so my sisters tell me,' she said, trying to overcome her shyness and enter into the spirit of the conversation.

'Everything a girl could want?'

She laughed. 'From what I've heard, many have wanted, and many have got!'

He grinned. 'But none have been disappointed.'

She was flattered by his attention – after all, he was the most eligible bachelor in town. But she was getting worried as to where it was leading.

'Sorry, Charlie, I have work to do. I really must get on.'

He sighed deeply. 'You have no heart.'

She smiled at his imitation of a dejected suitor. 'You'll get over it.'

'I have a Christmas present for you.'

She turned to look at him. He caught hold of her chin and held a piece of mistletoe over her head. Before she could object, he kissed her lightly on her lips. The kiss wasn't unpleasant, and it *was* Christmas after all. She barely resisted as he pulled her from her chair to kiss her more easily. But it soon became obvious that this was no longer just a friendly kiss, but one of ruttish passion: one of his hands was fondling her breast, while the other gripped an arm behind her back to prevent her from freeing herself. The more she struggled, the more fervent his kissing.

'You're too used to boys,' he teased.

It wasn't so much what he said but the way he said it that sent alarm bells ringing in her brain – his voice was lecherous. Before she could answer, his mouth was on hers again, but this time he caught her with her lips apart.

She struggled hard to free herself. A friendly kiss was one thing, but having his tongue forced into her mouth was another. It disgusted her: stale tobacco, whisky and peppermints mingled together on the rough tongue that was being rammed into her throat. She could hardly breathe and felt horribly sick. She tried to kick him, but her foot barely caught his shin.

He withdrew his tongue and, half-laughing, whispered in her ear, 'Come on, you know you want it, you little minx.'

She brought her knee up hard. 'Let me go! You–'

But she missed her target, lost her balance and toppled to the floor, bringing him down with her.

'Ah! So *this* is what you want,' he said, grinning as he stretched a leg across her body.

She began to protest, but he quickly shut her up with his mouth over hers. She kicked her legs wildly, struggling to free herself, but he merely forced her knees apart with his own, his weight rendering her helpless. Her struggles seemed to excite him and make him even more determined to have his way with her. He pushed a hand up her jumper.

'No bra? You little minx, you came ready for me.'

It was ridiculous; the bra fastening had snapped when she was putting it on that morning and her other one was in the wash. How dare he think she'd wanted him to grope her! She tried to bite him, but he was too wily.

'No knickers either? Let's find out.'

Terror seized her. 'No, Charlie, no. Let me go!'

'Come on, you know you want it.'

She was scared now. Kicking had lifted her pleated tartan skirt and cotton petticoat way up her thighs. She felt his hand moving up her leg. Tears flooded her eyes as she realised how utterly powerless she was. Charles was strong, sexually roused, and so convinced that she wanted him that her struggles only increased his passion.

'No, Charlie, I don't. I *really* don't. Please… please don't hurt me.'

He stopped what he was doing. Through her tears she saw his puzzled face, a hint of pain drawing his eyes together, knitting his brow in concern. He pulled his hand away. 'June, I'm so–'

The Colonel's authoritative voice boomed from the doorway.

'Charles! Leave the girl alone. Get out! Take a shower and sober up. Now!'

Flinching at his father's commanding voice, Charles pulled himself together and quickly stood up. He held out a hand to help her to her feet. 'I'm so sorry. I don't know what came over me.'

'Out, Charles!' thundered his father.

Utterly embarrassed at her predicament, she watched as Charles assumed a military bearing and headed to the door. He passed his tweed-suited father and then staggered towards the stairs in the hall. Suddenly realising her dishevelled appearance, she quickly straightened her clothing.

'I'm sorry, sir,' she said, hanging her head in shame.

Colonel Rogers moved to her side and put a fatherly arm around her. She felt the roughness of his suit pressed against her cheek and resented the gesture. He irritated her in more ways than one. Deep within her, she laughed hysterically at the incongruity of her thoughts.

'It's not your fault, child. But you must try to forgive Charles. Of course, his behaviour is not that of a gentleman.' He noisily cleared his throat. 'Like most things, you must put it down to the war – what he went through – that sort of thing. I know it does not excuse such shameful conduct, but...' He cleared his throat again. 'No harm has actually been done, has it?'

Shaken by her experience and trying to control her mixed emotions, June began trembling and was unable to answer him.

'Go and wash your face in the cloakroom,' he said. It was practically an order. 'Make yourself respectable and come back here. I want us to have a little talk, my dear.'

She picked up her bag and cardigan, and gratefully hurried away. As soon as she reached the cloakroom, she threw up in the toilet.

Why had Charlie done this to her? Was it her fault that men wanted her in ways that were forbidden? Sinful ways that her mother said were dirty? She was confused and ashamed. What would Arthur say if he found out? Would he think it was her fault for teasing his brother? Would he think her a tart, a tramp, a trollop?

She cleaned herself up and went back to the waiting Colonel, wanting to get it over with. She felt just as she had done when she had been summoned to the headmistress's office knowing that she was about to be caned. She had been caught kissing boys from the school next door. Miss Jones refused to believe that she had tried to stop it from happening, or that the boys had been holding her down. As far as her spinster headmistress was concerned, June must have encouraged them, because things like that did *not* happen to nice girls. *It had certainly never happened to her,* Miss Jones informed her.

Colonel Rogers was sitting waiting for her, but he stood up as she entered the room.

'June, my dear, I want you to promise me that you will say nothing to anyone about what happened this morning. I know it was not your fault, but you are a pretty little thing, and sometimes men do silly things when they are not in charge of their senses. Do you understand?'

June nodded.

'Good. Now, I know this might sound harsh, but I want you to keep away from Bloomfield for a while. Charles will be returning to the navy shortly, and Arthur will be going abroad. When they have gone, you will be free to visit Clare at any time.'

June couldn't believe what she was hearing.

The Colonel continued, 'I realise that you will be unable to sew for the family for a while, so take this Christmas bonus. You deserve it for your hard work.'

She was stunned. She looked at the envelope, and then at the Colonel. She wanted to ask questions but she was too overawed by his commanding presence. A feeling of shame swept over her once more. 'Thank you, Colonel Rogers,' she whispered.

'Good girl. We will see you again in the not too distant future.'

He helped her on with her coat and led her to the door.

'I will inform Mrs Rogers. She will find someone else to finish her dress, so don't you worry about that. Goodbye, my dear.'

Keeping her head bowed, June walked down the long drive. Horrible feelings were tearing her apart. She turned into the lane just as Arthur came round the corner. He looked at her in puzzlement and she quickly lowered her eyes. He took her arm, but she pulled it away.

'What is it, June? You look feverish. Tell me what's the matter?'

How could she tell him? He was part of the problem. She hated men: they let her down. They played with her and then humiliated her. How could she have thought Arthur that loved her? How could she have thought that Charlie liked her? How could she have thought that the Colonel was a gentleman? How long had he been standing there before he called Charlie off? Why did she let him buy her silence? It was all so *squalid!*

When she didn't answer him, Arthur pressed her to say what had upset her, refusing to let her go until he knew. But she was too upset to speak.

Then she raised her eyes to his, and saw his deep concern. Perhaps he did love her. But then why hadn't he told her he was going away? She couldn't tell him what had happened with Charlie; she was too ashamed anyway. With tears rolling down her cheeks, she murmured, 'You're leaving, aren't you? You didn't tell me. But why should you? I don't mean anything to you.'

His face twisted at the sting of her words. 'Look, June,' he said tenderly, 'I was going to tell you but I wanted it to be the right moment. There are other things I want to say too. I'm not just going off, as you seem to think. How did you find out anyway?'

She turned her head to avoid his eyes.

'Please don't turn away. Meet me after the carol service tonight. Seven o'clock, under the big yew by the churchyard path. I'll be waiting, and I'll explain everything and put things right. Will you promise to come?'

Too choked with emotion, she said nothing. She was about to walk off when Arthur pleaded with her.

'Don't just walk away. Please, my darling, see me tonight, I must talk to you.'

She felt a little thrill at the urgency in his voice. She *did* mean something to him. 'Yes, Arthur, I will come,' she whispered through her tears.

'And, June,' he said as she was turning to go, 'thanks for the gift, I'll treasure it always.'

She smiled; to treasure her gift was surely to treasure her. But as she walked home, the pleasant feeling Arthur had engendered soon faded as the memory of her ordeal crashed through her brain in flashes of Technicolor. How could Charlie have been so horrible?

When she arrived home, she went straight up the stairs to avoid seeing her family. Her mother called up to ask her why she was back so soon. She decided that the growing pain in her head was reason enough.

She tried to keep her voice steady. 'I've got a bad headache, Mam. Can't do any more sewing today. I'm going to lie down for a bit. I'll be down for dinner.'

She went to the bathroom and rinsed her face in cold water. Taking off her clothes, she flannelled herself roughly where Charlie had put his hands on her. Her flesh became bright pink, but she still didn't feel clean. She scrubbed her teeth and tongue with brush and toothpaste, but his foul kissing still lingered in her mouth.

It wasn't just Charlie who had defiled her; Colonel Rogers loomed in her consciousness like a dark spreading stain. How long had he been home? Had he heard her yelling? Had he been standing at the door enjoying watching his son do what he would enjoy doing himself if he could?

No! That was a horrible thing to think about the Colonel; he was an honourable man. But he'd seen her on the floor with her jumper pushed above her breasts, and her skirt nearly up to her knickers, with Charlie's hand about to... No! She couldn't bear to think about what might have happened, or what the Colonel had seen and heard. It was humiliating, nauseating, and it should never have happened.

But it did – it had. A terrible thought entered her mind: was it *her* fault for teasing him?

She pulled herself together. That evening she'd be seeing Arthur. Dear, dear Arthur. *He* surely loved her. He wanted to put things right. But where was he going? Would he be away for long? Why had the Colonel mentioned Arthur leaving? Did he think Arthur was being tempted like Charlie, or did he know what was going on? Her head was spinning. She had to stop herself from thinking, thinking, thinking. She combed her hair and put on a smile. Forcing herself to sing a carol, she went downstairs to set the table for dinner.

As usual, the meal was served with the family crowded around the oilcloth-covered kitchen table. June watched her family eating hungrily and talking noisily with their mouths full. Her two younger brothers were jostling each other to get more elbow space. Her two elder sisters were discussing what they were going to wear for the carol service that evening. Muttering to no one in particular, her mother, still in her pinny, was concentrating on watching a pan on the cooker; she was boiling a tongue to press for the Christmas feast. Her father suddenly slammed the table with the palm of his broad hand.

'You boys, sit still or get out! You girls, shut up! I can't hear the bloody wireless for your stupid chatter.'

When they had all finished their beef dinner, June stood up and collected the plates, putting them in the sink to be washed. She took the rice pudding out of the oven and placed it on a board in front of her mother, ready to serve.

She thought about the Rogers family, sitting dignified in their elegant dining room, talking politely whilst having their meal served to them by Mrs Craven. It was a totally different world.

During the afternoon, she helped her mother in the kitchen. The rest of the family were either out or trimming up the front room with the paper chains they'd been making for the past few weeks. Her mother, now dressed in a clean floral pinny and with her greying dark hair in curlers, was pressing the boiled tongue in a small saucepan. She'd put a tin plate on top of the meat and was tying a couple of smoothing irons on top of it to weigh it down.

'There, that should do it,' she said with a smile of satisfaction. 'Now to boil them 'ocks... or shall I roast one of them?' she muttered, placing a finger to her lips in thought. It wasn't really a question for her daughter to answer, and June knew better than to give one.

June set about shredding suet, washing dried fruit and stoning raisins. Being alone with her mother gave her the opportunity for a little chat. She wanted her mother's opinion about someone of Arthur's age being attracted to a teenager.

'Mam, someone Clare knows has a boyfriend… he's twenty years older than her, but he's ever so nice. She really likes him. Her parents don't know, and she's frightened they'll stop her seeing him if they did. What do you think?'

'That's she's a silly girl. A man that age should know better. 'E's only after one thing. She'll get 'erself pregnant and they'll 'ave to marry – that's if 'e doesn't clear off first, and leave 'er 'oldin' the baby.'

'But he seems a perfect gentleman, from what Clare says.'

'Some gentleman! There's too much 'anky-panky going on these days. It's no use blaming the war. I've 'eard that someone in Clare's school got 'erself pregnant. Now you'd think posh girls like that would know better. It'll do 'er no good. No nice boy will want to marry damaged goods – she's no better than a tart.'

June decided to say no more. Carols started to play on the wireless and her mother joined in the singing. Had her mother ever thought about Mary being a teenage mother? And how old was Joseph? She chastised herself for thinking irreverent thoughts and tried to concentrate on mincing the sweetmeats for the pies.

Chapter Five

Arthur had been truly shocked to see how much June was suffering. She looked older, weary, as though carrying all the burdens of the world. He walked up the drive thinking about what she had said. He knew she was more than just fond of him, but she seemed completely distraught. It wasn't as if he was going for good, or that he'd thrown her over for someone else. He felt her distress as a heavy emotional burden that pulled at his heartstrings. But how did she come to find out about his going away? Clearly it should have come from him, but he couldn't change things now.

When he entered the house, he caught a glimpse of Charles helping himself to a glass of whisky. He was worried about his brother. His drinking had increased lately and he seemed unsure of himself. Plainly, something was getting at him. He would soon be back on active service and it wasn't good for him to be so unsettled. He would have to try and catch him in the right mood for a brotherly chat.

The whole family attended church that evening. As soon as the service came to an end, Arthur made his way outside, leaving the others to chat. He turned towards the path and waited under the yew tree, both hands kept warm in the deep pockets of his heavy camel overcoat. One hand lovingly embraced the little lighter, his fingers feeling the smooth metal and his thumb rubbing the golden eye. Shining through the branches of the yew, patchy light from the church windows cast wavering shadows across the churchyard. He didn't expect anyone except June to come that way, as the path meandered to a small gate that led to a field. Around the corner was a toilet, so no one would question why June was turning towards the footpath.

The sound of people leaving the church began to dwindle. He could no longer hear the vicar's jovial voice saying how splendidly the children had performed and that he expected to see the adults again at the midnight Holy Communion. But the sound of a few people saying farewells, plus an urgent 'Gotta go' reached his ears, along with a hurrying of footsteps towards the toilet. Eventually, he heard June calling to her mother, 'I'll be home later, Mam,' and there she was, walking towards him, dressed as usual in her brown coat with the fur bobbles.

He wrapped an arm around her and drew her under the dark shadow of the tree. 'What is it, June? It isn't just that I'm going away, is it?'

'No,' she answered, with a slight quiver to her voice.

'Tell me then. What's the matter? Are you tired of the way we keep things secret? Do want an open relationship? You know, my darling, you're free to go out with someone younger. A boy you can take home to meet your parents, someone who'll go out with you and your young friends. Is that it? Do you want a normal youthful relationship… something I can't give you?'

'No, I only want you, Arthur,' she whispered.

He pulled her to him and pressed his face to her soft hair. 'I adore you, my darling. I want you more than anything else on earth. But you're so much younger than I am and people could make life very difficult for both of us. When you're just a bit older, the age difference won't appear so great and no one will call you unpleasant names. Do you understand what I'm saying?'

She nodded

'We've never talked about the difference in our ages, but I have thought about it a lot. I have so much experience of the world, but you've never been more than a few miles from your home. Your adult life has barely begun.'

He kissed the top of her head as she snuggled up to him.

He smiled with pleasure at her response. 'How I dread not seeing you for weeks at a time. But it has to be. I know it's difficult but please understand, your presence does things to me that I'm finding increasingly difficult to control.'

'Oh Arthur, I do understand, and I'm sorry.'

'I'm the one to be sorry,' he told her, regretting his honesty. 'I shouldn't have spoken like that. I'm not blaming you for my problem; you're just an innocent child.'

She stiffened and turned to face him. 'I may be innocent, Arthur, but I am not a child. You seem to be the only man who thinks I am.' As soon as she said the words, she bit her lip and snuggled back to him.

He was puzzled by the sharpness of her reaction. 'I'm sorry, I didn't mean to imply…' But he was at a loss to know what to say without upsetting her further.

She reached up and kissed his cheek. 'It's all right. I understand what you're saying. You've made me so happy, just to know that you love me.'

The church suddenly went dark and they were left with just the stars to brighten the churchyard. In a sudden release of passion, he kissed her hard on her lips, but quickly withdrew lest he leave her with telling bruises. 'My dearest darling,' he whispered in her ear. 'Dear God, how I love you.'

After a few minutes, his inner urges moved him to undo the buttons of both their coats. 'Trust me, my love; I just want us to come closer together, nothing more.'

She wrapped her arms around his waist beneath his coat, and pressed her face against the softness of his cashmere jumper. He held her close and nuzzled into her hair, feeling the warmth of her body deliciously close to his own.

'June, my sweetest treasure,' he murmured softly, 'I love you so very, very much.'

'Oh Arthur,' she sighed, and lifted her head for him to kiss her.

He pressed his lips against hers, moving them gently to stimulate her delicate senses as well as his own. They cuddled, and he tenderly caressed her. With little moans, she pressed herself up to him. Her instinctive response increased his lust for her. He gently pushed her away.

He held her hands. 'My darling, there are things we have to talk about,' he said, giving her a kiss on her forehead.

Her fingers tightened around his. 'What things, Arthur?'

'I'll be away on business for quite a while. It involves a fair bit of travelling on the continent; France, mostly. The new offices are being set up in Paris. I can't go into details at present.'

'Paris? How long will you be away?'

'It depends on how things go, but I'll try and get home occasionally.'

'Oh Arthur, I wish you weren't going. I'm afraid you'll... well... you know, forget me, and... well, French women... they know how to please men, don't they?'

'There may have been a few women in my life, my dearest June, but I have never been fully intimate with any of them. Do you understand me?'

'Yes, I know what you mean,' she whispered.

'I intend to remain as I am until I'm married. I have my needs – all men do – but I'll wait for you, no matter how long, just for the possibility that one day you'll be mine alone.'

'I've told you, I don't want anyone else. I love you, Arthur. Only you.'

He agonised within himself. He didn't want her to be fondled by young men trying out their sexual prowess on her beautiful body. He didn't want them to injure her warmth or make ugly those things that were intimately beautiful.

He held her to him and sighed. She was so young and vulnerable. How easy it would be to take her – at least, to have the pleasure of exploring her body and enjoying each other's intimate caresses. He knew how to set a woman on fire – he'd done so on a number of occasions – but it wasn't so easy to cool the blaze.

He wanted to leave her with something to remember him by. That thought brought to mind the wonderful gift she had given him. He put his hand in his pocket and pulled out the little lighter.

'It's beautiful,' he said softly. 'I love it. While I'm away, I will keep it with me always. Every day it will remind me of you. When I see the flame, I will feel the warmth of your love for me.'

He lit the flame, and in its warm glow he saw her eager, loving face. For a moment, her eyes reflected the little blaze and seemed to be on fire. He extinguished the flame and put the lighter back in his pocket, knowing he would see June's eyes every time he used it. He came to a decision. An idea had been going through his brain for a little while, now was the time for him to act.

'I have a present for you too, something to give you comfort while I'm away. I must see you again before I leave on Friday. When do you finish work?'

'The factory will close early on Tuesday,' she said eagerly. But then her excitement quickly faded. 'Oh, but it's Christmas Eve. I promised Mam I'd give her a hand with the baking. She's relying on me.'

'You'll be coming to Bloomfield sometime, won't you?'

She shook her head and looked away.

'I'm sure Clare said she was expecting you to join the family for tea and carols on Christmas evening. Hasn't Mother asked you over? You can meet the rest of the clan. They'll all be over, including the children. I can take you home afterwards and make an excuse to be late back... seeing a friend before I leave.'

'I can't come to Bloomfield. Please don't ask me why, I just can't.'

She seemed distressed, and it worried him deeply.

'I don't understand. Why can't you come to my home? Has someone upset you? Have you fallen out with Clare? Do your parents object?'

'I don't want to talk about it. Please don't ask me.'

Something was definitely wrong. He wanted to know what it was, but he couldn't press her and spoil their time together.

'We must find time to be alone,' he said gently. 'I'll meet you wherever you want. What do you suggest?'

'Can you meet me tomorrow? I leave work at five-thirty.'

'Of course. Tell me where you want me to wait.'

She gave him careful instructions, saying she would get there as soon as she could. 'I wish I could leave earlier, but I have a lot of work to clear up before the holiday. There would be dreadful trouble if I left before the bell.'

'Won't your parents be expecting you home?'

She pressed her face to his chest. 'I'll find an excuse to be late. I want to be with you.'

He held her close once more and kissed her tenderly. Time was getting on and they would both be missed.

Keeping to the shadows, he walked her home. At the crossroads, she was about to leave him when she stopped, delved into her pocket and took out an envelope. She pressed it into his hand.

'Your father paid me for the sewing I've done for your mother, but he gave me far too much. Please give him this.'

She ran off before he could question her.

There was a lot of activity going on at Bloomfield. Branches of red-berried holly and a variety of evergreens, paper decorations and shiny glass balls were already hanging from ceilings and walls. Christmas cards were now being displayed, and nuts, sugared almonds, petits fours and glacé fruits put out on tables, ready to be uncovered when needed. His mother intended to have a real old-fashioned Christmas, especially for the children coming from London.

Arthur was supposed to be helping with the huge tree standing in the hall stairwell. His father, balanced on a stepladder, looked down and saw him waiting to be given instructions.

'Where have you been, Arthur? We could have done with your assistance ages ago. We've had problems with the lights.'

'Sorry, I had to see a friend after the service, and then I bumped into June on her way home. She asked me to give you this envelope. She said something about you having paid her too much for some sewing.'

Arthur noticed a change come over his father's face. He came down the steps and accepted the envelope. 'Did June say anything else?'

'Should she have done?'

'No, I guess not.'

'Sir, perhaps I ought to have a chat with you before I leave on Friday.'

His father nodded. 'I would like that.' He cleared his throat. 'It's time for straight talking. Perhaps tomorrow evening before we retire for the night?'

That night, in her bedroom, June went over in her mind the warmth of Arthur's embrace. As she lay in her bed cuddling her hot-water bottle, she relived his kissing and caressing. She had felt again that strange power over him, and her body had reacted with new and wonderful feelings.

When he'd held her close to him, she had felt him tensing with lust for her. And yet, unlike Charlie, he had been so wonderfully controlled and considerate. A warm glow had swept over her in response to his sexual longing. She so wanted to give herself to him, to let him touch and caress her, and… and what? She dared not even think it. Was she wicked, and no better than a tart? Maybe, but she couldn't help herself.

Chapter Six

There she was, as sweet and lovely as ever, even after a long day working in what she described as a 'stuffy hellhole'. His step grew lighter and quicker as he walked to meet her by the gate of the ancient St Mary's church. He immediately pulled her into the shadows and kissed her tenderly.

Leaving his Rover parked at the roadside, they walked arm in arm to find a café. He asked her how her day had been.

'The office girls are planning tomorrow's lunchtime party. They're plotting to grab the managers under the mistletoe. They do it every year. I don't know why – they're a ghastly lot. I'm staying well clear of *my* boss, that's for certain. He's all hands when he's had a drink.'

She went on talking to him, her tinkling laughter brightening his sad spirit, yet making him even more aware of how much he was going to miss her. Her joyful chatter attracted a group of women nearby. One of them recognised her.

'Hey, June, where yer off to wi' yer dad?'

The women laughed and moved on, their raucous voices piercing the frosty air.

June looked at him apologetically. 'I'm sorry, Arthur. They're just jealous.'

'Forget it, I already have. Look, we'll go over the road to the Black Boy.'

The remark had come as no surprise, but it pained him just the same. He could do without reminders of their age difference.

Once they were sitting down, he ordered coffee and ham sandwiches for them both. When the waiter had gone, he slipped his hand inside his pocket and took out a small, gift-wrapped parcel. He placed it in June's hand.

'Happy Christmas, June. Open it, I want to see if you like it.'

She took off the pretty tissue paper and opened the purple velvet box. Her face lit up at the sight of a dainty locket. 'It's beautiful! I love it. Does the locket open? I can keep your picture inside.'

Arthur opened the locket for her. Inside the hollow golden heart was a magnificent jewel; she gave a cry of delight.

He held her hand and looked into her excited, sparkling eyes. 'I want you to keep the diamond fixed inside the locket until we have it set on a ring. There's no pressure,' he told her softly. 'It's yours forever, whether you marry me or not. But for now, keep the locket hidden under your dress. Promise me you'll always wear it, my dearest. I want you to remember me every time you feel that little heart next to your own.'

'Darling Arthur, how could I ever forget you?'

Her eyes were wet with tears of happiness, her face radiant. Arthur had never seen her look so happy, and his heart glowed. As soon as they had finished their meal, he intended getting her alone. Words would not be enough to express his love for her.

Holding hands, they walked to the arboretum as Arthur told her all about the coming job abroad. It was important to him that she knew something about his work; should they marry, she would be entertaining his business colleagues and their wives. He also believed that her knowing about what he did would strengthen the bond between them, drawing them closer together when they were apart.

Only a few people were in the park, mostly taking a shortcut to town. But one or two couples were taking an opportunity to do their courting in the shadows under the arboretum trees. With his arm around her, they walked silently along the paths lit up by the park lamps. Spotting a gap in the evergreen bushes at the edge of the path, he pulled her through into the deep shade of a dark yew tree. He found her lips and kissed her passionately, as if it had been years since they were last together.

Eventually, he pulled away. 'Let me put the locket around your neck. I want to see it there and keep it in my mind while I'm away.'

They moved into the light and June handed him the velvet box. She took off her woollen gloves and stuffed them into her pocket, then unbuttoned her coat and pulled back the collar. Arthur took the locket from its box, and while June held back her hair, he carefully undid the intricate fastening, put the chain around her neck, and closed the little hook securely. The locket fell down over her jumper.

'Yes, just right.' He put his arm around her and they moved back into the shadows. 'Now place it next to your heart, and keep it there always.'

'Will you put it there? I want you to do it.' She sounded a little nervous, and he knew why.

Pulling the neck of her jumper open, he let the little heart fall between her swelling breasts. Then he carefully put his hand inside her clothing to place the locket where he wanted it to be. Moving his palm over her heart, he felt its strong excited rhythm. June put her hand over his, drawing her breath in sharply and letting out a sigh of pleasure.

It was too much for him. After a few moments of blissful torment, he withdrew his hand. 'We must go now, my darling. I must get you home.'

The sky was clear and starry and frost was beginning to form, sparkling under the street lamps as they strolled back into town. June looked so wonderfully happy that he had no wish to disturb her mood, but some things needed to be said. He told her that he was seeing his father that evening.

'I want him to know about us. I know he won't approve. He'll think you're too young for me.'

Knowing his father only too well, he could also have added 'and socially inferior.' Arthur hated social distinctions, but at least his father understood sexual matters. Evidently he had had quite a reputation himself in his younger days, rather like Charles, who took after him.

'My father already suspects something is going on, I'm sure of it. But after I speak to him we can rely on him to be discreet. I'm sorry I can't speak to your father yet, but I want you to be sure of your own feelings first.'

'I know what I want. I want you, Arthur – now and always. But you're right about my dad. He doesn't even like me seeing Clare. He thinks I'll get posh ideas.' She looked at him with troubled eyes. 'Do you really have to tell your father?'

Sensing her discomfort, he stopped walking and took her by the shoulders, searching her worried face. 'Is there something you want to tell me?'

'Yes. But not now. Promise me, if your father says anything against me, you'll tell me before you go away. Please, Arthur, I must know what he says. Do you promise?'

He sighed. She was clearly anticipating trouble. Better to tell her his fears. 'I know he likes you, but he won't be pleased with what I tell him. He's bound to object for a number of reasons. I'm really sorry about that, but it won't make any difference to my intentions.'

She nodded, but said nothing. What was it that she couldn't tell him? He kissed her forehead and gave her a squeeze. 'I love you,' he said. 'Nothing can ever change that.'

As they walked to the parked car, they made arrangements to see each other again before Arthur's train left on Friday. They decided on Christmas evening. June's parents were meeting up with friends in the local for a session of Christmas cheer, and the rest of her family were having a party of their own.

'I'll slip out of Bloomfield while the adults are recovering from the children's Christmas party,' he told her. 'I'll find somewhere for us to go, even if we have to sit in the car.'

They reached the Rover, parked near to St Mary's, and Arthur opened the passenger door. June hesitated. 'Perhaps I'd better catch the bus home. Someone is bound to see me in the car, or getting out of it. I don't want folk being nosey and gossiping to my parents. I'm supposed to be working late.'

He knew she was right. He locked up the car again and walked her to within sight of the bus stop. Reluctantly he said goodnight, and kissed her on the cheek. Standing by a telephone box, he watched her board the bus, turn and give a little wave. Both joy and sadness filled his heart. His mind was rich with memories of her sweet, warm body pressed to his own as he made his way back to his car, already planning their future meetings.

Arriving home, he went to the kitchen to get himself a drink. Mrs Craven, the domestic, had been busy baking and hadn't yet gone home. She gave him a broad smile.

'Good evening, Mr Rogers,' she said, in her deferential manner.

'I keep telling you, Annie: call me Arthur.'

He received a disapproving glance from his mother as she came out of the pantry where she had been putting away cakes and pastries. He hated her snobbery, but he loved her dearly. He put an arm around her shoulders and kissed her cheek. 'How about a nice mince pie for your wayward son?'

She smiled and shook her head. 'Arthur, wayward is one thing you will never be. Sit down, I'll get you a cup of tea.'

Having drunk his tea and eaten a freshly-baked pie, he left the kitchen and went in search of his father. He found him in his study reading through the latest delivery of Christmas cards.

'Hello, sir, ready for that chat?'

'Come in, my boy and close the door, I think we should keep this private.'

Arthur sat down and faced his father. 'I want to talk to you about June,' he said.

His father cleared his throat. 'About June?' A frown creased his forehead. 'Are you *still* seeing that girl, Arthur, in spite of what I said?'

'Not only am I seeing her, I'm hoping that in a few years she'll become my wife.'

'Damn it, Arthur, you can't be serious! It's one thing to have an affair with a girl like that, but marriage is another matter entirely. She's still a child, much too young for you, and the wrong sort. How could she mix socially with people of our class? Even Clare only sees her at home.'

'What do you mean "a girl *like that*"? June is intelligent, honest and hard-working. You've said so yourself. She's fresh and innocent and wonderful to be with. She'll make me a perfect wife.' He softened the aggressive tone of his voice. 'Of course, our marriage is not yet certain. June needs time.'

The Colonel appeared to sigh with relief, much to Arthur's annoyance.

'It's up to June,' he told his father, forcefully. 'I know my own mind. We have an understanding, but we're keeping our relationship secret until I return from abroad. I don't intend for us to marry until she has more experience of life. You and Mother must get used to the idea.'

'Oh, *must* we indeed!'

'My going away will give her a bit of space. I want her to meet people outside of her workplace, and beyond her immediate environment. Her evening classes are helping there, and I hope she'll go on to the Nottingham College of Art and Crafts. She's intelligent, as well as artistic.'

'And crafty, too!' his father added bitterly.

'Exactly what do you mean by that? June is an innocent young woman. Certainly, she's ready to earn a bit of extra money, but crafty? She even sent you back quite a bit of cash. No, you just can't accept that she's good enough for your son.'

'No, Arthur, I cannot. And I never will. Apart from her being socially inferior, and far too young for someone of your age and situation, she is also the wrong sort of woman. Young and sweet as she is, she attracts men like bees to honey!'

'Sir, I think you'd better explain yourself,' said Arthur angrily, 'or I'll walk out of this house and never enter it again.'

His father shuffled awkwardly in his chair, noisily clearing his throat as he did so.

'I'm sorry, Arthur, that was unforgivable of me. What I meant was, she attracts men to her innocence. Some girls are like that. Her sweetness is tantalising and alluring. I have no doubt that she is a virgin; inexperience just oozes out of her. But that is what men find attractive. Girls like that make older men feel young and virile.'

'Including you, Father?'

The question appeared to be too near the truth for the Colonel's comfort. Arthur knew his father would never admit it, not even to himself, but he'd seen the way his eyes followed June when she was around the house.

'I suggest you retract that remark!' his father said furiously, his face going purple.

Arthur regretted his outburst; it hadn't helped the situation. 'Yes, all right, I *do* apologise. But you can't put me off June. I'm willing to wait for her to know her own mind. I don't know which way it will go, but I really do love her. Yes, she does make me feel young, and I can't deny that her lack of experience is a challenge to my male ego. I long to possess her. But I can wait. Isn't that a sign of genuine love?'

'It shows a responsible attitude, certainly, but I would expect that from you, Arthur.'

'I think perhaps we should leave it at that, don't you, Father?'

'Certainly. There is nothing more to be said.'

Arthur rose from his chair. 'I know you'll respect the need for secrecy.'

The Colonel stood up with him. 'Of course,' he said, 'as you say, there's time yet to see how things go.'

Arthur reached the door, when his father called him back.

'Do you want me to drive you to the station on Friday?'

By the time Arthur left the room, his father was in a better mood, but he knew it was going to take time for him to accept June as a future daughter-in-law.

On Christmas Eve, Arthur helped to collect the two visiting families from the railway station. He hadn't seen his brother Jack or his sister Jane for some time. Their spouses and five young children were almost strangers. The two families had travelled together from London on the early morning train, so a lot of hugging and hand-shaking was taking place.

By the time everyone arrived at Bloomfield, it was bedlam inside the house. Family members were greeting each other under the overhanging decorations, exchanging gossip and consuming coffee, sherry, lemonade and mince pies. The children were searching the Christmas tree, hoping to find little presents among the decorations. Excited whoops filled the air as small gift-wrapped objects were discovered.

Mrs Craven was taking bags and parcels to various bedrooms. Arthur picked up a pair of heavy bags and asked her where they were to go. She hesitated, but he was most insistent. She looked up at him and smiled. 'Follow me,' she said, picking up a couple of parcels. 'These go to the back rooms.'

All the bedrooms were now in use. Arthur's sister Kate had agreed that he could sleep on a camp bed in her attic flat, because Jane and her husband Frank were occupying his room. Three of the children were together in the large spare room, while Jack, his wife Rachel and young Mary had Charlie's room. Charlie had moved in with his younger brother George, and Clare had her niece, Alice, sharing her room.

Arthur helped Mrs Craven take all of the baggage to their respective rooms.

'It's very kind of you, Mr Arthur,' she told him, when the last bag had been delivered.

'Just Arthur, please, Annie. Anyway, it seems to me that you have far too much to do, especially with this lot here as well.'

'Bless you, it's no problem, Mr Arthur. Jenny's here today and she's staying the night in the servant's room. We'll both be here all day tomorrow and Boxing Day, and then it's just me for the rest of the week. I get time off later on. Mrs Rogers will be getting someone else in to help out.'

'Doesn't sound like much of a bargain to me, Annie, but it seems to suit you. I hope you manage to get a happy Christmas.'

After a visit to the bathroom, Arthur joined the family in the main dining room for a buffet lunch. They usually dined in the breakfast-dining room, except on special family occasions or if his parents were entertaining guests. But with all the family present, the extra space was definitely needed. All the main rooms had been beautifully trimmed, and with all the children in the house Arthur thought that tomorrow was going to be a truly magnificent old-fashioned Christmas. How he wished June could be there, meeting the family and joining in the singing. Once more, he wondered why she had turned down the invitation. What had happened to put her off?

He decided that Annie Craven might prove a useful ally, so during the afternoon he went in search of her. He found her preparing the sofa bed in the servants' sitting room at the back of the kitchen. Jenny would be sleeping there that night, as she always did when she was needed at breakfast time.

'Annie, I wonder if you would do something for me?'

She gave him a beaming smile. 'Mr Arthur, I'd do anything for you. Just you name it.'

'It has to be kept secret. Would that make things difficult for you?'

'What is it you want, Mr Arthur, sir?'

'Annie, forget the *sir,* just plain Arthur will do. Now, tomorrow evening, I'd like to bring a friend home with me. All quite innocent, I assure you, but I want it kept from the rest of the family. Kate will be going out after tea. As I'm staying in her flat, I'd like to bring my friend in through the back door and go up the back stairs. Could you make sure the door is open just after seven-thirty?'

'That's no problem, Mr Arthur, I'm glad to help out. But perhaps I should tell you something.' Annie's voice dropped to a whisper. 'I heard Miss Kate say that she'd be bringing *her* friend back here. Staying the evening… you understand. Would you like to use this room instead? It's quite warm, and no one else will be using it then.'

'Annie, you're a perfect angel. That will be splendid.'

She glowed with pleasure. 'I'll leave a guarded fire burning in the grate. It'll be nice and cosy for you and your friend.'

Arthur gave her shoulders a squeeze. 'You're a romantic softie.'

'And, Mr Arthur, there's a lock on the door. But you don't have to worry, no one will disturb you here. This room is regarded as my private space; even your mother never comes in here.'

In the afternoon most of the men went for a round of golf, but not Arthur; he still needed to prepare for his trip abroad. By the time he went downstairs, the house was filled with joyful sounds. The children were getting excited as presents were put under the huge tree. George was seated at the grand piano and most of the adults, including the returned golfers, were singing a jolly mix of songs and carols. Arthur imagined June there by his side. Yes, she would fit in perfectly, no matter what his father thought. He could see and hear her joining in the singing, laughing with the children, and chatting with his brothers and sisters. He decided to talk to his mother.

He went to look for her in the morning room, her favourite quiet place. The door was open and he heard her speaking to his father. He hesitated, not wanting to break up a private conversation. June's name was mentioned. Although he felt guilty of eavesdropping, he couldn't help but listen at the door.

'His infatuation with June will only end in heartache for both of them.'

'They're totally unsuited, I agree,' said his father, 'but if we don't interfere the relationship will die a natural death – bound to.'

'Do you really think so?'

'I have to admit, I tackled it badly. After all, he hasn't yet had time to settle down after the war. Coming home to find his fiancée had gone off with that damn Yank must have hit him hard. He's just infatuated with a fresh-faced chit of a girl who happened to be around at the time. It's a rebound thing, that's all. They aren't even engaged. There's plenty of time for him to see sense.'

His mother sighed deeply. 'My poor dear Arthur. So much like myself, letting his heart rule his head.'

'Well, my dear, we have all our family around us this Christmas, and that's cause for celebration.'

'Yes, all of them home and together. We are greatly blessed. We may have known the sufferings of war but we have all come through.' She sighed deeply once more. 'Dear Arthur wounded and missing for so long. Charles shattered by that terrible incident. Kate injured in that raid on London. Jack taken prisoner and shot in the leg while escaping. And poor Jane and Frank bombed out of their home. Oh Arthur, so much heartache, but we have all survived, thank God.'

'Well, Mary, tonight we'll all be thanking God together in the Christmas Communion. I'm proud of our children, but even more so of their mother.'

Through the crack in the door, Arthur saw his father embrace his mother, kissing her with considerable passion. He decided that now was not the time to disturb them.

Chapter Seven

June, along with the rest of the junior staff, was trying to work normally up to three o'clock. Since most of the office managers were taking things easy, it was proving rather difficult. The bosses didn't get back from their lunch break until after two-thirty. A strong smell of spirits filled the air as they passed by, and it was apparent from their unusually friendly demeanour that most of them were half-drunk. It wasn't long before the randier ones were kissing any girl sporty enough to hang around.

Knowing that her boss, Henry Brown, had his eye on her, June kept well clear. But he caught her just as she was leaving the ladies' toilet. His hands were all over her and his breath was foul, not just from the alcohol but with garlic and whatever else he'd been consuming.

She tried to push him away. 'Please leave me alone, Mr Brown, I don't like it.'

He started pulling her towards an empty office. 'Come on, little Junie, let me give you a great big Christmas bonus.'

She struggled with him. 'Get off! Leave me alone!'

He soon had her through the open door. 'Give me a kiss, you little minx,' he muttered, trying to get at her lips.

'No!' she shrieked.

He dragged her further into the room, kicking the door shut behind him.

She would have kicked him but she needed both her feet to keep her balance; she didn't want to end up on the floor with Brown on top of her. That didn't stop her using her fists though. 'Let go of me, you rotten swine!'

Laughing, he caught hold of her flailing arms and pulled them behind her back. 'Junie, you don't mean that. Be nice to me and I'll be nice to you. That's fair, isn't it?'

He sandwiched her between himself and the wall, his bulk preventing any chance of escape. Suddenly, he belched, letting out a disgusting stench of foul gases full in her face. She twisted round, trying to avoid his mouth, but he took hold of her face and tried to kiss her. She held her lips tight together but he was slobbering all over her. One of his hands moved to grasp a breast.

She was more furious than afraid. While his hands were occupied and his legs parted to keep his balance, she seized her chance. She brought her knee up hard into his groin. As the pain registered, he squealed like a pig and bounced around, grasping himself in agony.

'Well, I hope you enjoyed *that,* Mr Brown, because I certainly did!'

While Henry Brown found other uses for his hands, June made her escape.

Sitting back at her desk, clearing up last-minute jobs, she thought about the consequences of her actions. She realised that Brown would get her sacked, so it would be better to resign now and get a new job after Christmas. It had been worth it. He was a horrid beast and revenge felt good – incredibly good. But she had no intention of telling anyone about the incident. It had been bad enough enduring it without going through an inquest with the staff at work, or with her mam and dad.

When she arrived home, she helped her mam with the housework as she had promised. First she went upstairs to make the beds and tidy the rooms. Her two younger brothers, Tom and Ted, shared an attic room and it was always a mess: dirty boots and socks thrown on the floor, empty cocoa mugs staining the embroidered cloth on top of the set of drawers, the beds all awry, and the mattresses in need of turning. Her two elder sisters, Rose and Pat, did their own bed making and dusting, so she passed by their door and sorted out her own room.

In her parents' room she found the bedclothes thrown back to air the bed, and decided to straighten it up for her mother. She couldn't help but notice the marks on the bottom sheet. She wondered if her parents still made love, and if they enjoyed it. Her mother had told her to leave that room for her to do; now she realised why. It was very embarrassing, as though she had been caught prying into their private lives.

Funny though, she would never have thought that making love would mess up the sheets. But she knew that the staining had something to do with sex. Bits of gossip, giggles behind cupped hands, pointing at a boy's wet trouser front, and all that sort of thing, told her it was so. She suddenly realised that she was totally ignorant about sex. Schoolgirl gossip got more things wrong than right. She guessed her horrid monthly periods were the same thing as animals being on heat. That idea did not please her. It was quite disgusting to think of what might be involved in making babies.

A man's personal area was called by many names, or so it seemed, but polite people, and that included herself, referred to it as his 'private'. She had never seen detailed pictures of private parts, male or female. Graffiti maybe, but the pictures were so absurd that it was hard to imagine them as representing the real thing. She suddenly realised that she had never seen or examined her own. It somehow seemed not a nice thing to do. She started thinking about these things – asking herself questions but having no answers.

Arthur had made her realise that a man's urges did strange things to his anatomy. There was no disguising what was happening in that area when he held her close to him. He felt hard against her, as muscles in her arm grew firm when she drew them up tight. She felt exhilarated by his stirring, and her body responded to his arousal in some way that she didn't understand. She felt alarmingly ignorant about the whole subject.

The way her mother dealt with the subject of her daughters' chastity didn't help. Seeing sex as something dirty, she always avoided discussion of the subject. Such negativity was making June's thoughts and emotions seem wicked. She felt stupid and ignorant and wondered what Arthur would think if he knew. She didn't know the correct name for his private – she didn't even know what her own bits were called! It was all so stupidly hush-hush. She decided it was time to grow up and learn the truth about sexual matters. Ignorance made her feel vulnerable to her emotions; knowledge would give her power over them. After Christmas, one way or another, she would find a book on the subject.

After tea, she did the ironing. They had no power points and her mother refused to have an electric iron that had to be plugged into the ceiling light, so as usual she used their two flat irons heated up on the range. Old-fashioned maybe, but very efficient. The kitchen table, covered with a folded tatty blanket and sheet, served as an ironing board. Things were done differently in the Rogers household. They had an electric iron with a proper ironing board – and a domestic to do the ironing for them. Even though her sisters did their own ironing, she knew it would take her two hours or more to complete her task. But at least it gave her time to think.

Life with Arthur was going be completely different from how she lived now. They would have dinner at night and entertain posh people. What would she say to them? What would she give them to eat? She didn't even know what to do with all the pieces of cutlery posh people used.

She sighed heavily and touched the little golden heart bearing its brilliant diamond. Did it promise happiness or heartache?

And what about the wedding? She imagined his family and their posh friends on one side of the church and her lot on the other. A quick registry wedding would have suited her best, but that would never be accepted. After all, Arthur was the eldest son of Colonel Arthur Percy Rogers. The Colonel would pay for a posh do and her dad would just hate that. Maybe if she worked and saved hard, she'd be able to pay for it herself... not likely! Oh well, too bad. But at least she could improve her social skills. Arthur was right, she did need time; she had a lot of learning and growing up to do. But she was determined to succeed and make him proud of her.

With her mind occupied the time passed quickly. She had done quite a bit of work – and a great deal of thinking – and it was soon time to go to Midnight Communion. Her dad was staying at home to take care of her young brothers, or so he said, but she knew it was to sleep off too much beer. All the womenfolk were going to church, and they wanted to be there in time to hear the choir singing carols by the crib. Tired out by the day's events, June went wearily up to her room to change into her best clothes. The only thing that kept her awake and cheerful was the thought of seeing Arthur.

She entered the church with her family, just in time to see Mrs Rogers, Clare, Kate and George, all dressed in their robes, preparing to process with the rest of the choir to the back of the church. Sitting at the end of the pew, she smiled at them as they passed. They were too busy singing to notice her. All the other members of the Rogers household were sitting in their usual seats near the front.

Her mother whispered, 'Most of the Rogers family must be 'ere tonight. Don't they look smart in their evenin' clothes and fur coats?'

There was no doubting that statement. How old the clothes were, or where they were made, June couldn't say, but none of them were likely to have utility labelling, like those belonging to her own family. But one day she would look just as smart – and she wouldn't need a husband to pay for her clothes either.

The service started. Before long, Colonel Rogers, being one of the churchwardens, walked up to the lectern to read one of the lessons. He read with clarity and authority. Then, to June's complete surprise, Arthur rose and went to the lectern.

The vicar explained that, as a prelude to his sermon, he had asked Arthur, as a representative of those who had fought in the war, to read a poem about the power of sacrificial love, and the truth that brings us freedom from fear. He said that Arthur had written the verses himself.

June felt a warm glow spread over her. How appropriate that Arthur should read his poem that evening. As she listened to him reciting the poem from memory, she imagined him as a strong but compassionate leader of men. And yet she knew almost nothing about his wartime experiences, or the decisions he'd had to make in the heat of battle. She was totally ignorant of the hardships he'd faced and the suffering he'd endured.

Arthur's voice was clear and strong, and yet not without emotion. Moved by the tenor of the words, she touched her little golden heart. Arthur finished the poem and looked around at the congregation. He met her eyes in silent communication, and she smiled back in acknowledgement.

At the end of the service, people crowded around the church doors, exchanging Christmas greetings before drifting homewards. As June walked with her family, chatting about the service, a powerful voice sounded behind them.

'Good evening, Mrs Armstrong and young ladies, and a merry Christmas to you all.'

Along with the rest of her family, she stopped walking, and turned to see Colonel Rogers and Arthur smiling at them. They all exchanged polite greetings and her mother, in her usual manner, engaged in a brief conversation with the Colonel concerning the weather. When they came to the crossroads, they parted and went their separate ways.

''E's nice, that Arthur,' said her mother when the men were out of earshot. 'I wonder why 'e's not married? 'E's been 'ome at least two years now.'

June's sisters agreed with their mother, and gave good reasons why they wouldn't turn him down given half a chance.

'Well, you can forget about Major Rogers, 'is sort's not for the likes of us.'

Under the street lights, June saw her mother looking rather wistful. Was she thinking how wonderful it would be if one her daughters could get a catch like that? She instinctively put her gloved hand to her chest and smiled.

The following morning, June rose early to find her mother lighting a fire in the old black-leaded kitchen range, ready to cook the Christmas goose.

'Happy Christmas, Mam. Do you want anything doing?'

'Light a fire in the front room, June, love. I don't want the family clutterin' up the kitchen all mornin' when there's so much to do.'

June was pleased to help out, and it gave her time on her own to think about Arthur.

The front room was cold and dull. She opened the curtains and was met by stillness and a hint of frost glistening under the street lamps. Then, somewhere distant, she heard the Salvation Army playing carols. Yes, it was definitely Christmas Day. Humming to herself, she shovelled dead ashes into a bucket and placed scrunched-up paper, sticks of wood and shiny bits of coal in the grate. Then she lit the paper and sat on the rug, chin on knees, thinking. Occasionally she gave the wood an encouraging blow, and saw to her satisfaction that the coal was beginning to catch alight.

Humming the carol she could faintly hear from a couple of streets away, she looked at their Christmas tree. It was just a large twig painted white and decorated with chipped pre-war baubles, frosted pine cones and shiny spiralled-metal icicles. She smiled: it wasn't quite the huge fir she'd seen being cut ready to be put up in Bloomfield's beautiful hall, but the presents underneath would be just as much appreciated as the expensive items awaiting the Rogers household.

Using their old leather and brass bellows, she forced air on the reddening coal and, like a young child, watched a few sparks from the remains of the wood fly up the chimney. Then she built over the blaze with larger lumps of coal and took great pleasure in seeing flames licking their way from underneath the pile. Within a short time, heat would spread into the cold room and she could relax in the growing warmth.

Like all of the family, she was used to a lack of warmth. The whole house, apart from the kitchen, was cold in winter, but it was grand to have a fire to sit by. She wrapped her arms around her knees and indulged herself, not only enjoying the heat from the fire, but also reliving the erotic sensations of Arthur's hand on her breast. 'My darling, darling Arthur,' she whispered, 'I love you so very much.'

She heard her father come down the stairs. Stirrings in the room above her, and shouts from elsewhere in the house, meant that the family would soon be buzzing around. She put a guard in front of the fire and returned to the kitchen with her bucket of ashes, which needed taking outside for sifting: clinker for the path, useless dust in the bin. As she approached the door, she heard her mother mention her name.

'June's botherin' me. The girl seems 'appy enough but she's ever so restless. Do you think she spends too much time at Bloomfield? Maybe she shouldn't be doin' all that sewin' for Mrs Rogers, what with 'er full-time job and night school as well.'

'She enjoys sewing, and it earns her a bit of money,' her father pointed out.

'It's not good for 'er to 'ave Clare as a friend either. She goes to a posh school and mixes with all them well-to-do girls and their families. June must feel out of things; she's just a workin' girl. I reckon Clare just uses our June to sew for 'er.'

June knew her mother was right; her so-called friend rarely spoke to her now, but it was painful to hear it said. Would they think Arthur was using her too? Until they were engaged, that would certainly be their reaction.

Sounds of excited voices and the thumping of feet down the stairs gave her a chance to enter the kitchen without it being obvious that she'd been listening. Greeting her father, she went through to the back door with the bucket. After disposing of the ashes, she washed her hands and then sat before the range to toast thick slices of bread. The warmth, the smell of singed bread mingling with delicious aromas of Christmas fare, and her brothers' exuberant chatter all combined to banish any unwelcome thoughts. She pressed the little heart to her breast and a thrill ran through her – soon she would be seeing Arthur.

One by one, the family came into the kitchen to eat a small breakfast and then go off to the front room to open their presents. Her mother came back into the kitchen carrying her presents, and also an envelope, which she handed to June.

'This was pushed through the letter box, it's for you,' she said.

Puzzled, June opened it and was surprised to find ten one pound notes inside. She took out a letter and read it aloud.

'"Thank you for all the sewing you have done for the family. It has been greatly appreciated. Enclosed is a little something to express our thanks. I understand that you hope to go to college after you finish night classes. We will be pleased to help you in any way we can. Should you need one, I am willing to provide you with a reference."' June looked at the stunned faces around the table. 'It's written and signed by Mrs Mary Rogers.'

'Well, it's nice to know my little girl is appreciated,' her father said proudly.

Her mother's eyes lit up. 'You'll be able to earn your livin' while you're at college.'

'If you can earn that much now, goodness knows what you'll get when you're proper trained,' said her father. 'I knew you were clever, but to think Mrs Rogers, the Colonel's wife, will give you a good reference. That's worth quite a bit, whether you go to college or not.'

June wondered what the Colonel and his wife were up to, but she quickly dismissed her ungracious thoughts. Mrs Rogers was simply acknowledging her skills and offering to help her get on in life. But having a working girl for a daughter-in-law would not suit them at all. Well, whatever influence they had over their eldest son, Arthur had a mind of his own.

The rest of Christmas Day at the Armstrong household passed by in simple amusements, and in eating and drinking. The fire was continually built up in the front room, and the unaccustomed warmth, on top of full stomachs, induced drowsiness. June read a book, her brothers read their comic annuals, her sisters went to their room to try out their new make-up, and her parents rested and listened to the wireless; at least her mother listened, her dad was mostly snoring. Later on, June helped her sisters prepare for tea in the front room, putting out the seldom-used best china on the even more rarely used drop-leaf dining table. They never used the small dining room; the chimney was blocked and they didn't have enough coal for another fire anyway. It had once been her grandmother's room and it still stored her old furniture – as though they were waiting for her to return from the grave. But in fact the furniture had been promised to the first of the girls to marry.

While they were busy making sandwiches in the kitchen, Pat and Rose discussed the merits of various men they knew. Apart from marrying a good-looking guy, neither of them seemed to have any ambitions. Nor were they interested in what June wanted from life.

'Hey, Junie, which boys do you fancy?' Rose asked her.

'I've no time for boys.'

She smiled to herself at the truth of her statement. Later on, her dad would make himself decent in his grey demob suit, her mother would discard her pinny and curlers and put on her best blue woollen dress and cardigan, and they'd go off to meet their pals for a pint or two. While the rest of the family entertained their friends in the front room, she would be in the arms of the mature Arthur Rogers – the man she loved. No, she certainly had no time for boys!

Chapter Eight

When the Rogers family arrived home after the Midnight Communion, most of the family went straight up to bed. Arthur went to the kitchen to make himself a cup of tea before going up to Kate's flat. It was pleasant in the kitchen. Delicious smells lingered from the baking earlier on, and the warmth from the huge cooking range was cosily inviting. He relaxed in a soft-cushioned tall-backed wooden armchair, and thought about June.

As he was sitting quietly, allowing sensual memories of the previous evening to stimulate his senses, he became aware of muffled voices coming from the back entry area. The noises continued, together with a few bumps and bangs. Worried that they might have intruders in the house, he rose from the chair and went to investigate. From the servants' sitting room came a rhythmic banging and voices raised in ecstatic crescendo. He didn't have to wonder what Jenny Craven was up to, but it did concern him as to whom she was doing it with. He hoped it wasn't young George.

He returned to his chair and sighed. He had to admit he found the noises sexually stimulating. He would soon be in that same room with June, but nothing like that must happen. He picked up his cup and slowly sipped his tea, trying to ignore what was happening just yards away, but finding it extremely difficult.

It had been a strange experience reading his poem in church. He knew it had moved quite a few of his listeners. He recalled the moment he saw June holding her hand against the little golden heart. He'd felt her love flowing out to him, as indeed, his love had flowed out to her. He sighed deeply. Was he being fair to that young girl?

Just as he was about to leave the kitchen, there was the sound of laughter and giggles and a door being closed loudly. Then the kitchen door opened and Charles stumbled into the room.

'What the hell are you doing still up?' he muttered.

Arthur shook his head. 'Well, I don't have to ask why you are.'

Charles burst out laughing. 'I like to pull a good Christmas cracker!'

'Isn't she a bit young for that sort of treatment?' Arthur asked him, disgusted at his brother's casual attitude to sex. 'She's just a teenager. I hope you were careful.'

'You worry too much, big brother. Being an army man, you should know that sometimes a tactical withdrawal is necessary – leads to further advances without depleting resources. Done a lot of manoeuvres tonight.' He gave a loud burp. 'With a final thrust, amply protected by a willy frog suit!'

Charles burst out laughing again. Sitting in a chair opposite Arthur, he calmed down and asked him to make him a strong cup of coffee. 'Young George will be asleep,' he mumbled, 'and I don't want to disturb him.'

Arthur was happy to get his brother a sobering drink. Charlie's consideration for his younger brother somewhat quelled his anger with him. Even so, it just wasn't on to make free with the domestics, even if she had been willing; and from her vocalisation in the sitting room, she had been more than just accommodating.

For a while, Charles sat morosely drinking his coffee. Suddenly, he burst out, 'Can't help it, Arthur; I'm just made that way. Good looks can be a curse, you know. Girls throw themselves at my feet. What am I expected to do – kick them away?'

He burst out laughing again. Before long, his laughter trailed away into sobs. Shaking with emotion, he sat in the armchair with his head in his hands.

Arthur put a hand on his shoulder. His heart went out to his younger brother.

'Whatever it is, Charles, let it all out.' It was as if he were back in the battle zone, comforting a distressed soldier. 'Can I help in any way?'

'I've had it with the old man. Your lecherous brother has let the side down… shamed the family name and all that. Just as well I'm off in the next few weeks.'

'Charles, whatever you've done, you really should make it up with Father. If anything happened to you, he would be beside himself. Just talk to him and ask his advice. It's this naval mission that's worrying you, isn't it? That frog suit quip gave it away. Perhaps it's not for you. You don't have to prove your bravery by volunteering; you've already demonstrated your courage in extreme circumstances. The accident at sea wasn't your fault. The enquiry completely exonerated you.'

'All the men died, and I, the man in charge, escaped with mere wounds!'

'Maybe, but that doesn't make it your fault. It just means you're carrying around a burden of responsibility for what happened. Heavens, man! You were badly wounded and nearly lost your own life trying to save your men.'

Arthur recalled how young Charles had been when he was put in command of the minesweeper. But that was war. The accident could have happened to anyone. In spite of his bravado, his laughing and joking, his offhand talk about the forthcoming secret mission, he was a broken man out to expunge his guilt.

'Talk to Father. Tell him how you feel. It's no way to go out facing danger, with a burden on your conscience. I'm pretty sure he already suspects why you do the things you do, but he doesn't want to diminish you by bringing it up himself. Talk to him, Charles, you have nothing to lose.'

Charles looked up at him with tears streaming down his cheeks. 'You don't know what I did to upset him.' He dropped his eyes again. 'Last Sunday he caught me on the floor with young June, making an ass of myself as usual. Poor kid. The worst of it is, I'm really fond of her. I thought she wanted it. I didn't want to hurt her.'

Arthur felt as if Charles had just thumped him on his chest. June, his sweet innocent June, found on the floor with his brother? Now everything fitted into place: her tears and her absence from the house. Had she been told to stay away? No wonder she was anxious to know what his father had said to him. He remembered the money she'd sent back. Had his father tried to buy her silence? How far did Charles go? It was a question that must never be asked, but he knew he would be tormented until he found out the answer.

Charles recovered a little and sat up straight. 'Thanks, Arthur. I feel better for having talked to you. I'll do as you say. As soon as possible, I'll have a chat with the old man. Apologise for my behaviour and take it from there. Perhaps this navy lark will make a new man of me.'

Despite everything, Arthur loved his brother, and his heart bled for him. He helped him out of the chair and walked him into the hall. Together they mounted the stairs. On the landing, Arthur put his arms around him and embraced him warmly.

'Have a good rest, Charles.'

Arthur turned towards the attic stairs. Before climbing them, he stopped and watched his brother make it to the bathroom. 'God bless you,' he said softly, 'and make you whole again.'

In Kate's sitting room, Arthur lay on his camp bed. Soon he would be seeing June. What would he say to her? Would his voice betray his knowledge of what had happened? He remembered her look of misery when she'd nearly bumped into him. Poor girl. He knew only too well Charlie's sexual appetite. Surely he hadn't tried to rape her?

He recalled his father saying 'a girl like that' and how she attracted men like bees to honey. And didn't he say something about her being crafty? What had he seen? Had June egged Charles on? Was she as innocent as she appeared to be?

Of course she was. She would have to be an exceedingly fine actress to deceive him for such a long time. But then, Barbara had done that very thing. She had deceived all of them. His work colleague, Ronald Cunningham, had told him recently how she had flirted with him, and a few others, while he was serving abroad.

No, no, June was different. Even his father believed in her virginal innocence, whatever else he might be thinking. But unpleasant thoughts continued to hound him.

He felt wretched for even considering the possibility of June being less than virtuous. She had never made advances to him or anyone else in the house. He himself had taken her by surprise. She hadn't even tried to attract him when he'd endeavoured to ignore her. Having justified his faith in his beloved, he turned over and allowed drowsiness to overtake him.

When he opened his eyes, his first thoughts were of June. That evening they would be alone together in a cosy room. He lay in bed thinking of the delectable possibilities. Then, reluctantly, he returned to the here and now. He rose from the bed, showered, dressed and went downstairs to breakfast.

The children had been up early: toys and wrapping paper were all over the place. He could hear someone on the piano playing carols, a number of people chatting, children yelling and, somewhere, an infant squealing. He went into the dining room and helped himself to coffee and toast.

Charles walked in and gave Arthur a nod. Sitting next to him, he said quietly, 'I'm seeing the old man later on. Wish me luck.'

'I'm pleased, Charles. I know you won't regret it. It might even draw you two closer together – stop you thinking of him as "the Colonel".'

Half an hour later, Charles sat facing his father in the study. He was offered a cigar but he politely refused, not wanting to be distracted from his task. Clearing his throat, he began his confession.

'Sir, I want to apologise for the way I behaved last Sunday morning. I know it was unforgivable, but I hope that, in time, you will be able to put it from your mind. I cannot offer an excuse. To say that I'd had too much to drink merely compounds the offence. I abused your trust, cast shame upon this household, and acted in a manner that is unworthy of a son of yours. My conduct was despicable. I have to confess that since I returned from active duty I have not behaved like a gentleman.'

He paused for a moment before getting to the heart of his problems.

'I cannot offer as an excuse the injuries I sustained in the accident. I surely deserved them – the entire incident was my responsibility. Yes, I was cleared of negligence and I came out of it with honour, but *I* know I failed the men under my command.'

He paused, choking back tears of sorrow for his lost friends and comrades. 'The nightmares persist. I've tried blotting them out, but it doesn't work...' He bit his lip in remorse. 'I end up hurting others.' Pulling back his drooping shoulders, he took a deep breath to gain control of his emotions. 'You know the work I'm going to do, and you know it will be dangerous. I hope to redeem myself and once more be worthy of your respect.'

His father appeared deeply moved. After a few moments, he bridged the distance between them and offered him his hand. Tears streaming down his face, Charles immediately stood up, and his father embraced him.

'I know what you've been through, Charles. War does terrible things to people. We can only do our best, and do our duty.'

His father released him from the embrace and patted him on the shoulder. 'Sometimes things go well and we are comfortable with ourselves. But quite often things happen beyond our control, however carefully and dutifully we follow our orders. We have no option but to trust in God and carry on.'

Colonel Rogers had a faraway look and a pained expression on his face. Charles realised how little he knew about his father – the staunch authoritarian was vulnerable after all. Clearing his throat, his father resumed the role of the confident senior officer that Charles had always known him to be: Colonel Arthur Percy Rogers. Retired or not, he would never let go of his rank. It was his recognised identity, the thing that held him together.

'You were exonerated, but I know it didn't help your feelings of failure towards your men. It was a huge responsibility for a young officer. Unfortunately, because of your wounds, you didn't get an opportunity to live out your doubts and fears by commanding another vessel.' His voice softened. 'But I'm proud of you, Charles, *really* proud. Your behaviour at that time was nothing less than heroic.'

Shaking his head, Charles stifled a sob. His father patted him on his shoulder.

'The nightmares will cease once you accept what happened and learn to live with it. But ignoring your pain and hiding your suffering with drink and sexual promiscuity can only destroy you. That has been my concern all along.'

Charles brushed away his tears with the back of his hand. 'I'm truly sorry. Please forgive me, Father.'

'My dear boy, you are already forgiven. And now that you've brought everything out into the open, I'm sure your inner wounds will heal, just as your body has recovered.'

Charles took on a manly stance and faced his father with a new confidence.

'Thank you, sir. You've been a great help to me.'

'I am your father, Charles. I only wish I could have helped you sooner.'

'I feel terrible about what I did to June. What must I do to make amends?'

His father gazed into the fire for a few moments, picked up a poker and, somewhat distractedly, made a few sparks fly up the chimney. He put down the poker and cleared his throat.

'If you insist on a personal apology, then I suggest it be in my presence. It would not do for you to be alone with the girl, at least, not yet. If she brought her parents into it then that would be another matter, but I doubt she will. Just one other thing: don't mention the incident to anyone, including members of this family.'

Charles felt somewhat abashed. 'I'm sorry, sir, I've already told Arthur. He was the one who persuaded me to talk to you.'

His father sighed and was silent for a moment or two. 'Then we will have to meet with Arthur later to continue this part of the conversation.' He turned to leave the room. 'I'm joining Frank and Jack for a game of billiards. Unless you want to join us, I'll see you later.'

Arthur returned from a short walk with his sister Jane to find the children beginning to flag. Young Mary had dropped off to sleep in the middle of the floor. The rest had decided to do a giant jigsaw puzzle. The women were either upstairs or in the kitchen helping Mrs Craven.

Jenny, obviously tired after her late night activity, was endeavouring to tidy up. She looked up at him with bleary eyes. 'Colonel Rogers is looking for you,' she said wearily.

Arthur found his father in the study with Charles.

'Arthur… at last. I've been looking for you. Do come and join us.' His father pointed to a chair by the fire. He then poured out a glass of sherry and handed it to him. 'I think it necessary to be frank and not beat about the bush. We have to discuss the unfortunate incident that took place last Sunday morning involving June Armstrong.'

Arthur glanced at his brother, who was looking much calmer than the last time they'd met. It was a good sign. 'Yes,' he said, 'I agree.'

'I understand Charles has told you something about what happened. He would like to formally apologise to the girl. Is there anything you wish to say about that, or about anything else to do with the matter?'

Arthur thought for a moment. He knew what his father was hinting at.

'Charles, there is a good reason why Father has asked me to comment. I happen to know June rather well. I've been attracted to her for quite a while. She may have been a child two years ago, but I've grown to love her as the young woman she is now. Eventually, I hope to make her my wife. But we aren't engaged yet; she's too young to know her own mind. She knows nothing of the world like we do. She's still an innocent, and ignorant about so many things in life.'

Arthur noticed Charles drop his eyes and he sensed his discomfort, but he felt it necessary to press on.

'June told me nothing of what happened. I knew she was distraught, but she only mentioned my going away as the cause. She also refused to come to the house. I thought it was overreaction to my leaving, and to the fact that I'd kept it from her. She wouldn't say how she'd found out.'

Colonel Rogers interjected. 'I mentioned it to her. I also asked her to stay away until you two had gone off. I was concerned that there could be trouble between you. And I have to say that I consider Miss Armstrong to be too young for either of you. I don't want the girl to be just used, but neither do I think marriage is appropriate, especially for you, Arthur. But you are men, and you have to decide for yourselves.'

As far as Arthur was concerned he had already decided, but now was not the time to argue about it.

Charles was looking shocked. 'I'm so sorry, Arthur, I had no idea about you and June. I've been a bloody fool. I would never have approached her with the mistletoe if I'd known she was yours. But I'm not trying to excuse what I did… please believe that.'

'Mistletoe?' Arthur queried.

'You know, just a friendly Christmas kiss under the mistletoe. She'd just arrived – looking jolly pretty – to do a bit of sewing, and I held a sprig of it over her head. She didn't resist. I thought she really enjoyed it. But I made no allowance for her youth and inexperience. I went on to treat her like all the women that crowd my life – you know the sort I mean. She put up a fight, but I thought she was just teasing – being coy, but really wanting a good romp.' He lowered his eyes. 'So I pressed myself on her.'

Arthur felt his anger rising. He blurted out, 'For goodness sake, Charles, she's just a teenager, not one of your women who enjoy a bit of rough stuff!'

'I wouldn't have gone any further, not when I realised she was distressed.' His face twisted with remorse. 'I must have given her a hell of a fright though. I'm deeply ashamed… awfully sorry.' He looked at Arthur with sorrow in his eyes. 'I'd like June to know that… have her forgive me. Even if we can never be back on friendly terms.'

Arthur was grateful to hear the truth. Of course, Charles had behaved like an utter cad, but now he understood. But it would take more than understanding to dispel the anger he felt towards him.

'I think she's too vulnerable to lift the load of guilt from you, Charles, at least for the present. But leave it to me to explain things to her. I'm sure she'll come to forgive you – I know my girl.'

The Colonel cleared his throat and stood up facing Charles. 'Well then, we'll leave this matter in your brother's capable hands.' He turned to Arthur. 'You know my feelings about your relationship with this young lady; your mother is of the same opinion. I beg of you, Arthur, don't rush into things.' He left the room.

'I must go too,' said Arthur. 'I have to change. Thank you for your honesty, Charles. I know you've learned by your mistake.'

'I have indeed; helped by your understanding.' Charles frowned. 'I only hope young June hasn't been damaged by this humiliating experience. I'm dreadfully sorry.'

As Arthur made his way to the attic flat, he thought about the things that had been said that morning. It seemed that Charles was really smitten with June. If he had approached her in a proper manner, would he have won her over? He was eight years his junior, and exceptionally handsome. Most women, young and old, fell for his looks and charm. When he was his true self, he was gentle, amusing, stimulating, and the perfect gentleman. Even though his inner wounds had started to heal, Charles might never be entirely his old self again, but he was probably the better man for June.

Arthur changed out of his walking gear – casual grey slacks, white open-necked shirt and blue cashmere jumper – into the formal dress expected for the Christmas feast. As he inspected himself in the mirror, he began to realise that the anger he was experiencing wasn't just indignation at the way Charles had treated June, but also good old-fashioned jealousy.

Charles made his way upstairs to freshen up. Seeing his reflection in the mirror, he realised he was beginning to look the way that he was now feeling – assured, confident, and relaxed. He understood how much alcohol had been sapping his brain, but it would do so no longer. Just to be able to discuss the whole matter of his disgrace had been a great relief. To be given the hope of absolution through June's forgiveness left him feeling both elated and humbled.

The Prodigal Son came to mind. His forgiving father had welcomed the wastrel returning from the world of the damned. But, unlike the elder brother in the story, Arthur had given him hope of restitution too. He knew, without any doubt, that he was a reformed character. He now wanted to enter his new sphere of work, not to punish himself or to bring about redemption by offering his own life for those of his men, but because it was a challenge to his manliness – the realisation of his full potential. His fears were now under control and he knew his nightmares would cease. With the help of his beloved father and his understanding brother, he had released the renegade within himself and faced it full square.

Ten minutes later, he joined the rest of the family for their Christmas dinner. He found the formality of the occasion rather amusing, but also pleasant and reassuring; it was a tradition going back as long as he could remember. Noisy children's chatter suddenly ceased as his father rose from his chair and loudly cleared his throat ready to say the Grace. A solemn silence descended, followed by what appeared to be a sermon rather than a thanksgiving, after which they were ordered to pull their crackers.

The fun was followed by a wonderful dinner that everyone enjoyed. The whole family being present made the meal all the more enjoyable. Charles looked across at Arthur and wondered how long it would be before June would be sitting by his side. He sighed… would she ever forgive him?

Jenny removed his empty plate. 'Nice time last night,' she whispered in his ear. He preferred not to be reminded.

When the last course was finished, his father stood up again and spoke briefly of the pleasure of having them all together. He then told them about his growing involvement in politics, of the need for a strong government, and of the pressure he was under to stand for Parliament at the next general election.

Charles smiled as the family gave his father a little applause. Arthur had been right. He could now see his father as the man he truly was – an ordinary father who could only cope with relationships when they were subject to regimental order. And to prove the point, they all immediately stood up with glass in hand – including the children – as the Colonel announced the toast for King and Country.

Just before seven-thirty that evening, having changed back into his casual clothes, Arthur was waiting for June at the agreed place. When she arrived, she seemed a little anxious.

He kissed her tenderly. 'Don't worry, all's well,' he said softly. 'I'll tell you what happened shortly. You know that sitting room Mrs Craven uses? We can talk there in private. I want us to be together in the warm where we can talk without being seen and heard. Annie is leaving the back door unlocked and making sure the coast is clear.'

As they approached the door, Arthur took her by the hand and led her inside. Light shone under the kitchen door but no sounds came from within. Doors to the cellar and the storerooms were closed, but the door into the sitting room was open and a blazing fire threw a golden light into the small hallway. It was an invitation to romantic love. Arthur closed the door behind them. They took off their coats and snuggled together on the sofa.

'No one will disturb us in here,' he said quietly, 'but we'll keep our voices down so as not to attract attention.'

He remembered the noises from the previous night. The sofa underneath them had been the bed for promiscuous sexual gratification. He tried to divert his mind.

'June, so much has happened since we last talked. I understand things much better now.'

She looked a little startled. Her eyes were wide open and little flames reflected in them from the fire. Arthur was fascinated and had to resist the urge to take her in his arms and set the whole of her body aflame.

'I had that talk with my father. I must be honest with you, my dearest; he wasn't overjoyed by the news. He sees you as a child with no knowledge of the world and far too young for someone of my age.'

June smiled, 'What does it matter? You make me feel like a woman: an adult, not a teenager. You don't have to soften things for me. I know I'm ignorant. But one day I'll make you proud of me.'

'Silly little goose, I *am* proud of you, and I love you dearly, whatever my father says.'

'What else did he say? He doesn't think I'm good enough for you, I know that. And it's true. I glanced at your family last night. You all looked so smart in your evening clothes and posh fur coats. And the lovely way you spoke, and the people you spoke to–'

'My love, we spoke to *you*, and your family – remember?' said Arthur, before she could finish putting herself and her family down. He wrapped an arm around her and rubbed his cheek against her soft hair. 'Of course there's a difference in our families. But my parents are as much concerned for you as they are for me. They believe that becoming my wife will put you under an impossible strain.'

June frowned a little, but said nothing.

'The fact that I'm the eldest son doesn't help. My father wants more time for politics. When I return from abroad, he'll be expecting to off-load some of the family's business commitments onto me. It's not so much the time involved but the responsibility that goes with it. Becoming my wife is a lot to expect of a young, inexperienced woman.'

She nodded. 'I understand what you're saying, and I know my parents would agree with yours. But we can make it work, can't we? I can learn. I'll do anything to please you.'

'I know, my love, and I have absolute faith in you.'

'Did your father tell you what happened last Sunday?'

He gave her a gentle squeeze. 'Yes, but I found out from Charles first. He feels quite wretched about what he's done. Not just because Father discovered him assaulting you, but because he's genuinely contrite. He knows he's hurt you badly.'

He explained what had happened, and why Charles had been behaving so badly.

'You see, my darling, I understand Charles because I've been in that position myself – taking responsibility for things beyond my control. But I was much older and more experienced than he was at the time. We men are supposed to be tough and brave and have no fears, but we are only vulnerable human beings, not supermen.'

June nodded her head but said nothing.

'If you can understand these things it will soften the hurt for you. It must have been a humiliating and frightening experience.'

'Charlie didn't tell you that I said he was everything a girl wanted, and other silly stuff. I was just joking – truly. He told you that he kissed me under a piece of mistletoe. It's true, Arthur, I did let him do it – willingly. I've always liked him, ever since he came home. I should have realised that he'd been drinking. Why else would he want to kiss someone like me? I'm really sorry, Arthur. It's my own fault for being so stupid. Please forgive me.'

Arthur held her close to him. 'My precious darling, of course it's not your fault. Don't move the blame onto yourself. Charles knew exactly what he was doing, even if he misread the signals. But he's desperately sorry. He wants to make amends before he goes away. He hopes that one day you'll forgive him, even if things can never be the same again.' He hesitated. 'Would you be willing to let him apologise in person?'

Staring into the fire, she was quiet for half a minute before she spoke. 'All right, yes. I will see him,' she said, with a determined nod of her head. 'It has to be done. Not just for his sake, but for mine.'

Arthur smiled; this young girl in his arms was far wiser than most people thought her to be. He was beginning to feel wretched at leaving her. She would go on learning about life while he was away, and he wouldn't be there to witness it.

The fire was beginning to burn low. He poked the coals so that the flames would give all the light they needed. Then he turned off the lamp and moved towards her. Her reaction told him she was eagerly anticipating his love and attention. Her cheeks were flushed, her eyes half closed, and her lips were slightly open. As his eyes swept over her body, two small enticing peaks suddenly appeared, pushing at her clothing. He kissed her gently, moving his lips in a tender caress. She moaned a little and pressed herself to him. Slipping his hand inside her open cardigan, he whispered softly, 'Do you mind, my darling? Please say if it offends you.'

'No. I want you to,' she said, her voice trembling in anticipation.

Gently, he unbuttoned her pretty white blouse and slipped her bra straps over her shoulders. He released her breasts from their restrictive cups and moved his palms to fondle her firm silky flesh, kissing her constantly and murmuring his love for her. She completely accepted his touch, and mewed with pleasure. Pressing her backwards onto the cushion, he caressed her breasts with his open lips. Her back arched with pleasure and the response moved him to use his mouth and tongue in a little love play. Her little moans of ecstasy were soon accompanied by his own soft groans of sensual delight.

For a few minutes he managed to resist his body's cravings to go further, but in the end he had to pull away. 'It's time to go, my dearest,' he said with a deep sigh.

He helped her dress. Seeing the locket, he held it in his hand. He opened the case and the diamond sparkled with little flames from the fire.

'I love you – more than I ever thought possible. It's so hard not to ask you to marry me, but I can't do that… not yet.' Closing the locket, he put it back where it belonged. 'I'll always remember tonight.'

'Me too, Arthur,' she said rather shyly.

He wondered if she had ever allowed a man to go that far with her before. No, it was quite impossible, his personal experience of women told him that much. The signs of virginity were all there: the way she trembled and caught her breath as he touched and fondled, kissed and caressed; her eyes that widened in wonder at the sensations she was experiencing; and the sharp little moans of unexpected delight. It was all so new to her. Yes, he was her first lover. God willing, he would be her only one. 'My darling, I must see you again tomorrow. Can you meet me at two-thirty?'

'Yes, Arthur,' she said, eagerly.

'Make your way towards the park. Keep to the pavement along the main road away from houses and the park gates. I'll pick you up and we'll go for a drive.'

She was like an excited child. 'How lovely, I've only been in a car a few times.'

'See if you can be away from home until the evening.' He took hold of her hand and looked into her eyes. He didn't want to spoil their time together, but it had to be done. 'If we go somewhere where we can meet Charles, would you be willing to see him?'

She nodded. 'I have to see him some time. The sooner the better.'

Arthur gave her a hug. 'You're wonderful!'

As Arthur entered by the front door, the big grandfather clock revealed the time to be almost ten o'clock. Sounds were coming from the floor above. Evidently, the children were resisting their parents' attempts to keep them in bed. He took off his coat and hung it in the cloakroom. When he emerged after a quick wash, he nearly bumped into Mrs Craven who was leaving the study with an empty tray.

'Good evening, Mr Arthur. Can I get you anything before I go at ten?'

'A cup of tea and one of your lovely tarts would be nice. By the way, do you know where Charles is?'

'He's in the study with Colonel Rogers. Would you like your tea there?'

'That would be nice.'

Arthur put his head around the study door and asked if he could join them for a few minutes.

'Glad to have you, Arthur,' his father said. 'Please come in and sit down by the fire. Would you like a drink?'

'Thanks, but Annie is bringing me a tray.'

Arthur took out his pipe and put it in his mouth, but didn't light it. For a pleasant few minutes he allowed the warm glow of the fire to relax him. Being with June had its gratifying pleasures but, inevitably, it also caused certain physical tensions.

Little was said. Arthur's companions seemed to sense his need to relax. There was a gentle knock on the door and Annie Craven entered bearing a tray. She put it on a table next to Arthur, and silently poured tea out of a small silver teapot into a white china cup.

Arthur smiled up at their faithful servant; she was always ready and willing to please them. 'Thanks, Annie, you're an angel. Mince pies too – I'll have one of those!'

When the door closed, Arthur told the others that he had spoken to June.

Charles perked up. 'What did she say, Arthur? Did you ask her?'

'Yes, I asked her. She will see you, Charles; she's willing to hear your apology. But I'd like it to take place while I'm still at home. I was wondering... could you meet us tomorrow afternoon?'

'I'd do anything to be able to apologise. Where do you want me to be, and at what time?'

'I'm going to take her for a drive and stop at the Grange Country Lodge for tea. How about meeting us there at four o'clock?'

'That sounds great. What a splendid girl she is. And what a brick you are. No one could have a more understanding brother. You two really deserve each other. Even if I hadn't been such a bloody idiot, I would never have stood a chance to win June with you around.'

Arthur doubted the truth of that remark, but he let it pass. 'Yes, she's being incredibly understanding. She just wants to get the whole sorry episode behind her as quickly as possible.'

Colonel Rogers sat listening to the conversation with a smile on his face. He was clearly pleased that the incident wasn't going to taint the family.

Jane knocked at the door to see if they wanted to join the rest of the family for charades in the lounge. 'The children have finally settled in bed. Now it's time for *us* to become youngsters again,' she said, laughing.

Arthur went to bed that night with a feeling of satisfaction. Soon he would be off, but he intended to make sure June had plenty of happy memories to hold on to.

Chapter Nine

Arthur woke up to find that it was eight o'clock – well beyond his usual time for rising. Massaging his head with his fingertips as if to make his brain more alert, he made his way to Kate's bathroom. The door was closed. From within came the sounds of muffled voices and the sort of groans and urgings that could mean only one thing. He smiled at his sister's supposed hatred of men. There she was, having it off in the shower! Well, she deserved a little happiness after her last disastrous affair.

He put on his dressing gown and went downstairs to use a bathroom. When he'd finished his ablutions, not wanting to disturb Kate, he jogged down to the kitchen to get tea and toast.

Charles was sitting in a chair by the range, looking relaxed with a cup in one hand and toast in the other. He smiled broadly. 'Good morning, Arthur; come and join me. There's plenty of tea in the pot and I've just buttered fresh toast. I'd be glad of your company.'

After a short while, Charles began to reminisce about his teenage years. 'You know, Arthur, in many ways you've been like a dad to me, especially when Father was away. You taught me the facts of life and got me out of scrapes. Do you remember when I was sixteen and that redhead friend of Jane's – Grace, I think her name was…'

Arthur smiled as he listened to his brother, his mind going back to days gone by when problems seemed so much simpler. And now, once again, he was helping his younger brother sort out an emotional difficulty, although this time he was personally involved himself. He looked at Charles with admiration. His normal charming personality seemed to have returned. And he could rival any film star with those looks and that physique. If only he hadn't been such a bloody fool then, without a doubt, he could easily win June's affections.

Coming to a decision, Arthur suddenly interrupted his brother's recollections of the pre-war years. 'Charles, when things are put right between you and June, would you do something for me?'

Charles looked puzzled. 'Of course. Anything – you have only to ask.'

'You'll be home more often than me. If it wouldn't disrupt your life too much, would you take June out for me occasionally?'

His brother was staggered by such a request. 'After all that's happened? Even supposing June would want me anywhere near her, which I very much doubt, how could you possibly trust me to take her out?'

'It's because of recent events that you are the only person I would trust with her. I'm sure she'll go out with you, and in the not too distant future. I know she liked you a lot before last Sunday. Now she understands what happened, she'll get over it – humiliating as it was. I'm not saying it'll be easy for her. Just meeting you again is going to be painful and deeply embarrassing for her, but it has to happen if you are to apologise. Taking her out is a step further. If I tell her she'll be safe with you from now on, she'll believe me. I just know it.'

But Charles was shaking his head in disbelief.

Arthur could see into his brother's mind. 'I'm not asking you to be alone with her – well, not exactly. I thought you could take her to the theatre to see a ballet or a good play, visit art galleries and museums, that sort of thing. Do you see what I want to do, Charles? I want her to experience some of the privileges we take for granted.

I want her to be able to mingle easily within a wide social mix. Call it training to be my wife, if you like. I want her to be happy and comfortable with the sort of people she's likely to meet.'

Charles nodded. 'I can understand that.'

'It'll be much easier for *you* to take her out socially. You're nearer her age, so it becomes a more acceptable relationship. And you're not the eldest son with heavy responsibilities.' He sighed with the burden of his thoughts. 'You've known each other longer, and played games with her and Clare. It's true, her parents might get expectations, but you won't see her *that* often. She'll be going home full of the things she's seen and heard, and will be able to tell them about it quite openly.'

'You're wrong, Arthur. She would have to be insane to go out with me. She thought I was going to rape her! What you're suggesting is absolutely crazy.'

'But if she agrees, will you? Please, Charles; she's delectable honey and I fear the bees, especially when she goes out more and meets attractive men. She's so vulnerable that any lecherous Don Juan could sweep her off her feet. But I want her to have freedom and never regret being attached to me.'

It wasn't just promiscuous Casanovas that worried Arthur but, now that Charles was a redeemed character, possible feelings she might develop for *him*. But he would rather risk June being exposed to his brother's charisma in an innocent, controlled manner now, than have him as a rival once they were formally matched.

'If I had to lose her to someone, Charles, I'd rather it be you.'

Charles stared at him in disbelief. 'You can't be serious? June is your woman; she could never love me. Yes, I'll do as you ask; I can see how important it is to you. And there's logic in her experiencing a bit of culture. But will she agree?' He shook his head. 'I doubt it.'

'We'll see,' said Arthur. Satisfied at the outcome of their discussion, he finished his tea and went upstairs to dress.

June was preparing the dinner while her mother had a bit of a rest. Her sisters were going out in the afternoon to meet their boyfriends, but her brothers said they were going to the park with their new football. She would have to be careful not to be seen getting into Arthur's car. When she thought about avoiding them a sense of guilt crept over her. All the family, including her mam and dad, had been led to believe that she'd be with the Rogers family for most of the day.

Rose came into the kitchen. 'Must be great at Bloomfield. Proper Christmas tree I bet, and loads to eat and drink. Wouldn't mind being there myself – I'd love to catch Charlie Rogers under the mistletoe. Can't you get us an invite?'

June carried on peeling the potatoes at the kitchen sink. 'Sorry, Rose – they've got a full house anyway. The families from London are there too.'

'What are they like?'

'Ordinary,' June told her, hoping she wouldn't be asked for details. 'They were in another room last night, so I didn't get chance to talk to them.'

'Did you see Charlie?'

'Not last night,' June said truthfully. 'You'll be seeing your boyfriend soon, how can you be thinking about another man?'

Rose gave a deep sigh. 'Easy, when the other man is Charlie. I don't want to end up like Mam, you know.'

'Meaning what?' June asked, glad that the conversation had moved away from Bloomfield.

'I heard Mam talking to that old buzzard who's always round borrowing something or other. She said she was only too pleased the family would be out this afternoon because Dad wanted her in bed with him for an hour or so. She told what's-her-name she doesn't much care for that sort of thing; just regards it as her duty. "Complying with my old man's wishes" she said.'

'Rose, really! You shouldn't have been listening.'

'Come off it, June, you listen at doors, I've seen you. Anyway, she said if Dad had been sent abroad during the war he'd never have managed without her.' Rose laughed. 'Good job he worked at the local Ordnance Depot, so he was still able to get his daily ration!'

June smiled at her sister's joke, but how sad that things should be that way for their mother, making love merely out of duty. She felt drawn to Arthur and wanted to have his babies. But would that part of sex turn out to be a big disappointment?

Just before two-thirty, Arthur left Bloomfield and headed towards the park in his Rover. Being smaller than his father's older but more luxurious model, and quite unlike Charlie's red MG, it was far too dull to draw attention. He soon spotted June walking slowly along the deserted length of road, and pulled up beside her. She quickly jumped into the passenger seat.

'That worked out well,' he said, driving swiftly away. He smiled across at her. 'Happy, my dearest?'

'I'm always happy with you,' she answered simply, but Arthur detected sadness in her voice. They would soon be parted.

Getting down to practicalities, he asked her, 'When are you expected home?'

'Not until this evening.'

'Good.'

'When are we seeing Charlie?' She sounded nervous.

Arthur slowed down and stopped the car in a lay-by. He turned to face her.

'First, we're going for a little drive. Then I'm taking you for tea in Bridgford. Charles will be joining us there. It's going to be fine, you'll see.'

She didn't look convinced.

He took her hand. 'He's a changed man; he won't ever hurt you again. I'd trust him with my life – and you, my dearest, *are* my life.'

She smiled. He moved towards her and she lifted her lips to his. He kissed her tenderly. Allowing his feelings to overrule caution, he slipped his hand inside her coat.

'Oh, Arthur,' she murmured, sighing deeply at his sensuous touch.

A car's engine sounded close behind them. He quickly sat back in his seat, but kept his eyes on hers. 'God alone knows how much I love you.'

Her eyes lowered. 'But you're leaving tomorrow. You'll soon meet all sorts of exciting women who know exactly how to please men. You'll soon forget about me.'

He smiled. 'Silly little goose. No doubt I will meet a number of women, but not to sleep with. I'll save all my kisses for you – every single one.'

He put his hand in his pocket and drew out the lighter. He flicked on the flame and watched the reflection flickering in her hazel eyes.

'My dearest, you will always be with me… you are the light of my life.' He extinguished the flame and put the lighter back in his pocket. 'I'll keep your present with me wherever I go. I'll light it every night before I sleep. How could I possibly forget you then?' He wiped away her tears and gently kissed her.

A number of cars were fast approaching.

'Let's move away from here.' He started the engine and they continued their journey. But his heart was heavy.

He stopped the car by a river and helped June out of her seat. Taking her by the hand, he guided her across a bridge and up a hillside path. They stood and looked at the view around them. The sun was setting low in the sky, but it was strong enough to give a brilliant glow to both heaven and earth. The river, flowing from the distant hills and snaking along the valley below, was ablaze with gold and red. He held her close and she sighed blissfully as she snuggled up to him. They were in complete harmony with nature and with each other, and no words were necessary.

But when the sun disappeared behind the hill, his heart was filled with wistful longing for unity of body as well as of soul. Somehow keeping control of his libido, he led her back to the car.

'When I'm home again, we'll go to lots of beautiful places together. We have the whole of our lives before us; our parting now will be nothing at all.'

For all his show of confidence, the memory of Barbara jilting him while he was away on active service was hard to erase. How he longed to consummate his love before leaving... then she would always be his. She wouldn't resist his advances but welcome them, of that he was certain. As he opened the car door he glanced at the back seat. No! It must never happen, not before they were married. He must never allow such a thought to linger in his mind again.

As Arthur started up the car, butterflies began to gather in June's tummy. She'd soon be seeing Charlie. How could she possibly look him in the eye after what had happened between them? Maybe he wouldn't have raped her, but he'd still touched intimate parts of her body and treated her most shamefully. And yet, she'd always been attracted to him. That's what made it so ugly and squalid.

She felt Arthur's hand on hers. She looked across at him and tried to smile.

'Don't worry,' he told her. 'It'll be fine, trust me.'

Less than half an hour later, Arthur was parking the car in front of the Grange Country Lodge. June had never been to such a grand place. The drive leading up to it was lined with lime trees, now frosted over and glinting in the car headlights. Light poured out from the tall windows, illuminating gravel paths and shrubbery. Through the glass she could see a magnificent hall with a twinkling crystal chandelier and a splendid branched staircase. On the walls were huge mirrors and ornately-framed oil paintings. A huge Christmas tree, decorated with lights, stood in the spacious porch and she could just make out a uniformed doorman welcoming some guests. She felt totally out of place.

Arthur parked the car and came round to open her door. Charlie's car was parked nearby. June looked up at Arthur and smiled nervously, but said nothing. As she entered the splendid reception hall she was completely overwhelmed by its ambience. And there was Charlie coming towards them. She felt herself blushing and quickly turned her head away. It was all too much to bear.

Arthur was offering his hand to his brother. 'So pleased you came, Charles. We've just had a little walk and we're both ready for a cup of tea.'

She felt, rather than saw, Charles turn towards her. He spoke softly, 'Hello, June. Fresh air becomes you. You look lovely.'

She knew it was his presence rather than the walk that had reddened her cheeks. 'Hello, Charlie,' she muttered, looking down at her feet.

Arthur was saying something to her, but she couldn't concentrate on what it was. She'd just noticed something that filled her with horror: one of her shoes had a thick patch of mud smeared over it from the walk. Now she felt even more uncomfortable; not only were her clothes unsuitable for such a posh place, she was even looking scruffy. Why, she asked herself, couldn't she clean her shoes properly on the mat? Should she go back and get them clean? But then she might trail mud across the beautiful blue and gold carpet. Mortified, she crossed one foot slightly over the over to hide her shame. People just didn't enter such expensive places as this wearing second-rate clothes and with mud on their shoes – it was definitely not the done thing!

She began to panic. She felt completely out of her depth and wished she hadn't come. Arthur shouldn't have brought her here. She didn't fit in, and he should have known she wouldn't. She felt gauche, awkward, inferior – working class! Is this what life was going to be like away from the known and familiar? To make matters worse, Charlie was there to witness her humiliation. She wanted to run away, out into the covering darkness, but fear rooted her to the spot. She suddenly realised that Charlie was speaking to her.

'June, my dear, would you slip off your coat and sit on that chair behind you?' He was pointing her to an elegant upright chair by a large potted plant. 'Please?' he added in a whisper.

Not wanting to make a fuss, she did as she was asked – anything to get away from all the demeaning glances she was convinced were coming her way. Charles surreptitiously knelt down, lifted her foot and carefully wiped the offending mud from her shoe into his handkerchief. She had to smile when, hidden by leaves, he shook the soil into the plant pot. He quickly buffed the leather to return it to its normal polished state.

Relieved but lost for words, she merely said, 'Thank you, Charlie.'

Rising, he took hold of her hand and tenderly kissed it. She considered that if anyone had noticed something happening behind the huge leaves of the plant, they'd have thought that he'd been engaging in a little romantic love-play, he was so charming and adroit in his movements. Minus the mud and having divested herself of the only coat she possessed, which was yesterday's fashion, she now felt more comfortable and relaxed and was able to take in the pleasant atmosphere. Somewhere she heard a piano playing, and sounds of voices and laughter. She could smell the trail of expensive perfume from a woman on her way to the ladies' rest room.

Arthur broke into her musings. 'If you'd like to follow that lady in pink, you'll find the ladies' room where you can freshen up and hang up your coat. We'll wait on these chairs. Take your time; we can order the tea while you're away.'

She picked up her coat and bag and did as he suggested, pleased to be able to use the toilet and smarten herself up. An attendant hung up her coat and she checked herself in the mirror. Her outfit – brown tweed skirt and waistcoat with a cream crèpe-de-chine blouse – wasn't luxurious like the clothes some of the women were wearing, but it was well-styled, and a perfect fit since she'd made it herself. She felt so much better. To think, it had been Charlie, not Arthur, who'd noticed her embarrassment, and like a knight in shining armour had come to her aid. It had been such a relief. Full of confidence now, she returned to the hall where a smiling Arthur came forward to meet her.

'Here she comes, as radiant as ever!'

A young waitress came along and showed them into the small lounge, saying that she would bring their tea shortly. June couldn't help but notice the girl's eyes lingering on the handsome Charles. Did she know him?

Logs were blazing in the hearth and they sat in three comfortable armchairs placed around the fire. Another waitress came in and started to prepare a table. Arthur said they'd take their tea on a trolley by the fire.

She smiled at him in acknowledgement. 'It'll be nice to have it there, sir. No one else is expected in here this afternoon. Most of the guests are listening to the piano in the other room. We have a celebrity playing today. Can't remember his name, but everyone knows him – he's made records.'

June watched her close the shutters to keep out the night. Soon the three of them were on their own, sitting in the mellow light of the fire and the shaded table lamps. She knew what was coming next, and began feeling a little awkward.

Charles broke the pregnant silence. 'June, what can I say? Sorry isn't enough. I hurt and humiliated you. And to make things worse for you, my father witnessed the scene. I don't deserve to have you listen to my apology, nor can I expect your forgiveness, but I do hope that some time, and in some way, I can make up a little for the suffering I've caused you.'

June wondered if he'd been practising his little speech, since it had been delivered so smoothly. She sat in silence, looking at her hands and wondering how to answer him. Meanwhile, he continued with his apology.

'I make no excuses for my behaviour, but I can honestly promise that I'll never do anything to hurt you again. I really am so very, very, sorry.'

Arthur moved closer to her and took her hand. She glanced at him and saw the concern on his face. She smiled but looked away; tears were threatening to overtake her.

'I know you didn't want to hurt me, Charlie, but it did hurt, and I can't say otherwise. You have to understand… I've had to fight off boys since I was twelve years old.

Their groping hands sicken me. But I didn't expect it from you... someone I really liked and thought was my friend. *That's* what hurt me, Charlie. *That's* what really hurt.'

'I understand and I'm sorry. You're right about everything. I can't take back what happened, but perhaps one day you'll let me be your friend again. I do hope so.'

She looked up and saw the pain of remorse in his face. His heavy brows were drawn together and his dark eyes appealed for forgiveness. The set of his chin – controlled, firm and determined – with lips held tightly together, was indeed that of a man who knew what he wanted.

In spite of herself, her heart went out to him. This wasn't the intoxicated brute who had assaulted her, nor was it the carefree Casanova she had known the last few years. It was a Charlie she had yet to know. What suffering must he have undergone to rob him of his true personality? She couldn't help but notice that even in his present emotional state he looked incredibly handsome. She shook her mind free of such a thought. Her mother had told her many times never to go by looks – deeds were what mattered. Could this new Charles be trusted? But the sorrowful look had won her over.

'I'd love to be your friend again, Charlie, and I do forgive you. One day, perhaps, I'll be able to forget what happened, but that might take a little longer.'

Charlie's face lit up, but as he was about to speak the door opened and the young waitress came in with the tea trolley. She poured the tea, and, giving Charles another little smile, left them to help themselves to sandwiches and cake.

While they were drinking and eating, Arthur asked June, 'Will you be busy when you get back to work?'

'I'm not going back,' she informed him, taking a sip of tea and putting down her cup. 'I'm giving in my notice before I get the sack.'

Both men stopped eating and stared at her. Arthur said, 'You didn't tell me! Why are you giving up your job? What's happened?'

'Let's say my boss, Mr Brown, had a rather painful Christmas.'

The men looked even more puzzled.

'On Christmas Eve, as usual, the managers went out for drinks,' she told them. 'They came back hours later, sozzled. My boss dragged me into an empty office. He couldn't keep his hands off me, so I let him have my knee – right in his groin! I made quite an impression on him – one he won't forget in a hurry.'

'Good for you!' said Arthur.

'It certainly felt good at the time,' she said, grinning.

Both men burst out laughing and June joined in.

'I'm sorry, June. I, of all people, should not be laughing,' said Charles. 'But I wish you'd done the same to me. I really admire your guts. How awful it must be for you. What are you going to do now?'

'I'm going to look for something more interesting until I can get to college.'

She told them of her plans to get into designing.

'You'll make it,' Charles said. 'You have everything you need to get you there... skill... guts... determination. We, that is, the family, would like to help you in any way we can. Please remember that, won't you?'

'Thank you, I will.'

Charles rose from his chair. Taking June's hand, he gently held it in his. 'You've made me completely happy. I can now make a new start, thanks to you. I hope I'll see you again before I leave to do my training. Have a pleasant evening with Arthur. I hope all goes well for both of you. He's a good chap and deserves the best. You're so right for each other. God bless you both.'

June was touched. She looked straight into his dark eyes and said with feeling, 'And you too, Charlie.'

'I'll see you later, Charles,' said Arthur. Holding up a key, he added, 'And thanks for this.'

His brother turned and grinned. 'Make the most of it.'

The door closed behind him. June vaguely wondered what they were talking about but decided it was none of her business. The room seemed strangely quiet now that Charles had left. She turned to Arthur and found him looking at her intently. She gave him a shy smile. What did he have planned for the rest of their time together? As though divining her thoughts, he smiled back – even his eyes seemed to be aglow with expectant pleasure.

'Charles has given me a key to a flat he shares with a friend of his. They have an arrangement: his friend lives there during the week, and when he goes home at weekends, Charles can use it for entertaining.'

'Entertaining?'

'Use your imagination,' Arthur said, grinning. 'Sometimes a little privacy is necessary.'

She spontaneously drew in her breath as she realised not only what Charlie did in the flat, but what Arthur might be planning. She was both shocked and excited. 'Oh, I see.' She felt herself blushing.

He seemed amused by her reaction. His whole face, including his eyes, was drawn into a bewitching smile. He took her hand and gave it a gentle squeeze. 'Don't worry, we won't do anything you don't want to. But we need time together before I go… you do agree, don't you?'

Her heart was thumping in her chest. 'Yes, Arthur. I do, I really do. More than anything.'

A few minutes later, Arthur was driving her to the flat. She was full of nervous excitement of what was to come. Whatever he had planned for her, she wanted it. Her body was telling her just how much. Thankfully, Arthur was a gentleman who could be trusted, so there was no need to worry. Everything was going to be wonderful.

'Happy?' Arthur asked her.

'Sad that you're going tomorrow, but yes, I'm happy. I somehow feel clean again. Do you know what I mean?'

'Yes, I think I do. Things went well with you and Charles today. I'm pleased.'

She smiled. After a pause, she said, 'I've had a lovely day… the drive… the walk, and that nice tea. It was lovely in the Grange. The ladies' room was like something from the films. Oh, I wish…'

She sat quietly pensive. She couldn't put into words what she really wanted to say. How could he possibly understand, coming from where he did? She knew she was ignorant of things that Arthur and his sort took for granted. She felt inferior; lacking in knowledge and in experience.

After a few moments, he asked her, 'What do you wish, my darling?'

She ignored his question and returned to the afternoon's events at the Grange.

'Thank you for taking me there, Arthur – the Grange, I mean. And thanks for making things right with Charlie; I can face him again now. I've always liked him, you know. But he seems somehow different now… more gentle… more thoughtful, more… I can't say what exactly.'

'I know what you mean. This is how he used to be all the time. Yes, he could be headstrong and foolish, but we all are when we're young.'

'Like me, you mean?' June said quietly. 'You think I'm foolish and stupid, Arthur? My mother would think so if she really knew me. If she knew I was going out with an older man – kissing and… you know. Oh Arthur, do you think I'm a tart for letting you kiss me the way you do? For wanting you to touch me?'

'Of course not, don't ever think that. Hold on, we're nearly there, and then we can talk about things properly.'

Once in the flat, Arthur put on a table lamp and the two-bar electric fire that glowed with artificial coals. The large room was furnished with a pre-war reddish-brown moquette suite of angular design, a small dining table, two dining chairs, a radiogram, glass-fronted cupboard, sideboard, coffee table and one or two other items tucked into corners. A thick, brightly-coloured fireside rug drew the eye to the marble-effect fireplace. Arthur pulled the two chairs over to the fire, facing each other, and they sat down. He took hold of her hands.

'I love you, my darling, and that's all that matters. Yes, you're young, although in some ways you're quite mature for your age. But I always want you to be childlike, even when you're old and grey. Yes, you have many things to learn, but none of us ever stops learning about life. Foolish? Some people might say you are because you're here with me – someone old enough to be your father.'

June shook her head and turned her face away, not wanting to believe what he had just said.

He cupped her chin with his hands and turned her face to his. 'Stupid? There's nothing stupid about you, my dearest. You're warm-hearted, and it's natural for you to respond to my love for you. You're a woman with God-given sexuality. It's not like youngsters experimenting. I'm not some boy who wants to satisfy his sexual curiosity with every girl he meets.'

She could see the depth of his love written in his eyes, and a warm glow spread throughout her body. She knew what he wanted, perhaps what he needed, and the thought of it made her tremble. But she also knew he had the strength of will to resist and keep his lovemaking within self-imposed bounds. She couldn't trust herself to speak.

He gently squeezed her hands. 'I won't do anything you're not ready for. But don't confuse things in your mind, my love. There is nothing dirty or obscene in my desire for you, nor in your desire for me.'

She listened carefully to every word, then sighed heavily. 'I know you're right, Arthur. It's just that sometimes I feel so wicked. I long for your touch and want to be with you all the time. I don't know what's right and wrong any more, only that I love you. Sometimes I can't understand what's happening to me… I'm so ignorant about sex and all that sort of thing. I feel so stupid. How can you love someone who doesn't know anything?'

Arthur pulled out her little locket and put it in her left hand, closing both of his hands over hers. 'That is the symbol of my love and my honest intentions. Always hold on to that.'

He took her over to the sofa, put an arm around her and held her close to his side. 'Now tell me, what don't you know about sex? It isn't good to be ignorant about something so fundamental to your wellbeing. Hasn't your mother told you anything?'

She hung her head and shook it. She told him how her teachers and her mother had made everything seem so mysterious, and yet so dirty and squalid. How sensations in her body thrilled her, yet frightened her. 'I don't even know what a–' She stopped. Did he really want to hear how stupid she was?

'Would you like me to explain things to you?' he asked her, tenderly rubbing his cheek against her hair.

It was just what she wanted. Arthur would tell her the truth. She nodded her head but remained silent.

'Some things *are* dirty and shameful and, yes, squalid,' he began, his voice serious. 'And people can, and do, misuse one another. Abusing a young child's trust is the most wretched thing of all. Your mother is right to want to protect her children from men who take advantage. But it's also wrong to make ugly what is so beautiful. Do you understand what I'm saying?'

June nodded. 'Yes, I do.'

'It can be quite dangerous for a girl to gain sexual experience without knowledge. I can tell you anything you want to know, but it might be better to read my books.'

'No, Arthur, I want *you* to tell me.'

It was now warm by the fire, and Arthur suggested they take off their coats. She willingly did so. Then she snuggled up close to him, breathing in his masculine scent; his body felt so warm and inviting. Comfortable and relaxed, she asked him to continue talking to her.

He held her close and began telling her the facts of life and what every girl should know: how a child is conceived. He was a good teacher, and so relaxed about it that she didn't feel the least bit embarrassed. She decided to ask him something that had been bothering her.

'I heard my mother tell my sister that sex hurts. Is that true, Arthur?'

'Perhaps I'm not the best person to answer that question. Not usually, I should think. Only if it's forced, or if there's a problem. But your virginity is something precious, my darling. Kissing and cuddling and enjoying an expression of mutual love is one thing, but full sex is a joining of body, mind and soul and is not to be done lightly.'

'When you kiss me… you know… the way you do, I sort of glow in parts of my body, and I get feelings, mm… you know… warm, tingly feelings.'

'So do I, my darling. You must have noticed that yourself. It's good that you feel pleasure too. We just have to keep control and be aware of what's happening. It's my responsibility to manage the situation, and sometimes I have to push you away for both our sakes.'

She nodded in understanding. There was no doubt about his strong desires; his groans and the stiffening of his body told her how much he wanted her.

He kissed the top of her head and pulled her closer to him. 'When you give yourself completely to a man for the first time, it's something that can never be repeated. For me, my dearest, it's holy ground and I could never rob a woman of her virginity – it would be a violation, a sacrilege. Before we come together, I want God's blessing on our union. I hope you feel the same.'

She nodded. Nothing was said for a while; it didn't seem necessary. She felt older and wiser and so much closer to Arthur. She looked up into his kind blue eyes to find him looking intently into her own.

He said softly, 'Dear God, how I love you. I hope one day soon we'll have that blessing. It's my greatest desire, more than anything else in the whole world.'

She smiled at the thought of what was in store for them. Would they be able to wait that long? Suddenly she remembered he was going abroad.

'What will I do when you're away? I'll really miss you.'

'I've been thinking about that. June, my darling, you've seen how different Charles is. Well, I've asked him if he'll escort you to all the places I so much want to take you myself: the theatre, museums, art galleries, dining in good restaurants… wherever you fancy going. He'll be home for another week or so before returning to the navy, and he'll be home on leave from time to time. I just know you'll enjoy his company and the places he'll take you. Promise me you'll think it over.'

She was completely taken by surprise at the suggestion. Part of her was unsure about being alone with Charlie, but the whole idea of going to such exciting places thrilled her. Surely if Arthur trusted his brother then she should accept his judgement.

'If that's what you want me to do, Arthur, then yes, I will.'

He lifted up her face and kissed her tenderly.

'When you're out with Charles, I'll be thinking of you and imagining myself with you. But right now I'm with you… and I want you to have an evening to remember.'

A thrill of anticipation ran through her body as he began to unbutton her waistcoat and blouse. She stretched out sensuously on the sofa with her arms above her head in open surrender, the little golden heart – the symbol of his love for her – resting between her breasts. She knew she was being provocative and what it would do to him, but she delighted in the pleasure her body gave him. Excitement welled up within her as she noticed his hungering look – a mixture of tenderness and lust. She was both tremulous and elated at the prospect of his touch and started to unbutton his shirt. He completed the process, stripping himself to his waist. She saw a scar running at an angle down his right side and gently followed it with her finger. Poor Arthur, how painful his wound must have been. She followed it with her lips as if to make it better, then lay back on the cushions admiring his body. He bent down to hold her in his arms and she lifted herself up to him. Their naked flesh touched. Seized by desire, she pulled him closer to her.

'Oh, Arthur,' she sighed, as he moved his body against hers.

'My beautiful darling,' he whispered between soft groans.

He pulled himself away and kissed her gently over her exposed body, lingering in those places where she responded the most to his caresses. She felt the pressure of his desire and freely responded. There was no shame, no tension – just guiltless pleasure. She found herself softly moaning.

'My darling, darling, Arthur. Ahhh…'

Their lips played and their bodies entwined in rapturous delight. She realised what was happening and something within her wanted to urge him on and on until she was full to overflowing with those magnificent feelings. 'Oh, yes! Yes!' she yelled.

He let out a groan of agony and tore himself away. She knew why and made no complaint. But her body was aching for him… longing for him to…

She stopped herself from even thinking such things. If Arthur knew her true desires, he might find it too hard to be alone with her in future. So she allowed the feeling to dissipate, and bathed in the pleasant memories of his touch instead. When she opened her eyes, she saw him looking at her and smiling.

'Let me help you dress,' he said.

She knew it was the signal for the end of love-play until he returned from abroad. Oh, how long the waiting would be.

Once dressed, she waited for him while he was in the bathroom. She tidied the room and turned off the fire, then sat down and looked around. What had been a warm and cosy love nest a few minutes ago now seemed a rather dull and lifeless place. It was dominated by shades of brown, with only a few bright cushions and the rug to add a little cheer. Funny, she hadn't noticed it before. She wondered if her life would return to the dull and ordinary now that Arthur was leaving. At least Charlie would be taking her to interesting places. But there would be no more loving until Arthur's return. She sighed and fought away the threatening tears.

It was almost nine o'clock when the Rover pulled up in a lane close to her home. Little had been said during the five-mile journey. They stepped out of the car and stood in the shadows.

'I guess this is it, my darling.' He put a hand over the little heart where it lay under her clothing. 'The symbol of my love. One day soon, God willing, you shall wear a diamond ring on your finger. Then a golden ring will join it. And on that blessed day, we two will become one.'

She wanted to tell him that she couldn't bear it, that she wanted to go with him, live with him, be with him always. Instead, she said quietly, 'I'll wait for you, Arthur. There will be no one else. Not ever.'

He kissed her with utmost tenderness, then quickly turned and left her. But she knew he'd be watching over her until she was safely home. At her door she turned and saw the car down the road. Fighting back tears of sadness, she watched it drive away.

As she entered her house, she heard the sound of laughter coming from the front room. Her parents had some friends in and they were responding to the comedians on the wireless. She popped her head around the door to say hello. Her mother asked her if she'd had a nice time.

'Lovely, but I'm tired. I think I'll go to bed. Goodnight, all.'

Giving a little wave to everyone in the room, she closed the door.

She stood a moment wondering if they'd talk about her. She was right. She heard her dad's voice.

'That girl looks a bit flushed. Is she coming down with something? I hope she hasn't been drinking.'

'Our June's not a boozer, she's a good girl,' her mother said crossly.

'Maybe,' said her dad. 'But sometimes she gets fancy ideas. Mixing with that Colonel Rogers family – doesn't do to mix the ranks.'

There was a roar of laugher as Mrs Mop joined the BBC *ITMA* team: 'Can I do you now, sir?'

From her bedroom, June heard the laughter continue for the next half an hour. She knew she could never be the same person with her family; there were too many secrets now. But it couldn't be helped. She was transcending childhood and becoming a fully mature adult. And she was on the threshold of a different world; one of which her parents knew almost nothing.

Arthur was both her lover and her guide into a new life of which she had so far only tasted. From now on it was the future that mattered, and only sweet memories would go with her. She took the locket from her neck, opened it and kissed the sparkling diamond.

'Goodnight, my darling Arthur. I'll be everything you want me to be.'

Chapter Ten

Arthur returned to his car and hung around until June was safely home. He then drove the short distance to Bloomfield. The memory of her last words pulled at his heartstrings. He wanted to forget their families, marry her as soon as possible and take her with him wherever he went, never to be parted. His whole being cried out for her. Dear God, how he needed her – now, right now!

Before he entered the house, he took a few minutes to gain control of his emotions. Then, once again the cool, responsible retired officer everyone expected him to be, he joined the merry throng.

A party was going on in the lounge. The double doors to the adjoining dining room had been thrown open, and the radiogram was playing dance music. The furniture had been moved aside and the carpet rolled up to allow spirited couples to show off their dancing skills. Arthur mingled with family and guests but he really wasn't in a party mood. Clare came over to speak to him.

'Don't be a fuddy-duddy, Arthur, come and dance with your little sister,' she said, grabbing at his arm.

'All right, but only one. We old men have to save our energy.'

'You're not that old – you only *look* ninety!' she laughed, dragging him on to the dance floor.

When the foxtrot came to an end, she pulled him into a corner.

'I want to speak to you in private. You're supposed to be old and wise. Anyway, there's no one else to ask.'

He detected a strong smell of alcohol on his sister's breath and it concerned him greatly. He'd caught her smoking on a number of occasions too. It was no use remonstrating; she'd just ignore his advice anyway. Now he wondered what was coming. Already that evening, his youngest brother George had asked him what he should do about his girlfriend who wanted more than kisses and petting.

Clare was acting a little coy, looking down at the floor while she was speaking to him. She kept giving furtive glances around the room to make sure she wasn't being overheard.

'A man has asked me out… in secret, you understand,' she whispered, only just loud enough for him to hear. 'I like him a lot but he's much older than I am. Well, he'll expect a lot more than the boys get, won't he? What should I do, Arthur?'

'Frankly, Clare, I don't know what your boyfriends get. But are you asking me if older men expect to sleep with every girl they take out? I dare say some might – and do – but certainly not all of them, not if they have any decency. How do you expect me to know what this particular man is after?'

'Well, I guess I'm assuming he'll want to… you know. What should I do about it?'

'You want me to tell you whether you should go out with him, knowing that he wants sexual favours? I think you already know the answer to that. Or are you really asking me about contraceptives? He shouldn't be doing anything to need them. You really should talk to Mother about these things.'

'I can't do that, Arthur, he's my games teacher.'

'He's your *what?* Oh, Clare, no! Not my little Clare! Why are you asking me?'

'Because, well, you know so much. George said you do. And I trust you.'

'You'll be eighteen soon. If he really loves you, he'll wait until you leave school and then he'll do things properly, with good intentions… you know, *marriage*.'

'*Marriage?* God, no, I don't want to *marry* him!' Her sudden outburst caused heads to turn their way.

Arthur waited a moment and then said quietly, 'He can wait to see what you do want. Believe me, he'll wait another few months if he really loves you. And he's your teacher for goodness sake; he's in a position of trust. He's being incredibly irresponsible. I can hardly believe it.'

'But Arthur, lots of girls have gone out with him. They say he's really good at kissing and… you know… all the other things.'

'Some things should be left until you're married. Leave him alone. He's definitely not for you. And you really should talk to Mother.'

'Oh, you're just an old misery. Get with it! Times have changed since you were young.'

'Some things *never* change. You talk to your mother.'

Arthur thought it ironic that she should ask him, of all people, about going out with an older man. What right had he to be her judge?

He went to bed. As he reached the attic hallway, a half-dressed girl came out of Kate's bedroom and quickly went to the bathroom. Apparently she didn't see him. Just as he was closing the door of the room where he slept, Kate, completely naked, also went into the bathroom. After changing, he put on his dressing gown and went to use a bathroom downstairs.

Afterwards, he went quietly back to his room. As he was getting into bed, he heard the same noises as he'd heard that morning, but he now realised they were both female voices. So Kate had a secret about her love life too. That could prove useful when he needed an ally.

He closed his eyes and thought of June. She had been so wonderfully yielding to his touch, like a blossom opening to the sun. So fresh, so innocently accepting, and so unlike any of the women in his past.

The following morning, he found time to have a friendly chat with Charles, and to return the key to the flat. Charles told him of one or two things he had in mind for June's outings.

'That's wonderful, Charles; she'll really enjoy everything you've planned.'

'My papers came through this morning. Unless I hear otherwise, I'll be home for another two weeks before I start my training. I've no other commitments during that time, so I'm free to start being your lieutenant now.'

Arthur smiled at his brother's idea of the role he was playing – it was so apt. 'There is something else,' he reminded Charles, 'June will be without a job now. She'll be keen to find another one as soon as possible. I know I can rely on you to give her a hand in finding something suitable.'

'Glad to, Arthur. Anything else?'

'Actually, yes. I want to write to June but I can't send letters to her home. And I don't want to ask Mother to collude in deceiving her parents. So for the next two weeks, will you pass them on to her? After you go, Kate is willing to take over.'

Charles looked up in surprise.

Arthur smiled at his response. 'You'd be even more amazed if you knew why I've been able to tell Kate about my relationship with June. We aren't the only ones with secrets in this house. But we've promised mutual secrecy, so don't ask – just use your imagination!'

Arthur met various members of the family around the house and they all wished him well. His mother kissed him goodbye, saying she would do everything she could to make June feel at home and she'd gladly help her with her career ambitions. 'I may not approve of your choice, but the girl is industrious and creative; she deserves to get on in life.'

His father, having retrieved his pre-war Rover from the garage, was waiting to take him to the station. Arthur loaded his bags, sat in the cold leather passenger seat, and they were off. He turned to see the children, along with the rest of the family, robustly waving their farewells. He smiled and returned a wave.

As he drove along the lane, Colonel Rogers glanced sideways at his son. 'Well, Arthur, it's getting on for three years since you came home. A lot has happened in that time. Word has it that you're to be made Director of Foreign Investments in the near future.'

'I can thank you for that, Father. It was your recommendation that secured me the position I started with.'

'Not really. Your pre-war experience in the City combined with your excellent army record meant the job was yours for the taking. You could have landed a good appointment anywhere. It was my selfishness that wanted you near home.'

Arthur told his father what had happened between June and Charles the previous day. He concluded, 'So you see, Charles is more likely to be her protector than her seducer. The shock of what he did finally broke his defences. He's a new man, or rather the one he's always been at heart.'

'Yes, I can see that, Arthur. And I'm really pleased at the way things have turned out. We – your mother and I – were quite worried about him.'

Arthur then mentioned the plans he'd made for June.

His father listened and, as he turned into the station yard, nearly knocked over a pile of luggage. 'I hope you know what you're doing,' he replied anxiously.

'I know what you're thinking,' Arthur told him, once he was over the shock of his father bringing the car to such a swift standstill. 'I'm fully aware of the risks I'm taking; please believe that. But all will be well.'

'I can only hope you are right,' his father answered, fiercely jerking the handbrake as if to make a point.

There was a long queue at the booking office. By the time his ticket was bought, the train's whistle could be heard in the near distance. As Arthur carried his suitcases to the platform, the express was already approaching the station. He turned to shake his father's hand.

'Goodbye, Father. I hope the political business goes well for you. You'll be good for the people here.'

His father held his hand firmly. 'Goodbye, Arthur. Do take care.'

As Arthur was about to pick up his bags, his father suddenly gave him a warm embrace.

'You're every bit an officer and a gentleman. I'm so proud of you, my son.'

Chapter Eleven

When the visiting families left after Christmas, Charles thought it was as if the house sighed with relief. Normal activities soon resumed, and things were likely to be quiet at home until New Year's Eve. But he had much to do, and it was going to be his pleasure to do it all with June.

On Sunday, he walked to church with his parents and Clare. George was still in bed. To his surprise, Kate, when asked if she intended going, had declared herself to be an atheist. He wondered how well he really knew her. She had always seemed at a distance from them all, especially since being called up during the war. Being a uniformed WAAF seemed to change her personality. Or was she now being her true self and no longer afraid of being so?

He saw June sitting in her usual pew with her mother and her sister Rose. He smiled at the three of them as he passed them. Rose flashed her eyes at him. He hoped she didn't think he was after her. Mrs Armstrong smiled charmingly, but June looked down at her hymn book and started turning the pages.

After the service, he asked Mrs Armstrong if he could have a word with her. He had hoped that June would be present too, but Clare butted in first and dragged her off. He just caught what she was saying:

'Come on, June, I want a word with you. We'll walk home together.'

June glanced back and gave him a brief smile and a little shrug of her shoulders. He wondered why she put up with his sister's bossy ways.

Walking home with Mrs Armstrong and Rose, Charles said that his mother had mentioned that June was hoping to go to art college.

'Yes, that's right, Commander Rogers. Our June's very keen.'

'I too have an interest in art. I'm going to an exhibition of Nativity art in Nottingham. It's on display at St Mary's. Do you think June would like to see it?'

'I'm sure she would. I'll tell 'er about it. St Mary's, did you say?'

'Yes, but the buses are so infrequent on Sundays. I'd be pleased to take her in my car. I take it you would have no objection if she came with me?'

'Of course not. Thank you, Commander Rogers, I'll ask 'er myself. If you don't 'ear anything, you can assume she's going. What time will you pick 'er up?'

'Would two-fifteen be convenient, Mrs Armstrong? We could have tea out and I'll get her home by seven.'

She gave him a beaming smile. 'That will do very nicely, Commander.'

He tipped his hat. 'Good day, Mrs Armstrong.' He smiled at Rose. 'Nice to have met you, Miss Armstrong.'

As he walked away, he heard Rose say, 'Why her?'

Mrs Armstrong said proudly, 'Because June is going to art college. Mrs Rogers said they'd do anything to 'elp 'er. Anyway, I think Commander Rogers likes our June.'

Rose didn't seem pleased. 'Huh! I can't see why. She…'

The rest of the conversation faded from his hearing.

Clare hung on to June's arm as they walked along the road. June wondered why she was being so friendly – she hardly ever spoke to her these days. She would much rather have been listening to what Charlie was saying to her mother.

'Don't tell anyone,' Clare said, looking around her. 'I've got a new boyfriend.'

'Really? Why the secrecy?'

'He's my games teacher. He's lovely... a real smasher! All the girls are crazy about him. He wants to take me out. He's at least ten years older than me. I think the age difference could be rather thrilling, don't you?'

June was shocked. 'You can't go out with a teacher! He could lose his job. Surely you can wait until you leave school?'

'That's what Arthur said when I told him.'

'Well, Arthur's right. He's older than you, and wise enough to know about these things.'

'Arthur's an old fuddy-duddy. He hasn't even got a girlfriend. He was quite shocked when I told him what the girls said about Ray... that he was good at... you know what!' she said with a giggle.

June didn't like the sound of it. 'Gosh! He's your teacher, Clare. Do be careful, there could be lots of trouble. Does this Ray know what he's doing? Is he really serious about a relationship?'

'Does it really matter? I don't want to get married. I want to get into Cambridge. But Ray's fun. Meeting him somewhere secret... doing you know what... it should be quite exciting.' She gave June a wink.

'Why did you tell Arthur?'

'Because I thought he'd help me. He's a man of the world. He was engaged for years, so he'll know about these things – bound to. If my parents found out about Ray, they'd either expect wedding bells or give him a good horsewhipping!'

'I still think Arthur's right. For goodness sake, be careful Clare. Didn't a girl in your class get pregnant?'

'Yes, but it wasn't Ray's kid. Sally wouldn't say who the father was. She went away to have the baby, and then it was adopted. She should have been more careful.'

'She shouldn't have been doing anything to get a baby in the first place. Her boyfriend was wicked and irresponsible.'

'Well, I won't get caught out, and it won't stop me having fun. We're only young once, you know!'

'Please don't do it, Clare, you'll regret it. What you're talking about should go with marriage. You've asked me and I've told you. Arthur would say the same.'

'The way you talk, I'm beginning to wonder if you've had chats with my brother too!'

'It's just common sense.'

'Huh, and I thought you'd help me… give me a few tips so as not to get pregnant. Someone said to do it standing up, but it sounds a bit dodgy to me.'

'You'll have to ask someone else about that; you know what I think.'

'No wonder boys call you the Ice Maiden!' Clare snapped.

They had come to the crossroads. Clare went off in a huff. June watched her go and smiled to herself – Ice Maiden!

At two-fifteen precisely, Charles arrived outside the Armstrong's house. As he pulled himself out of his MG and approached the front door, Rose and Pat were behind a curtain upstairs, making sure they had a good view. Rose was almost swooning with ecstasy and envy.

'Lucky old June. Gosh, he's terrific. He's better than Cary Grant!'

'And Tyrone Power,' said Pat.

'And Gary Cooper.'

'And Gregory Peck.'

While Charles was being let in at the front door, Rose turned her attention to his car. 'Look at that red sports – tight, fast and thrilling. What I'd give for a ride.'

In between giggles, Pat said, 'I'd give it *without* a ride in the car – tight, fast and thrilling!'

'Oh Pat, you are awful! Good job Mam can't hear you. Well, he won't get *that* from our June, car or no car. Did you know that boys call her the Ice Maiden?'

'I'm not surprised.'

Seeing June and Charles leaving the house, Rose said in a sexy voice, 'Oh, Charlie, come and melt me anytime.'

Both girls broke out into fits of laughter.

June felt strange sitting next to Charles in his posh sports car. Before Arthur had taken over her life, she would have welcomed the event with the awe and excitement of a possible romance in sight. She knew her sisters had been watching from the upstairs window. They were clearly envious and couldn't understand why she was taking his invitation so calmly. She wondered how they would have reacted if they'd been assaulted by him. Knowing Rose, she'd have been egging him on!

'You're rather quiet. Are you all right?' Charles asked her, sounding concerned.

'Yes, thanks. I was just thinking.' She smiled to herself… just as well he couldn't read her thoughts.

Soon they were passing the Nottingham University Park. Beyond the lake, she could see the grand white building standing out against a grey-blue sky. She couldn't help but wonder what it would be like to study there.

'I suppose you have to have lots of money and brains to go to a university,' she said wistfully, as much to herself as to Charles.

'I guess money helps,' he replied. 'But university isn't everything. It's what you are that matters, and what you do with what you've got. Art college will give you new windows on life, and open up doors of opportunity.'

She smiled at his view of her situation. 'You make it seem as if it's already a certainty. I still have to finish night school first, and get enrolled on a college course. And I've no job now. I posted off my resignation yesterday, and I need to earn money to pay my way.'

Charles pulled up near the park's central gateway, giving her a rich view of the gardens, the ornamental boating lake beyond, and the lawns sweeping up to the main building. The university tower was suddenly caught in a ray of sun that faded as quickly as it had appeared. For just a moment, it was like a beacon of hope for her future.

Charles stopped the engine and turned to face her.

'June, Arthur has asked me to act for him, so I can say this to you in all honesty. He wants to back you financially in anything you want to do. He knows you want to stand on your own feet and get ahead by yourself, and he respects you for that. But sometimes we all need a little help to get us started.'

She wasn't entirely surprised to hear of Arthur's generosity. If he could give her an expensive diamond, no strings attached, then he would surely give her anything she needed. But she didn't want anyone, especially her parents, to think that a man was keeping her. She was however prepared to be taken out and educated culturally, for Arthur's good as much as her own.

'I'd rather not take money from Arthur. It would be difficult to explain it to my parents anyway. But I do want him to be proud of me, and to be able to take me anywhere... without mud on my shoes.' She looked at Charles and saw him smiling at the reference to her embarrassment. 'So I'm happy to be here with you, Charlie.'

'I have the next two weeks free before I go off for training. Starting tomorrow, I'll take you anywhere you want to go. How about we call at the Labour Exchange first? And we can look through the local papers too. We'll soon get you back to work, hopefully in a job more suited to your talents.' He grinned and gave a little salute. 'The car and its driver are at your disposal, my lady.'

'Oh, Charlie, you do make me laugh. You're so kind. I really do appreciate what you're doing for me, you know.'

She looked up into his face. What she saw in his eyes moved her deeply. But she refused to analyse either his or her own emotions. She turned her head away quickly.

'Right then, better get on,' said Charles, starting the engine and putting the car into gear. 'Hold tight, we're off!'

In less than fifteen minutes, they arrived at the Nativity art exhibition. June had never seen anything like the pictures on display. The icons drew her attention and Charles explained how they should be viewed – not really as works of art, but in spiritual terms. She nodded her head in understanding.

He told her: 'Icons were painted and blessed as visual aids, to teach, in a simple way, the mystery of the Incarnation. The symbols represent the truth that all Creation is to be redeemed.'

June tried to interpret the icons in a new light, experiencing them rather than looking at them as an art form. She looked deeply into the one in front of her. 'Redeemed?'

'Yes. Reclaimed and made whole again. It's about sacrifice and forgiveness. The Prodigal Son is free to return to his home, to the Father who loves him. The icon is merely a window you see through. Somehow you know and understand.'

Noticing strong emotion creep into his voice, she looked up at his face and said quietly, 'I think you know something personal about that story, Charlie. You're different. Something happened to you this Christmas, didn't it?'

He whispered, 'Yes,' and June understood. Charlie was a redeemed man.

After viewing the art, Charles guided her around the lovely old church, explaining details of the architecture and the symbolic representations. His knowledge and obvious interest in religious objects fascinated her. She thanked him profusely as they left the building.

'It's been wonderful… beautiful. I had no idea how knowledgeable you are about such things. I'd never have thought it.'

'Hardly surprising, the sort of life I was living. Actually, it was Arthur who taught me about religious art. He's been my guide throughout most of my life. I guess I've often let him down – sometimes quite badly.'

'But not any more,' she said with conviction. She couldn't imagine the new Charles doing anything that would hurt his brother or bring shame to his family.

'No, quite right, not any more,' he replied brightly, but in his eyes she saw pain where there should have been gladness.

His expression suddenly lifted. 'Time for tea!' he exclaimed with a grin.

'That'll be nice, I'm quite hungry.' She was happy to see him cheerful again.

He told her they could get to the Grange Lodge in just a few minutes and have a light meal there. She thought it was a lovely idea – it would bring Arthur closer to her. She touched the hidden heart with its secret message inside. Then she noticed Charlie watching her with a little smile on his face. Did he know about the locket?

Ten minutes later they pulled up outside the Grange. Charles jumped out, smartly opened the passenger door, and helped her out. She glanced at her shoes. All was well! She went confidently inside on Charlie's arm.

Inside the grand entrance hall, he courteously removed her coat. His delight at her appearance was obvious.

She had made her dress herself during her evening classes and this was the first time she had worn it. It was cut in Dior's latest style. The curving white piqué collar, which contrasted with the chestnut-brown of the soft woollen fabric, crossed over and fell to below the bust-line; the shoulders were softly rounded, and the waist nipped in. The three-quarter length sleeves had white cuffs to match the collar. The bodice was shaped to closely fit her figure. The skirt, cut on the bias, fell to mid-calf in a sweeping flare. To complete the look, she was wearing neat white court shoes borrowed from Pat.

'You look absolutely stunning,' he told her. 'I feel proud to be your escort.'

She felt herself blushing.

A receptionist came forward. 'Good afternoon, Commander Rogers,' she said, smiling at him somewhat coquettishly. She took their coats and handed them to a young assistant standing behind the desk. She ushered them through to the large lounge, where the pianist was playing tunes by Ivor Novello. 'We reserved you a table close to the window, as you requested, Commander. The waitress will bring your tea shortly.'

The woman guided them to their table, gave Charles another of her coded smiles, and left them to seat themselves.

June looked at Charles, who was grinning sheepishly. 'You intended us coming here then? Don't worry, I'm rather pleased.'

Sitting down, she glanced at the retreating receptionist and whispered, 'She seems to know you. Are you a regular visitor here?'

'Used to be. In case she lets it out, I'd better tell you. We went out a few times, but it wasn't serious. She was working somewhere else then. I didn't know she was here, I'm really sorry.'

'Don't be. I expect you to be well-known.' She nearly added, 'Especially by pretty women,' but she thought he might take it the wrong way.

She had noticed, ever since she had first met him, that women couldn't take their eyes off him; whether he was in immaculate uniform, casual country clothes, tennis gear or, as he was now, in a smart dark-brown suit and white shirt. 'Our clothes sort of match; isn't that nice?' she told him, for want of something to say.

He looked at her and smiled. 'I hadn't noticed, but yes, I guess they do. We look a perfect c–' He hesitated, cleared his throat and said, 'What a propitious coincidence.'

Had she embarrassed him? She changed the subject. 'I love the music. Makes you feel like singing.'

'Yes, doesn't it just. I've heard you singing with Clare at Bloomfield. You have a lovely voice.'

'Thank you,' she answered, dropping her eyes shyly – his gaze was too penetrating for comfort. 'You sing well, too.'

Tea arrived and while they ate the dainty food, Charles asked her about the books she liked to read and the films she liked to see.

'When I was younger, I was always at the pictures,' she told him. 'You see, during the war we were short of coal… we still are in winter. The house gets cold and damp. Of course, we have a fire in the kitchen every day, for hot water. The room can get quite crowded, but it's not often we're all at home and sitting together, except for mealtimes. Sometimes my sisters go out to meet their boyfriends and my brothers go to Boys' Brigade and Scouts. Dad goes to the pub when he's flush – weekends mostly. Before I started sewing a lot, I went to the pictures every week, sometimes twice if I had the money. It was good when I met Clare and we did the singing and dancing. I guess I started spending more time at your house than I did my own. Then when I started sewing for your mother I was home even less. I haven't been to the pictures for quite a while now, what with working during the day and often during the evening too.'

'Then we'll see what's on and I'll take you; it will be my pleasure,' he told her with a broad smile. She could see he really meant it.

On the way home, Charles asked, 'Have you told your parents about what happened at the office? Do they know that you've sent in your resignation?'

'Yes,' she said, remembering graphically the previous morning when she'd told them that she had resigned from her despised job. 'My dad was furious. He wanted to go and have it out with my boss. But, as I told him, it's my word against his, and they might not give me a reference.'

Charles was clearly angry. 'But he shouldn't be allowed to get away with it.'

'That's all right for others to say, but I have to get another job. As it is, if a prospective employer gets in touch with my old manager, I don't know what he might say. He could say he'd sacked me for insolence before I resigned.'

'I see the problem. I'm sorry; it's a rotten business. But you'll let me help you find a new position, won't you?'

It felt good to have an older person, one with more experience of life, ready and willing to support her. 'Thanks, Charlie, I'd appreciate it.'

'In that case, I'll call tomorrow and tell your mother that I'd like to help you find a new job. I'll tell her that my mother is interested and will give you a reference. That way, everything is out in the open with no strings attached.'

He helped her out of the car and escorted her to the door. She was finding such unaccustomed attention most agreeable.

He took off a driving glove and offered his hand. 'Goodnight, June. I've really enjoyed today.'

'So have I,' she said. Taking his firm masculine hand in hers, she added softly, 'I'm glad we're friends again.'

Charles arrived back at Bloomfield. His brother would be ringing soon and he had much to tell him. But some things would have to remain in his own heart; he was falling deeply in love with the girl Arthur was going to marry. At the exhibition she had told him something had happened to him. How he wished he could have told her that she herself had happened to him – that she had been the catalyst that had brought him to his senses. She was a wonderful woman: unaffected and innocent, courageous, and determined to succeed on her own terms. So unlike the women he had known and slept with over the years. But to simply be her friend and escort? His brother just didn't know what he was asking of him. Or did he?

Chapter Twelve

When June opened the door to Charles on Monday morning, she seemed a little flustered.

'Do come in,' she said, briefly glancing outside as if expecting to see nosey neighbours watching them. 'The boys are out and the others are back at work. I've told Mam what you said. Actually, she's not expecting you yet.'

'Oh, shall I come back later?'

'No, it's okay,' she said, shutting the door behind him.

The atmosphere in the house was cold and damp. He shivered involuntarily. 'I guess I *am* a bit early,' he told her, hoping she wouldn't notice his reaction. 'I didn't want to keep you waiting.'

'That's kind of you, Charlie.' She gave him a shy smile. 'I'm sorry I'm a bit of a mess, but I'm giving my mother a hand with the washing. Come through to the kitchen, it's really cold in the front room. You don't mind, do you?'

'Take me anywhere. It's good to see you again. I love the turban and pinny – they look quite fetching on you.'

She laughed. 'Oh Charlie, you are a charmer.'

Looking more relaxed, she led him up a short passage and into the kitchen. He could see Mrs Armstrong busy in the scullery; she seemed to be wringing out sodden clothes in a shallow sink. He could just make out an old mangle with its wooden rollers draped over with damp linen, and a basket filled with bright white washing. Judging by the amount of steam coming from the scullery, he guessed there must be some kind of boiler in there.

Dirty clothes were soaking in a dolly tub just inside the door. He found the combined odour of stale sweat and Sunlight soap quite nauseating.

In the kitchen, in front of a black-leaded range, sheets were already hanging on a clothes airer drawn up almost to the ceiling by a pulley. A small airer covered with socks stood in front of the open oven door of the gas cooker. A huge pan boiled on the fire, its lid continually bobbing up and exposing something white beneath the bubbling suds. Fascinated, he nearly tripped over a pail of dirty handkerchiefs – obviously well used – soaking in greyish water with a hint of greenish slime floating on top. On the table there were two baths of water, one coloured with dolly-blue, the other thickened with starch. The rest of the table and the kitchen chairs were taken up with clothes waiting to be aired or ironed: a mountain of knickers, bloomers and brassieres; a pile of vests and underpants; a stack of neatly folded blouses, shirts, pillowcases and handkerchiefs, and a mound of unidentifiable objects. A slightly open window allowed steam to exit and cold air to enter, but water hung in the air and condensed on every cold surface.

June chased a cat out of a little armchair by the fire and invited him to sit down and make himself at home. Charles smiled – home was never like this! What's more, the chair was covered in cat's fur and he imagined his navy coat turning into a moggy rug. He smiled to himself at the thought of his mother's reaction when she saw the state of his tailor-made officer's overcoat.

Mrs Armstrong hurried in carrying the cat. 'What's Tabs doin' in–' Her free hand slapped against her chest. 'Oh, my goodness!' She threw the cat under the table. 'June should 'ave taken you to the front room, I don't know what she's thinkin' of.' Her hands straightened her pinny and smoothed back her damp, untidy hair. 'I'll get you a nice cup of tea, Commander Rogers.'

He stood up. 'That's very kind. But please don't bother, Mrs Armstrong.'

'It's no trouble, I can…' Her eyes had settled on his coat. 'Good 'eavens, your clothes are covered in cat 'airs. Take the commander to the other room, Junie, while I get the tea.'

'It's cold in there, Mam. Charles doesn't mind being in here. I've often seen him in the kitchen at Bloomfield. That's right, isn't it, Charlie?'

'I love kitchens,' said Charles, wanting to put them both at ease. 'They're so homely and it's where all the real work gets done.' Then, drawing in a whiff of the soaking washing, he added, 'Thanks for the offer of tea, but I just had a cup before I came out.'

Mrs Armstrong pushed aside a pile of coats hanging from hooks on the back of the kitchen door and produced a clothes brush. 'Stand still a minute, Commander, I'll brush your coat.'

While she was fussing with his overcoat, Charles broke into her mutterings: 'Mrs Armstrong, would you mind if I help your daughter find a job? I have plenty of time at present. I can run her around in my car.'

'She did mention it. It's most kind of you, Commander, 'specially with the petrol shortages. June should be very grateful.'

'Of course I am,' June said, dipping collars into the starch. 'But I'll finish helping you here first.'

'Oh, no, you won't. You've done enough already. Get dressed properly. What ever will Commander Rogers think of you, lookin' like a washerwoman?'

June looked at him and grinned. 'I won't be long.'

He grinned back. 'Take as long as you need.'

Mrs Armstrong covered the chair with a clean cloth and signalled him to sit down again.

'We're 'avin' dreadful weather,' she groused. 'But then, what can we expect in winter? It could be much worse, don't you think?'

He opened his mouth to answer but she went on to complain about the state of the country. So he kept his mouth shut and just listened, nodding his head in appropriate places. Soon she was chatting about the Royal family. 'Fancy them namin' the baby Charles... Philip... Arthur... George. Three of them names belong to your family.'

Charles smiled. 'Yes, indeed. Quite a coincidence.'

Next came the benefits of the new National Health Service, the continuing shortages and rationing, communists, trouble abroad, and the death penalty. 'They should 'ang murderers. "A life for a life" is what the Bible says.'

Without a break in her chatter, she poked the boiling mass in the saucepan with a wooden spoon, dipped pillowcases in the dolly-blue and collars in the starch, built up the fire and checked the clothes on the airer. Tired of the cat purring around her legs, she picked it up and threw it in the back yard. She talked non-stop; Charles was glad to keep silent. Eventually, June arrived in the kitchen ready to go. Almost sighing with relief, he stood up to leave.

As they were leaving, Mrs Armstrong shouted, 'There's a storm brewin' – snow I shouldn't wonder. Don't catch cold.' She came hurrying after them, yelling loud enough for the street to hear, 'And thank you, Commander Rogers, it's very good of you.'

When they were both seated in the car, June told him, 'Ever since they found out you're returning to active service, you've gained a higher level of respect from my parents.'

'Is that so? I don't know why.'

'Well, instead of you being a bit of a lad, you're now an officer and a gentleman!'

A painful shaft of guilt stabbed at his heart. He wondered if they'd be saying the same thing if they knew how appallingly he had treated their daughter recently. But he accepted the remark in the spirit in which it was given. He laughed and started up the engine. 'Well, I'll do my best to live up to their expectations.'

'You're doing that all right!'

He glanced towards her and saw her winsome smile. How was it possible for her to be so relaxed in his presence? Dare he hope that one day... no! Thoughts of love must never enter his mind. Forgiveness, yes. Love – never!

As they drove away, he told her, 'I had a phone call from Arthur last night. He sends you his love.'

He noticed her hand go to her chest as though grasping something with her fingers. Was it the locket Arthur had told him about?

She glanced at him shyly. 'I hope I'm not stopping you from seeing your friends. I'm sure there must be lots of people you want to see before you go away.'

'I've plenty of time to see those I want to see.'

He suddenly remembered something. Keeping his eyes on the road, he reached into his pocket, pulled out an envelope and handed it to her. 'Mother asked me to give you this. She hopes it'll help you.'

'How kind.'

'Another thing. Mother would like you to come to her little get-together to usher in the coming year.'

'Really? She actually wants me there?'

'Yes. Do come. It would please Arthur. He'd like you to meet friends of the family. You could be introduced to them as Clare's friend. I'm sure your parents wouldn't object. And I'll make sure you get home safely afterwards.'

She seemed uncertain, and he didn't want to press her. He concentrated on his driving and left her to think about it.

After a few minutes, she opened the envelope. He already knew what was inside: a glowing testimonial to her skills, intelligence, personality and trustworthiness.

'How kind of your mother.'

'It's not just Mother who thinks well of you; we all do. Even my father is prepared to use his influence to help you into a more suitable job. He's very well-connected in the business world.'

'That's kind of him, but I'll see if I can get a job myself first.'

Charles smiled, but said nothing. Her reaction was exactly what he'd expected.

He stopped the car by the side of the Employment Exchange and waited while she went inside. Spotting a newspaper shop opposite, he stepped out of the car and crossed the road to buy a copy of the local morning paper.

After half an hour, June returned with a list of suitable job vacancies. Charles folded up his paper. 'I've been looking at jobs in the Morning News. I've marked one or two that could be interesting. We'll find a restaurant, have a meal and have a closer look at them.'

The restaurant was obviously far grander than June had been expecting. She seemed nervous when confronted by a rather snooty waiter. But it was a style of living she would have to get used to, and he intended her to enjoy it. He went through the menu with her, pointing out the dishes the chef was noted for. After the waiter left, she looked around the room, frowning. He could read her mind: being Mrs Arthur Rogers was going to completely change her way of life.

'Gosh, everything is so expensive. We could feed our whole family on fish and chips for the cost of that plaice I'm getting – and with rice pudding for afters!'

By the time they left the restaurant the weather had turned quite nasty, and as they ran to the car the sleet was slanting straight at them. June quickly snuggled into the warm rug he placed over her knees.

'Thank you, Charlie. I'm glad I'm not having to walk.'

For the next hour or so he drove her around the area looking for the firms on the list they'd made. She visited each one and enquired about the vacancy they'd advertised. One job had already been taken, two needed forms filling in, and the others told her to apply by letter.

She was grateful for everything. 'Gosh, the weather has been so lousy; I'd have got wet through on my own. You're giving me so much of your time, and I must be costing you a fortune with all these super meals. Thanks ever so much.'

'I'm just my brother's lieutenant, happily doing my duty. I enjoy helping you. In fact, I find it quite exciting.' He grinned. 'Remember me when you're famous.'

She laughed. 'Oh Charlie, you're such a lovely man.'

Her words truly delighted him. But even more wonderful was to see her looking so happy and relaxed in his presence. It was a miracle he did not deserve.

On the way home, he suggested that she might like to write the letters and fill in the forms at Bloomfield the following day.

'You can use my typewriter if you want to. And I can help you write the letters if you like. My job for the last couple of years has involved interviewing large numbers of candidates for jobs.'

'That would be lovely. No wonder Arthur asked you to help me.'

Charles just smiled. He knew exactly why Arthur had asked him – and his usefulness was only a small part of it.

He mentioned the New Year's celebration again. 'You'd meet some very interesting people. And I'd be around to make the introductions.'

She frowned. 'Trouble is, I don't have an evening dress. I'd shame Arthur if I turned up in my old bridesmaid's dress, even if I smartened it up a bit.'

'If you're short of that sort of thing, Kate will lend you a suitable frock; she's about your size. In fact, she says you can have one for keeps. She hardly ever wears them these days. Arthur arranged it with her before he went away; they seem to have become rather friendly all of a sudden.'

He told her about the clandestine letter delivery service.

'So Kate knows about us too? Well, I suppose that makes it easier. Arthur obviously has his reasons for trusting her,' she said thoughtfully. 'And it would be great to have someone else to talk to when you go away. I find it rather difficult to talk to your parents – especially your father.'

'I can understand that,' Charles said, thinking about the Sunday before Christmas. 'I'm so sorry.'

'Oh, Charlie, I didn't mean because of *that*. I meant because he's so… well… you know.'

'I certainly do. It's his military style.' Imitating his father, he barked: 'Jump to it, my girl! Get yourself to the party. Arthur needs you there!'

'Yes, sir! I'll be there at the double, sir.'

'Twice as fast. No excuses!'

She burst out laughing. 'You *are* funny!'

Soon, they were both laughing helplessly. He stopped the car, afraid that he might crash it.

When he calmed down, he said, 'Come back to the house with me now. Kate has put out a number of nice frocks for you to try on. She told me this morning before she went off on her motorbike. You don't have to accept Kate's cast-offs, of course. Arthur would dearly love to buy you a new one. Your parents wouldn't have to know it was new.'

She shook her head.

Within ten minutes they were at Bloomfield. As they entered the hall, Charles called to his mother. Mrs Craven appeared from the kitchen and said that everyone was out.

'If Mother comes in, tell her I'm with June in Kate's flat.' He noticed the shadow of a frown pass over the domestic's face. 'It's all right, Annie, you needn't look like that; Kate has left out some dresses for her.'

'Oh, sir! I didn't mean to suggest anything. When Mrs Rogers comes in, I'll tell her what you said. Would you and June like a cup of tea and a bit of cake?'

'Thank you, Annie. We'll have a cup when we come down. We won't be long.'

Charles guided June up the attic stairs. 'I can't blame Annie for being suspicious, she knows what I'm like – or *was* like, before the Prodigal repented.'

'You *are* different, Charlie... you're gentle and thoughtful now. Arthur told me you'd changed, and he's right.'

He led her into Kate's bedroom. Spread on the bed in front of them were the latest styles from top designers. He watched with pleasure as her face lit up. 'Some of these have never been worn,' he told her. 'Kate's last boyfriend gave her most of them. He was in the fashion trade. But he cleared off with a wealthy Canadian twice his age.

Kate doesn't want anything to do with men now, and that includes their taste in clothes. So take your pick!'

June lifted up each one in turn, her face a picture of disbelief.

'These are all absolutely stunning. I can't believe she doesn't want them. Gosh, I just don't understand her… well, okay, maybe I do. What a rotter! It's a wonder she didn't burn them all.'

'She nearly did. At least, the ones he gave her.'

'I think they're my size too. Might have to pinch the waist in a tiny bit, but that's no problem.' She turned to face him, her cheeks flushed and her eyes bright with excitement. 'Which one do you like best?'

'I think you'd look quite splendid in that red silky one. But anything, even a sack, would look lovely on you.' Thinking he'd gone too far, he added, 'I know that's what Arthur would say.'

She turned her eyes away. 'You know, Charlie, you don't have to be Arthur's lieutenant all the time. You are allowed to be yourself sometimes.'

Picking up the red dress, she looked at the label with the price tag still attached. 'This was bought in Paris!' she shrieked in delight. 'You knew, didn't you?'

It was true, he did know; he wanted her to have the best. Kate had been about to put her scissors through it, but he'd persuaded her not to. But June didn't need to know that.

'Now how would I know that? Kate is a very private person,' he said, smiling to himself. He walked towards the door. 'I'll leave you to try it on.'

A minute or so later, she called for him to return.

'What do you think?' she asked, swirling around, her face radiant with joy.

'Absolutely gorgeous! If only Arthur could see you now. I'll tell you what, tomorrow I'll take a photograph of you wearing the dress. I'll send a copy to Arthur, he'll be absolutely thrilled.'

'Oh, will you, Charlie? How lovely. Do you have his address yet?'

'No, not yet, he's still moving around at present. But he's booked a call to my parents for tomorrow evening at nine. You'll be able to say hello to him.'

Her hand immediately went to her chest and fell on a little golden locket revealed by the deep cut neckline. 'That's wonderful,' she said softly.

He looked at her quizzically. 'Arthur gave you that sweet little locket, didn't he?'

'Yes. It's a symbol of his love. It brings him closer to me. I don't think he'd mind you knowing.'

He not only knew about the locket, but what it contained. Fighting the jealousy that welled up within him, he said pensively, 'That's beautiful. I really hope things work out for you both. True love is hard to find.'

She looked at him tenderly. 'You'll find your dream girl one day; I just know it.'

He nodded and forced a smile. 'I'll go downstairs while you change,' he said, pulling himself away reluctantly. 'I'll see you in the kitchen. Annie will have made the tea by now.'

He found Mrs Craven spooning tea into a heated teapot.

'June should fit into Miss Kate's dresses very nicely,' she said as she poured boiling water over the leaves.

'She does, Annie,' he replied, the image of June in the red dress still burning in his brain. To change the subject, he said, 'That cake you're cutting looks nice.'

'Freshly made this afternoon. I thought you might like a slice.'

June came in with the red dress over her arm. She held it up for Mrs Craven to see. 'It's a lovely dress, don't you think, Annie? I'm wearing it tomorrow for the party. Mrs Rogers has asked me to come. As a friend of Clare's, of course. Wasn't that kind of her?'

'It certainly was. Very kind indeed. It'll be quite a do.'

After the tea and cake, he took June home. Just before they reached her house, he suggested: 'How about coming over at ten tomorrow? You can stay for lunch and get everything posted off by mid-afternoon. Then you'll have plenty of time to get ready for the party.'

She looked uncertain. 'Are you sure your mother won't mind, Charlie? I don't want her to think I'm pushing myself into the household.'

'Mother sort of suggested it herself. I think she wants to get to know you better. You know, more intimately. After all, you're likely to be her daughter-in-law one day.'

She was frowning and it worried him. Was she feeling his mother's rejection of her as a suitable wife for Arthur? Certainly, he had detected disapproval in his mother's voice – despite all her talk of wanting to help June get on. Arthur was the eldest son and the most favoured – and with good reason. No woman would *ever* be good enough for her dear Arthur. But socially well-placed single women were occasionally invited to dinner parties, and the reason was obvious. She had aspirations for all her sons – but *especially* for Arthur. Now June was being invited to a Bloomfield party. But did his mother have aspirations for her too? Or was she hoping she would feel outclassed?

Before he left June at her door, he had a word with Mrs Armstrong and told her about the party arrangements.

''Ow lovely. Are you sure it won't be a bother to collect 'er, Commander?'

'No bother, Mrs Armstrong. Your daughter is a delight to be with... a credit to her parents.'

Mrs Armstrong beamed.

'Didn't I say 'e was a proper gentleman?' June's mother said to her later that evening. 'It's lovely 'e takes an interest in you. You're a lucky girl. Fancy, all the family seem to 'ave taken to my little Junie. And why not? You're a good girl... been brought up to know right from wrong.'

June remained silent and went on altering the red dress to make it a perfect fit. She was being talked about as though she were a child. A credit to her parents, indeed! But she had to smile; Charlie was just buttering them up. A good girl and knowing right from wrong? Arthur had changed her perceptions about such things. Her mother might think differently if she knew of her rather intimate relationship with a man old enough to be her father.

The following morning a letter arrived in the post for her. It concerned her resignation. Mr Brown had written of his regret at losing such a valuable worker, but there were no inducements for her to stay with the firm. The letter also contained back pay and the usual sign of final separation from one's employer: her 'cards'.

When she arrived at Bloomfield, Clare opened the door and led her to the kitchen. 'We can have a chat while you wait for Charlie. He knows you're here. I haven't had my breakfast yet – up late last night.'

June could guess why, but she said nothing. They sat down at the well-scrubbed table and Clare poured tea into two pretty china cups. She offered June some buttered toast, but she politely refused. Clare shrugged her shoulders, reached for the marmalade pot and heaped a large spoonful on to her plate.

'Charlie says he's helping you find a new job. What happened to your old one?'

June told her about her resignation and why.

Clare nearly choked on her toast when she told her about kneeing Mr Brown in the groin. 'Good for you!' she said, after swallowing down some tea to clear the problem. 'But it's jolly unfair that you lost your job. They should have given you a medal!'

June grinned. 'I don't know about that. My boss has suffered the pain of parting, not me!'

'What a rat! Dirty old men should have it chopped off.'

Charles came in carrying a typewriter and sheets of paper. He said hello to June and then turned to his sister.

'What was that, Clare? Are you planning a bit of surgery?'

Smirking, Clare stood up and walked off, toast in hand. As she was going into the hallway, she turned to June and said pointedly, 'Watch it with my brother. There's a sharp knife on the worktop if you need it.'

June felt herself blushing.

'I apologise for my sister,' Charles said. 'She doesn't know I'm a reformed character. Now, lets take this lot up to Kate's flat. We have her permission and we won't be disturbed there.'

June dropped an envelope on the small table in the hall as she passed. It was a letter of thanks to Mrs Rogers. She felt a formal reply would be expected, apart from which she didn't particularly want to meet her just yet. She followed Charles upstairs. When they reached Kate's sitting room, she saw a pile of clothes thrown over the sofa.

'Is Kate having a jumble sale?' she asked Charles.

'Actually, she's having a clear out. She seems to prefer trouser suits to dresses these days – probably because of her motorbike. She's throwing that lot out. She offered them to Clare, but she said she didn't want her cast-offs. And why should she? Clare has her own taste in clothes, and she's never been short of anything she wants, clothes rationing or not.'

June thought of all the dresses she had willingly received from her sisters. The material could always be re-used, even if the clothes themselves were shabby. She smiled wistfully and lied, 'I can understand that.'

'Kate says to help yourself if you want any of them. She knows you're good at renovating and that sort of thing.'

She couldn't hold back her excitement. 'Really? I can have any of them? Those evening dresses are here, and those smart suits I like to see Kate in. Blouses and skirts as well. Oh Charlie, I can't believe it!'

Charles seemed as pleased as she was. 'I'll tell you what, when we finish here, we can pack the clothes into cases and take them to your house. You can have a good sort out and throw out the ones you don't want.'

June was appalled at such waste. 'You must be joking! You can't throw away good clothes like these – the material alone is worth a lot of money.'

'Well, whatever,' Charles said, smiling broadly at her enthusiasm. 'Such a thrifty wife Arthur will be getting; you'll put the Rogers womenfolk to shame. Now, before you get out your needle and thread, we'd better get on with these job applications.'

Putting aside the clothes, they set to work sorting out the paperwork and who was doing what. June filled in the forms while Charles typed out copies of his mother's testimonials. When he'd finished, he made some tea in Kate's kitchen and brought her a cup.

'How's it going?' he asked.

'I'm ready to start on the letters now. I've written one out in rough.' She handed him a piece of paper. 'What do you think?'

Charles carefully read the letter while she sipped her tea. He seemed to be frowning – did he disapprove?

He put down her rough draft and sat on the corner of the table she was using. 'You know, June,' he said, his head to one side in a thoughtful pose. 'One of these companies happens to be a clothing manufacturer. Although the job is for a clerk in the manager's office, it might be helpful if you pushed your artistic talents a bit. In my experience, it's always good to let your employer know what else you can do, especially when it's relevant to the firm's business.'

She frowned. It was something she'd thought of herself, but had rejected. 'Do you really think so? I don't want to put them off. They might think I only want a temporary job until I can get to college.'

'But that's true, isn't it?' he said, splaying his hands in an open gesture. 'It'll come out that that's what you really want to do before long, especially if you get a good interviewer. Being honest from the start might be the best policy.'

She was still uncertain. 'Mm, maybe.'

'Someone who's prepared to help out, say, in the design department, when things in the office are slack, might be a good selling point,' he told her with enthusiasm. 'When I've interviewed prospective staff, flexibility is something I've always looked for.'

'I see what you mean,' she said, now convinced that he was right. 'Thanks, Charlie. Will you check it for me after I've written it?'

'Certainly, and anything else I can do to help.'

By twelve-fifty, she had typed the letters and all the applications had been put into envelopes and addressed.

'Right, let's hope you get some replies before I go,' said Charles as he stuck on the last stamp. 'I insist on driving you to any interviews. You must present yourself looking smart and attractively dressed. You can do that all right, but I can make sure you arrive the way you start out.'

June looked at his eager, handsome face. 'You're being awfully kind to me, Charlie. I really do appreciate it.'

Their eyes met and her heart suddenly started to beat faster. Feeling drawn to him, she quickly turned away, afraid of her emotions.

Mrs Craven called up from the bottom of Kate's stairs wanting to know if they'd be joining the rest of the family for lunch. The spell was immediately broken, and her heart calmed down.

She had often eaten at the Rogers' house, but only in the capacity of the sewing help or Clare's friend, and the meal had always been taken in the kitchen. To sit as a guest in the breakfast-dining room with Colonel and Mrs Rogers, Clare and George, as well as Charles, was an unaccustomed privilege. She felt a little awkward eating with Arthur's parents, knowing they disapproved of her relationship with their eldest son. But they were pleasant enough – they were too polite to be otherwise.

After the meal, she asked Mrs Rogers if she needed help with anything. Her offer was gratefully accepted.

'Actually, June, that dress you were making for me before Christmas was not finished properly. Lily, who took it over, made a mess of the hem. Would you have time to alter it for me please?'

'I'd love to, Mrs Rogers. Can we do it now?'

'Certainly. We will go to my bedroom.' She rose from her chair and turned to Charles. 'Would you like to post June's letters while she's helping me?' It was more of a command than a question.

As soon as they arrived in the bedroom, Mrs Rogers mentioned that she had read June's letter of thanks for the testimonial. 'If I can do anything further to help you, my dear, please ask. You work hard and deserve to get on.' She pointed to a comfortable-looking armchair by the window. 'Just sit down a moment while I put the dress on in my bathroom.'

It wasn't the first time June had been in that bedroom. She loved it. It had tall windows overlooking the garden, where trees screened the distant houses. They could have been in the middle of the countryside. The dressing table – of polished walnut like the rest of the bedroom suite – was resplendent with silver-backed brushes, trinket boxes and perfume bottles. The furnishings were plush, as was to be expected in such a household, with the pink, beige and green Chinese carpet nicely matching the heavy brocade curtains that reached down to the floor. Such luxury! Even the pink of the quilted silk bedcover matched perfectly with the silk-panelled walls. Mrs Rogers seemed to lack nothing – except a suitable match for her dear Arthur!

Mary Rogers returned, wearing the offending dress. June quickly summed up the problem and dropped to her knees with a box of pins.

'I see what you mean. It won't take long to fix it.'

While she marked the new hemline with pins, Mrs Rogers cleared her throat and said primly, 'I have to be honest with you, my dear.' She paused and genteelly cleared her throat again. 'Although I like you a lot and I think you will make someone a splendid wife, this affair with Arthur troubles me.'

It was what she had been expecting, if not dreading. Although shaken, she tried to stay composed and went on with her pinning, waiting for Mrs Rogers to finish her little speech.

'You must understand, this is nothing personal.' Her tone was now conciliatory. 'If it had been George, I would be much happier about you coming into the family. Is Arthur being *fair* to you? That is the question that needs consideration. Have you any idea what it will be like as the wife of a top director? Not only that, but he is also the eldest son, and in this family that means heavy responsibilities.'

June said nothing, but felt the full weight of what was being said to her. Her guts were playing havoc with the lunch she'd just eaten, and the fingers holding the pins were beginning to shake. She took a deep breath and forced herself to keep calm, but the words had been like a dagger to her heart. She wasn't good enough and belonged where she was – on the floor, serving the mistress of the house!

No, no, that was unfair. As things stood at the moment, Arthur's mother was probably right. Her own father had said many a time that it didn't do to mix the ranks.

'You are so young, my dear; do give it time,' Mrs Rogers continued in a motherly manner. 'But it is so sad for Arthur that he will have to wait for you.' She sighed deeply. 'He waited over the war years for Barbara Lightfoot only to be disappointed. A man has his needs.' She hesitated. 'I do hope you are both careful in that respect. You do know what I mean, don't you?' A concerned frown wrinkled her forehead – a bastard child, or having Arthur trapped into wedlock, would never do.

Fighting to control her nervousness, June lifted herself from her knees and sat on the floor. She looked up at this woman who had been so honest with her and gave her a smile.

'You have no need to worry, Mrs Rogers. Arthur and I have no intention of doing anything that would bring shame on his family. Some things are best left until we're married.' She paused a moment to let it sink in. 'I realise I'm not what you wanted for your son. It's true, he could do much better. I appreciate all that you and your family are doing for me, and I promise I won't let you down. What I don't know, I'll learn. I'm determined to make Arthur proud to have me as his wife.'

Mrs Rogers seemed relieved, even if not entirely happy. Indicating that the conversation was over, she offered June a hand to rise to her feet. Unexpectedly, she gave her a restrained hug. Clearly, she was making an effort to accept the situation.

'I'm glad we had this little talk, June. I don't want to interfere, but I think it best to keep knowledge of the affair restricted, at least until it can be formally announced. We agree on that, I think?'

'Yes, we do. And it's what Arthur wants too. I'm sorry I can't tell my parents, but they'd find it hard to accept things as they are.'

Mary Rogers nodded in agreement and a hint of a smile appeared at the corners of her mouth. Did she think there was still time to find a more acceptable wife for her son?

'Arthur might not want us to get engaged until I'm older, but I know he loves me. We love each other. We can wait until the time is right. I just want what Arthur wants. I really do, Mrs Rogers.'

Sighing heavily, Mary Rogers said, 'I know, my dear. We both do.'

Chapter Thirteen

At eight o'clock, Charles pulled up outside the Armstrong's terraced house. He picked up an umbrella from the back of the car and hurried to the front door, which was opened immediately by June's father.

'Come in, Commander Rogers, June will be down in just a minute. We want to thank you for what you're doing for her. She's had a bad break with that swine at work. I'd like to get hold of him and make sure he don't harm any other innocent kid.'

Charles felt a little uncomfortable as he entered the house. What would Armstrong do to him – quite justifiably – if he knew what had happened to his daughter the Sunday before Christmas? Certainly, he wouldn't be talking to him now as though he were her benefactor!

'It was a bad business, sir. I can understand your anger,' he said as the door was closed behind him. 'But I have an idea that June will triumph from this situation. She's a bright young woman and deserves to get on in life.'

'Thank you, Commander. We've always done our best to encourage our Junie, but people in your position know how things are done. She was thrilled with that art exhibition. A bit more of that sort of thing – that's what she needs. I hope she thanked Miss Kate for those lovely dresses. She'll have some grand clothes to start her next job with. Do thank Miss Kate for us, will you?'

'I'm sure Kate was pleased that someone could do something with them.'

He turned as he heard someone coming down the stairs. As he'd hoped, it was June – looking delightfully flushed. She joined them in the small, narrow hallway.

'Sorry to keep you waiting, Charlie. I should have been ready.'

'But that's a lady's prerogative,' he told her gallantly.

'Tell a woman that and she'll keep you waiting every time,' Armstrong muttered with a sniff. 'You'd soon know if you had a wife and three daughters.'

'That's not likely to happen for a long time yet,' Charles told him, grinning at the thought of Armstrong's problem. He studied June more closely. She was wearing an open coat over her dress, but he thought she looked gorgeous in her make-up and with a white chiffon scarf floating over her hair. 'You look lovely, June. Well worth waiting for.'

Mrs Armstrong came into the hallway from the kitchen. 'Is June keeping you waiting, Commander?'

'No, not at all, we're just off.'

He took hold of June's arm and steered her quickly away before the rest of the family arrived. He'd already seen her sisters at the top of the stairs.

Arriving at Bloomfield, Charles moved quickly to open the passenger door and help June out. Once inside the deserted hall, she went straight to the cloakroom to take off her coat and uncover her hair. Charles heard a few guests chatting and laughing in one of the rooms, but he had no intention of deserting June. His parents joined him in the hall just as she emerged from the cloaks.

'Good evening, Colonel and Mrs Rogers, I'm so pleased to be invited,' June smiled with pleasure.

'My dear, you look absolutely splendid!' exclaimed Colonel Rogers, his cheeks a little pink.

'Beautiful!' said Mary Rogers, sweeping her eyes over June's figure – a little enviously, Charles thought.

'Ravishing!' he said. 'I think you've altered that dress. It certainly is a perfect fit.' He pulled his eyes away and hoped his parents didn't dwell on the implications of his remark.

June beamed at the compliments. 'How clever of you to notice, Charlie. I've taken in the waist, and lifted the neckline a little. I thought it was a bit too low for me.'

Charles saw his mother smile and nod her approval. But she also glanced at him somewhat quizzically.

Kate suddenly appeared, telling her mother that her friend would be staying overnight in her flat. She then caught sight of June.

'Well, my goodness! Surely that's one of the frocks I put out for you. You certainly have made it fit well. I'm glad you had it, it really suits you.'

Clare appeared from the kitchen area. She stood in awe of June. 'Gosh, you look lovely! Where did you get that dress?'

Charles nearly burst out laughing. His young sister had turned down all of Kate's dresses without even looking at them. But he was glad that she had.

More guests started to arrive and Charles took it upon himself to introduce June, saying that she was Clare's friend. The rooms were getting crowded. He was annoyed that Clare hardly came near June; she was too busy chatting up his men friends most of the evening. He noticed her slip away to the conservatory with his old pal Lionel, a known womaniser. Well, he could hardly criticise – only a week earlier he'd been in bed with a girl not much older than Clare. George, looking moonstruck, came along and took June away with him to get food and drink in the main dining room.

George didn't look at all pleased when, at almost nine o'clock, Charles took June by the elbow and led her to the study. He explained that it was about a job June had applied for, but his brother obviously didn't believe him. Jealousy and anger showed in his eyes and his tight-lipped smile.

The phone rang and Charles picked it up straight away. He told Arthur that he was passing the phone over to a beautiful lady sitting beside him. Then he left the room to join the noisy crowd in the hall. After allowing them time to talk, he told his mother that Arthur was on the phone. He called out loud enough for June to hear, 'In here, Mother. I took the call in the study. June's holding the phone while I get everyone.'

Charles put his hand on June's shoulder and steered her to the morning room. 'Now to get my camera,' he said, 'before someone else sweeps you away from me.'

He had just taken the last photograph when the door burst open and an old girlfriend of his burst in.

'Charlie! I've been looking for you everywhere. What are you doing in here? Surely you're not leading this young girl astray? Shame on you; come and seduce someone nearer your own age.'

He was about to protest when June said, 'It's okay, Charlie, go with your friend.'

'Do call me Angela,' she said, sweeping her eyes over June. She turned to Charles. 'Come on, Charlie. Time for dancing.'

'Yes,' said June, 'please go with Angela. George is waiting to dance with me anyway. Thanks for taking the photographs. You must take some of Angela.'

She hurried out of the room with Charles calling after her, 'I'll see you later.'

'Mm, taking pictures eh, Charlie,' said Angela. 'Would you like me to strip off?'

Angela was looking provocative in a close-fitting pink satin gown. It was slashed deeply at the front, partially revealing her smooth, full breasts. With her blonde hair, pouting pink lips, blue eyes and tall shapely figure, she looked exceedingly enticing. The way Charles was feeling, he'd have liked her to do more than just strip off. But he was determined to control his appetite for women.

'Sorry, Angela, but I'm all out of film,' he told her apologetically. 'June wanted a photograph for her parents. Anyway, let's dance!'

At twelve-thirty, June said she was ready to go home. Charles obliged.

'Thanks, Charlie,' she said, when he took her to her door. 'I've had a lovely time. Sorry I've dragged you away, but I'm really tired. Angela looks nice. You must get back to her before someone takes her off.'

Did he detect a little jealousy? Ridiculous! Just wishful thinking on his part.

Angela was waiting for his return. He knew what she wanted all right. He'd given way to her desires in the past – and most enjoyable it had been. The frustrating situation he found himself in did nothing to quell his desire for her. He longed to be consumed by her lusty appetite. Sweating as they danced, and with Angela pressed up to him, he continued to wrestle with himself.

New Year's Day was cold and wet. June was ready for Charles to pick her up at twelve o'clock, as arranged. He was taking her to lunch at one of the city's finest hotels, and she was looking forward to it with both excitement and trepidation. Would she be wearing the right clothes? Would she let Charles down through her ignorance of social niceties?

Fortunately, he sensed her nervousness and tried to put her at ease. 'Relax, you don't have to worry about a thing; I'll make sure you enjoy the experience. The food here is great, the wine superb, and the service couldn't be better.'

She would never admit it, but it was the service that worried her most. The waiters would know she was clueless and they'd look down their noses at her. She didn't want to show her ignorance, so when they walked into the hotel restaurant she asked Charles to order for them both. She was pleased she had, for when they sat down to dine she found that the menu was entirely in French.

'Next September, I'm going to join a night class for French,' she told Charles as soon as the waiter had gone.

'That would be rather splendid. A real asset for a society lady.'

'You're teasing me,' she told him crossly.

'No, *really*. Arthur will definitely want to take you to France with him. Knowledge of the language would be useful anyway – I could give you a few lessons before I go away. Would you like that?'

'Oh, Charlie, I'd love you to teach me.'

After the meal, they sat in the red-carpeted and gold-pillared ornate lounge, drinking coffee from dainty cups. June soaked in the atmosphere, looking around her and taking in the behaviour patterns and dress of the other diners and hotel guests. She saw Charles watching her.

'It's rather grand here, Charlie. Do you come here often?'

'Not often – special occasions. There are other places I prefer, but I thought you'd like to sample the food here. They have the two dining rooms, both of them excellent, but I thought you'd like to taste the French cuisine.'

'It's very good, but the beef wasn't cooked, it was quite bloody.' Just the thought of it made her feel sick. 'I'm sorry, Charlie, I couldn't eat most of it.'

'So I noticed. The French cook it that way. I'm sorry, I should have warned you.'

'But it wasn't cooked. It was just… singed.'

He shrugged his shoulders and smiled. 'You get used to it. You'll probably enjoy it eventually.'

Raw meat? She didn't want to get used to that.

After lunch, the rain cleared and they walked along the river bank for an hour, chatting about their different school days. More than ever, she realised that Charles and his family lived in an entirely different world to hers. It wasn't so much the material things – they were only too obvious – but attitudes and expectations.

While he was driving her home, she told him, 'It's been really grand. You make me feel like a proper lady.'

'You *are* a lady, June, and it's a real pleasure to take you out. It's too bad that Arthur's isn't able to do so, but it's given me a chance to make up for other things.'

She heard the sorrow in his voice. 'Not sure what you mean, Charlie,' she said softly. 'I can't remember anything of the sort.'

He smiled. 'As generous as you are beautiful.'

She said nothing, but the warmth of his words touched her deeply.

They soon arrived at her home. He turned to face her. 'How about we start those lessons tomorrow morning?'

'Golly, I'll be able to speak a few words in French to Arthur when he gets home.'

'I've always thought of French as the language of love,' he said wistfully.

It wasn't hard to imagine his deep melodic voice whispering soft words to melt the coldest heart, and she wondered how many young women had succumbed to his romancing. From what she'd heard about him, he had no need to seduce *any* woman – they were only too willing to fall into his arms. If things had been different that Sunday, if he'd been in his right mind, if only…

'Thanks again, Charlie,' she said briskly, pushing her disturbing thoughts aside. 'I'll see you in the morning then.'

He helped her from his car. Before she went inside the house, he picked up her hand and lightly kissed it. 'Until tomorrow, *au revoir*.'

It was just a brief gesture, but a thrill of pleasure shot through her body. It was most disconcerting. She entered the house determined to think only of Arthur.

'Very romantic,' said Rose, who was coming down the stairs.

'You were watching us? That's rotten! Anyway, it meant nothing, Charlie was just being polite.'

'Oh, yes?'

'Yes!'

'What does he kiss like? You know, *proper* kiss and all that?'

'I wouldn't know, Rose, we don't do that sort of thing.'

'What? I don't believe it.'

'You can believe what you like. I'm not interested in kissing him, and Charles is a gentleman. He's just escorting me places – partly because his mother has asked him to and partly because he wants a bit of company… someone who *doesn't* expect the sort of thing *you're* talking about.'

But she knew how he *really* felt about her. She could see it in his look, hear it in his voice, and catch it in his smile. What's more, when she saw him looking at her, wonderful sensations flowed through her body. No, she mustn't even think it. She dismissed her thoughts and told herself that it was just because she was missing Arthur. Of course she wasn't interested in kissing Charlie. Well, at least she could be totally honest about one thing: Charlie *was* behaving like a perfect gentleman.

As arranged, she went to Bloomfield the following day for her lesson in French. Charles suggested it might be a good idea for her to learn a few common words and phrases that they could practise during the day. So in the afternoon, while they walked around the city, visiting the castle and other places of interest, she practised her French, laughing and joking when she made a mess of it. They went by the theatres and halls to see what was on during the coming months. A touring company was putting on *Swan Lake* at the Royal late in February. Charles delighted her by buying two tickets.

'Hopefully, Arthur will be back to take you,' he said, smiling his gorgeous smile, but with a certain sad look in his eyes.

He also booked for an orchestral concert on Saturday night, and promised to take her to the cinema to see *The Tales of Hoffman*. By the time he took her home she was dizzy with mixed emotions. So much was happening to give her pleasure, but she was experiencing it with the wrong man. Or was she? Charlie seemed so right by her side; knowledgeable, funny, and a wonderful companion. *But Arthur will be even more so when he has a chance to be,* she told herself. Charlie was just Arthur's lieutenant, doing what had been asked of him. He wasn't her boyfriend, and never would be.

She asked him to drop her off near Bloomfield so she could walk the short distance home. Turning up in his car all the time was attracting attention from the neighbours. A good-looking guy like him driving a sports car was hard to miss in *any* street, but in her road, practically on her doorstep, he was a head-turner and a cause for gossip – especially with her sisters watching out for him.

He looked puzzled. 'Are you sure? It's no problem driving you home.'

'I'm sure. Anyway, I want to call at the corner shop,' she lied.

She jumped out of the car before he had time to help her. 'Thanks, Charlie, it's been a lovely day. See you in the morning.'

Afraid of her feelings, she walked home quickly, turning just once to wave farewell. She spent the evening sewing in the kitchen, oblivious to the sounds coming from the wireless and the chatting of family members. Later, in her cold bedroom, a water bottle on her knees, she wrote a long loving letter to Arthur.

Two letters dropped through the Armstrong's letter box the following morning, both of them for June. They were replies from firms she had written to, and each was offering her an interview on the same day. Much to her delight, one of the firms wanted her to bring samples of her artistic work with her. But the other job had good prospects for promotion, and they were offering a good salary. She couldn't wait to tell Charlie.

She arrived for her French lesson at ten o'clock. Charles opened the door. 'I have something for you,' he said quietly, and slipped a letter into her hand. She knew immediately that it was from Arthur.

Talking in whispers, they headed to the breakfast-dining room where they'd be able to do an hour of French undisturbed. But the room was already being used by Clare, who was sitting by a crackling apple-log fire reading a book. She looked up as they entered.

'What's all this whispering, you two? French lessons? I think I'll stay and watch your technique, brother Charlie.'

'It would do you good to brush up on the basics, Clare. Do join us.'

She gave a little snort and left the room.

Sitting at the table, June showed him the letters she'd received.

'This really is good news,' he said, quickly scanning them. 'I suggest you ring from here and confirm the interview with Watson's, the garment manufacturer. As for the other one, I think you should ask them if they can offer an alternative day later in the week and risk them saying no.'

'I knew you'd know what to do, Charlie. Can I ring now?'

He stood up and led the way. 'We'll use the phone in the study, come on.'

Having sorted out the interviews and worked hard at her French, June went home at eleven-fifteen. She was anxious to open the letter from Arthur. In fact, it said very little. There were no expressions of undying love, just information about the weather and things he'd seen. Clearly, knowing the sort of household she lived in, he wasn't taking any chances. There was also a postcard in the envelope. On one side was a sketch of a village church. Turning it over, she saw that he'd written a little poem.

In the silence of the starlight, under the old yew tree
I linger a while and silently ponder
The love I've known, so sweet and tender
As she gave her heart to me.

She was delighted. Clever, clever Arthur! She pressed her little golden heart to her breast and read the letter over and over. Then she hid it inside a folder among her night class things; it was the only place safe from her sisters' prying eyes.

Still thinking about Arthur and the poem, she started on an alteration to one of Kate's outfits. She had used some of the money Mrs Rogers had given her to buy a second-hand sewing machine from a neighbour, and it was proving tremendously useful. Soon she would be well-equipped to go anywhere and look smart whatever the occasion. She was on her way up and nothing was going to stop her.

Charles was picking her up at one-thirty. He'd told her to dress reasonably smartly, but not fussily. She was also to ask her mother's permission to be out with him until just after eleven. Her mother wanted to know where she was going but June couldn't tell her. 'It's a surprise, Mam. I don't know where he's taking me.'

When the MG arrived outside the house, her mother followed her to the door. Charles, immaculate as ever, was crossing the pavement with his umbrella. 'Well, ave a nice time, love, wherever you're goin'. The Commander's a lovely man,' she said wistfully.

June was soon seated in the car, glowing with pleasure. 'This is so exciting!'

'I hope you won't be disappointed,' he said grinning. 'We're going to be kids again.'

Within twenty minutes, the car was parked and they were hurrying towards the theatre. She soon realised where they were heading.

'Oh! We're going to the pantomime!'

'Are you disappointed?'

'No, I love it. My favourite uncle took me to one, years ago.'

'It's been a long time for me too – before the war.'

'Before the war? That's when *I* went. I was just seven.'

'Well, let's pretend you're seven and I'm your favourite uncle.'

'No, I don't want you to be my uncle; you've got to be a child like me.'

He took her hand and swung it as they walked. 'Whatever you want, little Junie,' he told her, laughing as he tried to speak with a childlike voice. 'Please will you sit next to me?'

June laughed with him. With a lisp, she said, 'Do we get an ice-cream at the interval?'

It began to rain. Charles clasped her hand more firmly and they ran the rest of the way.

They arrived at the theatre damp and breathless, but still laughing. The place was crowded with excited youngsters, all bright-eyed and shiny-faced. Throughout the whole performance, with Charlie egging her on, she behaved just like one of the little ones around them.

When they came out, they hurried to the car, repeating all the catchphrases they'd shouted during the performance. They were still laughing and joking as they reached the car park and slid inside Charlie's MG.

'That really was fun. I haven't laughed so much since I was a kid,' she said, settling in and covering her knees with the rug.

'Oh, yes, you have,' he told her in a squeaky pantomime voice.

'Oh, no, I haven't.'

'Oh, yes, you have. Hasn't she, boys and girls?'

They both burst out laughing again. Charles took a clean handkerchief from his pocket and dabbed at her damp cheeks. 'I don't want folks thinking I've made you cry.'

For a few seconds they gazed into each other's eyes. Her heart started a rapid beat, but he moved away and the moment was lost.

'We're booked in at Grange Lodge for an early dinner,' he said, starting the engine and slipping the car into gear. 'And I have something else planned for afterwards – but you'll have to wait and see what it is.'

Excitement once again sent her nerves tingling. 'Oh, Charlie, I'm having such a wonderful time. You're spoiling me and I'm loving every minute of it.'

At Grange Lodge, a receptionist came forward to greet them. 'Good afternoon, Commander Rogers. Would you and your lady care to wait in the small lounge and study the menu for this evening?'

When they were alone by the fire, June whispered to him, 'I'm beginning to feel really posh. Such luxury! Being waited on, good food to eat, and sitting here with you – the town's most eligible bachelor. I'm the envy of every girl around.'

He gave a little laugh and assumed the role of the wicked villain: 'Flattery will get you everywhere, my dear.' He suddenly looked embarrassed. Shamefaced, he stammered, 'S-sorry.'

For a moment her mind had been taken back to the last time she'd flattered him in jest – and the devastating consequences. She wouldn't easily forget it, no matter what she had said to the contrary. She pushed aside the horrid memories of lustful kisses and groping, and looked at the unhappy Charles.

'I thought I was with the Big Bad Wolf for a second there. "Oh Grandma, what big eyes you have!"' she said, mimicking Little Red Riding Hood. She touched his hand.

'The panto was smashing! Terrific fun. I really enjoyed it. Thank you, Charlie.'

He looked at her with a grateful smile, then took her hand and tenderly touched it with his lips. 'You're a very gracious lady.'

A tingle of pleasure caught her off-guard. Avoiding his gaze, she leaned back in her comfortable armchair and looked at the flames flickering in the fire. Her thoughts immediately turned to Arthur, and memories of his lovemaking warmed her heart. She must think only of him... always, only of him.

Sitting in the balcony of the Regal cinema, they were watching the film that she had told Charles she wanted to see – *The Tales Of Hoffmann*. But Charles was finding the closeness of her presence deeply disturbing. It would be so easy to put an arm around her and lay his cheek on her soft hair. When she looked up at him, he desperately desired to kiss her beautiful smiling lips. But all he did was return her smile. Could she sense the tension building within him? He dug his nails hard into his hands and reproved himself. He must control his imagination. If she knew what he was thinking, she would surely never go near him again.

Offenbach's *Barcarole* was now playing. Who wouldn't be moved by it? With an aching heart he turned from the film to look at her. Tears sparkled in her eyes as she sat, entranced by the music. He could see her hand clasping the locket under her dress; there could be no doubting where her thoughts lay. He bit his lip and tried to contain his jealousy. Then, much to his surprise and delight, she casually leaned towards him, resting her head on his shoulder. He refused to let his heart rule his head by holding her hand – she might be offended and that would break the spell. So he sat there, feeling her so close and yet so untouchable. He knew where she was, and it wasn't with him. If only…

As the music faded away, she suddenly became aware of what she was doing and moved her head from his shoulder. Embarrassed, she whispered an apology: 'Sorry.'

He gave her a little smile in acknowledgement, as if it was nothing, and they went on watching the film. Oh, why did she have to spoil it by apologising? Clearly, she was only too aware of what she did to him; the apology was meant to distance herself from her action, and from him. To have had her so close in a gentle, loving way – even if by mistake – had been a touch of heaven, and he didn't want an apology. He wanted to revel in her closeness, not have each precious moment turned into a reason for her to be sorry. And what exactly was she apologising for? For using him as his brother's stand-in? Or for arousing his masculinity? To be pitied was almost as bad as being hated.

When they left the cinema, they hardly spoke. On the way home, she was quiet and pensive. He left her to sort out her feelings; he had enough of his own to deal with.

After a while, without looking at him, she said, 'I'm so sorry, Charlie. I guess I was tired… and sort of dreamy. I didn't realise what I was doing.'

There it was again, a reminder that even such a simple innocent act should never have happened – she belonged to his brother.

'Don't apologise,' he told her lightly. 'It was nice having my little sister resting on my shoulder.'

She smiled. 'I like the "little sister" bit. Arthur was so right to make you his lieutenant. You're always so courteous and understanding.'

Charles kept his thoughts to himself. Arthur knew what he was doing all right – throwing them together in the knowledge that he was honour bound not to betray his trust. But he couldn't complain; there was no one else he would rather be with. Instead of resentment, he felt true gratitude for his appointed task.

Suddenly, a cyclist shot across the road in front of him.

'Bloody hell!'

He braked hard and the car skidded, but he brought it to a halt safely. In the beam of the headlights, the cyclist turned, laughed, gave them a two-finger insult and rode off – no lights front or rear.

'Are you all right?' he asked, turning to her.

She'd shrieked when the car came within inches of the cyclist, and instinctively she'd put her hands hard on the dashboard to protect herself. She was looking a little wild-eyed and flushed.

'I'm okay,' she said, shaking a little. 'Stupid fool, he could have got himself killed.' She turned to face him. 'Are *you* all right, Charlie? I don't know how you missed him.'

'I'm fine.' Adrenaline raced through his veins, stirring parts of his body he preferred to let rest. 'It was a hell of a shock though.' He leaned forward, his lips hovering above hers. 'Are you absolutely sure you're all right?'

'Perfectly,' she whispered, her lips in line with his.

He felt her breath on his face – sweet and alluring. Beckoning warmth from her body rose to meet him. Desire was tearing him apart. In his imagination their lips were already meeting...

He pulled back, sweat rising on his brow. He dug his nails into his palms and turned to face the windscreen. 'Good,' he said in a strained voice. 'By God, that could have been nasty.'

The rest of the journey took place in near silence.

Arthur put down the phone and thought about what Charles had just told him. But what about the things he hadn't told him? He felt convinced that his brother was holding something back.

He shook off the unwelcome feeling and took out the little lighter from his travel-bag. He lit the flame and said aloud the words of the poem he'd written on June's postcard. His mind drifted to the precious moments they'd spent together so recently. Extinguishing the flame, he picked up his pen and quickly wrote another poem.

The flame of love, it never fades
Fed by the heat of desire
It twists, and flares, and burns the breast
And never rests, till hearts be blessed
To assuage the raging fire.

On Saturday, June had two more letters offering her interviews. She would tell Charlie when he picked her up at six-thirty. There was a lot of sewing to be done before she started work again; her own, as well as some for Mrs Rogers. It was going to be a busy day.

After tea, she changed into a three-quarter length blue evening gown – a cut-down of Kate's. She looked at herself in the mirror. Yes, it would do very nicely. The plunge neckline was reasonably modest, the fitted top with its gathers crossing under the bust-line accentuated her slim waist and full, shapely breasts, while the narrow shoulders made the most of her slender arms. The gathered full skirt gave a perfect balance. She could hear Charles arriving in his car, so she slipped on a fur-collared blue coat – another item of Kate's – and hurried quietly down the stairs. Her sisters were in the front room discussing her and Charlie; she could hear them from the hall. No doubt they'd been watching for him from the window.

'What a terrible waste,' Rose was saying to Pat. 'What does he get out of taking June anywhere?'

'He's only escorting her places. But maybe she's not as icy as we think. She never talks about him, though.'

'He's a lot older than her; he'd be much better off with me,' sighed Rose.

'Huh! What's age got to do with it? They all want the same thing.'

'Hard luck! He won't get it from June,' said Rose sniggering.

'Just as well. She'd freeze it off!'

'You are awful!'

'I know. That's why I've got a better feller than you.'

'Says who?'

'Me. They call my Jim *"Hot Rod,"* said Pat, giggling.

'That's because of his bike.'

'You think what you like – I say what I know!'

'Ooh, here he comes. Isn't he gorgeous?' cooed Rose. 'If my Jerry wore that suit he'd look like a waiter.'

'June said we could have one of Kate's dresses if we could get into them.'

'Fat chance! Better odds on getting off with Charlie Boy!'

They both went into fits of giggles.

June rushed out before they caught her in the hall. She hurried with Charles to the car and they were off before any of the family could stop them.

It was the first time she had been to an orchestral concert. Her gown made her feel grand, and Charlie's compliments gave her the confidence she needed for the occasion. During the interval, he explained some of the finer points of the music, and the parts played by the different sections of the orchestra. She studied the programme and soaked up knowledge like a sponge.

It was fantastic – wonderful! The concert hall was far removed from the cinema that she was more used to, but the company, and her clothes, helped her to relax and enjoy the music without feeling self-conscious.

When Charlie took her home, they parted politely. Just as she was closing the door, she saw Rose further down the road, giving her a wave as she was coming home with her boyfriend. Rose and Jerry stopped to kiss under a street lamp, the young man groping inside her coat. No doubt Rose would have noticed that Charlie hadn't even given her a peck on the cheek to say goodnight. She could almost hear her sister saying, 'What a waste!' It was true that Charles didn't seem to be getting much out of the relationship. Perhaps her sister was right. Charlie would soon be off on active service… surely he deserved better than he was getting?

Charles wasn't with his family at the Sunday service. June heard Rose whispering to Pat, 'Do you think he's got frostbite?'

The two sisters giggled, provoking a disapproving look from their mother. June sighed; they'd clearly intended her to hear their disparaging remarks. What on earth would they say if they knew about Arthur?

Chapter Fourteen

June was up early on Monday morning. Well before time, she was spruced up and ready for her interview at Watson's. When Charles arrived to pick her up, she tucked a portfolio of her artwork under her arm and ran out to meet him. But her mother wanted a word with Charlie before they drove off.

'Commander Rogers, this is very good of you. If our Junie gets this job, she'll 'ave you and your family to thank.'

'Not at all, Mrs Armstrong. Your daughter is bright and intelligent. If she passes the interview, it will be on her own merits.'

'I'm glad you think so. I must say she's brighter than 'er sisters. She's good around the 'ouse too. She's a very good cook. And she's thrifty – knows 'ow to look after money.'

June was getting more and more embarrassed and interrupted her mother. 'Mam, we have to go, I'll be late for the interview.'

'Sorry, love. 'Ope all goes well. See you later.'

Charles helped June in with her portfolio. Then he quickly went to his own side, slipped into his seat, waved to Mrs Armstrong, and they were off.

June said, 'I'm so sorry, Charlie. I feel most embarrassed. I think my mother fancies having you for a son-in-law. She's so obvious about it!'

'Actually, I feel quite honoured. And maybe it'll make it easier for her to accept Arthur.'

'Yes… perhaps. But not at the moment. You're younger and you have a boyish charm. I know the navy title helps but…' She hesitated. 'Well, there's something about you. It's not just the women in our house who like you; my dad thinks a lot of you, you know. I'm afraid they'll be in for a big disappointment.'

'I think you worry too much. I assure you, they'll find Arthur a much bigger catch. When you're a little older, the difference in your ages won't seem nearly as much. In any case, I get the impression that your parents love their little Junie and want her to be happy.'

'Yes, they do. But Dad was a sergeant in the army. With Arthur having been a major, and your father being a colonel, he's going to feel very awkward in their presence.' She sighed. She didn't say it but she could have added, 'And your parents won't be keen to meet him, either.'

'Well, you seem to think they'd be happy enough to have *me* for a son-in-law, and I'm Arthur's brother. And I'm much older than you too. Not as much as Arthur, maybe, but it's still twelve years. Your parents will love Arthur when they get to know him. There's no wiser, kinder, gentler person alive.' He glanced across at her. 'You look smashing. Exactly right for an interview – *especially* this one,' he said, changing the subject.

She was pleased with the compliment. 'Thank you,' she said shyly. 'But I'm terrified. What shall I say if they ask why I left my last job? I can't tell the truth. They wouldn't accept it, it's always the girl's fault.'

'You said on all your forms and letters that you wanted a change. There has to be a pretty compelling reason for someone to leave a job before getting another. But it's obvious that you're not a slacker. After all, you go to night classes and do paid sewing. Your lively interest in the world of fashion will come over very well. So don't worry about the past; think positively.'

'Yes, I will. Thanks, Charlie.'

'You know, my father has a name in this city. I'm not saying that it'll get you a job, but Mother's reference will mean something – that you're a person to be trusted.'

'Your mother has been very kind. She's given me a lovely photograph of herself. It was taken at some big do where she was presenting an award. It might be at Clare's school. She's wearing an outfit I designed for her not long after I started night school.'

'There you are then, that can give you a starter. Say you wanted to be free to look around for something better than you had, and that you intend to keep busy with paid needlework until you find something suitable.'

'Mmm,' she murmured. He was right, she *did* have a good excuse if it became necessary to give one. In fact, if she couldn't get the job she wanted, it might be worth having a go at working for herself and seeing if she could build up a reputation. She would give it some thought.

'Well, here we are,' said Charles, as he pulled up at a forbidding arched gateway. Beyond it stood the old, smut-laden factory building. 'I'll wait for you just along the road. Best of luck. I'm sure you'll do well. Just be confident – you have every right to be.'

A young office girl met her at the gatekeeper's office and took her up two flights of well-worn stone steps to the Outerwear Department. From every direction, the sound of machinery met her ears. The girl told her that the interview was taking place in the factory showroom, situated on the floor where the managers and designers had their offices and workrooms. She took her inside the room, pointed to seats placed around a coffee table near the window, and suggested she sit down. Then she left, closing the door behind her. A muffled silence fell like a heavy blanket.

The showroom was fairly large and appeared to have a false ceiling that dampened the noise coming from the floor above. A thick brown wall-to-wall carpet muffled the sounds from rooms below. Pale gold curtains screened two walls. On the wall opposite the door, a window with slatted blinds was framed with the same curtain material. The remainder of that wall was hung with framed pictures of dress designs since the beginning of the century. Cupboards, reaching to the ceiling, ran across the door wall. Tall-backed, leather-cushioned chairs were placed around a table at the centre of the room, and matching low armchairs around the coffee table where she was sitting. All the wood in the room was of light oak. She could see a number of lights along the picture wall and fixed to the ceiling, but only one dull central lamp was switched on.

All alone in the dim, hot, claustrophobic atmosphere, she tried to keep calm, but barely succeeded. She was beginning to wonder if they'd forgotten her when the door suddenly opened and in came a rush of fresh air and noise, followed by a smartly dressed middle-aged man talking to someone in the corridor behind him. The door closed and silence descended once more. The man pushed a switch and the room blazed with lights.

'Good morning, Miss Armstrong. I'm John Watson. I run the outerwear clothing business in this organisation. My colleagues will be joining us shortly.'

He quickly shook her hand, then sat himself down and looked at her intently. After about ten seconds, he said briskly, 'I don't normally interview office staff; I leave that to my deputy. But I am interested in other aspects of what you have to offer. I want to deal with that first. Now, will you please stand up and take off your coat.'

She was shocked; what did he think she was there for?

He raised his brown eyes to the ceiling and let out a sigh of contempt. 'Do not be alarmed, Miss Armstrong, I am only interested in what you are wearing, not what is underneath.'

She was amazed at his interviewing technique. Was he trying to make her feel stupid to catch her off guard? But she refused to be intimidated. She stood up and serenely removed her coat.

'Turn around. No, right around. Yes, excellent! Obviously you have good dress sense. Did you design that outfit yourself?'

'I renovated it from a good quality suit, Mr Watson. I reshaped it to be more fashionable, and to make it fit better. I added my own touches too – the velvet collar and pocket flaps.' She thought she sounded confident, even if she didn't feel it.

'I'm impressed.' He stood up and walked over to one of the curtains. 'Now come over here.'

Feeling better about herself, she obeyed. What on earth was coming next? This was nothing at all like she had expected. Watson pulled aside the huge curtain, exposing rails of dresses and suits.

'Now, I want you to look quickly along these rails. Tell me what you think of the collection.'

She started to look at each one in turn, weighing up in her mind not only what she thought of the clothes but what she thought he was expecting her to say.

'Please, Miss Armstrong, just look quickly, we haven't got all day,' he said impatiently. 'I only want your overall impression, not a detailed analysis.'

She hurried along the rails. She didn't like his brusque tone, nor the way he was hurrying her. Well, she would give him a truthful answer and take the consequences. Charlie had told her to be honest, and she trusted his advice.

'Frankly, Mr Watson, there's nothing here that *I'd* want to buy. They're obviously aimed at the older woman. To tell you the truth–'

'The truth is what I asked for,' he interrupted. 'I want your impression of what you have just viewed. I don't want platitudes, I want honest opinion. I was watching you closely. I can tell what you think – just say it straight out.'

'I think they're behind the times. Most of them are dowdy.'

'Good! Now sit down please. Quickly go through your portfolio.'

She showed him various designs and then, finally, produced the photograph of Mrs Rogers, explaining that she had designed the outfit being worn.

Mr Watson perused her work in silence, but when she handed him the photograph he exclaimed, 'I know this lady. She's the wife of Colonel Rogers. I've met her at the Conservative Club. Come to think of it, she gave you a testimonial. I thought I knew the name.'

He looked thoughtful for a few moments.

'You criticised our frocks as being dowdy. Tell me the difference between those garments and the one you designed for Mrs Rogers.'

She was staggered by the question. Somehow, she summoned her wits together.

'In that photograph, Mrs Rogers looks chic. If she'd been in one of those garments, at least the more fashionable of the selection, she'd have looked smart but nothing more. But then, Mrs Rogers has the elegance and finesse to look good in all the clothes she buys.'

She was surprised at her own audacity.

'Well done! I could not have put it better.'

She tried not to show her relief.

'Now we can get on with the interview and I'll tell you why I asked you to come here today.'

He relaxed a little in his chair, interlaced the fingers of his hands and rubbed the cleft in his chin with his two forefingers. He looked at her pensively.

'Miss Armstrong, if you really want the office clerk's job, I'll fetch someone else to interview you. I am interested in your other talents. You are, of course, very young and inexperienced, but your youth could be an asset, not a hindrance.'

She wondered where this was all heading. Surely he wasn't going to offer her a job in the design department? She tried to keep her excitement from showing.

He waved a hand towards the dress rails. 'Our present range satisfies our older customers, but we have to think of the future. We want to expand our range to include a more youthful element – in fact, just like you are dressed today.' He paused while he swept his eyes over her in admiration. 'So far we have not advertised for a young designer; it was something that was to come up at the next board meeting. But when we received your letter of application, my deputy passed it to me to see if I would be interested. I looked at your letter and found it intriguing. I read Mrs Rogers's testimonial and was impressed.

'I left it to my deputy, Bill Potter, to ring your former employer. Should you decide to go for the office position he may wish to question you on that matter. Now, you wrote that you hope to go to college this year.'

She nodded in assent. 'I want to be a designer, Mr Watson, and I'll do whatever it takes to get me there.'

'I admire your ambition, but what I have to offer may well present a reasonable compromise. I would like to take you on as a trainee designer. We have a room that you could use as your office, but most of the time you would be assisting my senior designer. That way, you will learn a lot about this particular business. You will need to know how to handle customers and what their individual requirements are. You will have to become familiar with the techniques of mass production and realise that there are limitations to design.'

He frowned, turning his facial lines and dimples into deep furrows. 'Believe me, Miss Armstrong, you have a great deal to learn and you won't get it from college. Here you will be given the opportunity to try out a small range of your own. You will be given your own sample-hand to sew the garments. She will teach you a lot about what can – and cannot – be done on the sort of scale we work to. Miss Martin, our senior designer, will go over those details with you.'

June quickly put a word in. 'Are you actually offering me a job, Mr Watson?'

'What I was *about* to suggest,' he continued, frowning a little at being interrupted, 'was that you come here on a six-month trial. If, at the end of that period, you are still keen on a college course, then you must of course go.' He leaned back in his chair and again attacked the cleft in his chin with his two forefingers. 'This is an old family firm. All our senior people got where they are through learning on the job. Whatever you gain from college will be minute compared with what you will acquire through experience. You must realise that every firm has its own methods. However, it would be a good idea for you to keep up with your night classes, especially in pattern cutting. You will learn from Miss Martin, but every designer needs to develop his or her own methods. Should you prove hopeless – a liability – then we will be asking you to go. But I cannot envisage that happening.'

'I don't know what to say, I–'

'You don't have to decide now. Think it over. I realise you had your heart set on going to college, but what I'm offering is surely worth thinking about. As far as pay is concerned, we are prepared to offer five pounds ten shillings per week. We will also give you an allowance to help you with your evening classes.'

June was overawed. 'That's very generous of you, sir. I would like to think it over very much.'

Watson picked up his folder. 'Ring me tomorrow morning. If you decide to accept the offer, you can start next Monday. I have to go now; I'll ask the others to come in.'

He rose to his feet, shook her hand and walked quickly out into the corridor. The room seemed suddenly empty.

She was left feeling breathless. What a speed that man moved at! So much to take in, and so much to consider. Her head was spinning and she was close to shaking. Actually being offered a job designing! Not in her wildest dreams had she expected such a thing to happen. Would she be up to it? Of course she would: she designed clothes for Mrs Rogers – the wife of Colonel Arthur Percy Rogers.

Before she could sort out her thoughts and emotions, another man walked in. He was younger than Watson, of medium height and build, with blue eyes and thinning fair hair that framed a pleasant, smiling face. Unlike Watson, he was without a jacket or waistcoat. The sleeves of his blue striped shirt were rolled up, and his red tie and braces added a jolly touch to his appearance.

'Good morning, Miss Armstrong. May I call you June?'

'Yes, please do, Mr…?'

'Potter. But you can call me Bill – except in the workrooms.'

His gentle manner had a calming effect on her. 'Thank you, Bill,' she said smiling.

He gave her a lot of information about various aspects of manufacture and distribution. After a mind-boggling ten minutes, he suddenly said to her, 'By the way, I can understand you wanting a change, but isn't it rather unusual to give up a job before finding another?'

She'd been dreading this, but she confidently repeated what Charlie had primed her to say. Bill seemed impressed.

'I'm pleased it wasn't a clash of personalities – it does happen. I just hope that if you accept this job, you won't walk out on us. If you have any problems, come straight to me. Okay?'

She breathed an inward sigh of relief. Had something been said to him by her last firm, and he was choosing to be on her side? She looked him in the eye and said pleasantly, 'Thank you, that's good to know.'

'I'll just let Miss Martin have a quick word with you. She's very busy, so she won't keep you long.' He rose to leave. 'Oh, I think I can hear Rob. I'll call him in.'

A young man in his mid-twenties entered the room. Slim but muscular, and above average height, he was neatly dressed in a casual sort of way. His dark-grey trousers were well pressed, his fancy blue-patterned waistcoat was a perfect fit, but his pale blue shirt was open at the neck. His brown eyes were under heavy brows and his thick, dark, curly hair flopped slightly over one eye in a rather rakish fashion. His likeness to John Watson was striking, especially the strong jaw line and deep chiselled dimples in chin and cheeks, but his youth gave him a more handsome, if rugged, appearance. She wasn't surprised to hear from Bill Potter that Rob was the Managing Director's son, Robert.

Rob Watson stood smiling at her while Bill continued his introduction.

'Rob spends quite a bit of time travelling, but you'll see him from time to time. He'll be pleased to get a bit of young talent on the design staff.'

'Especially such good-looking talent,' Rob said, his penetrating eyes sweeping over her body. 'Good morning, Miss Armstrong. I do hope you'll be joining the firm. It'll be nice to see a fresh face when I return from my travels.'

She felt a warm glow creep over her and her heart began to beat faster. Rob was an exceedingly sexy individual who made the most of his charms – she was going to have to be careful.

A middle-aged woman swept in and the two men said they had to be off. Before Bill disappeared, he introduced the newcomer as Miss Martin. She was tall and slender – some might say skinny – and smartly dressed. She was wearing a white silk blouse with a high neckband that finished off in a large soft bow tied under her chin. An expensive brooch, pinned to the lapel of her smart grey suit, sparkled with diamonds and sapphires. June could hardly take her eyes off it. She wondered if Miss Martin wore the brooch as an affirmation of her successful career. Though far from beautiful, she was certainly impressive.

'Now, my dear – June, is it? I will give you some idea of what will be expected from you if you take up Mr Watson's offer,' she said rather imperiously, her voice sharp and clipped. Did Miss Martin object to having someone younger working by her side?

Giving her no chance to comment, she spent ten minutes going over various aspects of the job. Suddenly, she looked at her watch. 'My goodness, is that the time?' She quickly rose from her chair and headed for the door. 'I have to go now, I'll send a junior to show you out.'

'Thank you,' June said, but Miss Martin was already speaking to someone in the corridor. The door closed and she was left alone again. She tidied the things in her portfolio and wondered if she would be able to keep up with the pace of these busy people.

The door opened again and a young girl entered. 'Follow me, please,' she said in a bored voice, and led the way to the factory entrance without saying another word. Only when the factory hooter sounded did she perk up. 'That way,' she said quickly, and disappeared back up the steps.

As June stepped out of the building, the cold air jolted her back into the outside world. It had been quite a morning. She walked towards Charlie's car. The roads were busy now, as workers on bicycles streamed out of the factories. Charles was sitting in his car reading a newspaper. He looked up and saw her coming. With a broad smile, he clambered out of the MG and walked towards her.

A surge of joy rushed through her and she eagerly ran to him, carelessly dropping her things on the wet pavement. She flung her arms around his neck and lifted herself up to kiss him on his cheek. All the emotions she had struggled to keep under control during her interview burst out unrestrained.

'Charlie! Charlie! Charlie! Thank you! Thank you so much. You've done it for me. *You!* Just *you!* I couldn't have got the job without you.'

He took her arms from around his neck. Still holding on to them, he pushed her away a little and looked into her face. He was about to speak when their eyes met. Her heart started a rapid beat. He was bending over her with his lips soft and moist. She could feel his breath on her face and sense his natural desires wrestling with his conscience. Her heart was racing, waiting… longing… for their mouths to meet. His lips were hovering over hers… now lightly touching them. Suddenly, he clasped his hands more tightly on her arms and moved away from her. She flinched, more from the shock of the sudden movement than the twinge of discomfort.

His face twisted with concern. 'Gosh, I'm so sorry – I didn't hurt you, did I?'

She dropped her eyes. 'No, not really. Just took me by surprise.'

The spell was broken and he released her. She suddenly became aware of workers streaming from the factories around them. A small group of men and women were hanging around watching them, laughing and giggling. A gruff voice shouted, 'Hey, I'll kiss yer, love!'

'And I'll 'ave Cary Grant,' yelled a woman wearing a wraparound pinny under a flapping-open coat. 'How about it, duck?'

The shouts and whistles continued as Charlie picked up June's things and hurried her to the car. He helped her into the passenger seat, and then she watched him run to the driver's side and slip his athletic frame into the seat. So lithe… so nimble… so handsome.

'Time for lunch,' he said briskly. 'Relax now, and tell me all about the job when we get there.'

She sat in silence, wrestling with her emotions. Surely it had been nothing more than a flash of desire, brought on by the excitement of the morning's events? Nothing had actually happened, and even if he *had* kissed her, it would have meant nothing more to her than… than what? She couldn't answer that question. She tried to think about Arthur, but it was impossible with Charlie sitting so close. His warmth, his masculine scent, his very presence, made her feel sexually alive.

Within fifteen minutes, he pulled up at a pleasant-looking inn.

'This is *The Boathouse*; highly recommended by a friend. I think you'll like it here – hotpot, log fires, and all that.'

She remembered her dad chopping up some old chairs to burn just before the war ended. 'I wish we had old trees to chop down for firewood. We all get chilblains in the winter. It's not so bad now there's more coal, but it's so nice to go to your place; you have lovely fires.'

Charles opened her door and helped winkle her out of the low seat. 'We cleared out a few old apple trees. I can assure you, it hasn't always been so warm at Bloomfield. My father believes that cold showers turn boys into men! But let's get inside, you must be freezing.'

It was busy in the inn, but a couple were just leaving and Charles led her over to the vacated table. It was in a cosy nook not too far from the welcoming hearth. After ordering hotpot, they settled themselves on the hefty but rather battered chairs, while the waitress cleared and wiped the equally battered and hefty table.

Charles went to the bar and came back with glasses of shandy. He placed her drink in front of her. 'Now then, young lady, perhaps you'd like to tell your Uncle Charles what all that delightful hugging was about?'

She felt herself blushing. 'You're a wonderful person, Charlie, how can I help but love you?' Seeing his brows draw together, she quickly added, 'Don't get me wrong, we love *all* our friends, don't we? Or they wouldn't be our friends.'

'Sounds like solid logic, but what happened at your interview? Or do I have to apply burning coals to your feet to get you to tell me?'

She laughed. 'I think my feet are warm enough, thanks.'

She spent the next ten minutes telling him about her interview and the details of the job she'd been offered.

'So you see why I'm so excited. I think I should accept it, don't you? The pay is fantastic, and it'll give me time to save some money. The experience alone will be worth quite a lot. If I'm useless at it and get thrown out, at least I'll know I'm on the wrong track. But I could still go to college and do other arty stuff.'

'I agree. I think it would be a wise move. Mother would agree with you, too.'

'Your mother has been a brick in all this. It was her testimonial that influenced their decision. But it's all the things *you* helped me with that really got me there. *And* you gave me the confidence I needed. I can't begin to tell you how grateful I am. I just wish I could make it up to you.'

'My darling little girl–'

She stopped him. 'No, Charlie, I'm not little, and I'm not a child. I know what you're trying to do, we both do. But can't I love you as an adult friend? Do you have to keep me at a distance all the time?'

Out of the corner of her eye she saw, alone at a table close by, a flashy woman of about thirty years turn to look at Charlie with a smile and a raised eyebrow. She would have to keep her voice down.

Unaware that they were being overheard, Charles said, 'I can see you want to be honest and open, but all the time we're together we play games with each other. My fault, I know.' He looked thoughtful for a moment. 'You're right, you're quite right, you're not a child. But you *are* Arthur's girl. I had my chance, but all I did was to hurt you.'

She could see the pain in his eyes. 'That's in the past, Charlie.'

He shook his head. 'You *know* I love you,' he whispered softly. 'Surely it's better to play pretend games than to risk losing your friendship?'

She was deeply moved. But what could she say? She was clearly putting him under a lot of strain. 'I'm so sorry. Would you rather keep away from me altogether? Many women would give anything to have you for a boyfriend. I'm just getting in the way.'

She dropped her eyes, unable to look at him. She had said the words and given him the option, but her whole being begged him not to desert her.

He took hold of her hand and held it gently. 'All I want is to keep the relationship we have. I don't want to do anything to spoil that. But if you want comfort at any time, or a shoulder to cry on, I'm here for you. I can't say it'll be easy, but I'll keep faith with you and Arthur.'

They sat in silence for a while. She loved the comfortable feel of his warm fingers embracing hers and the message of devotion that came with it.

'Right. No more games,' she said, reluctantly retrieving her hand. 'I acknowledge that you love me.' She looked up into his eyes and noticed they were glistening. 'You make me feel greatly blessed to have you as a friend,' she whispered.

He smiled. 'Then our friendship must never be broken.'

Their lunch arrived and they ate mostly in silence. She felt heady with emotion and could hardly trust herself to speak. As they rose to leave, she told him that she had definitely decided to accept the job offer.

'I *can* do it – and I will succeed!' she said triumphantly.

'I never thought otherwise,' Charles told her. Grinning, he added, 'I'll tell Arthur the good news tonight and get his permission for us to spend tomorrow night celebrating.'

As they squeezed past the table next to them, June noticed the flashy-looking woman slip a piece of paper into Charlie's pocket.

'Hello, Charlie,' she said. 'I don't suppose you remember me.'

'Grace! I didn't see you sitting there,' he said, obviously surprised.

She gave him a provocative smile. 'Call me sometime and we can get reacquainted.'

'Thanks for the invitation, but I'm off shortly – going back to the navy. Nice to have seen you again. You're looking as lovely as ever. Can't stop. Bye now – take care.'

June felt a pang of jealousy and she hated herself for it.

As they settled back into the MG, Charlie said, 'Sorry about that. I guess my past tends to catch up with me. Grace is an old girlfriend going back to my youth. She used to be a redhead; I didn't recognise her straight away. Fancy meeting her here.'

'Forget it, Charlie. It's nice that you have so many friends.' But the incident continued to nag her. Would he take up her invitation?

Back home, her parents were delighted with her good news. Her father put down his newspaper in awe at her announcement.

'To think our little Junie will be earning all that money,' he said in amazement. 'And what prospects! I reckon it's the young Commander that's helped you get the job. I think he's taken a shine to my little girl.'

'I hope not, Dad. He's lovely to go out with, but I don't think about him in *that* sort of way. He's a lot older than me and he calls me his little sister. Anyway, he's going away soon – he's just filling in time for a couple of weeks. He gets a kick out of taking me places I haven't been, and helping me to get a job.'

As she climbed the stairs, she heard her father talking to her mother in the kitchen. She couldn't help but stop and listen.

'I reckon he's keen on her right enough, but she doesn't seem bothered. Probably just as well – they're too good for us.'

'What a grand lad 'e is, though,' her mother sighed. 'Pity Rose and Pat can't find someone better than their two layabouts. It'll be a good thing when those girls marry. They're too forward; they need to settle down.'

When Charles told his mother about June's job she was equally delighted.

'I hope it will give the girl something positive to aim for and get thoroughly involved in. Perhaps it will divert her away from Arthur.'

He raised his eyebrows. His mother noticed.

'Yes, Charles. Knowing about the affair does not mean that I approve of it. I was more than happy to help her get a suitable position.'

He was appalled by his mother's attitude. 'I think you're wrong, Mother. They really do love each other.'

'That may be, but a woman fully occupied in her own affairs will not make a suitable wife for my eldest son. He will surely realise the impossibility of such a marriage. Clearly, you are also keen on the girl. I must admit, a match in that direction would be less disturbing. June is far superior to some of the women who throw themselves at you.'

'Really, Mother, I know I made an ass of myself before Christmas, but that's all finished with. I'm merely escorting Arthur's future wife. Please don't make an issue out of it.'

Mrs Rogers sighed. 'I have a deep foreboding that one of you is going get hurt by all this. Please be careful, Charles. Frankly, I hope that June will soon find someone more suitable and nearer her own age. She is far too young for either of you, you must know that. Goodness knows what the rest of the family will think. June is no more than Clare's age, and Clare is just an innocent schoolgirl.'

'Age has no place where love is concerned,' he said as he made to leave the room. 'Just accept it, Mother: Arthur *will* marry June.'

Chapter Fifteen

June arrived at Bloomfield just before nine-thirty the following morning. Charles was ready for her. By ten-thirty, the necessary letters had been written and the phone call to John Watson had been made.

'How about a little drive in the country?' Charles asked, knowing full well what her answer would be.

It was a pleasant if slightly frosty morning, and everywhere was touched by the glow of the winter sun. A perfect day, he decided, for getting away from the dull, dirty streets in smoky towns and enjoying the fresh, clean air of the open roads.

They stopped for coffee at a lovely old manor house. In the lounge, customers gathered by a blazing fire. Charles steered her to a table by a window overlooking the garden. It was not only more private there, but pleasantly free of cigarette smoke.

Once seated, against a background of cheerful gossip and laughter, he gave her a report of his evening's talk with Arthur, and passed on his brother's tender words of love. It wasn't hard to put meaning into the words, as they could have come from his own heart. But it was hard to speak them without giving away his own feelings. His next message from his brother came more easily.

'Arthur was pleased about the job. *Very* pleased. But he says that if you aren't happy there then you must leave and enrol at the college. He'll support you financially.'

She smiled but shook her head.

'Don't refuse to even consider his offer, June, it wouldn't do for his future wife to be struggling.'

She was silent for a moment. 'I really don't think it'll come to that. The job seems ideal, and who knows where it might lead? But I understand his concern and I'll keep it in mind.'

Charles smiled. 'Good. Arthur said, and these are his exact words, "You can pay me back by being successful. And if I have to find someone else to care for me in my old age, you can design her wedding dress."'

They both laughed.

'He really puts your happiness above everything else,' he told her tenderly.

'I know he does. How did I ever come to deserve such love?'

To hide the longing in his heart, he quickly turned away. 'By just being you.'

They sat looking out of the window, enjoying the view. Wild birds were flying around and eating food scattered on a bird-table. A robin hopped around on the ground picking up fallen cake crumbs. Charles couldn't help but identify with that little bird. He didn't want to be jealous of Arthur, but it was a constant battle. Through his thoughts, he heard June saying something about how pretty it looked outside. He smiled at her, but thought that he preferred what was just in front of him. Now was a good time to tell her about his plans for later.

'Arthur wants us to celebrate this evening. He asked me to take you to dine and dance at the Grand. I've made a provisional booking already. You can wear one of your evening dresses and show off your locket. Think of it as Arthur being with you – he certainly will be in spirit.'

'What a lovely thought,' she said, her eyes looking far away and misty.

'We can stop here and have a bit of lunch. Then I'll take you home and ask your mother if I can keep her daughter out late tonight.'

They took a little walk in the grounds of the house, and she told him how much she loved the rustic opulence of the place. Contrasting her new experiences with what she was used to, she marvelled at how her life was changing so rapidly.

'You know, Charlie, more than ever I feel the separation from my family roots. Don't get me wrong; this is where I want to be. Everything else seems a world apart.'

'I can understand that. And it's not just you. Since the war ended things have been changing, and it's affecting many people. Divisions between the social classes are becoming less relevant. A good thing too. But there's still a long way to go.'

The ground was slippery in places and he just managed to prevent her from going over.

'Oops, blimey!' she blurted out. She put a hand to her mouth. 'That's not very elegant, is it? I sound just like my dad. I'll have to watch my step – in more ways than one!'

He laughed with her. 'Well, I don't intend teaching you *my* swear words – they're certainly not fit for a young lady. Let me assure you, being an elegant speaker only affects the *manner* in which you swear.' He slipped her arm into his. 'I'll give you a hand. Don't want you breaking a leg or I'll be short of a dance partner tonight.'

They headed back to the house. She slipped again, but he caught her and held her firm in his arms. She looked up into his eyes. 'What would I do without you, Charlie?'

Her warm breath touched his cold cheek. Her plump lips looked so deliciously enticing, stirring to life his virile manhood.

'It's easy to slip on dodgy ground and fall head-over-heels,' he said.

Her eyes told him that she understood the double-meaning in his message.

'Yes, you're right,' she said. 'I'd better be more careful.'

They entered the manor by the rear door and made their way to the dining room. A waitress showed them to their reserved table.

'This is wonderful, I really do love it here,' June said, taking in the beamed ceiling and the refined yet relaxed ambience of the place.

He watched her as she leaned forward like an excited child. Her eyes swept around the room, dwelling on framed sepia photographs of anglers covering one wall, and old pottery plates and dishes decorating the rest. Copper jugs hung from the beams. He saw her smile at the genteel customers lunching with their friends, spouses, and business associates. She seemed comfortably at home with them.

'Fancy,' she sighed happily, 'we're out *again* tonight. I'll be a little piggy by the time you leave.' Her smiling face suddenly changed to one of sadness. 'You'll be leaving next Monday, won't you?'

'Yes, unless I hear differently. I'm going to miss taking you out.'

'Not as much as I'll miss being with you – enjoying all this,' she said, waving a hand around. Her eyes came to rest on his. 'My dear Arthur's faithful lieutenant.'

The waitress arrived with two steaming plates of steak and kidney pie, breaking the tension. They ate their meal in silence. An hour later, as he drove her home, he wondered if the coming evening was going to put too much of a strain on their relationship.

He called for her at seven. Her father opened the door and bid him a hearty welcome.

'Come in, Commander. June's about ready.'

'I really appreciate my being allowed to take your daughter out tonight, sir.'

'I hope you both have a good time. Don't keep her out *too* late, though.'

'June will have told you that we are dining as well as dancing. It's a great pleasure to escort your daughter to places I enjoy visiting. I'm only sorry that I will be going away in a few days, but duty calls.'

'So, you'll soon be leaving. What a pity,' Armstrong told him, sounding genuinely disappointed. 'I know June has enjoyed your company.'

There were sounds of footsteps on the stairs. Charles caught his breath in surprise as June appeared, looking absolutely stunning. She had altered another of Kate's dresses. He recognised it at once, having seen it on Kate's bed and imagined June wearing it. It was made of white satin and had a deep plunging neckline, which she had modestly drawn together with a brooch. He didn't need to see the back; he knew it was pitched almost to the waistline. Sleeveless with very narrow shoulders, the bodice was so perfectly styled as to envelop her breasts without the need for a bra. The smooth line followed her shapely body until it reached her hips, where the skirt then flared out into a wide hem.

Armstrong called to his wife. 'Come and look at our lovely daughter. My goodness, she looks just like you at her age.'

'Come on, let's go,' June whispered to Charlie, quickly putting on her coat and pulling him towards the door. 'We'll be here all night at this rate.'

When they arrived at the Grand, they mounted the steps of the portico. Charles handed over his car keys to the doorman, who stepped forward to open the huge glass door to the foyer. June looked completely overawed by the hotel's interior.

'Oh, Charlie, this place is a palace!'

'And you are the beautiful princess,' he told her, smiling at her childlike response.

She made her way to the ladies' rest room while he checked in his coat. While he waited for her in the ornate Romanesque atrium, he was taken by surprise by another old flame.

'Charlie! I haven't seen you for ages. I've missed you, darling,' she lamented in a whiny voice.

At the same time, he saw June approaching. Much to his delight, she had removed her modesty brooch. A deep cleavage exposed more than the little golden locket. She looked an exceedingly desirable woman.

Charles touched his ex-girlfriend's shoulder and smiled in June's direction. 'Ruby, you must meet the lady I'm with tonight,' he said.

While Charles made the introductions, Ruby gave June a thorough going over. 'Well, dearie,' she said. 'How do you like our Charlie? *"Charlie is my darling, my darling, my darling,"* she sang in a sing-song voice. 'In fact, Charlie's everybody's darling! Make the most of him, ducky, he'll soon be snatched away.'

She didn't wait for a reply; she turned her back on them and headed towards her escort. He was clearly much older than her. With black hair – probably a wig – hard, chiselled face, and a scrawny body that even his expensive suit couldn't make elegant, he was not the most handsome of men. His thin lips and shifty, baggy-lidded eyes seemed to leer at June, while regarding Charles with distinct hatred. Charles had heard that he was an incredibly rich financier and fond of what money could buy. He knew, to his cost, that Ruby was an expensive lady with a fondness for diamonds.

He felt embarrassed. 'I'm sorry about that. We knew each other once, but not for long… too demanding. But you don't want to know about her. Let me have a look at you.' He took her hand and twirled her around. 'What can I say? An angel has come out with me tonight. I shall be the envy of every man here.'

'I think I'm the one being envied, *"Charlie, darling."*

He laughed at her imitation of his ex-lover. 'Well, it appears Ruby has now found her true heart's desire. Good luck to both of them.'

Before long, they were being seated at their table and handed menus. While Charles ordered for them both, June was alert to what was happening around her, her eyes glancing in all directions. The band began playing *Moonlight Serenade* and she hummed along with the music, her shoulders swaying alluringly.

Having ordered the food and wine, he asked her to dance with him. He stood up and bent down to take her hand. The sight of the deep cleavage formed by her unfettered breasts set his imagination alight… and the evening had only just begun!

He took her hand and guided her to the dance floor. Perfectly in time with the music, he swayed her to the silky rhythm of the melodic beat. Totally relaxed, she followed his movements perfectly, as though they were joined at the hip. He was in complete control, and he found her yielding closeness quite intoxicating.

Occasionally, he looked down at her and caught the glint of gold next to her heart. Arthur was with them too. No matter, he was content to feel her in his arms and look down at her lovely body, so close to his. It thrilled him to see those enticing breasts peeping from the neckline of her gown, and to have them pressing up to him as he pulled her closer to his chest. He felt her soft brown hair brushing seductively under his chin as her head moved to his shoulder. Moved by an urging difficult to control, he allowed his hand to slide further down her slender back. He felt, rather than heard, her gentle sighing as their bodies gained further contact. He was in heaven and dancing with an angel.

When the music stopped they returned to their table. She glanced up shyly. 'Thank you, Charlie, that was lovely,' she said, sitting down and keeping her eyes lowered.

'It was entirely my pleasure,' he told her, lightly touching her hand.

The waiter arrived with the first course, but Charles wasn't hungry for food. Between courses they chatted a little about their families, but he knew it was only a camouflage to drown a communication of unspoken words. As much as he honoured his brother, he wanted the woman beside him; wanted her body and soul. Part of him had wanted her from the day he saw her in that white ballet dress, but he'd resisted such yearnings… until that Sunday best forgotten. Now here she was, again dressed in white, and looking incredibly beautiful. Clearly, Arthur had caused her to bloom into womanhood. How far had she been with him? No! He shook his head; he really must not think about such things. She was Arthur's, and what they did together was none of his business.

'You're shaking your head, Charlie, don't you like the trifle?'

'Delicious – far too delicious. I was just thinking that I'm going to miss food like this when I start training,' he lied, pushing away his dish.

She put down her spoon and wiped a dab of cream from the corner of her mouth with her napkin. 'I suppose you'll miss *lots* of things. I hope there'll be compensations,' she said, giving him a sympathetic look.

'Certainly, there's more to life than food. Excitement, adventure, the feel of adrenaline running through your veins, pushing your body to its limits, the sweet taste of success… need I go on?'

'The sweet taste of success? *That* I can understand.'

'Then there's something that drives both of us. I haven't the slightest doubt that you'll achieve what you want.'

'And so will you, Charlie.'

He smiled ironically at his thoughts. The sooner he was back in training the sooner he'd get over his lovesickness and concentrate on new goals. Until then, he'd make the most of what had been granted him.

Coffee arrived and they sat back in their chairs looking at the dancers. Charles was wondering at the wisdom of returning to the dance floor. Suddenly, he stood up. 'Arthur wants us to have a good time,' he said briskly. 'Come on – let's dance.'

The band was playing a romantic melody. He held her close to him; she with her hands around his neck, resting her head against his shoulder, he with both hands low on her back, feeling the erotic smoothness of her dress against his palms. Moving as one, they slowly made their way around the dance floor, aware of what was happening but refusing to acknowledge it.

The tune ended, and they were returning to their table when the band struck up a tango. The bandleader requested the dancers to stay on the floor and invited others to join them. Raising his eyebrows, Charles smiled at her. 'Let's show them how it's done,' he said, moving her back to the floor.

She was startled by such a suggestion and held back. 'I know the steps,' she told him, her eyes flashing excitedly, 'but I've seldom had partners brave enough to attempt anything intricate.'

'Then we'll *both* be brave,' he said, putting her firmly into position. He straightened himself up to his full height and set off, leading her across the dance floor.

Before long, the other dancers stopped to watch them, and diners suspended eating to observe the impromptu floor show. Charles was a confident dancer and she had not the slightest difficulty in following him. Her dress swirled in a white cloud about her as he spun her to the rhythm of the music. Drawing her back to his side, he began further manoeuvres, jerking, swaying, bending, spinning, pulling her back and holding tight. Pulling her close to his body, they swayed and completed an intricate step formation, leading to a finale of swinging her round and bending her backwards, her head almost touching the floor. Clapping and cheering filled the room. Exhilarated, they walked back to their table.

He looked at her. She was glowing, ecstatic with delight. She caught his glance and laughed nervously.

'That was fun,' she said.

'Arthur will be so pleased that you're enjoying yourself. I know *I* am.'

'You're such a marvellous dancer, any girl would enjoy being here with you.'

'I've never danced so well before. You're an inspiration – a perfect partner. No wonder my brother has fallen head-over-heels in love with you.'

She clasped the locket and a frown wrinkled her brow. He squeezed her hand and she gave him a wan smile. He thought it was time to go.

On the way home, June sat quietly, holding on to her locket. Charles tried to assess her mood. Did she feel that she had betrayed Arthur? And yet it was Arthur who had wanted her to go out and enjoy herself. She was clearly in a state of confusion, having responded to the rhythm of the dance and the exhilaration and excitement of being at one with him. Was she now wondering if it had been more than that? Damn it! Arthur knew how well he could dance; surely he also knew that holding June in his arms would move her emotionally. Was his brother testing her? Or testing them both?

But he also needed to work out his own sense of guilt. He'd lured her on to the dance floor, and into the erotic movement of the dance, fully aware that it would excite her. He had possessed her, and she'd responded to his will. She'd been helplessly at his mercy, and yet enjoying every moment of it. The finale had been an orgasm of victorious delight. And he knew beyond doubt that she was with him... body and soul.

He stopped the car not far from her home and looked at her sitting quietly gazing at the little golden heart. He took hold of her hand. 'June, just for a moment, please give me your locket.'

She looked up. In the dimness of starlight, he could see puzzlement in her eyes. But obediently, she took the locket from her neck and handed it to him. He placed it in his pocket for safekeeping.

'Just this once, please let me be myself, not Arthur's lieutenant,' he pleaded. 'Let this night be mine; something that will live with me forever. Tomorrow you can be Arthur's again, and his for the rest of your lives together. You know I love you. I'll never do anything to hurt you again. Please, my darling, just this once, allow me to kiss you goodnight.'

She slowly lifted up her head for his lips to meet hers. Her lips were full and moist as she yielded to his touch. Savouring the delight of close intimacy, he kissed her tenderly. She had the power to move him in a way no woman had ever done before. There was far more to it than mere sex; this was something too deep for words. Fearful that carnal desire would overtake him and destroy the purity of the moment, he reluctantly drew away.

'I love you so very much, my darling. Soon you'll be wearing Arthur's ring, I respect that. But I want you to know, I'll always be there–'

'Don't say it, Charlie, I can't bear it,' she blurted out. 'I want you to find someone worthy of your love. You've given me so much already. I love you for it, but you can't always be Arthur's lieutenant.'

He sighed. Worthy of his love? What was his love worth? Had she any idea how many women he'd slept with? Women who meant nothing more to him than a good time? There was only one woman he could ever give his heart to.

'It's not that easy, my love.'

'No, Charlie, I'm not your love. Your love is waiting for you somewhere. You'll find her, if only you'll give yourself the chance.'

He thought over her last remark. 'I think you're telling me that forbidden fruit is always the most desired. Is that it?'

'Something like that. Yes, I want you as a dear friend, but I want you to be happy with someone else. I know you think you love me, but you have to let me go.'

'I know. You're quite right.'

'It's been your night – no, sorry, our night. We'll end it now. Kiss me again – as you really want to, I know you were holding back before. Make it a goodbye kiss and let's begin again tomorrow as just good friends. Please, Charlie?'

Her body was relaxed and she gazed into his eyes expectantly. He hesitated for just a moment, fearful that he wouldn't be able to keep control of his aroused feelings. But how could he possibly resist the chance to prove his love and desire? If only he could blot out those humiliating kisses that must surely be imprinted on her memory.

He gently traced his fingers around her eyes, her nose, her mouth, and with the tip of one finger, he slightly parted her lips. She didn't resist as his mouth closed on hers. He felt a slight tremble of her body. As their lips pressed together, he put his arms around her and pulled her closer to him. With slightly open mouth, he gently wandered his lips against hers, touching them with the tip of his tongue. Still there was no resistance; her lips parted for him to enter. What blissful agony!

June wasn't exactly sure what to expect. The tender kiss was pleasant enough but the memory of that forced, revolting kiss had made her think she was immune to his embraces. She was prepared to sit back and simply accept what came. But *this* was different. Not only was she deeply attracted to his touch, she found her body responding in no less a way than it did to Arthur's kissing. She felt her nipples harden and push against the fabric of her gown, increasing pleasurable sensations and causing her juices to flow.

The rhythm of the dance music tangoed through her brain as their tongues glided in a unity of pleasure. Just for a moment she thought of Arthur, but the moment's guilt vanished as his words came back to her. He wanted her to experience her youth, just as he had done.

So she gave herself up to her primitive desires. When Charles slipped his hand inside her open coat, she didn't resist – the pleasure he gave her was intense. As he pushed back the fur collar to kiss her neck and shoulders, delightful sensations made her long for more. When his hand moved down her bare back, thrills ran down her spine, causing her to draw in her breath. Her heart beat rapidly as his mouth closed over hers once again and she welcomed his sensuous lips and the gentle thrust of his tongue. Hot with passion, and moaning with the pleasure of his love play, she was ready for him to go on and on unheeded…

But he gently pulled himself away from her and, excusing himself, left the car.

She straightened her clothing and sat up straight, feeling a little bemused. What had happened to her to allow Arthur's brother to kiss her in such a sensuous way?

Charles returned to the car and slipped into his seat, perfectly composed. They sat in silence. She didn't know what to say, and surely he must be feeling the same. He had brought her body to life in the most powerful way. No, it was more than that; she had *wanted* his closeness, *wanted* to be part of him and he part of her. It was wrong, utterly wrong; she belonged to another. She had given no thought to what powerful emotions might be unleashed when she'd asked him to kiss her again. But oh, how wonderful it had been.

Charles turned to her. 'Thank you, June. As you say, we start afresh tomorrow, but I do have this night to remember.'

Would she ever be able to forget what had happened, and would her times with Arthur ever be the same? She looked at him through misting eyes.

'Yes, tomorrow is another day,' she said shakily. 'Things will be back to normal.'

But what is normal? June asked herself. Her world was changing rapidly – too rapidly. At that moment, she appeared to be floating on a cloud of emotion. Would she come to earth with a bump?

It was after twelve when he pulled up outside her home. He helped her out of the car and took her to the door. He was about to speak when the door opened. Her father appeared in front of them.

'Sorry, we're later than usual,' said Charles, before objections could be raised. 'I guess we were having a good time and the hours flew by. I had better not keep you up. Goodnight, sir, and thank you.'

When Charles arrived home, he found that his father had only just arrived before him. Although clearly tired, the Colonel asked if he could spare him a minute. They went through to the kitchen where it was warm from the cooking range.

'I'm proud of you, Charles. You did an excellent job helping young June land that position. No doubt she is benefiting from your company too. How about inviting her here on Saturday evening? We have a few guests coming for dinner, as you know. You can steer her through it.'

If his father was hoping she would feel out of her depth and be put off from joining the family, he was going to be bitterly disappointed, Charles thought.

'Good idea, Father, I'll ask her tomorrow.'

'I hope you're coping with the situation on a personal level.' He slowly shook his head. 'You could get badly hurt.'

'No need to worry; everything is fine. I'm away in a few days and things are working out splendidly. June is going to be a perfect wife for Arthur, I can promise you that.'

A little later, as he was getting ready for bed, he discovered that he still had June's locket in his pocket. He held the little heart in his hand. The symbolism did not escape him.

Chapter Sixteen

June had arranged to see Charles after lunch the next day. Since he was the only one at home, he let her into the house himself, and they decided to have that day's French lesson in the kitchen. She seemed a little shy, which was hardly surprising, but he had no intention of intruding into her thoughts. What had happened last night must remain in the past and be no more than a magnificent dream.

As they settled in their chairs, he gave her back her locket and she returned it to its rightful place. He then produced a letter from Arthur, which she slipped quickly into her bag. 'I'll look at it later,' she told him. He couldn't blame her for wanting to keep it to herself.

Then he gave her another envelope, which she immediately opened. Her eyes widened in surprise when she saw its contents. 'It's me in my red dress! You've had it tinted too. Gosh, I really do look glamorous, don't I? May I send it to Arthur?'

She sounded like a child asking a favour. It was a reminder of her unsophisticated youth, and he loved her for it.

'No need,' he told her. 'I sent him one this morning. You'll be pleased to know that we have an address for him now. So any letters you've been writing and storing up under your mattress can now be sent.'

He handed her a slip of paper with Arthur's address, which she put in her bag, along with the photograph. Then, to his surprise, she jumped up, hurried to the back of his chair and threw her arms around his shoulders.

'What would we do without you?' she said, putting her cheek against his head.

'You'll do very well,' he said, quite seriously, though it wasn't an easy thing to do with her clinging to him.

She sat down and looked at him searchingly. 'What are you saying, Charlie?'

'On Monday morning, I'll take you to work.' He took hold of her hands. 'Then that'll be it, June,' he told her gently. 'I'll be off, and I won't be coming home for a while. And you're going to be a busy lady too. What with learning a new job, going to night classes, writing letters to Arthur and doing your French lessons, the weeks will soon pass. And it's time I looked for that girl you tell me is just around the corner.'

She said nothing. Her head was down, and he suspected tears were gathering.

'You know I'm right.' He squeezed her hands. 'Of course, when I do come home on leave, I can always loan you a shoulder to cry on. That's what friends are for.'

She gave a little sniff and wiped a hand across her eyes. He passed her his big white handkerchief.

'But I'm not gone yet. So cheer up, Mr Armstrong's little Junie, and I'll tell you what I've got planned before I leave. First, let me give you the theatre tickets for the ballet. Arthur should be home that weekend. If he isn't, take Clare, or someone else.'

She thanked him without enthusiasm, and put the tickets in her bag.

He told her about the opera on Friday – another chance for her to look and feel radiant.

'That's great, thank you, Charlie.'

'And then, young lady, you're invited to join us here on Saturday evening. My parents are having a dinner party for their political friends. Probably terribly boring, but it'll be a taste of what it'll be like to be Mrs Arthur

Rogers, daughter-in-law of Colonel and Mrs Arthur Percy Rogers.'

'I might do something dreadful and shame you all,' she said glumly.

'No you won't, *I'll* be there to guide you. George has other plans for that night and Clare says she's staying the night with a friend, so you can partner *me*.' He gave her a big smile: 'That's not so bad, is it?'

'No, you're quite right, Charlie – as usual. It'll be a good experience. And I'll be able to dress up again. You know what a big show-off I am.'

She gave him a cheerful smile, but he knew it was only for his benefit. She was probably scared stiff.

'A show-off? Not at all. Beauty *should* be on display – we men love it! Of course, we'll all be doing our best to look incredibly handsome and wealthy; that's part of the social ritual. Some might say it's more about power. Or maybe the mating game. Strutting peacocks, that's what we are. So why shouldn't you show off your fine feathers?'

She laughed. 'Yes, I suppose you're right.'

He opened up the French language book and she soon regained her enthusiasm for learning.

Mid-afternoon, he told her that she'd studied enough and it was time for tea. They drove to one of the best city hotels and took tea in the lounge. But she seemed preoccupied. She wasn't really listening to his cheerful banter. Occasionally she looked up and smiled, but her eyes told him she wasn't interested in what he was saying; her mind was elsewhere.

'I'm really going to miss you,' she said with deep feeling when he asked her if she was all right.

'Then let's make the most of me while I'm still here. You can start by answering my question. Shall we visit Nottingham tomorrow, and make a day of it?'

'Yes, of course – I'd love that. Thanks.'

He picked her up early the next day, saying he had a busy programme to fill. She was pleased. After arriving home the previous day, she had gone to her room feeling quite depressed. Over her bright patchwork quilt, she had spread Arthur's letter and address, the photograph of herself, and the tickets for *Swan Lake*. Memories of both Arthur and Charlie crowded her mind. She had thought Charlie would be seeing her when he was home on leave. But no; either he wasn't going to come home or he was going to look for another girl to marry. She'd told him to do just that, so why was she so upset? It was the best thing that could happen. After all, she had Arthur. It was truly selfish to want him to spend his leave with her. Arthur's letter was full of encouragement and love. She felt ashamed of her self-centred emotions. 'Oh Arthur, I'm so confused. Please forgive me.'

But now Charlie was with her, and he was giving her no time for moping or speculating on her future. Telling her there was much to see, he kept her on the move.

In the middle of the afternoon, he took her into Griffin and Spalding, a top department store. First, he guided her to the perfume department and insisted on buying her a bottle of their finest.

'This will remind you of our French lessons together,' he told her, picking up her hand and lightly kissing it.

She'd never had expensive perfume before. 'Oh, Charlie, you're so thoughtful.' Ignoring the grinning assistant, she looked lovingly into his eyes. 'Thank you. But I'll really miss those lessons; they've been such fun.'

She heard giggling from customers behind her and a voice whispering, 'French lessons? I bet!'

He took her arm and led the way to the clothing department, saying she must have new shoes for her new job. 'They'll remind you that you're going places,' he told her.

In spite of her protestations, he bought her the most expensive pair. To please him, she accepted them with gracious thanks, although, not being used to such extravagance, she would rather have had a cheaper pair; they fitted her feet just as well. Such indulgence made her feel uneasy.

After a cup of tea in the restaurant they left the store, and as they walked down the road he told her about his earlier life with Arthur as his mentor. Suddenly, he pulled her into an expensive jewellery shop. Much to her astonishment, he bought her a beautiful gold bracelet-watch. He'd picked it out a few days earlier and it was wound ready for wearing.

'Use every minute to enjoy life,' he told her, slipping it over her wrist and fastening the catch.

'I can't possibly accept this, Charlie. It's far too expensive. I don't deserve such generosity.'

'Nonsense! You've given me a lot to treasure during these last two weeks. It's been a joy to escort you to so many places. Maybe I *have* been doing it at Arthur's request, but it's been my pleasure. Arthur has been the loser.'

Overcome with emotion, she stretched herself on her toes and kissed him on the cheek. 'Thank you, Charlie, I'll cherish it always.'

A smiling assistant looked at him. 'Is your lady to wear the watch now, or do you want it in a box?'

'I'll wear it,' she said. 'I'll always wear it,' she added, looking up into his eyes. 'And I'll remember all the good times we've spent together.'

The assistant looked from June to Charles. 'We've an excellent selection of rings, sir,' she said.

'I'm sure you have. But not today, thank you,' he answered, his face creasing into a curious mixture of smile and frown.

June was acutely embarrassed and kept her eyes from his. It was even worse as they left the shop. She heard another assistant remark, 'They'll be back for certain, anyone can see they're in love.'

'Isn't he gorgeous? I–'

The door closed behind them. She slipped her arm in Charlie's, but kept her thoughts to herself. In love? No, it was Arthur she loved. And Charles…? Just fondness.

She didn't see him the following day until he collected her for the opera. He told her father he would do his best not to be late getting back, but they might be held up by the snow.

Once in the car, she turned to him. 'You have a wonderful way with my parents. I guess they're going to be sad when you go, especially when I tell them we won't be going out together again. They'll think I put you off. My sisters might be pleased though. Don't be surprised if Rose hangs around Bloomfield every time you come home on leave.'

'No doubt I'll meet your sisters socially sometime. Bound to when you and Arthur get married. Somehow, I don't think it'll be a double wedding though.'

She laughed. 'Rose is lovely; but you're quite right, she's not for you. Anyway, she's already got a boyfriend.'

Charles was silent for a while. Falling snow was making driving hazardous and he needed to concentrate. But as they entered the city, the weather eased. He glanced at her and smiled.

'Would you like me to write to you? And send saucy postcards from the seaside? I'd like an odd line from you occasionally. I can let you have a forwarding address.'

She was glad the suggestion had come from him. 'I'd love to. Friends should always keep in touch.'

'That's what I think too,' he said, and then fell silent again as traffic built up on the roads.

June was entranced with *La Boheme* and became completely involved in the performance. During the tender parts, tears formed in her eyes and rolled down her cheeks unheeded. Charles passed her his big handkerchief and she took it with gratitude.

During the interval, he took her to the lounge area where people were having refreshments, and bought soft drinks for them to sip while they strolled around stretching their legs.

'You look very elegant in that black frock,' he told her. 'And I like the little added touches. You know, I get a real kick out of the way people look at you.'

'They're looking at you just as much – and smiling too. You must be quite well known here.'

'I do come quite often. Mother supports the place.'

A middle-aged couple standing nearby turned and smiled when they saw him. The man said something about the political scene, though she didn't quite catch what he said. Charles introduced them to her as Councillor Jim Baker and his wife Enid, and then skilfully brought her into the conversation.

The Councillor asked her, 'As a young woman, what is your opinion of the present Socialist Government?'

'Too often workers are oppressed, especially women intimidated by their male employers,' she told him with feeling. 'If Labour can make things better, then their candidate will get my vote – when I'm eligible to vote, that is.'

Jim Baker grinned. 'I admire your honesty, young lady, especially as you're with the son of our next Conservative Parliamentary candidate.'

Back in their seats, Charles told her that the Bakers were personal friends of his parents, and that she'd be meeting them again at the dinner party the following evening. She was shocked.

'Oh no !, I'm *so* sorry, Charlie,' she whispered. 'What will your parents say if they find out? I've let you down badly.'

'Quite the contrary – a bit of honesty is jolly refreshing. Don't be sorry, stick to your guns; Jim will respect you for it. And don't worry about my parents, just enjoy the rest of the show.'

By the time they left the theatre, the snow had stopped falling. Light shed by the moon and stars created a magical wonderland. Charles drove carefully until they were outside the city. Then, quite unexpectedly, he turned off the main road, stopped the car, and switched off the lights. June was apprehensive, although part of her was also sexually excited and that truly worried her.

He sensed her emotions. 'Don't worry, I'm not up to anything. I just want you to feel the silence of the night and see the lovely view.'

She relaxed and began to enjoy the wonder of it all. Lights from houses glimmered in the wooded countryside around them. In the velvet sky, myriad stars twinkled and sparkled like the diamond in her locket. Moonlight cast deep shadows over the snow-covered ground.

To her surprise, Charles stepped out of the car and reached in the back for an old waterproof cape, which he spread on the ground beneath a nearby cedar tree. He opened the passenger door – an invitation for her to join him under the stars.

'It's all right,' he said, smiling as he registered her wariness. 'It's too cold for any canoodling. I just want you to stand outside without getting your shoes too wet.'

She pushed aside her warm knee rug and joined him in the chill of the night. He put an arm around her and pulled her to the warmth of his body.

'Look around and feel the silence – its magical!' he whispered.

The beauty was overwhelming in its simplicity. A dog barked in the village half a mile away, disturbing the peace. A voice could be heard calling, and then silence. An owl hooted softly close by. There was a flutter among some trees, followed by a cascade of snow falling gently to the ground. Far away, the sound of a train could just be heard as it came closer, soon to steam away into the far distance. Then, apart from the sound of his breathing, the silence became absolute.

'It's wonderful,' she said softly, fearful that words would break the spell.

He lightly kissed her cheek. 'Yes, isn't it. Somehow, infinite space puts things into a better perspective.'

'You mean we worry too much, Charlie?'

'Something like that. But we'd better get going. No use philosophising to your dad if we get you home late.'

Back in the car, she leaned her head against his shoulder and wrestled with her feelings.

'I'm going to feel so alone when you leave.'

'That's inevitable; we've done so much together,' he said, rubbing his cheek against her hair. 'But that's how things are in life: meetings and partings. Believe me, when you start work on Monday you'll be so absorbed in what you're doing that you won't even notice I'm not around.'

She found that very difficult to believe.

She spent Saturday morning preparing for the evening's big event. She was making a shaped jacket of black and white striped taffeta to wear with her black dress. She was nervous about the dinner, feeling rather vulnerable, but knowing that it was something that had to be faced. Her future life with Arthur wasn't just going to be the two of them living intimately together. As soon as they were engaged a new life would begin and she was determined to be an asset to him, not a hindrance.

Charlie called for her at eight, looking ever so handsome in his dinner jacket, bow tie, and dress shirt resplendent with gold and jet cufflinks. She could hear her sisters twittering about him in the front room. Before they, or either of her parents, had chance to meet him, she took his arm and swept him off to his car. 'Come on Charlie, we'll be here all night if anyone catches you.'

Arriving at Bloomfield, he helped her with her coat. 'You look beautiful,' he said. 'I recognise the black dress but that little jacket is *your* design, I can see that. And it's perfect for the occasion.'

Mary Rogers welcomed her warmly, and also remarked on how chic she looked.

'I do hope you will continue dressing me, June,' she told her pleasantly, 'you have such a flair for good design.'

Her confidence began to rise. At least she knew how to dress correctly.

Charles whispered in her ear, 'Mother is always right about clothes; you really do look fantastic... in *every* respect.'

She turned to face him. 'You look pretty good yourself, Charlie.'

He grinned. 'Not much you can do with a suit – except spill your soup on it!'

A man's voice sounded loudly as a couple of guests entered the hall. 'Well, here's that young lady we met last night. Miss Armstrong, if I remember correctly.'

She smiled. 'You're quite right, Mr Baker.'

'And very beautiful you look, my dear. In fact, you and Charles make quite a handsome couple.'

'Sorry, Jim,' said Charles, 'but we're just good friends.'

Another voice sounded close by: 'Ah, then there's hope for *me*, is there?'

June turned to see who the newcomer was. A dapper man in his sixties was grinning at her.

'I think not,' she told him, giving him a look of regret, 'but if my secret lover deserts me, I'll let you know.'

Everyone laughed. She relaxed. Everything was going to be all right.

When Charles took her home, he kissed her on the cheek and told her that Arthur would have been proud of her. 'You looked so confident, so much part of the social scene – even if you don't agree with their politics. They all recognised that you were plucky to speak your mind, especially as the women didn't back you up.'

She recalled the women's supercilious smiles. 'They would have done,' she said adamantly, 'if they knew what it was like to work hard for your living, domineered by bullying bosses.'

He gave a little laugh. 'Some might say they know already – that's how their husbands treat them!'

She had to laugh with him. He was probably right; the men did seem to be a chauvinistic bunch.

He took her hand. 'I won't be seeing you tomorrow. I have a lot to do before I go.'

The words were spoken gently, but they came like icy water poured on bare flesh.

'I understand,' she said, rather too cheerfully. 'I don't know how you've managed to give me so much of your time. I really do appreciate it.'

It sounded terribly polite and formal but she knew it could be no other way. A certain distance had to be maintained or she'd be in tears.

'I'll pick you up at eight-thirty Monday morning, as we planned.' His voice became heavy with emotion. 'I'll only have time to say goodbye. I have to be off down south – it's a long way to go.'

In the light of the street lamps, she looked up and saw a glistening in his dark eyes. She put her arms around his neck and stood on the tips of her toes to reach towards his lips. Wrapping his arms around her, he bent down and kissed her tenderly. He rubbed his cheek against her hair. When he spoke, his voice was strained.

'Be happy with Arthur. You couldn't have a better man to love and take care of you.'

Before she could answer, the front door opened and her father was standing there looking cross. 'You're late – again!'

Charles let go of her and cleared his throat. 'I promise you, Mr Armstrong,' he said in a controlled voice, 'I'll not be keeping June out late ever again. After I've taken her to work on Monday, I'm off to take up my commission. I don't know where it will lead me or when I'll be home again. Goodnight, sir, and thank you for allowing me to escort your daughter. It has been a great pleasure. June is a lovely young lady who does you credit.'

June felt tears rising to her eyes; it was all so definite, so final.

Charles turned to her. 'I will see you Monday morning, June. Goodnight, God bless you.'

When she arrived in her bedroom, she opened her locket to look at the diamond. Then she reread Arthur's letters, her heart aching for his presence. She felt lost. On Monday she would see Charlie for just a short time, and then that would be it. He'd made it clear that he wouldn't be coming home very often, and when he did it could no longer be as Arthur's lieutenant. At least he'd continue to be a friend… a much loved, but rather distant friend.

Surely, she thought, it couldn't be love that was driving her to tears. No, it must be loneliness. Her family were at a distance from her now. She had set herself on the road to a better life than they had ever dreamed of. She thought differently, behaved differently, even spoke differently. She could no longer talk to them in their language. It wasn't because she thought herself better than them. No, they were perfectly happy with their lives. But she wanted little to do with that style of living. They had so little in common to talk about anyway. She couldn't be open about either Arthur or Charlie. She was the Ice Maiden, the butt of her sisters' jokes. And that was another thing: what would her parents think of their innocent little Junie if they'd seen her half-naked in Arthur's arms?

Charles was her link to her new life – more so than Arthur had been. And now he was leaving her. With Charlie gone, who would be her guide until Arthur came home for good? She sighed deeply. There was no use moping; she must write a letter to Arthur. It would bring him closer to her.

On Monday morning, Charlie drove his car just beyond the factory entrance. He opened her door and helped her out.

'I guess this is goodbye,' he said, handing her the various bags she'd brought with her.

Full of emotion at the changes taking place in her life, she looked up at his face, wanting to keep a picture of him in her mind. She took in the dark, heavy brows and the brown eyes lightly tinged with hazel that, according to his mood, sometimes gave the impression of turning darker. His thick, dark hair was now cut short at the sides and back – had he paid a visit to the barbers before picking her up? But his handsome face with its strong features looked serious and concerned.

'Oh, Charlie,' she whispered, fighting back the threatening tears, 'I'm frightened I'll never see you again. Take care of yourself – don't try to be too brave. You will send me that card you promised, won't you?'

'Yes, I'll do that. And you must write to me,' he told her, his eyes giving away the pain of parting even though his lips were smiling.

'I will. Thanks for everything.'

She began walking towards the factory entrance. Suddenly she turned, ran back to him, dropped her bags on the pavement, and lifted up her arms for him to pull her up and kiss her. He kissed her long and tenderly. Then, holding her face to his chest, he rubbed his cheek against her hair. Then he gently pushed her aside.

'Don't make this harder for us, my love. I just want to whisk you away and make you my own. It can't be done. Can't you see you're tearing me apart?'

'I love you, Charlie. I don't want to let you go. I know I'm being unfair to both you and Arthur but I can't help myself.'

'Young people are always thinking they're in love. You won't even miss me after a while. It's just my manly charm, you know!' he said, lightening up the situation in his usual affable manner.

She smiled. He certainly had the charm.

He picked up the bags she'd dropped and handed them to her. 'Now off you go and get some work done. Make us both proud of you.'

She forced a smile, then turned and walked towards the factory once more. It was the beginning of a new chapter in her life, and she was determined not to look back again.

Chapter Seventeen

At five minutes to nine, June arrived on the dress production floor of the huge factory building and found Robert Watson waiting for her. Rob reintroduced himself and guided her into his office.

'It's nice to see you again, Miss Armstrong. Come this way. I've been given the job of showing you around the factory, but first a word or two.' He perched on the corner of his desk, pointing to his chair for her to sit on. 'Don't you think you'd better take your coat off?' It was more of a command than a suggestion.

While she unbuttoned her coat, he watched her thoughtfully, his right thumb rubbing the deep dimple of his chin. Then he ran a hand through his thick, curly hair, pushing it back from his forehead. As she straightened her soft woollen suit, she saw his eyes narrow slightly, his gaze almost penetrating her body.

'Nice outfit,' he said. 'Fits you perfectly.'

She couldn't help but admire his strong facial features, and broad-shouldered, slim-hipped, athletic build. He looked like a rugby player – and a fit one too. He noticed her eyeing him, and his lips twisted into a smile. She quickly glanced away, embarrassed at being caught out.

She straightened her skirt over her knees and casually looked around the room. It was a busy place. Garment rails were filled with dresses, rolls of fabric were propped against a wall, and a long table was strewn with sketches, papers, buttons and embroidery samples.

'Right, now that you're settled,' he said pleasantly, 'let's begin. The workers start at eight o'clock. The junior staff get here spot on nine, but they're lazy blighters, most of them. The senior members of staff are at their desks well before then. If you intend to get on, I suggest you do the same.'

'Of course. I'm not a clock-watcher,' she told him.

'Good, that's what I like to hear. I think we'll get along fine. Let me give you some idea of our clientele...'

For the next few minutes he told her about the type of shops that bought their stock from the wholesalers that Watson's supplied, then he took her to a small office next to his own. It was simply furnished with an old desk, a chair with a worn seat, and a cutting bench. A dress rail, with a few wooden hangers, stood next to a wall, and some tatty looking patterns hung from a rail in a corner. Rolls of fabric were scattered on the bench and piled on the floor. Boxes of buttons and trimmings spilled their contents over the desk, the bench, and all over the floor.

'This is yours. We'll tidy it up a bit, but you won't be in here much for the first few weeks anyway, you'll be assisting Miss Martin – though everyone here knows her as Miss M. She's only in need of assistance while we're rushing out our new range, so after that you can come in here and twiddle your pencil. Once you've proved capable of doing what's required, you'll have more time to do your own work.'

The prospect of seeing her designs made up and in the shops was enormously exciting. 'That's wonderful,' she told him, 'I'm looking forward to the challenge.'

'Mm, good, I like a woman with enthusiasm. We want you to try out one or two garments to start with, just to see how it goes. It's my responsibility to get our younger range moving. Since you'll be designing for that end of the market, you'll see quite a bit of me; we could end up doing a lot of work together. You'll also have to meet the customers who don't come to our showroom. Will you be able to join me on the odd visit to London? It'll mean staying over, perhaps a night or two.'

'That sounds wonderful, Mr Watson,' she responded, trying to keep calm, but finding it hard to contain her enthusiasm.

He raised a heavy eyebrow. 'Are you sure your boyfriend won't object?'

'Boyfriend?'

'That tall, handsome-looking guy I saw you kissing from my window.'

'Oh, you mean Charlie. No, he's just a good friend. He won't mind if I go to London on business.'

'Well, if you say so. I'll take you around the factory now. Bill Potter was going to do that, but since I'm in this morning I thought it would be best if I showed you what's what. It'll give us the chance to get to know each other. People who work together should get on together, don't you think?'

'I'm sure you're right,' she said, thinking about the sorry state of her previous employer. 'I feel certain that we'll get on, Mr Watson. We both want the same thing.' She saw him grinning, and feared that she was being misunderstood. 'We both want to succeed at it,' she added quickly. 'Getting on, I mean.' Seeing an even broader smile on his face, she explained, 'We're in this together, Mr Watson. The new youth range, that is.' She felt herself blushing.

'Well, let's start by you calling me Rob.' His smile encompassed the whole of his face, emphasising his rugged good looks. 'We are *certainly* in this together, June. Perhaps one evening we can drink to that?'

She felt a little alarmed at that suggestion, but she didn't want to antagonise him; he was probably just being friendly. 'I'd love to, Rob, but I'm not old enough to drink alcohol yet, and what with night classes starting up again, and other things, I've very little time in the evenings.'

'What a busy girl!' He shook his head and grinned affably. 'But you have to relax sometimes. Anyway, let me show you around the shop floor.'

By the end of her first week at Watson and Sons, June was exhausted. There was so much to take in: names to learn, processes to think through, and the terms and language used in the bulk manufacture of garments to remember. It was all so different from what she'd imagined. There were no designers sitting at drawing-boards in bright airy offices, and no light workrooms full of genteel ladies sewing by hand or machine in the way that she'd always done.

Factory conditions opened her eyes to the workers' lot. The huge workroom had dirty windows and worn floorboards that smelled of oil. The odour of women's bodies hung in the air. Rotating machinery drummed remorselessly throughout the whole of the day. The sewing machines added to the din as each machinist picked up the rotational drive with an individual foot pedal. On the same floor were many other noisy machines, working on numerous processes. From other floors came the constant drum of knitted cloth manufacture and the muffled rattling and droning of machinery producing jumpers and cardigans. And above it all was the sound of music to keep the workers happy. The girls seemed cheerful enough – though it was the good rate of pay that mattered most to them. Their movements were swift and accurate as they sang along with the latest popular songs.

No individual garments were sewn in that room; everything was done in bulk. After cutting, different types of machine embroidery would be added first, if they were needed. Decorations like pin-tucking and quilted embroidery would have to be pressed and the piece reshaped. Each lockstitcher had a bundle of garments to do her bit of the process. Some parts, such as collars, would need pressing before moving on to the overlocker for seaming, the blindstitcher for hemming, and the buttonholer as required. Speed was essential to keep prices low.

Only in the finishing rooms could she make her voice heard without shouting. But even there the girls sang as their fingers worked swiftly with fine needles; each button, hook and eye, press-stud or piece of hand-stitching earning the worker another penny. Next door was the ironing and steam pressing room. It was just as grubby as the rest of the place, and hot and steamy too. She marvelled that the dresses didn't get dirty as they were constantly dragged across the shiny ancient floorboards.

Miss M's office was nothing like the designer's rooms she'd seen in Hollywood films. It was purely functional: a covered dress rail, a large oak utilitarian desk with a matching armchair, and a long bench with sliding-door cupboards. Huge rolls of thick craft paper stood at one end of the room. A pile of sample fabrics and some attractive material draped over a dressmaker's dummy provided the only softening touches.

June spent most of the week at Miss M's bench. Her right thumb became sore from using the large cutting shears, but after initially protecting it with plasters the skin and joint soon toughened up. She cut patterns strictly according to Miss M's instructions and had them checked and modified by her. She was shown how to cut out the garments so as to be as economical as possible with the material. She also learned how to do a sketch of the lay of the pattern as it had been placed, ready for cutting further samples and, finally, mass production.

On one occasion, she missed a piece of pattern off the sketch of a lay – a costly error if Miss M hadn't spotted it. Mr Watson senior had been right; she had a lot to learn.

Apart from the initial samples, all garments were cut in bulk according to each customer's order. This was limited only by the number of layers of fabric the cutters could easily and accurately cut through with their sharp shears. Too much wastage in any department could mean the difference between profit and loss.

Each pattern was graded into the required sizes and the patterns placed on fabric-width craft paper. The pattern lines were then perforated on a special long-armed machine. On the long cutting benches, material was cut to length and built up in multiple layers, and then the perforated paper lay rolled out and placed carefully on top. Soft bags of powdered chalk were then patted over the holes, transferring the pattern to the fabric. Within a very short time many garments could be cut and bundled ready for sewing. This method didn't work on all fabrics however, so tailor's chalk was sometimes used to mark out the lays, just as it was on the sample. But this was time-consuming and added pennies to the cost of each garment.

Another of June's many tasks was to rush around with Miss M's garments to get them through all the separate processes. Speed was of the essence here, as the samples had to be ready for viewing by the firm's most important customers, who always arrived early to get the pick of the new designs.

By the time she arrived home from work or night school, she was completely worn out. Yet she was still working for Mrs Rogers, designing, helping her choose fabric, and making up garments. When Kate slipped her a letter from Arthur one Saturday afternoon, she felt ashamed that her life was now so full that she hadn't even thought about her beloved. She wrote back straight away.

She soon adjusted to the routine of industrial manufacture, and began looking forward to working on her own designs. Eventually, she decided to mention it to Robert Watson. Since he was travelling so much of the time, it was difficult to catch him when he wasn't busy; any time was inconvenient. But that morning he'd been called out of his office to look at some dubious fabric that had just arrived from the dyers. She bumped into him on her way to the finishing room with one of Miss M's dresses, and reminded him of what he'd said at her interview.

'You'll get your chance,' he told her rather brusquely, as he mulled over the still-warm material.

Embarrassed, she hung her head and wished that she'd waited for a more appropriate moment.

'After all,' he said more softly, 'that's why the old man took you on, not just to cheer the place up – although you certainly do that!'

Flustered by his sudden change in attitude and the way in which he was now looking at her – practically undressing her with his eyes – she felt her cheeks turn bright red. But now that she had his attention she decided to make the most of it.

'By the time I'm allowed to try my hand, it'll be too late for the present range.'

Rob threw aside the fabric, nodded to the waiting cutter to go ahead and use it, and gave her his full attention. Rubbing the dimple in his chin with his thumb, his eyes narrowed and he screwed up his face in thought.

'No, not really,' he said, after a moment or two. 'There are always a few customers hoping to find something new. But it's important to present what we know will sell, and you are an unknown quantity. But you should still give a youthful lift to the end of this season's range, even if no one buys your stuff.'

She was shocked. Was she there just to do a bit of window dressing? Or was he being deliberately cruel? She was hurt and puzzled. A feeling of frustration came over her, and it didn't escape his notice.

'Tell you what,' he said, his broad, friendly smile indicating a change of humour. 'Design some dresses in your own time and pass them to me. I'll see if any of them have potential for what I have in mind – something a little bit different. I'll pick out the best and pass them on to the old man, and ask him to give you a chance to do something for us now. Miss M will just have to do her own donkey work for a bit.'

June's spirits rose to fever pitch. Rob was on her side and was going to get things moving for her. She would see her designs made up for viewing by potential buyers. Already she could see her dresses going through production, and eventually arriving in the High Street. Hundreds – maybe thousands – of women would be wearing clothes she had designed!

'Thanks, Rob,' she said, unable to keep the excitement out of her voice. 'You're an angel. I won't let you down.'

He burst out laughing. 'I get called a lot of things, but I think "angel" might prove a bit too restrictive for me!'

She saw the girls on the nearby cutting bench grin and give each other knowing looks. She'd heard their crude jokes and Rob was often at the centre of them. Whenever he passed by their benches, they always looked up and gave him a smile – as all the female workers did. And the office girls were no different. It hadn't taken her long to realise that the manager's son had quite a reputation where women were concerned.

Eager to prove her abilities, she arrived at work extra early the following morning. Designs were already popping into her head as if they had a will of their own, and she wanted to examine all the buttons and trimmings available. She made her way to the partitioned store at the end of the cutting benches. It was eerie in the huge workroom with no lighting or sounds of voices and machinery. With all the racks stacked with rolls of fabric, it was rather gloomy and claustrophobic inside the store, but not wanting to explain her presence to anyone, she decided not to press the light switch. Anyway, what she wanted was by the window, which was passing early morning daylight through its dirty panes. On shelving screwed to grubby whitewashed walls, boxes were piled in neat rows, with a picture of each design clearly visible; the trimmings were next to them. Miss M and the other designers already had samples of the old and new stock, of course, but she thought it better to get her own, rather than be told to do so.

Before long she had a small pile of boxes and bags on the floor, and was busy helping herself to some samples when a woman's voice sounded by the entrance to the store.

'Are you in there, Mr Watson?'

'No, I'm right behind you, Jane. I really appreciate your coming in early; we need those samples urgently.'

'How appreciative?'

'Okay, but it'll have to be a quickie. Get 'em off and keep your voice down.'

There was lewd merriment in Rob's voice. Surely they weren't going to do it... not right there in the stockroom! No, he was just joking; the man's reputation was fuelling her imagination. She was about to reveal her presence when she realised how embarrassing it would be for all concerned. So she sat on the floor amid her trimming collection, hoping they'd go away. Moments later she knew they were going to be there for a while. Jane, the cutter she had seen with Rob the previous day, was, in rather crude terms, being appreciative of his assets.

She tried to quell her imagination as Jane's groans of pleasure, coinciding with Rob's grunts of effort, reached her ears. Rhythmic bumping pinpointed their position to the partition wall near the entrance. Were they doing it standing up?

Activity suddenly halted. Rob mumbled something and Jane gasped – a curious sound of both pain and intense pleasure. What *had* he done to her?

No more than five minutes after entering the store they were gone, leaving June feeling shattered by her voyeurism. Erotic feelings had set her body ablaze, and she realised she was jealous of Jane's profound orgasmic experience. But this self-realisation also made her deeply ashamed, and she resolved never to think of such desires again… at least until she and Arthur were married.

Within a week, everything happened as Rob had predicted. She made up a few numbers that he thought sufficiently viable to be included in their range. When the firm's model tried them on for Rob, John Watson and Miss M to see, she was filled with both euphoria and fearful apprehension. But to her delight, their opinion was favourable – although they all said that alterations would be needed to make them less avant-garde.

Unexpectedly, Rob said, 'I think we should let June do a few more so we can offer a small range of youthful designs.'

The others agreed with him. June couldn't believe what she was hearing. Her own range! It was beyond her wildest dreams. She looked at Rob, who was grinning at her reaction. He must have thought her eyes were popping out of her head! She took a deep breath and calmed herself.

'Thank you all very much,' she said serenely, 'I'll do my best not to let you down.'

'Oh, you won't do that,' said Rob smiling, 'I know a winner when I see one.'

For a moment their eyes met, and she felt a thrill run through her body. There was something about that man that was totally compelling. It wasn't just his rugged good looks, but something much more earthy and dynamic; she had never met anyone quite like him. She strongly suspected that he could be just as ruthless as he was charming. Another shiver ran through her as she recalled the stockroom incident and realised that it was the dark side of him that truly fascinated her.

Her designs soon caught the eyes of customers. As predicted, they'd needed toning down, but at least she was getting somewhere. She felt exceedingly grateful to Rob for his encouragement. She looked forward to his nods and smiles and, she had to admit, the way he looked at her. He made her feel like a woman – a woman who was going places!

When she arrived home on the last Friday of February, she found a postcard waiting for her. It had a picture of a row of bathers dressed in tutus, tripping across a stormy lake and shouting, 'It's so bracing here!' The card was from Charles. All he had written was 'Hope you enjoy the ballet'. She suddenly remembered the tickets for *Swan Lake*… it was tomorrow! Work had been dominating her life; even her letters to Arthur were getting shorter and less frequent. She really needed to go to the factory in the morning and finish off a job ready for Monday. But she decided that after finishing up there she'd treat herself to lunch, spend the afternoon in the library, and then go to the ballet on her own and imagine Arthur sitting next to her.

She took out her writing paper and wrote a loving letter to Arthur and a friendly update of her life to Charlie. Then she lay in a warm bath, thinking about Arthur and imagining his touch. Pleasurable thoughts filled her mind, but they also made her ache for his presence. After a good soak – in emotions as well as water – she put on her dressing gown and went down to the kitchen to finish her sewing. But she soon had to give it up. Saying goodnight to her parents, she struggled back up the stairs to bed, and as soon as her head hit the pillow she fell fast asleep.

Refreshed after a good night's rest, she rose early and had a quick breakfast. By taking the train instead of the bus, she arrived at work just after eight, thinking she might have to get the gatekeeper to let her into the design offices. She was surprised to find the door to the offices already open and Rob Watson busy at his desk. He looked up and saw her standing in the corridor. He seemed as surprised as she was.

'Hi there! What are you doing in the factory this morning, young lady?'

She joined him in his office. 'I've some work I want to get finished. I can get a lot done when I'm on my own. I hope that's all right?'

He raised his eyebrows and smiled. 'No one is going to object to someone working for nothing. Go ahead with whatever you want to do, and let me know if you need anything.'

She left the room, taking off her coat as she did so. Rob called her back. 'Where are you going dressed like that? You look fantastic!'

She suddenly became conscious of what she was wearing. It was a new outfit that she'd recently made for herself. The mushroom-coloured soft woollen suit had a figure-hugging jacket designed with collar and revers in a lighter shade of fabric, and the skirt flared out to reveal godets of the same paler material. The rather low neck, made only slightly more modest by a see-through chemise, revealed a hint of shapely breasts.

'It's just a little number I'm wearing to the theatre tonight,' she said rather coyly.

He shook his head. 'I hope you're not planning on working here all day. That's taking loyalty too far.'

She told him of her plans and he listened with interest.

'Mm, but you shouldn't be on your own,' he said, gazing at her appreciatively, 'especially looking so beautiful.' He stood up and sat on the edge of his desk. 'What a pity I don't have a ticket. Suppose I give the theatre a ring and see if they have any cancellations? Perhaps they'll take yours in part exchange for a pair.'

'If you really would like to go, I do have two tickets. My friend wasn't able to go,' she told him, pushing aside all thoughts of the consequences.

'Really?' he said, lifting an eyebrow. 'Could this be the friend I saw you with?' But before she could reply, he added, 'Poor him – lucky me!'

She smiled and turned her eyes away. He was flirting with her, but she knew it was just his way with women. But she enjoyed his attention, and the sensual feelings that rose unbidden whenever his searching eyes penetrated her defences. 'I wasn't speaking of him. Clare, my girlfriend, is busy tonight.'

'Obviously meant to be. Tell you what, I'll take you to an early dinner before the show.'

'It *would* be nice to have some company,' she said, trying not to sound too enthusiastic. 'But are you sure that's what you want to do?'

'I'm completely sure. In fact, I want to talk to you about something important. I can't tell you now because I have to get this job finished by lunchtime. Can you abandon your afternoon plans? You look too elegant to be sitting in a library anyway. I'll take you to lunch. We can sit and have our discussion and then I'll drive you out somewhere. Then we'll have an early dinner and get back for the ballet. I'll drive you home, of course.'

'You seem to be offering rather a lot for the price of one ticket,' she said, beginning to feel suspicious of his motives.

He grinned. 'Don't worry, it's mostly business. You'll understand when we have our chat. It's highly confidential and I'd rather not talk about it here. I wasn't going to say anything yet, but seeing that outfit you're wearing has convinced me I'm on the right track.' He raised his eyebrows. 'Got you interested?'

'Very intriguing. Thank you, I look forward to it.'

He sat down and gave a little wave of his hand. 'Right. I must get on now. Be ready for twelve-thirty. Is that okay?'

He didn't even look up when she answered him. Feeling dismissed, she went to her own room and began working.

Before one o'clock, they were sharing a light lunch in Barker's coffee bar. He asked her about her likes and dislikes, and her hobbies. Then things became more personal.

'I see you don't wear a ring. Does that mean no serious attachments?'

She knew that some employers weren't keen on employing married women in key positions. 'I'm not married or engaged, if that's what you mean.' Feeling a little guilty, as though Arthur had been dismissed from her life, she added, 'I do see someone from time to time.'

'A casual relationship? Lucky man,' Rob said, grinning. 'I'm only interested because I want to know if you're serious about your ambitions. Too many young women give up their work, or lose their dedication, once Mr Right comes along. I don't want my plans jeopardised by the arrival of babies. You'll understand when we have our discussion.'

'It all sounds very intriguing,' she said, trying hard to ignore the feeling of guilt at deceiving him. She was consumed with curiosity. The way he was talking, it must be something big. Opportunities had to be grasped; surely Arthur would understand? The words of Mrs Rogers shot through her mind: 'A man has his needs.' Well, she would supply his needs, whatever they were. But marriage and a family could come later. Anyway, Arthur had wanted her to wait.

'When we finish here, we'll go to my club and I'll explain everything over a drink.'

It was a new experience to be sitting in a men's club. The strong masculine feel of the place was a little off-putting, and even though other women were present in the visitors' lounge, she felt awkward. A waiter came over and asked what they'd like to drink. Rob ordered coffee with rum for both of them.

'Rob, you *know* I'm below drinking age,' she told him, as soon as the waiter was out of earshot.

'June, my sweetie,' he said in a tone that she found profoundly irritating, 'you're a woman, not a kid. If you want to be treated like a woman, act like one. You'll enjoy the special coffee – it's served with cream as well as rum. And when we have dinner tonight, I shall expect you to share a bottle of wine with me. You know, my girl, in that outfit you look a million dollars, and wearing that French perfume you even smell a million dollars. Now, let's have a little sophistication to go with it please. In the sort of circles we'll be moving in, the sweet innocent child act is definitely *not* on.'

She coloured up. 'I'm not acting, I – '

She suddenly felt shy and awkward, as though she had been discovered playing a part. She felt out of her depth. She didn't belong there. She should be planning her future with Arthur, not denying their relationship. Although her head was turned away from Rob, she knew his eyes were watching her closely. She felt trapped in her own deception.

But when he spoke, his voice was contrite. 'I'm sorry, that was terribly rude of me. I'm afraid I've hurt you. Now you won't be interested in my plans for us.'

She was confused by his sudden change of attitude. She looked up. 'For *us*? What do you mean?' After all the stories she'd heard about him, she was suspicious of his motives.

'I don't mean anything personal… it's a business idea. Are you interested? Or do you just want to go on as you are, working for Miss M and having all your designs neutered? That's exactly what happened to the other members of the design team, by the way. But they didn't have your flair anyway.'

She pulled herself together, warmed by his opinion of her abilities. That she could be part of his business plan meant a great deal of trust on his part. He didn't see her as a kid who needed to learn social skills, but as a *woman*, a talented designer, capable of going places. She wanted to know more. 'I'm sorry, Rob. You're right about everything. I *do* want to get on and get somewhere in the fashion world… but I don't see how.'

The waiter arrived with their coffee; it was heavily laced with rum. She put a good spoonful of sugar into the glass and helped herself to cream, pouring it over the back of a spoon as Rob instructed her. She sipped it cautiously.

'It's delicious!'

Sitting back in her low-backed easy chair, the ambience of the place suddenly seemed perfect for why she was there – to discuss business plans in a man's world – and she was able to relax. But not for long. Within minutes, she was sitting upright and alert as Rob outlined his plans.

'As you know, our trade is strictly wholesale. This restricts how well our garments can keep abreast of fashion; too avant-garde and by the time they reach the stores they're last season's news. But if we don't keep up with fashion trends then our sales will drop off. The women who buy our clothes like to have something they can go on wearing for years and still look smart. It means spotting that little something in fashion that's enduring. That's why your creations have been neutered. It's not because they're a bad design. Far from it – it's because they're too good!'

She smiled at the encouraging remark.

He continued, 'But times are changing and we have to move with them. If we don't then our business will slowly decline. More women are working these days, and in higher-paid jobs. They're no longer the skivvies of the rich, cheap factory fodder, or downtrodden housewives… well, not entirely, but things are moving that way. Women can afford to be more fashion conscious. That's why I want us to have a retail section. I want to go straight to the top outlets, show them the latest designs, and be able to get the garments direct to their shops while the styles are still hot.'

He paused, looking at her intently. 'You might need to go to the shows to get an idea of what the top designers are pushing. But it would then be up to you to express the new trends in your own way. This is a totally different market to what we do at present. I've been working hard at getting introductions to the top people, and I think we're in with a very good chance indeed. Eventually, I hope we'll get our own designer label. The only problem, of course, is convincing the old man to let us strike out in a new direction.' He sat back in his chair and picked up his coffee, but his eyes were studying her reactions.

She was delirious with interest, but she had to avert her eyes from the intensity of his gaze. It did things to her beyond her understanding; things she could never admit to, not even to herself. But what he was saying was something really big, and he was drawing her – June Armstrong – into it! It was the stuff of dreams – of cinema and theatre! She tried to calm her wildly beating heart and be objective; nothing was set in stone yet. Mr Watson senior was evidently a barrier to his son's aspirations, and therefore to her own.

'It all sounds great, but I don't understand… why would your father object?'

With his left arm supporting his right elbow, he stabbed at his chin's cleft with his right thumb in suppressed anger. 'Old traditions die hard. Our firm goes back a long way. Dad wants a younger element adding to our range, but he only sees it as an extension of what we already do.'

He leaned forward, eagerness lifting his frown. Let's face it, Christian Dior launched the New Look in February '47. Here we are two years later and our range is barely influenced at all by Paris. But with the two of us working together – you and me – we could change all that.'

Excitement was bubbling away inside her. If she understood him correctly, she was the key to his new enterprise. Wow! She took a deep breath. 'Okay… so what do you have in mind?'

'I'm not sure yet. One possibility is to get a range of designs together and use contract firms to do the making up. The other is to start up entirely on my own.'

Her nerves were now jangling. She gripped her hands to stop them shaking. 'Which would you prefer?'

He finished off his coffee and put down his glass, licking a little stray cream from his top lip. He remained silent for a few moments, as if summing her up.

'I'll try to get the old man interested first, then go on from there. If he agrees, we'll keep the big plan for the future.'

She loved the 'we' bit.

He grasped her hand. His eyes were compelling, reaching into the depths of her soul. 'Are you with me, June? Be a woman; give me an honest answer. Does it thrill you? Does the whole idea set you on fire? Because if it doesn't then we can just forget the whole idea – you'll be no use to me.'

Rob Watson, the manager's entrepreneurial son, wanted *her* beside him in a great business adventure! He hardly knew her, but he obviously had enormous faith in her talents. It seemed impossible. Quite impossible. Yet it was true! Her excitement was now spilling over. In the whole of her life nothing had ever gripped her with such passion.

'Yes! Oh, Rob, yes, yes! If you think I can do it then I'm with you all the way.'

'Right then, it's champagne for us tonight!'

While Rob drove his Daimler into the damp misty countryside, he talked of the exciting things happening in the world of fashion, and the post-war perception of what women wanted: clothes with sex appeal. He was completely animated, obviously delighted that he had someone with whom he could share his obsession. June sat listening, fascinated by both him and his ideas. To have someone she could talk to – an enthusiast who understood her ambitions and wanted to take her with him into realms beyond her imaginings – completely intoxicated her.

They dined at a city hotel, but she was far too excited to eat the delicious food set before them. She merely picked at it whilst listening to Rob and gulping down the champagne that he kept topping up in her glass. He told her about his spell in the army before returning to work with his father, and how he'd increased their business through aggressive salesmanship and more creative methods of marketing.

'In spite of my father dragging me back on a choke chain, output has doubled these last three years. Even so, if we don't move with the times we'll soon be finished. Dad won't shift without proof. *We* have to give it to him.'

They finished with coffee, Rob having his strong and black.

'Well, we'd better be going before the swans fly off the lake and vanish without trace.'

She laughed. She'd been so fired up by his plans that she'd forgotten about the ballet.

Rob called the waiter and asked for the bill. In the foyer, he insisted on holding her coat while she put it on. 'I *love* that perfume,' he whispered softly. His cheek brushed against her hair. 'I'm really looking forward to this evening.'

Through her alcoholic haze, alarm bells sounded in her brain, but she dismissed them. Life was too good, too exciting, to respond to negative signals. And the truth was, she was drawn to Rob Watson from the very depth of her being. Yes, there was the promise of a fulfilling career. And he brought her innate creativity to life. But surely it was more than that...?

Rob gazed at her as she was immersed in the ballet. Her eyes were sparkling, her face was flushed from the champagne, and she looked fantastically gorgeous in that figure-revealing outfit. He knew what he'd rather be doing. She was on a high, just as he was, and it would be so easy to get her under him. After all, she wasn't attached to anyone, so why not? She obviously accepted casual relationships. The way that guy was kissing her on her first morning must have had something behind it, and yet she'd just dismissed him as a friend. Yes, she was his for the taking. A very pleasant evening lay ahead.

He thought he detected a tear running down her cheek. Well, it *was* a moving episode in the ballet… at least for a girl. Flat-chested women and men prancing around in tights did nothing for him. But the emotional situation provided him with the perfect opportunity; he took her hand and held it in his. Since she made no objection, he thought it augured well for the rest of the evening. Very well indeed.

As soon as the ballet ended, they went straight to the Daimler. Should he take her to his flat? No, too obvious. Easier to drive to a quiet spot and take advantage of her vulnerability on the back seat. But he'd have to be careful: she *must* want him. She might have been nothing without him, but his future plans now revolved around her and her creative potential. He couldn't afford to drive her away.

He turned off the main road and stopped the car in a gateway. He looked across at her. Worn out by the day's activities and groggy from the champagne, she had fallen asleep. He stretched out a hand to slip it under her skirt. She half-opened her eyes and smiled.

'Arthur?' She blinked and shook her head. 'Mr Watson! Rob, I'm so sorry, I must have dropped off. How rude of me. Am I home?'

'No,' he said, starting the engine. 'I just took a wrong turning.'

She slept in late on Sunday morning, but she dressed quickly and arrived at Bloomfield soon after the family had left for Morning Prayer. Mrs Craven let her in and gave her a letter from Arthur.

'Thank you, Annie. Did Kate ask you to give it me?'

Mrs Craven's eyes darted around the hall, her face the mask of a conspirator. She whispered, 'Yes, and she gave me a message for you. She's asked me to receive the letters at my house and to pass them on to you. She wants you to let Mr Arthur know straight away so your letters won't get lost.'

Although she was sure no one else was in the house, June kept her own voice low. 'What's happened, Annie? Have I upset Kate? I thought we were friends. She's been so kind to me. I don't understand.'

'She's left. There was a lot of unpleasantness. Something to do with her friend staying in her flat most nights. Evidently, someone told Colonel Rogers something nasty about Miss Kate. I heard things said but I can't repeat them, so don't ask me.'

'It's a puzzle. It must be serious for Kate to leave that lovely flat.'

She pushed the letter into her bag and went into the room now set aside for her sewing. There was a lot to do. Mrs Rogers might not approve of her missing church, but it couldn't be helped. Anyway, she would be at the evening service and surely once on Sunday was enough. She pulled out a ready-tacked dress from her bag. Arthur's letter fell out with it. She felt a sudden pang of guilt; was her beloved also taking second place in her life? She moved over to a small armchair by the electric fire and opened the envelope.

Arthur's letters were getting shorter and the poetry was often missing. She read the single sheet. Being under pressure of work was something she now understood.

But his letters were constant, and his love shone through the simple lines. Kissing the paper, she returned it to its envelope with a deep sigh. 'Darling Arthur, please come home to me soon. I need you, I really do. I miss you so very much.'

The following week, another postcard arrived from Charles. On the back were simple words of greeting, but on the front was a picture of Westminster's Big Ben. She looked at her precious watch and smiled. She remembered his last words, telling her to work hard and make them both proud of her. It was hard to believe how quickly things had moved on since then.

The weeks passed by and little had been seen of Rob since he'd told her of his plans. He was travelling to see clients most of the time, but he called in whenever he could to confer with his colleagues and to bring his office work up to date. On one of these occasions he opened her door and put up his thumbs. 'Getting there!' he said, and was gone again. Eventually, he called in to tell her there were only a few more people to see before speaking to his father. 'Oh, and by the way, you'll find your pay has increased,' he said, grinning. 'I like to keep my key workers happy. Can't risk losing you at this stage of the game.'

Mary Rogers invited her to one or two of their social functions, introducing her as a young designer. So now other women began asking her to design clothes just for them. Not wanting to refuse an opportunity to create exclusive designs, she looked like being busier than ever. But her growing reputation boosted her self-esteem. Even if Rob's plan came to nothing, she was, in a small way, already producing the latest in fashion. The financial rewards were also welcome; if she lost her job, which was most unlikely, she could survive very nicely.

On the Friday of the first week in April, she was surprised to find Rob waiting in her office. It was only just after eight.

'Good morning, June. Nice to see you're still keen,' he told her, 'but it's no more than I expect from you.'

'I'm determined to get as many designs done as I can before it's too late for the present range,' she said, walking to the dress rail and picking up a hanger bearing a blue dress.

'I've just been looking at them. They're pretty good,' he said with a casual wave of his hand.

She was disappointed that he showed no more interest in them. Instead, he was waiting impatiently while she slipped off her coat and took her latest sketches from her bag. The muscles in his face tensed up. 'For goodness sake, sit down, woman, I've got news for you.'

It was definitely a command, not an invitation. His aggressive urgency, although demeaning, excited her and she willingly obeyed. 'Sorry, Mr Watson… Rob.'

Perched on the corner of her desk with his hands gripping the edge, he told her about his meeting with his father and the rest of the management team. His eyes watched her closely.

'So, yes, they *are* prepared to consider a fashion retail section as a separate department. But it'll mean putting the bulk of the manufacturing out to contract. Neither the old man nor any of the others are willing to see the present trade put at risk. But the designs, samples, and the rest of the running of the new business can all be done from here. You'll still be doing some designing for the main trade, at least until we prove the new project viable.' He fixed her with his penetrating gaze, eye-to-eye. 'Can you do that? It's a hell of a lot of extra work for us both. But it's the start of something big – really big!'

She caught the excitement in his voice and it thrilled her. She was going to be an essential part of a brand new enterprise – no longer a hopeful dream, but a reality!

'Rob, that's fantastic! Yes, yes, of course I can.'

Rob was like a wound-up spring. He jumped from the edge of her desk and paced the floor.

'We might catch the last of the summer trade,' he said, thumping his left palm with his right fist. 'We have to visit London straight away. You need to see what's happening in current fashion.' He turned to face her, his eyes wild. 'Well, June, are you game?'

'Game? You bet! When do we go?'

He gripped her by the shoulders, searching her eyes. 'Monday! We'll stay overnight and come back Tuesday evening.'

'My bags will be packed tonight!'

He pulled her from her chair and hugged her tight. Releasing her, he cupped her face in his hands and said with utter conviction, 'You know what? We have a great future together.'

Their eyes met and she felt the power of his irresistible magnetism. A rush of adrenaline flushed her face and the whole of her body became alive to his touch. He pulled her to him and kissed her hard on the lips. The passion of the kiss both consumed and exhilarated her. There was no time to think of the rightness or wrongness of what was happening, or where it might lead. She felt no desire to resist the pleasure – and pleasure it most certainly was. It seemed part and parcel of the new relationship.

'Now I know why some folk come in early,' said a grinning Bill Potter, standing by the open door. 'Rob, if you've finished with that young lady, could you come to my office please?'

'We'll talk later,' Rob said to her, and left with Bill, both of them grinning.

She sat for a few moments, calming her rapidly beating heart. Then her rational mind took over. She must never get carried away by Rob again, at least as regards that sort of kissing. But then, why should she feel guilty or anxious? It was just the heat of the moment; it probably meant nothing to him. Even Bill Potter seemed to accept it as normal behaviour for Robert Watson. So why dwell on it? Ridiculous!

But he'd stirred something deep within her that wouldn't be easily dismissed. She turned her thoughts to Arthur. *Come home soon, my darling.*

'Miss Armstrong, could you come to my office for a chat?' The authoritative voice of John Watson, speaking from the corridor, snapped her out of her self-absorption.

By five-thirty she was ready to drop. Clearing up ready for Monday's trip hadn't been easy with so much on her mind. She'd hardly seen anything of Rob all day. He was a human dynamo, dashing about the factory and talking animatedly to people in the workrooms, his office, or on the end of a phone. Just as she was preparing to leave, he called in to fix a time to pick her up.

'And don't say you have to ask your dad first. Just tell him you're a big girl now – one that's going places. If he kicks you out, get a place of your own... or come and join me in mine!'

She had to laugh. 'You say that to all the girls. All talk and no action!'

He laughed. 'Give me the opportunity and you'll soon find out!'

'No thanks. Our relationship is strictly business.' She said the words, but part of her didn't believe them.

They went out into the yard, deep in conversation about their forthcoming trip, just as the last few workers were hurrying home. Rob put his hand on her shoulder and guided her towards his car. She was about to get inside when she looked up and was amazed to see Arthur, dressed in his camel coat and trilby hat, standing just outside the factory gates.

She quickly pulled herself away from Rob's guiding hand and nodded towards the gates. 'I'm sorry, but would you mind if I went home with Arthur? He's obviously come to pick me up. It's months since we've met. He's been abroad. Come and meet him, he's a dear old friend of mine.'

'Old friend? I thought he must be your uncle or something. Thanks, but I'll meet him some other time. You go and have your reunion; I'll get home and do some planning. But just remember what I told you: ambition and entanglements don't go together. Keep it strictly platonic or make a meal of sex, but don't get caught in the web of marriage.'

She stood, shocked by his remarks.

'See you Monday, seven-thirty – prompt!' he shouted, as he slipped into the driver's seat. 'And don't do anything I wouldn't do!'

He drove off laughing, waving to Arthur as he passed.

She was excited but confused, and not a little guilty. She wanted Arthur badly, but part of her also wanted to be with Rob. To make matters worse, Arthur was looking tired and grey. And yet he'd made the effort to come and meet her. He must have been waiting there for ages.

She flung her arms around his neck. 'Arthur, how wonderful to see you!'

He wrapped his arms around her. 'Darling, how I've missed you.'

She felt the strength of his longing for her in his passionate kissing. Oblivious to her surroundings, she responded without reserve. It felt so good... so very good.

A chorus of cheering and lewd remarks arose from the maintenance men who were just arriving for work.

Arthur let go of her. 'Let's get out of here, my love. We need to be alone.'

Chapter Eighteen

Arthur asked June what time she was expected home.

'Well, I go straight to evening class some nights, and work late others, so I'm not expected for meals. I always get a bite to eat before I go home. I'm usually home before ten-thirty unless I'm going somewhere special.'

It couldn't have worked out better. 'How about an early dinner at the Grange?'

'Lovely!' She squeezed his arm affectionately. 'I'm so pleased to see you, Arthur. You've no idea how much. Why didn't you say you were coming?'

He opened the passenger door of his Rover. 'I *did* tell you, a few letters back. I couldn't be certain, but I said it was a strong possibility… if not this week, then next.' He helped her into her seat. 'Didn't you get the letter?'

'No. Perhaps it's still waiting for Kate or Mrs Craven to pass on.'

'Quite possibly.'

He settled into his seat, started the engine, and they were on their way. He told her that George had written to him about his sister's affair – and his parents' anger. Of course Kate should have been more discreet, but even so, he was unhappy at the way she'd been treated. But there was nothing that could be done about it; their father was in a delicate situation politically.

'But why did they object to Kate having friends to stay?' she asked him.

'It's not that simple.'

'Then tell me,' she insisted.

He sighed heavily. He may not have approved of his father's actions, but he preferred not to say so. 'The flat is part of the family home and Father has his reputation to think of, especially now that he's in politics.'

'Yes, but what's that got to do with it? I could understand if they were men. But just her friends – that's stupid!'

'They weren't just friends. Not in the sense you mean.'

'What other kind are there? Friends are friends.'

'You really don't know, do you?' It was at times like this that her youth and naivety really hit him. 'It's just that some women prefer women. Just as some men prefer men.'

'I'm not *that* stupid, Arthur. Most people have friends of the same sex. What's wrong with that?'

She sounded annoyed, as though he was treating her like a child. Clearly, she had no idea about alternative sexual relationships. That was hardly surprising, since homosexuals kept their lives private if they didn't want to end up in prison. Few people would suspect two spinsters of living together in a lesbian relationship, unless they drew attention to themselves. He tried to explain.

'Two people don't have to be of different sexes to enjoy sexual activity.'

'What? I don't believe it! It's not possible.' She gave a bit of a giggle. 'You're just kidding me.'

Trying to concentrate on his driving, he slowed the car as he turned a bend. The traffic lights ahead were just turning amber. He brought the car to a halt and turned to face her.

'I think it's time to bring you up to date with your education. There are many ways for a couple to express their love for one another… use your imagination. Kate happens to be in love with another woman. If *you* find that shocking, what do you think Father's future voters would think? Especially since it was happening under his own roof. Two women sleeping together, and one of them his own daughter.'

'Kate and Rachel? That friend I met once or twice in her flat? I find that hard to believe.'

'Just accept it and try to understand. But don't say anything to my parents. It's been a terrible shock to them both. Given time, they'll eventually come to accept it.'

The lights changed and he put the car into gear.

'I've enjoyed reading your letters,' he told her, once they were moving again. 'I'm really pleased that things are working out for you. It all sounds fantastic.'

'It is, Arthur. It really is. It's quite unbelievable.'

'That young man I saw you with… was he my stand-in for the ballet? Robert Watson – the one who's going to whisk you from my arms and set you on a pinnacle of fame?'

He instantly regretted speaking from his heart. Would she detect the jealousy in his voice, or his fear of losing her to a younger man? He glanced in her direction. She looked serious.

'Well, yes, he did come with me that night. And yes, he does intend for me to get on. But he isn't going to take me from you. No one will ever do *that*, Arthur.' She sounded hurt.

He sighed. Why was she so defensive?

'I have to be honest with you though,' she said, as if reading his thoughts. 'We *have* kissed. A sort of celebration kiss – nothing for you to worry about. I'm not going to hide anything from you, I love you too much for that.'

He stopped the car in a lay-by. There were things he had to get off his chest before suspicion started eating away at their relationship. He turned to her and took her hand.

'I think I should tell you, my dearest. A short while ago, I had to stay over in London for the night. While I was there I met up with Charles. I didn't mention it in my letters; I couldn't have said much in writing anyway and I didn't want you to worry.'

She bowed her head and looked down at his hand holding hers.

'It's all right, I know about the kissing and the dancing and… everything,' he told her. 'He kept nothing from me. He told me about the gifts as well. And I'm pleased that he did. I realised a while ago how much he cared for you. I knew you'd eventually fall for his charms. All women do – young and old alike.'

'Oh, Arthur, I'm sorry. I–' she began, but he didn't let her to finish.

'Charles honestly believes you love me, not him. Why should I doubt him? Of course I'm jealous, what lover wouldn't be? But I wouldn't deny you those experiences. God knows, I've had plenty myself. I wouldn't want you to go through life wondering if you'd married the wrong man.'

He lifted her chin and lightly kissed her lips. He felt the warmth of her response.

'Everything's all right, my darling, it really is. I'm home for the whole week and we can make up for lost time. I'll wait for you each lunchtime and we'll go for a meal. I can pick you up every afternoon after work. If you skip your night classes we'll have whole evenings together.'

He felt her stiffen. Something was wrong. He didn't need his Cambridge degree or years of experience as an army officer and executive to sense that she was deeply troubled by his suggestion.

'What's the matter? Am I spoiling things for you?'

She looked awkward, shrinking back from him. 'It's just that…'

He realised he'd put her in an impossible situation. 'I'm sorry, I shouldn't have come barging back into your life.

You must have plans of your own.' He hesitated before stating his greatest fear. 'Perhaps you're going out with that young man from the factory, is that it?'

'No! Well... not exactly. It's just business. You must believe that?'

He wasn't entirely convinced, but he had no alternative but to trust her. 'Forget what I said just now. Just tell me when you're free and we'll take it from there.'

'Oh, Arthur, you're so wonderfully kind. I really don't deserve you. The truth is, I'm going to London with Rob on Monday. For a couple of days. Purely business.'

He was taken by surprise. 'To London? With Robert Watson?'

'We aren't sharing bedrooms or anything like that,' she added quickly. 'But I won't be back until late Tuesday evening. It's something we can't put off for another week.'

It was impossible to hide his disappointment. 'Obviously, it's important to you.'

Her face registered her torn emotions. 'It *is*, Arthur, it really *is*. Please believe me. I want to be here with you. I love you and I need you so much. But I want to get on and get somewhere. I want to be a top designer. And *this* is my big chance. Don't you see? I just *have* to go to London with Rob.'

She was right, of course. She couldn't cry off for the sake of being with her man. It wouldn't do; businesses weren't run like that. He himself would think twice about promoting an assistant if she put her boyfriend before her work.

'Yes, of course you must go. I told you I'd support you, whatever you want to do. When we marry, I wouldn't want you to be sat at home wishing you were somewhere else. Tonight, we'll work out what we can do together without spoiling your plans. All right?'

She smiled and cuddled up to him. 'Yes, that would be wonderful. It's lovely to have you home, it really is.'

After an excellent dinner, he took her to the flat for an hour or so. He switched on the electric fire and the living room soon warmed up. They took off their coats.

'I like that blue outfit you're wearing. Close fitting clothes really suit you; you have the right figure to wear them.'

She subconsciously straightened her shoulders and held herself well, showing her breasts and neat waist to their best advantage. 'I have to look decent in my job. It's important for a designer to look smart and attractive, especially when customers visit the factory. I'm glad you like this colour... it reminds me of your eyes,' she added, smiling at him coquettishly.

He grinned at her attempt at allurement. 'How about some background music?'

She helped him look for the records Charlie had told him about. Then he put the ones she had chosen on the automatic record player. Bing Crosby, Perry Como and Frank Sinatra were soon crooning romantic melodies.

Sitting quietly on the sofa listening to Crosby's melodic rendering of *You Belong to My Heart,* with June's head on his shoulder, Arthur recalled their first kiss. He stroked her hair with his cheek. 'You know, you seem so much more self-assured, more confident. You're not that young girl who turned me into a crazy fool. Do you remember that first kiss? I really shocked you, didn't I?'

'I couldn't believe what was happening. The mature Major Arthur Rogers, kissing someone like me – just a naive kid!' She giggled and snuggled up to him. 'Somehow, I couldn't resist you. Still can't.'

He stood up, took off his jacket and threw it onto a nearby chair. Then he bent over her and stared meaningfully into her eyes. She caught his mood, but pretended to be startled and ran to the other side of the room, where she stood with her back to the wall, excitedly waiting for him to catch her. Taking her in his arms, he kissed her with all the passion he'd denied himself for so long. He could sense her heart quickening and her body trembling with expectation. It was time to pick up the threads of where they had left off.

He led her to the sofa and slowly, very slowly, took off most of her clothing, lightly touching her nipples as he pulled off her blouse. She lifted her body, encouraging him all the way. For an enchanted moment he stood gazing at her young silky skin. She looked so adorable. Her flimsy white knickers and bra were pretty and heavily trimmed with lace, far more sophisticated and expensive than she could have afforded not so long ago. Her black nylon stockings were hooked to suspenders that disappeared under the frothy softness of her knickers. His fingers longed to follow their tracks and reach across to the gentle mound where dark hair was just visible through the fine fabric. She stretched her arms above her head in a beckoning pose. He smiled, because the little minx knew exactly what she was doing to him – it was perfectly obvious. But he loved her for it. His girl was practically eighteen, no longer a child but a beautiful, elegant and alluring woman. Yes, he wanted her to charm him, to send him wild with desire and force him to the limit of his powers of restraint. His personal battle had begun, and his heart was beating wildly with joy.

He looked at the little golden heart resting between her lovely firm round breasts, her nipples pushing pink and proud against their delicate but restricting cups. Breathing in the sweet warmth of her body, he unfastened the locket's chain and put it safely aside; she would have his own heart close to hers and nothing must get in the way. He stripped to his waist, slipped off her bra and pulled their bodies together. She responded with gasps of delight, clinging to his back with her fingernails. The pain only urged him on. Clearly, she was desperate to be loved and he knew he could do anything with her; she wouldn't resist. He hovered over her body. Kisses, long and tender, moist with passion, united his mouth with hers and led the way to intimate caresses. She yielded totally to his touch, sighing and moaning, tinkling sounds swelling up and bursting out in expressions of love and urgent desire.

'Oh Arthur, I love you. More, more. Yes, yes, my darling.'

He rolled to the floor, pulling her down on top of him, savouring the delightful pressure of her body on his before moving to lie beside her. Holding her close, with his loins hard against her, he felt the power of earthy passion urging them both to complete their union. But he could, and would, resist; there was so much to enjoy without breaking his vow. With practised skill, he followed the route of his exploring fingers to caress with moist lips and tongue where she reacted most to his touch, relishing the pleasure as she tensed and squirmed with desire.

'Mmm, lovely,' she sighed. 'More – please more. Ah – yes – yes!'

Sweating with the sweet agony of restrained passion, he pleasured them both for some time, drawing it out for as long as he could. But eventually he had to force himself to kiss her gently on the lips and move away.

'I'm so sorry my darling, I must leave you now.'

He left her to get dressed while he went to the bathroom, taking his clothes with him. When he returned, he found her tidying the room. He took her over to the sofa and discussed his plans for the coming week, with June quietly resting in his arms. She was distressed about being away for two whole days.

'I'm so sorry, Arthur, I've ruined things for you.'

He hid his jealousy and made light of her absence. 'Don't worry, I'll get a rest from your insatiable appetite!'

She laughed and beat him with a cushion. 'Beast! Horrid beast!'

She asked him about his meeting her at the factory. He told her that his mother had given him all the information he needed.

'She's really impressed with you,' he told her. It was the only thing he was certain about as far as his mother's relationship with June was concerned. 'In fact, she's arranged a get-together for tomorrow night and would like you to come. Kate won't be there, and neither will Clare, but George is back for Easter, and…' He hesitated, looking at her closely, 'Charles is coming home for the weekend. He'll be wanting to see you again.'

A look of joyful surprise flashed across her face, and once again jealousy clutched at his heart. Ridiculous – of course she'd be pleased to see Charles again, it was only natural. He mustn't let unfounded suspicions ruin their relationship.

'I'd love to come,' she said with a smile. 'Is anyone else invited?'

'Mother has a couple of eligible ladies lined up for Charles and me. You'll be partnering George as he's nearer your age. Don't worry, it's only for formality – the seating plan and so on. Mother could hardly have just one young lady surrounded by three handsome men all after her scent!'

She laughed, and he laughed with her. But, even so, he was concerned that his mother hadn't yet accepted the idea of June being his wife.

On the way home, June brought up Kate's situation. 'It's a pity she won't be there tomorrow. She's always been so nice to me. I really like her.'

'June, my love, do you want *four* of our family panting after you? Five maybe – I dare say my father enjoys your presence too.'

She laughed. 'Oh, Arthur, you're teasing me again.'

'Maybe.'

'I still don't understand about Kate though.'

He did his best to explain the attraction that people could have for their own sex. 'No less affection than we have for each other. And you must realise, especially after tonight, that there are many ways to express and enjoy that affection.'

He negotiated a sharp bend and slowed down at a Belisha beacon. A man with a dog hobbled slowly over the crossing. Arthur watched him. He was dressed in an army greatcoat and an old pair of boots. As light from a street lamp caught his face, it became obvious that he was a middle-aged down-and-out, a piece of flotsam drifting nowhere in particular. Was he ex-army?

With social problems as they were, what did it matter if some people preferred a homosexual lifestyle?

'I see,' June was saying. 'Well, no, not quite… it doesn't seem natural. But why are people so horrid about it all? Kate is a lovely person who wouldn't hurt anyone.'

He had to agree. 'But that's life,' he said, letting in the clutch. 'Unfortunately the same applies to anyone who doesn't conform to what society regards as normal. But don't even mention it at Bloomfield.' He didn't want anything to make June's acceptance more difficult than it already was. 'We don't want to upset my parents. There's already a lot of tension at home. George has been in trouble with Father – over money, I think – and now Clare is being awkward and upsetting Mother.'

June sat thinking. 'Clare told you about her games teacher, didn't she?'

'Yes, but I don't expect she took my advice. The affair has probably died a natural death by now anyway. I must admit, Mother was pretty cross at Clare for refusing to come to dinner. Do you think she's still seeing him?'

'I don't know, Arthur. She hardly ever talks to me now. She was really strong on him though. Not as a marriage prospect but, well, you know.'

He sighed. 'I'm really concerned about her, but she's eighteen now – a young woman, not a kid.' He slowed the car as they approached her home. 'But never mind Clare, what about us? Can I pick you up near the bus stop at ten tomorrow morning? We'll have lunch out. I'll get you back by mid-afternoon.'

'Yes, please,' she said eagerly, getting out of the car. 'Darling Arthur, I'm so pleased you're home. You've no idea how much I miss you.'

Alone in her room, June stripped off her clothes ready for bed and went over her time with Arthur. Her lover was no beginner at pleasing women, that much was obvious. A pang of jealousy gripped her heart. But she smiled as she remembered that no woman had yet had the pleasure of being totally possessed by him. That would be her privilege alone. Dreamily, she walked to the bathroom and sponged clean her intimate areas. Warm feelings flowed wildly within her. It had been an evening of delicious intimacy and yet, as pleasurable as it had been, she had also experienced a yearning deep within her for something more. Feeling him so hard against her had triggered an earthy passion that welled up in powerful gushes. She climbed into bed and indulged in memories of his lovemaking, her skin alive to every sensation. In her mind he was with her. Panting from the feel of his touch, her loins were soon aching with desire. There was no denying her heart's desire to be joined to him body and soul. She drew up her knees and groaned. No – no – not until their wedding day. For now, she would have to be satisfied with the wonderful gifts of love he gave her with such finesse. Contentment descended with a glow of happiness. 'Ah, yes, my darling Arthur. Until that sweet day…'

In the morning, she awoke with feelings of joyful expectation. Arthur picked her up as planned. One or two people saw her get into the car, but she wasn't concerned. If word got back to her parents, it wouldn't entirely surprise them. She was a friend of the Rogers family, and being given a lift into town by one of them would appear quite normal.

To her surprise, he took her to a jeweller. He left her looking at brooches displayed in brightly-lit glass cabinets, and disappeared into a back office. He came out smiling. She was completely taken aback as he placed a pair of magnificent clip-on earrings in front of her. They each had a brilliant diamond surrounded by a circle of little rubies.

'Arthur, they're beautiful! Thank you – thank you!'

'Not as lovely as the wearer,' he told her, his face made younger by his charming smile and twinkling eyes. 'Happy birthday, my darling. When you celebrate your eighteenth, you'll know I'll be thinking of you.'

'Arthur, you've remembered.'

'How could I forget such a special occasion? Wear that red dress tonight; the one in the photograph. The earrings should match perfectly. Will you do that for me?'

She was already thinking of wearing the dress and it delighted her that he had the same idea. She threw her arms around his neck.

'Of course I will. I'll do anything for you. Anything you want me to.' In a state of excitement, she kissed him full on the lips.

Suddenly, she became conscious of the people around them and quickly pulled herself away from him in embarrassment. 'Sorry,' she said, her eyes lowered coyly.

'I'm not,' he smiled back at her. 'But let's get out of here and go somewhere private.'

As soon as the earrings were neatly parcelled, he led her out of the shop. As they reached the street, she just caught the words of a woman near the door.

'I wouldn't mind a sugar daddy like she's got!'

With pain in her heart, she glanced sideways at Arthur and saw him wince.

A red MG arrived at June's home promptly at seven. When he'd dropped her off that afternoon, Arthur had told her that someone else would be picking her up in the evening. Seeing the car, she assumed that it was Charles and her heart quickened. Her father went to the door while she put on her coat and scarf.

'Do I know you, young man?' she heard him say.

'I'm George Rogers, sir. I've come for June.'

'Of course, the Colonel's youngest son. Nice to meet you. Please come in.'

'Thank you, Mr Armstrong,' said George. He turned and saw her waiting just inside the front room. 'Hello, June. Have you been waiting long?'

'No,' she told him, feeling a little disappointed that he wasn't Charlie. 'Only a minute or two.'

Although they knew each other well, George seemed unusually shy. She put it down to the formality of the occasion. Other than, 'I'm pleased you're coming tonight,' he said nothing until they reached the house.

'Here we are then,' he said, sounding even more tense as he helped her out of the low seat and ushered her inside.

She went straight to the cloakroom to hang up her coat and tidy her hair, leaving him staring after her. Just as she returned to the hall, the front door opened again and in came Arthur dressed in formal dinner wear. He was escorting two laughing and chatting ladies who were wrapped in fur stoles. She recognised one of them as Charlie's old flame, Angela Buxton. Arthur noticed her immediately and raised his eyebrows in admiration. A broad smile spread across his face and he gave a sideways nod of his head to communicate his pleasure at seeing her. As their eyes met, a wave of emotion washed right through her.

Colonel and Mrs Rogers came into the hall to greet their guests. Introductions were just about over when she heard a familiar voice behind her. Her heart skipped a beat.

'Hello everyone. Now which of you lovely ladies is sitting by me tonight?'

'I guess you're stuck with me, Charlie darling,' said Angela, eying him adoringly.

'Who could object to sitting next to Venus herself?' he gallantly answered.

Angela was dressed far more demurely than the last time they'd met, June thought. Her breasts were less exposed and her back was completely covered by a loose-fitting jacket. Instead of pink satin, her outfit was a pleasant coffee-coloured crèpe. A floral pattern, worked in gold thread, decorated the jacket.

The other lady, Betty Butler, was wearing a simple dinner dress of dusky-pink moiré silk. She gazed admiringly at Arthur.

'It's good to see you again, Arthur. It's been quite a while.'

He made a suitable reply, which June didn't entirely catch, and the two new arrivals went off to the cloakroom. Mrs Rogers went to the kitchen to see how Mrs Craven was coping, and the Colonel said he had to visit his study for a few minutes to finish an urgent letter. June was left alone with the three brothers.

George was gazing at her in adoration. He seemed to be transfixed to the spot.

'Why don't you take this beautiful lady into the other room and get her a drink?' suggested Arthur.

George didn't seem to hear.

'Tell you what, George,' said Charles, 'you wait here for Angela and then bring her through and I'll take June into the lounge.'

Without waiting for his brother to answer, Charles took her arm and steered her forward. She took a quick glance over her shoulder at Arthur, but he was smiling and giving her a nod of approval.

When they were out of earshot, Charles told her, 'I just wanted to say that Arthur knows all that happened and it's all right.'

She didn't want to discuss the past; it was too disconcerting for comfort. Just having him touch her arm was enough to stir up erotic memories of dancing with him.

'Yes, Arthur told me,' she said without looking at him.

'I have to admit I've missed you, but I was right, wasn't I?'

It was true that being busy had given her no time to miss anyone. But seeing him again pulled at her heartstrings. And yet she loved Arthur – her rock, her counsellor and her lover. It was so confusing.

'I guess you were. Time soon flies when you're busy, and now Arthur's home again – at least, for a week.'

'He tells me you're off to London on business on Monday. Things are really moving for you. Stick at it, June, and don't let anyone hold you back. We're all behind you.'

She smiled up at him. 'Thanks, Charlie. I'm sorry I haven't written very often, especially as you did so much for me.'

'That's okay. I see you're wearing those gorgeous earrings. Arthur told me about them. I doubt if anyone will believe they're just cheap paste, but let folk speculate; it adds to your alluring mystery. Now, since it's almost your eighteenth birthday, how about a glass of sherry?'

'I'd love one.' No need to tell him about the alcohol she'd already consumed with Robert Watson.

She may have been talking calmly, but she felt incredibly excited by his presence. What was it about him that stirred her so? Images of them kissing in his car flashed into her mind but she tried to push them aside and concentrate on the present.

The rest of the party entered the room. George came over to her and awkwardly apologised.

'I'm sorry, you must think I'm a right idiot!'

'No, not at all,' she assured him with a smile. 'We all get tongue-tied sometimes.'

'You look so beautiful, you'd take any man's breath away.'

'I bet you say that to all the girls. But you're looking pretty good yourself, George. It's the first time I've seen you dressed up in your finery.'

Colonel Rogers arrived and immediately dominated the scene. Politics took over until they were all sitting down to dinner. She noticed Mrs Rogers giving her husband a cautionary glance. He took the hint and allowed the others a change of subject.

George took her home at eleven, driving Arthur's Rover. Charlie had gone off in his MG with Angela. As soon as they stopped outside her house, George leant over and kissed her on the cheek.

'Can I see you again before I go back?' he asked, rather shyly.

She was touched. George had been splendid throughout the evening. At the dinner table, he'd given her a mental tour of Cambridge, and she'd listened with enthusiasm, picturing the ancient mellow buildings, life among the students, relaxing in a punt whilst drifting under the old stone bridges and overhanging willows... it all seemed so dreamy.

'Thank you ever so much for asking me, George, I really appreciate it. But I'm already seeing someone, and I have so much work to do. If I ever visit Cambridge though, you can definitely take me punting. I'd really love it!'

Sitting on her bed, rolling down her stockings, June let her thoughts drift over the evening's events. The dinner party had gone well. She'd noticed Mary Rogers looking at her three sons and smiling contentedly. No doubt she thought they were all well matched. Betty Butler was so right for Arthur – in every respect. Her age, breeding, education and social contacts would be real assets to a man on his way to the top. Angela Buxton appeared to come from a good family and seemed keen on Charles. And as for George... Mrs Rogers probably hoped he would take over from Arthur as being a more suitable partner for *her*. In a way, she felt sorry for the Colonel's wife; she lived in a passing world.

June slipped into bed and cuddled up to a hot-water bottle, believing that she was the luckiest woman alive. As drowsiness overtook her, many wonderful images flowed through her mind. She felt herself floating on air with Arthur, punting on the Cam with George, sailing in a boat with Charlie, and then all of these experiences pleasantly intertwining. Then the thoughts melted away and a new image came into her mind: Rob's heavy-browed dark eyes stared deeply into hers. 'No entanglements, June. Fashion is your future. Remember you are now mine. We belong together.' He was pulling her away, drifting… drifting…

She woke up to find her mother standing by her bed.

'If you want to go to church this mornin', you'd better get up. You're overdoin' things, you know. Burnin' the candle at both ends. Early to work, non-stop all day, 'ome late every night, parties at the weekend. You'll do yourself in, my girl!'

After taking Betty home, Arthur retired to his room, stripped off his evening clothes and lay on his bed with his hands under his head. His thoughts centred on June as he stretched an arm towards his bedside table and grasped the lighter she'd given him – an action he'd repeated many times in the last few months. He smoothed it in his hand, thinking of the day she'd given it to him. Things had moved on a lot since then. He smiled as he thought of their last intimate time together, then he closed his eyes and relived the pleasurable sensations.

There was a knock at the door and Charles came in, asking if he could speak to him. He settled himself in a comfy chair by the electric fire and grinned at his naked brother.

'There's a fine figure of a man. Pity you're not sharing that bed with your beloved.'

'We do all right, Charles, thanks to your flat. But I presume my love life isn't why you're here… is it?'

'I need your advice, Arthur. It's Angela. She wants to renew our relationship.' He sighed deeply. 'If Mother knew what that girl is really like, I don't think she'd be so eager to have her as a daughter-in-law. She had her hand in my crotch before I'd even put the car in gear… just like the first time I took her home.'

Arthur laughed. 'Some might say you're a lucky fellow.'

'Seriously, Arthur. My job may be a challenge, but what with no alcohol, tobacco or women, and having to keep myself fit on a restrictive diet, life's been jolly dull. A man needs to relax after the sort of action I'm engaged in.'

Arthur fully realised the sacrifice his brother had made in not pursuing June any further than he had. 'I understand the problem,' he said sympathetically. 'So tell me about the demure Miss Angela Buxton.'

'As I said, the very first time I took her home she made it plain that she wanted my body. It was a bit tight in the MG, but where there's a will and all that! She was great, I can't deny it. So we took it from there. But after a while, things cooled off a bit. Seeing young June's sweet innocence made me yearn for something different from all that Herculean stuff she kept demanding. Then she said I'd gone off the boil, and found someone else to keep her hot.'

Arthur nodded his understanding.

'I had to prise Angela off me tonight. And I have to say, it took a bit of effort – my body was crying out for it.'

Erotic pictures of Charles's predicament flooded Arthur's mind. 'It must have been difficult for you.'

'To be honest, Arthur, seeing your June looking so desirable didn't help matters.'

'I truly sympathise. My darling girl has bloomed into a beautiful woman.'

'I go back early Monday morning. Angela's begged me to meet her at the Richmond tomorrow and book in for the night. I'm thinking of doing just that. But I'm worried that she might have wedding bells on her mind. And why *did* Mother invite her best friend's daughter to be my partner tonight? Do you think something's being hatched?'

Arthur thought for a few moments before answering. Their mother could certainly be devious. But from what Charles had told him, Angela had a mind of her own and didn't need any help in getting what she wanted. And it seemed she wanted his handsome, athletic brother.

'Staying the night in a hotel could be a very compromising situation. Personally, I'd leave her alone. But that's easy for me to say.'

Charles frowned. 'I guess you're right.'

'Take her out if you must,' said Arthur after a moment's thought, for he knew how hard it was for his brother to be without a woman. 'But be careful, Charles. Don't let her trap you into marriage. Make it plain from the start that you're not intending the relationship to be a serious one.'

June made it to church in time for Sunday morning service. Her mother and sisters were already in their usual pew. Rose and Pat glanced in her direction and started whispering together. She heard 'snooty', 'posh', 'money' and 'clothes', and guessed they were talking about her and the Rogers family. The Colonel and Mrs Rogers were with Arthur, Charles and George. Charles, followed by each of his brothers, turned and smiled in their direction. Out of the corner of her eye, she saw Rose give them a little wave. She smiled and looked down at her hands.

Just as the service was starting, Clare hurried in. As she passed, she whispered, 'I need to see you after the service.'

That was typical of Clare, she thought. She always expected her to be ready and waiting when she wanted something. It was her own fault for being so compliant. Well not any more. It was time to be assertive.

She went straight out after the service, but found Clare already waiting for her. George had followed her out and asked to walk with them. Clare pushed him away. 'Get lost!' she said, in a most unladylike manner.

George looked at June wistfully. She gave him a smile and shrugged her shoulders. 'We have personal things to talk about,' she told him kindly.

Clare appeared angry. 'I don't know what's wrong with my brothers. You'd think you were a bitch on heat the way he's sniffing around.'

She decided to ignore the crude remark. 'So, what's the problem, Clare? We haven't talked for ages, so why now?'

Clare looked around her. 'It's that bastard Ray,' she muttered furiously. 'The damn fool's got me pregnant!'

June was shocked. She glanced at her friend, who was wearing an expensive dark-green fitted suit. If anything, she looked slimmer than she usually did. 'Clare, are you sure? Have you seen a doctor?'

'*Yes*, I'm sure. And I don't need a doctor to tell me.'

'Are you getting married – you and Ray, I mean?'

'*Married?* You must be joking! I'm not marrying *anyone*. Certainly not a randy school teacher!'

Life could be hard for an unmarried mother, and she was concerned about her. 'What are you going to do then? Do your parents know? Will they help you look after the baby?'

'Really, June, do you think I'm telling my parents? They'd kill me! I *don't* want a shotgun wedding, and I *don't* want this thing inside me. I've got to get rid of it before anyone finds out.'

'Clare, you don't know what you're saying. You can't get rid of the baby, it's not right.'

'I'm going to *Cambridge*, not to nappy land! It's got to go. I need help. You've always worked in a factory; lots of those girls must get pregnant. Find out how they get rid of the bloody things.'

'It's a baby, not a thing!' She was shocked at Clare's attitude. 'And it's jolly insulting to think that factory girls are less moral than your lot.'

'I'm sorry,' Clare muttered. She grabbed her by the arm and stopped walking. 'But will you help me? I've got to get rid of it before it shows.'

'Clare, you have to tell your mother. She's bound to be angry, but more with Ray than with you. It's disgraceful. Teachers are supposed to protect their pupils, not get them pregnant!'

'Ray would get sacked and I'd be forced to have the baby. Is that what you want? It'd be hushed up of course, so poor Daddy wouldn't lose his votes. It's been bad enough with Kate. They mustn't find out, or I'll never get to Cambridge. Come on, June, help me please – you're supposed to be my friend.'

'I'm sorry, Clare, but I really don't think I can. I wouldn't know who to ask anyway. You have to see a doctor. You can't just do things to yourself, or let other people do things. You don't know what might happen.'

'I know what'll happen if I *don't* do anything,' Clare said tetchily. 'You don't know what it's like to want something really badly. I've worked jolly hard to get into Cambridge and I'm not letting it go now that I have a place. It's what I want – what I really want.'

June was incensed. Clare might have worked hard with her studies, but everything she had in life had been handed to her on a plate. Getting into Cambridge probably had as much to do with her posh school and family background as her own efforts.

'Nothing is worth killing your child for,' she told Clare angrily. 'You should have thought about the consequences before doing what you did. And actually I *do* know what it's like to really want something and have to work to get it.'

'What, slaving in a factory all your life and sewing for other people? Huh, I should think you *would* want something better! You haven't even got a sex life. It was obvious that Charlie was sweating after you, and now you've got George panting to get your knickers off. Why don't you melt a bit, Miss Ice Maiden? Then maybe you'd understand my problems and be more helpful.'

She stormed off in a huff. June sighed deeply. Poor girl. She had to sympathise with her plight, for she now realised how easy it was to be swept away by sexual feelings. Thankfully, Arthur was such a responsible person; he wouldn't let things get out of hand. She suddenly felt enormously grateful.

Arthur picked June up in the early afternoon. Before going to hear Handel's *Messiah* at St Peter's church, they visited the arboretum. Spring flowers bloomed in the borders, almond trees were shrouded in misty pink, and green leaves were beginning to burst from their tight buds. On the pond, ducks paddled and splashed as they fought for scraps of bread thrown by excited children. Although the air was a little chilly, the sun was shining and as far as Arthur was concerned it was a perfect afternoon. One day, perhaps he and June would take their children to feed the ducks and play on the swings. What a wonderful prospect: marriage and a big family! But would she want a family? After all, her work meant so much to her.

'I love children,' she said, as if reading his thoughts. 'I hope you do too. We can work it out, can't we? You know, with me working?'

He held her in his arms and kissed her. People looked at them and smiled, but he didn't care.

'We can work out anything you want,' he said, content that she was on his wavelength. 'You'll get all the help you need.'

After a pot of tea and sandwiches in the arboretum tearoom, they went on to the concert. From time to time he glanced at her. He could tell she was enthralled by the music and singing, and her eyes glistened with tears. She'd certainly be in the mood for love afterwards! He smiled to himself. She was such a sentimental girl and he loved her for it.

'Maybe we don't need to eat,' he said, as they left the church.

'You're right about everything,' she whispered.

'Charles goes back first thing in the morning. He's using the flat tonight. But we'll get by.'

He drove the car to a lonely spot in the country where they enjoyed an hour's cuddle on the back seat. She was eager for his kisses and touches… sighing and pleading for more. As his mouth tenderly embraced her breasts, she squirmed and groaned, pulling herself up to him. He allowed his tongue to stimulate her nipples into hard peaks, and then gently sucked and nipped as his hand slid up the inside of her thighs.

'Oh Arthur, Arthur, Arthur…'

But he could go no further. His own need was becoming too great to be controlled.

Not wanting her to be tired the following morning, he took her home just after ten.

He wouldn't see her again until Wednesday evening. With an aching heart, he kissed her goodnight and wished her a lovely time in London. His beloved was going out into the world and he knew it would be a very different June that would return to him. Would she still be dreaming of marriage and babies?

Chapter Nineteen

At seven-thirty the following morning Rob was waiting, with engine running, for June to appear outside her house. The front door opened and out she came in a hurry, carrying an overnight bag and waving to someone behind her. He certainly approved of the way she was dressed. Her pale green suit, trimmed with velvet appliqué, had a nipped-in waist and flaring skirt, and the cute velvet hat perched on her dark curly hair was a perfect match. The high heels of her matching shoes added curves to her already shapely legs. Yes indeed, if the rest of her clothes were as good as this, she was going to make an excellent impression on the people he wanted her to meet.

She threw her case onto the back seat and slipped in beside him. 'Good morning, Rob,' she said, her voice brimming with excitement.

'Good morning, June. You look quite splendid. Keep that radiant smile, it's good for business.' He let in the clutch and bellowed, 'Hold tight, we're off!'

Rob travelled thousands of miles a year, mostly by car, and he didn't hang about; time was money. They were soon passing the station, only just getting beyond the barrier gates before they closed for an incoming train.

June turned and waved to two men who were getting out of a car.

'Seems as though you prefer men to boys,' he told her, grinning. He liked the idea. 'Mature wine, eh?'

'They're both just friends.' She sounded embarrassed.

'Come off it, June. I recognised the older man – Arthur, isn't it? He's still wearing that camel coat and hat. And the tall guy in naval uniform? He looks like the one I saw you kissing the day you started. Gosh, that seems like years ago now. Can't be much more than three months though.'

'I know! Isn't it incredible? I seem to have come a very long way. And I owe it all to you.'

He knew it was true. Without him she'd still be the kid pining to be given a chance. But now wasn't the time to capitalise on it; he needed her to be strong and confident.

'Don't sell yourself short,' he said, flashing her a smile. 'We're going to meet some important people today. Be confident. Get rid of any shyness and act the part I want you to play. We're going places. It might only be small to start with, but think big – that's important. If we don't have confidence in ourselves then no businessman worth dealing with will touch us with a bargepole.'

Taking advantage of a break in the heavy morning traffic, he turned the car onto the A6, slipped easily through the gears, and put his foot down. The Daimler quickly reached maximum speed. He had a lot on his mind; no time to waste on social chat. So he got straight down to business and told her about the people she'd be meeting.

'Remember: be confident. They won't discuss business with a kid. You don't have to lie. Just let them think you've been a successful designer for a few years. I'll be supporting you, so you don't have to worry. Dressed like that – very elegant, I must say – they'll think you're a youthful twenty-something. Let them think that. You have the flair, just let it out. Fresh ideas are what they're after. If we work together, we can deliver the goods.'

Once in London he drove straight to their hotel, where he'd booked adjoining rooms. He told her it was to make it easier for them to get together to discuss business. But he also had other things in mind if things went his way – and they usually did. He allowed her just ten minutes for a quick brush-up before joining him for a snack in the bar.

There was no time for sightseeing or enjoying the spring sunshine. They left the Daimler in the hotel garage and did a quick sweep of the top stores, which were busy with customers taking advantage of the end of clothes rationing. Then they visited the boutiques where so-called 'exclusive models' were sold. He wanted her to make snap decisions based on her first impressions of what she liked. He could spot winners himself, but he didn't want direct copies, he needed to know what she could do with them. By six o'clock, he could see that she was tired but exhilarated. Her excitement at buying clothes, even though they weren't for herself, rather amused him. Unlike most of the women he knew, she wasn't used to spending money – especially on clothes that she could make herself.

Back at the hotel he gave her just enough time for a quick wash and a change of clothes and then they were off again, this time to have dinner with a business contact. He was pleased with her choice of outfit for the evening: a trendy, figure-hugging, silk-embroidered black dress with coat to match. It was exactly right for the occasion – sexy yet modest. In the taxi on the way to the restaurant, he explained that the man they were meeting, Phil Jones, ran a successful outworking firm. They made up garments for some of the top design houses.

'June, remember this is a very important person; he can help us a lot. He might be able to manufacture some of the stuff for us. More importantly, he can give us tips on the styles that are moving fast. He may well get us some introductions to top retailers, and names of contacts. Of course, I have contacts in those areas myself – you'll meet some tomorrow – but the garments Phil produces go to a particular niche in the market. That's where we should be, competing with the top names.'

She shook her head. 'It's sounds so ambitious, Rob. I don't think I'm up to it.'

Her reticence angered him. He turned to her and shook her shoulders. 'Snap out of it. You're up to anything you want to do. You have the *gift*, damn it! All you need is confidence, and *I'll* give you that. But you have to drop this little girl routine. Think *big*, June. You're a full-blooded woman. You not only have flair, you have beauty – enough to turn the head of the most hard-bitten male.'

She blushed but he ignored it. 'It's a fantastic combination: flair, beauty and sex-appeal. You're a very desirable woman. So play on it for God's sake.'

She looked a little startled. 'Play on it?'

'Yes, play on your assets. Well-packaged goods have an immediate appeal, especially to a man like Phil Jones. Buyers will soon find out what you can do, how good you are. Before long, your name will be made. Once we have a reputation for delivering the goods, no door will be closed to us. Look, when we get back to the hotel tonight you can try on what we bought today. I'll give you a lesson in self-presentation. It's just a matter of having confidence in yourself.'

She looked dazed. Was she too young and inexperienced for all this? No, he was never wrong about people – especially women. His judgement had served him well when building up his father's business, and now he was going to create one for himself. His own little empire. He smiled at the thought. June Armstrong was not only right for the job; with her fondness for older men, she was going to be a knockout with Phil Jones! He gripped her shoulders even more firmly.

'Snap out of it. Be the woman you are.'

She opened her mouth to catch her breath and he pulled her to him and kissed her passionately, forcing her to breathe in his breath. She made no attempt to resist; rather, he felt her body tremble with the intensity of the embrace. As far as he was concerned, she was now infused with his life force. He looked into her startled eyes and said menacingly, 'We're a team. Together we can do anything – anything at all. Don't you ever forget it.'

'Yes, Rob,' she said meekly. 'You're right. I'm sorry, I think I was just tired.'

He smiled to himself; he knew what women needed more than they did themselves. He wiped his mouth with his handkerchief to remove all traces of lipstick and then made sure her make-up was in order.

'Good, you now have a natural bloom on your face. Just relax. You'll be fine. Once we start discussing business, your adrenaline will shoot through your veins and you'll come to life. I'm never wrong about these things.'

The taxi pulled up at the kerb and the bright lights of the restaurant streamed out to meet the pavement. He looked intently into her eyes. 'Right, the show has started; you'll soon be centre-stage.'

Phil Jones was a powerful looking man in his mid-forties. His heavy-lidded, penetrating steely-grey eyes, set in a square face sculptured with deep lines, gave him an air of utter self-confidence. His fair hair was neatly combed back, which tended to emphasise his large nose, wide mouth, and strong chin. His broad, well-padded frame was made elegant by a superb dark-blue suit. His white shirt was finely striped with blue, and he wore a blue and yellow tie – a perfect match for his bright yellow waistcoat. June thought his character matched his clothes. The man had a vibrant personality and was clearly no numbskull.

After ordering their meals, he sat back in his chair while Rob discussed his plans. Phil interrupted every so often to make a valid and precise comment.

Occasionally, he glanced her way, eyeing her up and down. Suddenly, he asked her a direct question.

'What do you think about all this? You seem a bit young for such a venture.'

This was it. She'd rehearsed what she would say to a number of questions, but the man obviously wanted more than stock answers; he wanted to know her in-depth thoughts on the subject.

'All the top designers started young,' she said, almost meekly. She caught Rob's dark stare, willing her to be confident. She instantly relived his sensuous kiss and his words: 'We're a team. Together we can do anything – anything at all.' He was right. His strength was now her strength.

'Youthful freshness, that's what's needed,' she said, knowing for certain that she was right. 'Most customers want to feel young and desirable. Don't you think so?'

Phil smiled and nodded.

She was beginning to enjoy herself; an important businessman was agreeing with her.

'Surely fashionable women dress to attract attention,' she continued, picking up a different tack. 'They want to look good and feel good. But they don't dress primarily for themselves, they dress for men.' She knew that was rather a bold statement to make, but it was what she truly believed. It was better to be honest than risk being caught out as a sham.

Phil raised his eyebrows and grinned. 'Don't tell my wife that!' he said, studying her with renewed interest.

'It's all about attraction,' she continued, now feeling completely confident. 'Isn't that what is meant by being attractive? Youth *is* attractive – otherwise women wouldn't spend most of their lives trying to stay young, and men wouldn't leave their wives for younger models.'

Phil's grin spread across his face. 'Looking at you, I certainly have to agree. If what you're wearing, Miss Armstrong, is an example of what you're saying, then I must say you've made your case.' He glanced across at Rob. 'From what Rob has told me, you're a woman with drive and ambition. You work hard, and are prepared to work even harder.' He swept his eyes over her body. 'I admire that in a beautiful woman. So many women take, but are not prepared to give something back in return.'

She was now feeling buoyant. 'Thank you, Mr Jones,' she said smiling, 'and please call me June.'

'A lovely name for a lovely lady. I hope you'll call me Phil.'

'Thank you, Phil,' she said, almost coyly, 'you're very kind.'

'I speak the truth; kindness has nothing to do with it. I hope to get to know you much better, June.'

She looked across at Rob, who was beaming contentedly. Obviously, as far as he was concerned, she was making all the right noises. Things were going well. She became more animated as both wine and conversation flowed. Having brought her into the conversation, Phil now included her in the rest of the discussion, and she loved every minute of it.

She was very much aware that he couldn't take his eyes off her. And with Rob continually smiling in her direction and sending out signals of approval, plus glass after glass of wine, she was feeling exuberant. She found it easy to join in the conversation, and she had a lot to say that was relevant to Rob's plans. Her enthusiasm knew no bounds. If this was what working alongside Rob was going to be like, then life was going to be wonderful.

At nine-thirty, Phil rose to leave, saying he still had important business at one of his factories. He shook Rob's hand and then took hers, as if to do the same. But he held onto it, telling her how pleased he was to have met her, and that he hoped to have the pleasure of her company again in the near future. He gave her hand a gentle squeeze. 'Perhaps you might allow me to entertain you tomorrow evening while Rob's busy elsewhere.' He surreptitiously stroked the palm of her hand. 'I can promise you a *very* interesting time.'

She wasn't entirely sure what he meant, but she had no intention of being alone with him to find out. At least she had a genuine excuse not to accept.

'Sorry, Phil, we're going home tomorrow afternoon. But it's been so nice to have met you.'

Rob put in quickly, 'We can stay another night, June, as long as we make an early start on Wednesday. A night out will do you good.'

'No, Rob. I'm sorry, but I have other arrangements,' she said quickly. 'I have to be home tomorrow evening.'

Phil looked disappointed. 'Ah, what a shame. Perhaps we can arrange something the next time you come?'

'We'll make sure we fit it into our schedule,' said Rob.

Oh, no, we won't, she thought, desperately searching for an excuse. 'I'm sure an evening out would be very nice, but you know how I always prefer work, Rob.'

'We can arrange that too,' said Phil, kissing her hand before releasing it.

Not knowing what to say, she smiled weakly and rose from her chair to collect her coat from the nearby hooks. Phil stepped forward and helped her into it. As she put her arms into the sleeves, she felt him touch her breasts as he pulled her coat around her. Surely it was no accident? She felt sick with disgust but, because of the delicate business situation, she tried not to let it show.

'Thank you,' she said without smiling. How she wanted to slap his face!

While Rob was paying the bill, she slowly threaded her way through tables of well-heeled diners until she reached the foyer. Thankfully, Phil was already disappearing through the swing doors into the street. She breathed a sigh of relief and waited for Rob, her anger building at the way she was being sexually exploited.

'I forgot to give this to Rob.'

Shocked, she turned to see Phil back inside and handing her something. She took the envelope from him and forced a weak smile. 'Thanks, I'll give it him.'

His powerful frame seemed to be looming over her. She took a step backwards but he caught her in his arms. Putting a hand behind her head to hold it still, he kissed her full on the lips. His mouth was large and wet. She pushed against his chest, but he only drew her closer to him, kissing her even more fervently. She stopped fighting and he soon released her.

'I do like a girl with spirit! I look forward to our next meeting,' he said, as much with his eyes as with his voice.

He was gone before she could get her wits together for a suitable riposte.

In the taxi back to their hotel, she told Rob about the incident. But he completely dismissed it as a fuss over nothing.

'Really, June, the way you were kissing your sailor friend in front of the factory a few months ago, not to mention the very public greeting you gave your ageing lover-boy last Friday, don't give me that sweet and innocent stuff. You didn't exactly push me away when I kissed you either. What's the matter with you? You're not engaged. You were great all evening – even giving Phil the come-on with all that talk about older married men preferring girls like you.'

She was aghast. 'That's ridiculous!'

'Then you have to go and put the stopper on everything. Why the hell wouldn't you stay over? You knew what he wanted. He could be a big help to us.'

'He's a filthy swine!'

'Make your mind up, woman. Do you, or don't you, want success as much as I do? This is one occasion when you can mix business with pleasure. You obviously enjoy men, so why play hard-to-get?'

'My private life has nothing to do with you,' she told him angrily.

'Rubbish! Phil could give you a really good time. He's not bad-looking either, you have to admit that. Well, at least you haven't put him off. We'll have to see how soon we can come again; he's really taken with you.'

She pulled a face. 'He's married. He should keep his hands off other women – especially me!'

'So what if he *is* married? You're an enigma, June. Sometimes you're so sophisticated, and yet there's still that sweet innocence about you. For goodness sake don't lose that, it's your attraction. But come on, loosen up a bit and enjoy life.'

'I won't see him again, Rob,' she told him forcefully. 'I'm not going to be a prostitute for you or anyone else. Get some other stooge to design for you. I want to carry on as I've been doing – or get another job.'

She saw his eyes narrow with fury and she prepared herself for battle, but he suddenly softened. 'It's been a busy day and you're tired. We've come a long way in a short time. You know I don't want to replace you; we work so well together.'

She'd won her stand for integrity, but she'd also seen a ruthless side of him that frightened her. Even so, his passionate ambitions thrilled her and it would have torn her apart if he'd dropped her. Making an effort to hide her relief, she said, 'Well, you know where I stand.' The words came out rather primly, and when she saw the corners of his mouth curl she felt herself blushing.

He took her hand. 'When we get back, try on the frocks. They'll make you feel better – get your creative juices going! It's been a fantastic day on the whole. You've done well and I'm really proud of you.'

She melted in the warmth of his praise and gave him a smile. The touch of his hand and the penetrating look of his dark eyes drew her to him like a magnet, and the memory of his passionate kiss sent her heart racing. She didn't want to be at odds with him; her future was tied to his. But was it more than that?

The taxi stopped suddenly, breaking the spell. Releasing her hand, he said gently, 'All right now?'

As they entered the hotel, he suggested that she freshen up with a shower while he sorted out the dresses. 'Together, we'll get an assessment of immediate fashion trends. I'll hang up what I can around the room and lay the rest on the bed.'

She undressed in the bathroom, carefully putting her locket in her toilet bag. The shower helped change her mood and she began to relax. She dressed in her underwear and put on a little of the perfume Charles had bought her. She suddenly thought of Charlie with Angela clinging to him as they left Bloomfield after the dinner party – with Angela giving him sloppy kisses. Angela had gone to the party with Betty and Arthur; it was only too obvious why she wanted to go home alone with Charlie.

Why couldn't she bear the thought of Charlie with another woman, making love to her and gaining that ultimate pleasure that she hadn't yet tasted – with Arthur or any other man? She sighed. How could she think of Charlie when she was practically engaged? It was ridiculous. Mere infatuation; being in love with love. She brushed her hair and turned her thoughts to Arthur, imagining him beside her, touching her and speaking words of love. She sighed once more. This wasn't the time for such indulgence. She pulled herself together; there was business to be done.

Assuming her confident designer role, she slipped on her dressing gown and went to join Rob in his bedroom.

The sight of the dresses on the bed and hung up around the room filled her with fresh verve. Rob was watching her carefully, his thumb working away at his chin as if to make the dimple even deeper. She looked at each dress in turn, then stood back and viewed them as a whole. Then she gave him her judgement.

He grinned. Without saying a word, he passed her a piece of paper on which he'd written his own appraisal. It was almost word for word what she'd just said. She looked at him and they both burst out laughing.

'You see, June, we think alike,' he told her, flinging his arms outwards to embrace the whole collection. 'We are perfect partners in this venture. Now, try them on and get some idea of how they make you feel.'

With Rob's back to her, she slipped on each dress in turn without leaving the room. There was no time for modesty, and she was wearing more than most women wore on the beach anyway. Nor was there time for a detailed analysis of each garment, but that was fine since they both wanted immediate impressions.

By eleven-thirty she was exhausted but exhilarated. She slipped her dressing gown back on and sank into a chair just as a waiter arrived with champagne – ordered by Rob. The waiter opened the bottle, poured bubbling liquid into two glasses, and left the room with a broad smile and a large tip.

'Oh, Rob, this is fantastic! I've never had so much fun. All these lovely clothes!'

'You can have the whole lot when we've finished with them. Think of it as a bonus for all the hard work you're doing. When the business takes off, you'll be earning *real* money.' His face became serious but with a hint of a smile. 'Money is *power*. Power over your own life.'

He'd said the words with deep feeling, and they moved her considerably. Power over her own life sounded a very desirable objective indeed. Isn't that what everyone wants but so rarely obtains? He came over, pulled her from her chair, and lightly kissed her cheek.

'I'm sorry about earlier on,' he said, sounding genuinely contrite. 'Please forgive me. We're a good team. I don't want to spoil things.'

She was touched by his gentleness and grateful for the apology. 'That's all right, Rob,' she said. 'I guess you think all women are the same. But some of us aren't tarts and don't want to be.'

He kissed her cheek again. 'You smell wonderful,' he said, nuzzling into her neck.

Her heart began to beat faster. Champagne, success and Rob's warmth and closeness were lifting her to dizzy heights. His lips touched her neck and she drew in her breath sharply. Delightful sensations flowed over her body and weakened the muscles of her legs…

Suddenly, he pulled away from her. 'I must let you sleep. Another busy day tomorrow.' His voice was deep, soft and tender.

She felt somewhat bemused as he ushered her out of his room. She wanted to stay, but of course he was right. She felt confused; he'd had her in his power but he hadn't taken advantage. She warmed to him even more. Her body began yearning for his embrace… no, *more* than just an embrace…

'Goodnight, June. Sleep well.'

'Goodnight, Rob,' she said, regretfully. She was suddenly finding it hard to concentrate. 'It's been a fantastic day. Thanks for everything.' Her voice seemed far away and not part of her.

She went into her bathroom and splashed her face with cold water, trying to get a grip on her emotions. Being full of champagne in a bedroom with a sexually exciting man was a situation to be avoided, for she could never deny his powerful sexuality. Overcome with guilt, she took out her little locket and kissed it.

'No one will ever come between us, Arthur.'

The following evening they were on their way home. June was tired but content. While Rob concentrated on his driving, she went over the day's events in her mind. It had all gone smoothly, if a little hectic.

She'd met several people connected with the retail trade. Some of the store buyers had been interested in viewing their range when it was ready for showing, but they'd need to preview some samples first. A handful of small retailers had said that if Rob was able to get a few impressive samples ready within a week, and if he could deliver before the end of May, they'd consider buying a small quantity for the midsummer trade.

She was going to have to put her full effort into her side of things. It would be an exciting but demanding challenge, and it would all begin tomorrow. Rob was going to pick her up and get her to work early. Rob! A thrill of excitement ran through her. Of course he thrilled her, she acknowledged to herself; he was her key to a fulfilling career. She refused to even consider any other reasons.

Rob glanced across at her, looking so happy and content, and thought how much he was going to enjoy their close – very close – association. It wouldn't do to antagonise her at this stage. There were ways and means of getting her to comply, and he'd enjoy the challenge. It had been hard to pull away just when she'd been ripe for picking, but better to leave her wanting than to have her moaning with regret later. No, she wasn't just one of his floozies. When he took her it would be at the peak of their relationship, and he wanted her to be sober and fully aware. Half an hour with the barmaid had taken the edge off his frustration. June had been left for another time – until her need for him had strengthened. Yes, what with business going so well, and handling June with such dexterity after the Phil Jones incident, he had every right to feel pleased with himself.

Chapter Twenty

In response to June's telephone call, Arthur was waiting outside the factory at eight o'clock the following evening. She left the building half an hour late. Sitting in his Rover, he watched with sinking heart as Rob walked her to the gates with his hand on her shoulder. They were deep in conversation. Suddenly they looked at each other and started laughing; they were like a couple in love. He could only hope that it was their mutual love of fashion rather than of each other. Rob looked towards the car, gave him a wave, patted June on the shoulder and turned to go back inside.

As he left his seat to open the passenger door, June was already running excitedly towards him. Still hyped up from the adrenaline rush and the sweet taste of success, she threw her things into the back and slipped into her seat. He leant over to kiss her. As delightfully as she responded, he knew that he had a serious rival for her affections. Her ambition to be a successful designer captivated her. There was nothing he could do but help her consummate her passion and be satisfied with the remnants of her love. That night, and the following two nights, she could only give him an hour or so of her company. But mentally and emotionally she wasn't with him at all. Her mind was on her work and where it was leading.

They agreed that he would pick her up at midday on Saturday, but she phoned to say she was running late, and would he be 'a precious dear' and collect her at six? He waited at the gates as arranged, but it was still another half an hour before she emerged… escorted by Rob. Arthur threw her things into the back of the car and she flopped into the passenger seat with a huge sigh – a mixture of tiredness and contentment. He leant over to kiss her as he always did, but there was little response; she was almost asleep. He took her for dinner, but she just picked at her food and said she wasn't hungry. Clearly, the small part of her mind that hadn't shut down through exhaustion was still working at the factory. With considerable concern, both for her health and their future together, he took her straight home to get some rest.

Sunday was the last day before he returned abroad. June had agreed that it would be *their* day, but she still went to work in the morning. He was sitting in his Rover outside the factory just before noon. To his great surprise, she didn't keep him waiting this time. As he opened the passenger door for her, she threw in her things, wrapped her arms around him and kissed him hard and long.

'I'm so sorry, Arthur. I know I've treated you badly, but you know how it is: everything's happening at once. We have to get a good start on the designs for our new customers. It won't always be like this.'

'I hope you're right – for your sake,' he told her, deliberately denying himself a genuine grumble.

'And now you're going away again. I feel awful. Please forgive me; I don't want to lose you.'

Of course he understood what it was like to be under pressure. The fact that she realised what was happening eased his pain. It was just circumstances keeping them apart, not her lack of love for him.

'It's all right, my darling, I understand. Things will be different when I'm back for good. We'll be able to work something out to suit us both. Now let's get well away from here before you change your mind.'

He drove her into the Derbyshire countryside, where they enjoyed lunch at a quiet inn. Delighted to see her face glowing from the fresh air, they set off to walk the footpaths in the April sunshine. Light played on the rippling water of the Dove and Manifold, lambs gambolled in the fields above the dales, and wild spring flowers surprised them at the side of the paths and beyond. They trod in mud and struggled over stiles and laughed with the joy of life and love as they walked hand-in-hand. Other walkers, dressed for hiking in bobble hats, leather boots, chunky sweaters, and with haversacks on their backs, hailed them cheerily as they passed by. Turning a bend at a lonely spot, he kissed her with fervent passion, but just as he was about to slip his hand inside her coat, a line of walkers came along the path. They gave up and made their way back to the car, laughing all the way.

'We must have time together, or we'll drift apart,' he said, as they drove to a hotel for dinner. 'You don't want that to happen, do you?'

'No, of course not. It's just that I–'

'I know, my love,' he cut in, not wanting yet another explanation. 'But don't think things will get any easier, because they won't. From now on, you're always going to be busy with your career. And I have my work too. If we're to stay together we'll have to work at it. So how about we do a bit of labouring today? Suppose I see if I can book us a room at the hotel? We could have a few hours alone together before I have to get you home.'

Her eyes lit up. 'That would be wonderful! But can we do that, Arthur? Will they let us have a room just for a few hours?'

He smiled at her enthusiasm. 'I don't see why not if we book in and pay for the night.'

He parked in front of the vine-covered building and went through to the reception desk. A few minutes later he joined her in the dining room.

'No problem, they're even going to light a fire for us in the bedroom.'

She was ecstatic. 'We'll make this the best ever – to last until you're home again. Let's not take too long over dinner. Please?'

'There is just one thing though,' he said, grinning. 'Just for tonight your name is Mrs Smith.'

Less than an hour later, they were sitting in their bedroom by a cosy fire. It was a pleasant room with an en-suite bathroom, just as he had requested. The curtains were drawn and the ceiling-light switched off. June looked at him expectantly.

'What are you teaching me about love tonight? I'm very willing to learn.'

'I thought we'd start with a clean slate. In a moment or two we'll take a shower, and then…' He kept her waiting, smiling at her eager expression. 'You'll just have to wait and see, my darling little student.'

Relaxing on pillows in front of the warm fire, he held her golden locket in his hand. He opened the case to reveal the diamond sparkling in the firelight. There was something that needed to be said and put out of the way.

'I want you to be happy, my darling. *Your* happiness is *my* happiness. I want you to be a successful designer and go far in the world of fashion.'

'I know you do, Arthur, and I love you for it.'

He sighed. Would she accept what he was about to say? He tried to keep his voice gentle and his words free from jealousy or blame.

'There must be a better way to achieve your goal than being a slave to Robert Watson. You're working all hours and burning yourself out. You could go to college as you once planned. Maybe develop the designing you do for Mother and her friends, turn it into a proper fashion business with rooms in the city. Somewhere prestigious… '

He went no further. She had pulled away from him and lay on the pillows watching the flames flickering over the coals in the hearth. As he waited for an answer, he realised that he should have waited until later on. He was spoiling their evening together. Now her mind would be on her work – and Robert Watson. He looked at her serious face, highlighted by the glow of the fire, and longed to stroke her hair and kiss away the frown. He wanted to tell her it was all right, that nothing had to change, and to forget what he'd just said. But more than anything else, he wanted their relationship to last forever. Was that even possible when another man loomed so large in her life – an attractive, virile entrepreneur who held her spellbound with his romantic promises of glory? Even he could see there was something of the Svengali about the man. He had the power to draw out her creative flair and play on it.

She kept her eyes away from his. 'I just don't know,' she said with a heavy sigh. 'Things are going so well right now.'

'I know. It's only too obvious how much you're enjoying yourself. All I ask is that you think it over while I'm away. You know I'll support you whatever you do. Now let's enjoy the rest of our last evening together. I'll make sure we both have something to remember in the weeks ahead.'

Their romancing began in the shower, where he pleasured her with new experiences – gentle, but erotic. Having brought Robert Watson to the surface, he had every intention of banishing the man and his business from her mind. When they returned to the fireside she was under his spell alone. Never had their time together been so good. But, oh, how he longed for their wedding night.

Chapter Twenty-One

Work became even more hectic for June. She had to prepare a complete range of samples for Rob, and make a start on the usual Watson's range. She was given another pay rise, and with it came a tremendous sense of achievement. But pressure mounted when Mrs Rogers invited her to design for more of her friends and acquaintances. She felt she couldn't refuse. Although she did the designing, she paid her sample-hands to make them up for her in their own time. Since she was creatively adapting patterns already in use to allow for individual size and style, the cutting of the garments could be done quickly before or after work. As well as designing, cutting had also become her forte.

One Saturday evening, while she was visiting Mrs Rogers to discuss her latest requirements, Clare was suddenly rushed off to hospital. Mrs Craven had found her slumped in a pool of blood on the bathroom floor. The following morning, June called at the house to see how she was faring. Both the Colonel and Mrs Rogers evaded her questions and declined to reveal the cause of her distress. 'A woman's problem' was the only explanation they would give for the sudden emergency.

After the conversation she'd had with Clare some weeks earlier, she could guess the nature of that problem for herself, and when she visited her at the hospital, she was proved right.

Clare was resting in bed, her face pale and drawn. She fixed June with a sullen stare. 'It's your fault. I had to do something – you wouldn't help me,' she said accusingly.

'I gave you good advice. If you'd taken it you wouldn't be in hospital. You've only yourself to blame. I'm sorry you're poorly, but... that poor little baby... how could you?'

'In my situation, easily! But it went wrong. Don't you dare say anything to anyone, or you'll be sorry. *Very* sorry,' she said menacingly. 'You'd be surprised what I know about you and my brothers.'

Unless she'd been listening at doors, what could she possibly know? But she thought it best not to call her bluff.

It was all hushed up. Clare denied having done anything to herself and refused to give the name of the aborted child's father. Her silence caused a terrible row with her parents, but she refused to give way. The atmosphere at Bloomfield was becoming increasingly unpleasant and June wished she could avoid being around when all the shouting was going on. In spite of what she'd told Clare, she did feel some responsibility for her near-death crisis. She had failed to act on her knowledge – she could at least have told Arthur.

To make matters worse, in Arthur's next letter he told her that Angela Buxton had written to Charlie to say that she was pregnant. Charles, accepting her word, had agreed to marry her. Evidently, Mrs Rogers wanted them to have a quick and quiet wedding, but Angela had insisted on a full ceremony with all the trimmings... and she wanted June to design the dresses.

She was convinced that Charlie had been trapped into marriage. But it was none of her business, and after all, hadn't she told him that a girl was waiting for him somewhere? Perhaps his marriage to Angela was meant to be. Even so, she had a bad feeling about it. Or was it jealousy? She put her unhappy thoughts aside and concentrated on her work.

Just a few weeks before Arthur was due home in August, June was in London with Rob. A top store had placed several large orders and he'd insisted on taking her out to celebrate. They went to a nightclub where, much to her displeasure, they met up with Phil Jones. At least Phil had a girl called Trudy with him. But her relief was short-lived – apparently the girl was for Rob's benefit.

They all drank champagne with their meal, Phil and Trudy drinking quite heavily. As they finished the last course, Trudy began giving Rob suggestive looks. He took the hint.

'I'm going to take Trudy home, June. I'll leave you in Phil's capable hands.'

Being in Phil's hands was the last thing she wanted. 'I won't hear of it. Phil has a wife to get back to. I'll just take a taxi back to the hotel.'

'Certainly not,' Phil said, emptying the bottle into her glass. 'I'll look after you. No hurry, June, my dear. Stay and finish this first.'

She watched as Rob disappeared with Trudy, leaving her alone with Phil. He was gazing at her with his pale, lecherous eyes, and she wished she'd put on something less revealing. What had she once said about women dressing to attract men? Did he think she was ready and willing for anything?

He stretched an arm across the white tablecloth and touched her hand. 'I have a nice little place for us to go,' he said. His tone of voice and the expression on his face told her exactly what to expect when they got there.

'Oh dear!' She held her mouth. 'I feel sick – too much champagne,' she muttered between her fingers. 'I'm going to the ladies' room.'

'I'll meet you outside,' he called after her. 'You just need a bit of fresh air. Don't worry, I'll look after you tonight.'

There was a phone outside the ladies' toilet, and she rang for a taxi to pick her up in five minutes. When she went outside, she found Phil waiting by his car.

'I've been sick, Phil. I'm going back to the hotel. I've rung for a taxi; I don't want to be ill in your lovely car.' She changed her voice to a conspiratorial whisper. 'It's the time of the month. I'm sure you understand.'

Back at the hotel, she fumed that she had been manoeuvred into such a compromising situation.

In the morning, she stormed into Rob's room for their pre-arranged breakfast discussion. She sat down and angrily told him what had happened the night before. Rob poured himself some coffee and casually shrugged off the incident.

'I really don't know what you're complaining about. A gentleman very considerately offers to take care of you, and you refuse and call him a lecher!'

'Not to his face, I didn't. But you know what he was after.'

Rob picked up a piece of toast and buttered it. 'Did he assault you?'

'I didn't give him the opportunity.'

He spooned thick chunky marmalade onto his plate and spread some over his toast. He pushed the slice into his mouth and chewed rhythmically, regarding her with a penetrating stare. After a few moments his lips curved into a grin.

'Exposing all that delectable flesh, some might say you were asking for it, my dear. But then, maybe you just like playing hard-to-get. Is that it?'

She felt herself blushing. 'That's ridiculous! You set me up – you know you did.'

He picked up his coffee. 'Set you up? You had a choice and you took it. What's the matter with you, woman? Are you a frozen bitch? The way you act with your lovers in public, I find that hard to believe. Phil's got a lot going for him. He isn't short of women but he seems to have taken a fancy to *you*. Heaven alone knows why, the way you treat him.'

'I was very polite to him. But I resent you throwing me at him like that. I've told you before: prostitution is not part of my contract. If you *ever* do that again, we're finished. I can walk out of this job, you know. There *are* alternatives.'

His eyes narrowed. 'Half-hearted effort won't get our venture off the ground. I need your heart and mind fully on what we're doing. I don't want to have to start looking for a replacement. But if I have to… I will!'

Was he bluffing? She shifted her gaze and took in the splendour of the room. This was no economical abode for thrifty travellers. Her own room was just as expensively furnished and decorated. With Rob, hard work brought rich rewards. She now had money in the bank, and her prospects were beyond anything she had ever imagined possible. He might make her angry, but he brought her creative gifts to life and put zest into the more mundane tasks. She put a spoonful of sugar in her coffee and stirred it aimlessly, allowing herself time to think. After a few moments, she looked up at him. He had another piece of toast in his hand, but his eyes were still fixed on hers, ready to mesmerise her with their penetrating gaze. She succumbed, as she knew she must.

'I love my job, you know that, Rob. I've put my heart and soul into it. But I don't want men touching me, or treating me as if I'm game for anything. I'm not like that, and you know it.'

He sat back in his chair, rubbing a thumb into the hollow of his chin, and mumbled a half-hearted apology. It was better than nothing. She dropped her eyes and started her breakfast. Somehow, eating together, especially within the privacy of his bedroom, was like a communion of souls. She began to relax and enjoy his company once more, and the conversation turned to the people they were about to visit. Before long, her anger had dissipated completely, and by the time the day's business was done, they were talking excitedly about how well things were progressing.

By the end of the week, her enthusiasm had fully returned; everything was going far better than they ever could have expected. Back at the factory, she began working all hours. She no longer attended night classes, and often ate her meals with Rob beside her talking business. It was all so thrilling.

The weeks went by quickly. She was so wrapped up in her work that there was little time to think about Arthur. Feelings of guilt made her determined to take time off to be with him during the first two weeks of August.

All too soon, the last Friday of July arrived. There was still so much to do, but she couldn't let Arthur down; she loved him far too much. When he did come to mind, usually when she was in bed late at night, her body cried out for him. Yes, she truly missed him – body as well as soul.

The factory was just about to close down for the annual holiday when Rob came into her office with details of an important assignment.

'Sorry, June, but we'll have to come in next week.'

Afraid to look him in the eye, she continued clearing her desk. 'You know I can't, Rob. I'm taking the annual fortnight. It's all arranged.'

'You can't let me down like this! Take a week off later.'

She kept her eyes lowered and repeated: 'The two weeks are all arranged.'

'What's so important that it can't wait? Damn it, June, look at me when I speak to you!'

She raised her head but kept her eyes turned away from him. 'Arthur is coming home. I haven't seen him for months. I want to spend the full fortnight with him.'

Rob was furious. 'You promised me no attachments! Remember? You *will* come in, June. Never mind Arthur – I need you here!'

'I will *not* come in! Things can wait until I get back. I'll do a few sketches at home.'

'For goodness sake, get a grip of the situation. We have this fantastic opportunity to move ahead of our competitors. Isn't that more important than fornicating with your precious Arthur? What can he give you that I can't? If you need a man that badly, we can easily fix it without you taking time off!'

'You're disgusting!'

'And what are you? A lying bitch? You told me your whole heart was in this enterprise.'

The factory bell sounded. The office staff had already gone. The rest of the workers were going off, either for the weekend or for the holiday fortnight. She reached for her coat hanging on a sample rail. 'Goodbye, Rob.'

'We haven't even finished discussing the Brown's order and you're clearing off as soon as the bell goes? That's not very professional of you. Are you so desperate to jump into bed with your lover?'

'That's *it,* Rob, you've made the decision for me. I'm going now. You can find someone else to sweat for you. I need time with Arthur – and I'm going to have it.'

She spun around sharply but caught her foot on the dress-rail and almost fell to the floor. Rob caught her and held her firmly. She looked up into his face, still defiant. But part of her didn't want to escape. She could never give up the work she loved. And the look in his dark, heavy-browed eyes and the firm grip of his hands were thrusting waves of wild, erotic feelings throughout her body…

Full of conflicting emotions, she quickly lowered her eyes and tried to think of Arthur. 'Let me go please, Rob. I have a bus to catch.'

'You're not deserting me now, there's too much at stake,' he growled. 'You agreed – no entanglements.'

She tried to justify her position while being true to Arthur. 'Yes, I know… and I'm not engaged… at least, not yet.'

'You're not in love with this man, you're in love with your *career*! We both know it's true. So does Arthur if he's half the man I think he is. Like a fool, he hung around waiting for you when he was last home. Well, he can do the same now.'

She was torn. 'No, Rob. It's not fair. We need our time together.'

'What for? I can give you what you need.' His grip tightened. 'And you can have it right now.'

He pulled her to him, kissing her with wild passion. He moved his mouth to her throat. Feeling herself powerless to resist, she threw back her head and drew in her breath sharply. Before she realised what was happening, he had closed his mouth over hers, forcing her to accept his breath along with his kissing. For a moment, she capitulated and became one with him, her whole body alive to his touch and her heart beating wildly. He excited her, thrilled her, in a way no one had ever done before. She wanted to pull away but was drawn to him like iron filings to a magnet. But then she felt his hand slide down her back and pull at her skirt. Alarmed, as much by her own desires as by his possible intentions, she tried to pull away.

'Leave me alone. I'll scream. I really will,' she told him, but she knew she didn't sound convincing.

He squeezed her buttocks as he pulled her closer to his hard body, his fingertips curling under the lace on her knickers. 'Take it easy. Everyone's gone home. King Arthur isn't here to rescue you either. So relax… just relax.'

She tugged at his hands. 'Let me go!'

'Oh, come on, June, give me a chance to prove we're a perfect team. You don't need anyone else for sex. Believe me, it doesn't come any better.'

She struggled to free herself. 'Let me go at once! I'm going home. You've no right to stop me.'

He gripped her arms and captivated her with his smouldering eyes. 'You're *nothing* without me. I've made you as a designer, now let me show you what else I can do for you.' He bent his head to kiss her again.

She turned her face away. 'No, Rob. Let me go!'

Still holding on to her arms, he pushed her a little way from him. A lecherous look crept over his face. His deep dimples became rugged clefts and his dark eyes glittered under their heavy brows. His smile twisted with lustful intent. When he spoke, his voice was deep and seductive. There was no mistaking the true meaning of his words: 'We have business to finish first.'

Excited by his compelling sexuality but fearful of what he might do, her heart raced inside her breast. 'I've had enough of your business for today.' Her voice quivered uncontrollably.

'We haven't done anything… yet!'

She was terrified by her inability to control the situation. 'Let me go! Let me go!'

But he pulled her to the carpeted floor and pinned her down.

'Come on, just relax,' he said calmly, as though talking to an overwrought child.

'Get off of me! Get off!'

She pushed and thumped but knew she was powerless to move him. Under his weight, struggling was quite useless; she was just burning up energy. She waited for him to make a move so she could act: kick, scratch, knee him in the groin.

'Okay, you win,' he said suddenly, lifting himself up and turning away.

She closed her eyes and breathed a sigh of relief. But when she moved to get up she saw his belt unbuckled and his fly flapping open. He'd tricked her!

Quickly pinning her down again, he murmured softly, 'Don't struggle. Do you want me to hurt you?'

Fear gripped her heart. 'No! No! No! Don't touch me! Let me go!'

She continued to struggle, but he was too strong for her. While kissing her with lips wet with passion, his hand went up her skirt.

She pulled her lips away from his. 'Oh, please, Rob, don't do it. I don't want you to. I really don't.' Her whole body shook with fear.

'See, my sweetie, you're trembling for it. You want me just as much as I want you. Admit it. I know the signs. Playing hard to get turns you on. Okay, let's do it your way.'

He tore at the bodice of her dress, stripping off the buttons. He pulled the widened neck over her shoulders, trapping her arms and exposing her breasts. She was powerless to stop his wet mouth moving sensuously over her peaked nipples. Her body was on fire and she was filled with a potent mixture of dread and guilt. Dread of what was going to happen, and guilt because part of her wanted, desperately, to experience his torrid lovemaking.

Her juices were flowing. Soon, very soon, he would discover it for himself and play on it. He mustn't get that far. She renewed her efforts to free herself, screaming again and again, but he merely increased the fervour of his love-play.

'Leave me alone! You can't do this to me!' she yelled. 'I'm Arthur's. He'll *kill* you!'

'Stop struggling and enjoy it. We both know what you want. Old Arthur's no match for a real man. You won't want him near you after this.'

'Please, Rob. Please. Please. Oh, please don't–'

He kissed her mouth and silenced her.

Chapter Twenty-Two

June lay on the floor with Rob by her side, unable to grasp what had happened to her – or what was happening now. Rob, so warm and tender, cooed over her as if she were a hurt child in need of his loving care.

'You'll be fine now. And you'll enjoy it even more next time.'

He'd removed the remains of her torn dress and was gently smoothing his lips over her reddened arms and thighs as if to make her better. He was no longer the aggressive entrepreneur and rapist, but a gentle, affectionate lover, genuinely concerned for her welfare.

'From now on we'll have perfect unity. Your marriage to your career has been consummated. You're too good to be just a housewife; that's strictly for the birds. You don't want a man to tie you down to a kitchen sink and fill the house with screaming kids. And you don't need marriage for sex, we've just proved that. I promise you, it doesn't come any better. You'll really enjoy it next time. Believe me, I know what I'm talking about.'

Still she said nothing. She couldn't concentrate on anything. His words were being overlaid by a replay of the last ten minutes.

She was pinned to the floor. He was pushing her trembling legs apart with his knees and groping inside her French knickers.

'Why, I do believe you're still a virgin. No wonder you're so frustrated. Well, well, Arthur isn't even man enough to make a woman of you. *That's* going to be my pleasure!'

'Please don't, I don't want you to. Please, Rob. Please, please – oh, please.' But the groping went on.

He was cooing in her ear now. 'Stop struggling. I don't want to hurt you. Come on now, my darling... relax, just relax.'

He came up hard against her. She panicked.

'No! You're hurting me! Oh, please, no. Nooooo...'

As she wrestled herself back to the present, the voices and movement faded away into the darkest corners of her mind. She was alone on the floor now. Rob was speaking to her.

'Come on, June, you'd better get dressed.'

He helped her up, smiling at her attempts to cover her nakedness with folded arms. He picked out one of her designs from the sample rail and handed it to her.

'Put this on and keep it; get another one cut. You deserve the best of everything. When we're in London, I'll get you some real silk underwear – it's great next to your skin. How about that?'

She looked at the dress and at Rob. He was smiling at her with his head on one side in a relaxed sort of way. Her brain was spinning with confusion. She was somehow being made to feel grateful and she couldn't understand why.

'I guess you're tired,' he said. 'You'll soon snap out of it. The first time is always a bit of a shock. Takes more energy than you think! Give it a day or two and you'll be asking for more – they all do.'

He picked up her bag and ushered her to the staff toilet. When she emerged, washed and tidy, he took her face in his hands and kissed her, ever so gently.

'You know, I could really fall in love with you. Things are going to be great from now on. Achievement comes from power over weakness. Together we'll conquer the market. No – we'll conquer the *world!*'

She collected her things together and he drove her home, acting as if nothing had happened. He talked continually about business and fashion. She nodded automatically, but she wasn't listening. Her emotions were in overdrive and her mind couldn't cope. She put her hand to her chest to feel her comforting locket. It wasn't there.

'My locket! I've lost my locket! We have to go back, Rob! I've lost my locket!'

'Calm down, June, I've got your locket. The chain broke. I'll get it repaired for you.'

She breathed a sigh of relief. 'Thank you.'

But why was she thanking him? Surely he must have broken the chain when he… No! She didn't want to think about that. She *mustn't* think about it. She couldn't accept it. It was too dark, too confusing, too painful. Better to think of the jobs she had to do that night.

They arrived outside her house. He turned to her and smiled.

'Just take a *few* days off. Then, next time we go to London, we'll make a bit of a holiday of it.'

Denying her true feelings, she washed and changed into a light suit and went to Bloomfield to see Angela. She had organised a trying-on session for the wedding dress and wanted to get it over with. By nine-thirty she had finished tacking the dress ready for her to try on again before the machinist had it back. She was on her own waiting for Angela, her strained emotions crying out for attention, when Charles walked into the room. He was casually dressed and looking incredibly virile with his tanned face and muscular arms. He smiled down at her and opened his arms in greeting.

'How's my girl?'

'Charlie!' she jumped up and threw her arms around his neck. 'I thought you weren't coming home for another week.'

He gave her a hug but quickly released her, then guided her back to her chair and sat down beside her.

'It's just an overnight stay. Angela wants to sort a few things out, so I managed to get away for a quick trip. I just popped in to say hello. How's the job going?'

Her control over her feelings suddenly vanished. She burst into tears.

He took hold of her hands. 'What's the matter, June? Don't cry, my darling girl. Tell me what's wrong. You're overdoing things, aren't you? You work much too hard. You shouldn't be doing this dress for Angela.'

She somehow managed to control her weeping. 'You've been so good to me, Charlie, I'm doing it more for *you* than for her.'

'I appreciate the thought, but she doesn't deserve it. Sackcloth and ashes would be more appropriate.'

She was shocked by the animosity in his voice. 'That's hardly fair, Charlie. She didn't get *herself* pregnant.'

'Ah, but she isn't pregnant. I realised that just before you arrived tonight. I won't go into details, but I've been duped.'

'Then why go along with it? Why marry someone you don't love?'

'Well, it'll suit Mother and the old man for one thing. Angie's been brought up to be a social asset. And someone's going to get me sooner or later. At least she knows how to make a man feel virile and all that. No, we deserve each other.'

She frowned. Surely there was more to marriage than social compatibility and sex. *Sex?* She mustn't even think about it.

He squeezed her hand. 'Don't worry, it'll all work out. She'll clear off as soon as I'm home for good. All she wants from marriage is plenty of money and the freedom to do as she pleases.'

'Charlie, I'm so sorry.'

'Don't be sorry for me, June. I'm going into this with my eyes wide open. You may have noticed that the Rogers progeny are not swayed by conventions, much to our dear mater and pater's regret. When the divorce happens, it'll be put down to my long and frequent absences and the fact that I'm such a lecherous rascal.'

It was written in his eyes which woman he'd rather be marrying. Confusion flooded her mind and a sudden pain stabbed at her heart. A fresh wave of tears overtook her.

'I hope those tears aren't for me,' he said softly, dabbing her cheeks with his handkerchief. 'I'm not the family man type anyway. Things will work out all right. You'll be very happy with Arthur. You both love each other and that's all that really matters.'

Her tears flowed even faster – for Charlie, yes, but mostly for Arthur and all their broken dreams.

He put a hand on her shoulder. 'Tell Arthur's lieutenant what the problem *really* is,' he said gently.

'I can't marry Arthur. I *can't,* Charlie. He'd be getting damaged goods. And I don't think I could ever let him do… you know… what you and Angela did.'

'Well, I certainly don't believe the damaged goods bit. And as for the other thing, Arthur would never do anything to hurt you. You'll see; it'll be the climax of your wedding vows. I know how he thinks about these things.'

'So do I, Charlie. But you don't understand – it can't happen like that anymore.'

He looked puzzled. 'Is it because of me?'

'No, not *you.'* Could she tell him? Yes, she had to let it out. 'My *boss,* Rob–'

Hysterical laughter overtook her. 'What a joke, Charlie. Can't you see it? *Rob – robbed?* I've been robbed of what was mine and Arthur's. Rob did it to me. He held me down. I couldn't stop him. *I couldn't,* Charlie. I tried, I really did, but I couldn't stop him.'

He held her tight while she sobbed away all the repressed pain that had come flooding back. As her tears lessened, he dried her eyes and tenderly kissed them.

'What a bastard,' he muttered angrily.

'It happened at work. Everyone had left. I don't understand it. He was so kind to me afterwards... so gentle... as if we were newly-weds. He said I'd really enjoy it next time. But I won't. I don't want anyone to touch me ever again. I feel dirty and wicked. Rob *must* have thought I wanted it though – he wouldn't want me to walk out on him. What's wrong with me, Charlie?'

She sobbed again on his shoulder.

'There's nothing wrong with you, my love,' he said, stroking her hair. 'Robert Watson's an arrogant devil. He shouldn't be allowed to get away with it. Have you reported him to the police?'

'I can't say anything to anyone! I can't, I can't. It would be so humiliating. It'd get around the town, maybe into the papers. No one would believe me. Especially Rob's father. And it would be dreadful for Arthur and your parents, and my family too. Please don't say anything, Charlie. I couldn't bear it, I really couldn't.'

'Forget my parents – Arthur would agree. But I can understand your concern.' His face twisted into an angry grimace. 'Suppose I pay the swine a personal visit?'

She knew exactly what he meant. But giving Robert Watson a beating wouldn't make her feel any better. Besides, Rob would make capital out of it one way or another. 'No, please no. It would only make things worse.'

He let out a frustrated sigh. 'Arthur will be home tomorrow. He'll sort it out – trust me.'

'I *did* say no to him, Charlie, I really did. You do believe me, don't you?'

'Of course I do. But some men are insensitive brutes.' His dark brows drew together in an expression of pain. 'Let's face it, I've proved that to you myself.'

'Oh, Charlie, I didn't want to remind you about that. That was different. You did stop when… you know. But Rob thinks he's sealed our partnership in his new venture. He's got me where he wants me – away from Arthur. He thinks he owns me, body and soul. "Achievement comes from power over weakness," those were his exact words. I'll never forget the way he said them.'

A tinkling voice sounded behind them. 'Well here's a pretty scene.'

They turned to see Angela watching them from the doorway.

'What did you do to little June, Charlie?'

'You say nothing of what you heard, Angie, and I'll keep quiet about your phantom pregnancy. We don't want anything to spoil our wedding, do we?'

'I won't say a dicky-bird. She turned to June and gave her a smirk of a smile. 'I'll try the dress on tomorrow morning. Make sure it's ready. Are you coming to bed, Charlie?' She drifted out of the room, humming to herself.

Charles turned to June. 'I'd better go or she'll kick up a fuss. I'll collect Arthur from the station before I leave in the morning and I'll have a word with him then. You'll be here tomorrow, won't you?'

'Yes, in the morning.'

He framed her face with his hands, gently wiping away her tears with his thumbs. 'Tell him everything. He'll comfort and advise you; it's what he's good at. Now don't you worry; my brother loves you more than anything in the whole wide world. He won't let you down – ever. Goodnight, June, God bless you.'

Full of mixed emotions, she packed up her things and trudged the short distance home. She headed straight for the bathroom and ran hot water into the bath. Her mother was soon shouting up the stairs.

'You only 'ad a bath last night, June, what are you doin' in there again? There'll be no 'ot water left.'

'It's the hot weather, Mother. I won't use much water.'

Her mother carried on grumbling, but she didn't care. She had to get into the water, scrub herself clean again and think through what had happened. Surely she'd lost Arthur now. And her career.

But it didn't have to be that way. Rob didn't want to lose her. He'd been really nice to her after what he'd done. Would he force himself on her again? Could she risk it? She suddenly threw up in the toilet pan. How could she even think of working with that man again? No career, however much it mattered to her, was worth that much. No, she was finished. Her wonderful, miraculous career was over. It could be the only outcome. Arthur had foreseen the dangers of working with Rob and she hadn't listened. Would he believe she'd resisted him? Maybe. But she was no longer a virgin. She couldn't marry him now – Rob had seen to that.

She lowered herself into the soothing water and started to scrub herself with the nailbrush, rubbing hard to get rid of any stuff he might have fouled her with. She looked at the bruises on her body caused by her struggles. She had actually let him kiss them better! But he wasn't a bit sorry. He thought he was doing her a favour, that it was now part of their relationship. But there could be no going back to Watson's. It was over; the dream had turned into a nightmare. She would write her resignation and get it over with.

She couldn't expect anyone else to employ her, of course. Rob, in his fury, would make sure of that. Neither could she expect any decent man to marry soiled goods. Rob had offered her a glorious future by his side. *He* could be her future. She was finished anyway, so why not go for it?

She shook her head. No! No! No! She was a slut to even think it. Somehow she would win through. She could still sew and earn her way to college. And then? Who knew?

She rinsed herself down and stepped out of the bath. It was time to make a clean start. And she would begin by confessing to Arthur what had happened.

Arthur walked into the room where June was working. She knew he had arrived home, and she'd been waiting nervously for him to come and see her. Hearing his familiar footsteps, she looked up anxiously. Seeing him standing there, his face twisted with concern, brought tears to her eyes. What could he possibly be thinking? His precious girl, the woman he'd intended making his wife, had been violated.

He took hold of the wedding dress and threw it on a chair. Then he pulled her to her feet, put his arms around her in a silent embrace, and guided her to the door.

'You're coming with me. No buts. Leave the bloody dress; you'll have plenty of time to finish it later.'

He drove her out of town. She could feel his anger, but she knew it wasn't aimed at her. There had been warmth and love in his embrace. He remained silent, allowing her to shed her tears while he concentrated on his driving. Eventually he turned down a country lane and parked the

Rover in a gateway. He helped her out and held her tight, pressing her head to his chest until she was out of tears.

'Now, you'll tell me what's happened. I'll keep quiet until you finish. I want to hear everything, no matter who's involved or where the blame may lie. Leave nothing out – we have all day.'

He led her along a footpath towards the river. With his arm around her, she calmed down and was able to tell him in detail what had happened. By the time she'd finished they were at the top of a small rise looking down over the Trent, which glittered in the golden sunlight of a fine summer's day. She glanced up at him and saw the thundering rage in his face.

She couldn't bear for him to be so hurt. She turned her gaze back towards the river. 'So you see, you were right, Arthur. But it's too late now. I can't keep the job. And how can you marry me? The thing you most wanted in a bride has been taken from you. It's my own fault. I was greedy for success. I was too ambitious to see what was happening. Perhaps I didn't want to see. And now I'll surely lose you as well.'

She glanced at him again and saw the muscles of his face twitch with pain. How could she comfort him? How could she relieve his anger? Sighing, she watched a family of white swans and grey-brown cygnets swimming silently with the current. Her life would go on too, and she would flow with it, but it would have to be without her beloved Arthur. Her eyes filled with tears.

He turned her to face him and lifted up her chin.

'Look straight at me, June. I want you to see that I'm sincere in what I'm about to say.'

She looked into his blue eyes, narrowed by the strain he was under. She knew he wouldn't lie to her, and she dreaded his honesty.

'My darling, I can't pretend this hasn't happened, or that it will make no difference. But we can work it out. You're going to need time to heal. Physically, of course, but that won't take long; it's your emotions that are most badly damaged. What Watson did was to make something beautiful seem ugly and dirty. I love you, June, and nothing can ever change that. Only you can make what happened divide us.'

'But you've saved yourself for–'

He stopped her. 'I'll still keep faith with you, my dearest. You didn't give yourself to this awful man, he abused you for his own aims. Trust me, and I will help you heal.'

'Darling Arthur, of course I trust you.'

He held her close to his chest and kissed her forehead.

'When our union comes, it will have no relation to what happened yesterday. It may take time, but one day you'll respond to love again. It's what I want, my darling – to be the one who awakens you to love in all its fullness. We'll experience it together. It'll be beautiful, rapturous, and for a few moments we'll be carried away with the angels. I promise you. Have I ever let you down?'

'Never.'

He wrapped an arm around her and they strolled along, enjoying the warmth of the sun. Children paddled in a shallow stream that fed the river, their happy voices drowning out the sounds of the riverbank. As they turned a sharp bend, the whispering of reeds and humming of insects greeted them once more and a new sound met their ears: the pattering of feet on water as swans winged their way skywards. She watched as their struggle for take-off turned into the beauty of graceful flight.

At that moment she was at peace with herself and with the world. Arthur loved her and wanted her. Whatever struggles lay ahead would all be worked out. She *would* succeed.

'We have to sort out your future,' Arthur said after a few minutes' silent meditation, 'but first I have to ask you something.'

He sounded serious. They sat down on an old wooden seat by the path and he held her face in his hands and kissed her swollen eyelids, leaving them feeling pleasantly cool and soothed.

'I love you,' he said softly, and tenderly kissed her lips. He gazed into her eyes. 'June, my beautiful darling girl, will you marry me?'

'What? Yes – yes – oh, yes!'

He kissed her again. 'You've made me a very happy man. Dear God, how I love you.'

She rested her head on his shoulder, thrilled that he still wanted her. How could she have doubted his love? Suddenly she remembered her missing locket bearing its precious stone. A tight knot wrenched at her stomach. She didn't want to bring up her dreadful ordeal again, not at a time like this.

'I've just remembered, Arthur, my locket chain is being repaired. But I'll have it back soon.'

'Don't worry, I'll get the ring done before I go back. Once our engagement is formalised, it'll be announced in the papers and everyone will know that we belong to each other. I'll speak to your father. From now on, we shall go about openly.'

Happiness welled up within her. 'Mrs Arthur Rogers. My parents will be amazed, I just know it.'

'They'll get used to the idea.' He was quiet for a moment. 'You're right of course; you'll have to leave the firm. You must not work anywhere near Robert Watson again. Even if you wanted to go on working for Watson senior, his son cannot be trusted. Losing you will be a severe punishment for him.' His voice tightened with suppressed rage. 'June, are you *sure* you don't want to go to the police? This is a very serious matter. He should not be allowed to get away with it.'

Tears welled up again and she began to shake. 'I couldn't bear it, Arthur. Please, please, don't make me.'

'Very well, you know best. Hush, my darling, we won't speak of it again.'

She cuddled up to him and calmed down.

'We'll see if you can get to college this year. I'll support you of course.'

'But, Arthur–'

'No arguments, June. I won't have my future wife short of money. You must have everything you need, and time to enjoy being young, not working all hours to scrape a living. When you know what you want to do, we can work out our future together.'

That night, Arthur told his father that June had agreed to marry him.

'We're getting formally engaged with a ring, but the marriage will have to wait. The way things are going I could be away for months yet. June is leaving her job and will be going to college. I'll help her all I can.'

His father slowly nodded. 'Bees to honey,' he grunted. 'Don't leave her alone too long, Arthur. She's too pretty for her own good.'

In view of what had happened the day before, Arthur could only think how right his father was, but he had no intention of mentioning her ordeal. 'I must try to get home more often. But it'll be good for her to study with people her own age and widen her circle of friends.'

His father merely nodded. Arthur refused to defend his decision to marry the girl he loved. His parents would just have to get used to the idea and admit defeat. June's father was an uncertainty though, for he had never even met the man. Her mother might be the best one to ease the way.

The following day, Arthur walked home from the church service with June and her family, with Mrs Armstrong talking nearly all the way. When he took hold of June's hand, Pat and Rose, much to his amusement, nudged each other and pulled faces. They were clearly taken by surprise. But Mrs Armstrong didn't even notice what was happening right next to her.

'He's old enough to be her dad,' he heard Rose whisper to Pat, while at the same time their mother was complaining that sweets were back on rationing.

When he managed to get a word in, he told Mrs Armstrong that he'd be taking June out in his car that afternoon. Although intending to be deferential to her parents, he was aware that he had an air of authority about him that forbade his judgement being questioned. It was partly army conditioning and partly who and what he was. Realising how he must sound, he added, 'I hope you have no objections?'

For once in her life, Mrs Armstrong was lost for words. 'No, Major Rogers,' was all that she could muster.

June's letter of resignation landed on John Watson's desk on Monday morning. With Bill Potter off for the holiday fortnight and his father away on business, Rob was taking care of the incoming mail, as well as coping with his own massive amount of work. By the time he got around to opening June's letter, he was already in a bad mood. And when he read the contents he was furious – as much with himself as with her. He'd thought he had her eating out of his hand, and now this! Arthur must be behind it. So much for having no attachments – she had lied to him.

'Oh, no, you don't, young lady. You'll be back – I'll make sure of it!' he bellowed. Standing up, he paced the office floor, trying to get his thoughts together. He suddenly thumped his fist on the desk. 'You ungrateful little bitch! After all I've done for you. Well you won't get away that easily. You'll be back, all right. You most certainly will be back. There's too much at stake for both of us.'

Deep in thought, he sat down and rubbed the hollow of his chin with his thumb. The thunder left him and his face gradually lit up. A smile spread across his face. He burst out laughing. 'I'll see you soon, my darling!'

On Tuesday, just before Arthur left Bloomfield to pick up June, a small parcel was put through the letter box. He picked it up and noticed that it was addressed to him. Curious, he took the package over to the hall table and slipped off the string and brown paper. He took out a flat red box. Opening it up, he saw June's little golden heart locket. Inside the box was a note:

'Perhaps you'll give this to June. She's careless with things. I found this on the back seat of my Daimler. You can guess how it got there. Let's get together sometime for a drink. Obviously, we have things in common! Robert Watson.'

Arthur was shocked and puzzled, but he refused to be angry. Watson was clearly trying to get at him. But it was up to June to tell him how, when and where the chain had been broken – if indeed it *had* been broken. He slipped the locket into the inner pocket of his jacket and went out to his car, thinking about how best to approach June without upsetting her. At least the jewel was safe and he could now get the engagement ring made.

As soon as he stopped outside her house, June came bursting out of the front door. She was holding on to a cute, yellow-bowed white hat perched on top of her bouncy hair, and clutching a white purse under her arm. She looked bright and cheerful in a floral yellow dress. The fitted bodice and full skirt, from which peeped a trimming of broderie anglaise along the hem of a petticoat, added to her vivacious appearance. Her hazel eyes sparkled with excitement as she came running towards him, all trace of her weariness now gone. *This* was the young girl he had fallen in love with – and the maturing woman he intended to marry.

Half an hour later, while they were drinking coffee, he took out the locket and gave it to her. She looked at him in surprise, and her face turned pale.

'I don't understand. Where did you find it?'

'I didn't find it. It was delivered just before I left the house this morning. Perhaps you took it to the jeweller who fixed the diamond for me; he knows my address. He should have put a note inside.'

'No, Arthur. Rob had the locket. The chain must have been broken when he… you know.' Her voice became shaky. 'He said he'd get it fixed and drop it through my letter box. I didn't want to tell you. I'm sorry. Of course he knew you'd be home, but I didn't expect him to do such an awful thing.'

'It's all right, June. He's playing games with us, but he won't win.'

The next day, Arthur took her to have her finger measured and to have the diamond removed from the locket. Before long he'd be putting the ring on her finger and they'd be officially engaged; one step nearer to his heart's desire.

They spent the rest of the afternoon shopping for a wedding gift for Charles and Angela.

'People will be doing this for *us* one day,' he told her, as they looked at silver cutlery and fine china. 'So you choose for Angela and Charles what you'd like for us.'

'Everything is so beautiful. How can I possibly decide? You'll have to help me. Everything is so expensive too. Golly, this set is a hundred pounds!'

'That's no problem, but it'll have to be twice the number of settings.'

Her eyes boggled. 'Can you afford it?'

He laughed. 'I'm sure I'll be able to scrape it together.'

He looked at her happy face and thought of the healing that was going on. When he went away again perhaps he could get George to take her out a few times, as Charles had done. It'd give her some company and stop her brooding over what had happened. That was his greatest fear: with no job, except for her odd bits of sewing and designing, she'd have too much time on her hands.

The week passed happily by. Eating out and walking in the fresh summer air worked wonders for June, and Arthur was feeling healthier and far more relaxed himself. Although they kissed and cuddled, he deliberately refrained from touching her, and kept their romancing low-key.

His mother insisted on putting on a party for them before he went abroad again, and Arthur decided that the time was right to approach June's father for permission to marry his daughter. On Friday, the eve of Charlie's wedding, he went home with her.

Mr Armstrong was overawed, as well as surprised, that the eldest of the Rogers sons, Major Arthur Henry Rogers, actually wanted to marry his youngest daughter.

'Marry June? *You* want to marry our little Junie, Major?'

'Yes, Mr Armstrong. But please call me Arthur. The wedding will not be just yet as I have business commitments to attend to abroad, but June has agreed to our getting engaged. My mother is putting on a little party a week on Saturday. You will all be receiving invitations of course, and we hope that you will all be able to come.'

'Well, you seem to have got it all worked out. And I expect you'll wed anyway, whatever we think. Right then, go ahead – and I hope you'll both be very happy.'

Charlie and Angela's wedding was a poignant time for June. Dressed in a cream linen suit with a cream-and-coffee blouse to match, she sat next to George with the Rogers family. Arthur was Charlie's best man. The two men she loved were side-by-side. If Arthur hadn't come on the scene when he did, and if Charlie hadn't made that stupid mistake... no, she mustn't think of Charlie in that way ever again. She was Arthur's now. He was her everything, and she loved him with the whole of her heart.

With only a week to go before Arthur's departure, she was determined to make each day one to remember. They walked in the countryside, visited the theatre twice, and dined out every evening. One afternoon he drove her to Chatsworth and she revelled in the beautiful gardens with their grandiose water features, and enjoyed the splendour of the magnificent house. There was so much to see and enjoy, so much creativity and history to take in, that her mind found it hard to cope. She imagined herself as the daughter of one of the estate workers, given the privilege of viewing the house and its contents, and wondered at the difference in their lifestyles.

On Friday evening, they revisited the country hotel where Arthur had previously booked a bedroom. It had been his idea and she was delighted to be there. Warm memories flooded her mind and stirred up sensuous feelings she had been trying to suppress.

Towards the end of their meal, he took her hand in his and gazed into her eyes. 'How do you feel about a little intimacy? Just a kiss and a cuddle, whatever you feel like doing, my darling. Don't feel under any pressure though. The room is booked, but it can easily be cancelled.'

'I'd like that very much.'

They entered the bedroom, the same one as previously. It gave her a warm glow as she remembered how happy she had been on their last visit.

They sat on the edge of the bed. 'I won't touch you unless you want me to,' he said, tenderly putting an arm around her. 'But I *would* like to look at you – you know, *all* of you – if you're happy to undress for me. I ask for nothing more.'

To please him, she stripped off her clothes in front of him and stretched out on the bed, the golden satin quilt feeling cool under her warm body. She wanted so much to make him happy. It thrilled her to feel his eyes piercing her body with loving desire. He looked younger; his smile lit up his face, turning the deep lines into expressions of happiness.

'You're so beautiful,' he whispered, sitting on the edge of the bed and stroking her face.

To be lying there naked while he remained fully dressed seemed ridiculous. 'Now you too,' she said. 'Let me help you undress.'

She unbuttoned his fine cotton shirt and pulled it from his body. Then she took off his vest and kissed his long jagged scar. His back arched with pleasure. He turned her to face him and held her close to his body, but she pushed him away.

'Hey, I haven't finished yet. *Everything* has to come off!'

Unbuttoning his fly was a bit awkward. She broke into giggles as she finally completed the task and his trousers fell to his ankles, followed by his underpants.

She looked at him in awed delight.

'Oh, Arthur!'

Under the shower, the soft bubbles ran over her shoulders, falling down her back, her legs and her feet. Arthur touched her lightly, sensitive to any adverse reaction, but there was none. He held her close, with her head resting on his shoulder.

It was bliss to be so close to her. That his passion was rising was becoming more and more obvious. He knew she wanted to please him, but he had no intention of bringing up painful memories. It was enough that she was naked and in his arms. That was definitely something he hadn't planned.

To his surprise, she took the initiative by touching him. She explored his body, noticing his reactions, and playing on her power over him. His whole being cried out to press up hard against her, but he resisted the urge. She sensed his desire and responded by increasing her love-play, her own excitement growing as he released involuntary groans of ecstasy. He wanted to tell her to stop, but he just couldn't do it. Finally, he pulled her hard against him and allowed his rapture to come.

'Have I hurt you?' she asked, slightly alarmed.

He smiled at her concern. 'Of course not. You've made me unbelievably happy. Dear God, how I love you.'

They stood in the shower, letting the water wash away the fruit of their labours. Of one thing Arthur was determined: their engagement must not be for long.

At June's request, Arthur collected the Armstrong women on Saturday evening to drive them to Bloomfield for the engagement party. Her father, brothers and her sisters' boyfriends agreed to walk the short distance. She thought they were like a flock of brightly-coloured starlings in the car, but Arthur just laughed and said that she had a jolly cheerful family.

Once inside the house, June took care of the womenfolk, introducing them to her future in-laws. When the men arrived, Arthur insisted on taking care of the formalities. Then the Colonel and Mrs Rogers took over and introduced June's family to the other guests. Much to June's dismay, it wasn't long before her father became embroiled in a heated political argument with Councillor Jim Baker.

Arthur took her into the study. 'Don't worry, political skirmishes are quite normal in this house. Forget about them, there's something else I have to do.'

He slipped her engagement ring onto her finger. The magnificent diamond sparkled from its bed of tiny rubies that formed the shape of a heart. When he spoke, his voice was soft with a tremor of restrained emotion.

'June, my dearest love, will you marry me and make me the happiest man alive?'

Spilling over with happiness, her tears flowed unheeded. She put her arms around his neck. 'Oh, Arthur, you know I will.'

The following morning, June felt proud to be sitting beside Arthur during the church service – even if she did hear deprecatory whispers about their respective ages. Dressed in a dark grey suit, white shirt and blue tie, Arthur stood up to read one of the lessons. She smiled when she heard a woman whisper, 'He ought to be a vicar.' There was no doubt about it; her fiancé and his family were well known and respected by a great many people. She had something to live up to.

After the service, many people offered them their congratulations and wanted to look at the exquisite ring. Some women said how lovely she looked in her cream linen suit, worn that morning with a pale pink blouse. But a number of others smiled to her face and whispered snide comments behind her back. She saw eyes rolled towards her mother, who was standing a few yards away loudly praising her daughter: 'Our Junie knows 'ow to cook and always looks after the pennies.' And she saw them nodding at Mrs Rogers as she stood serenely by the church door talking with the vicar. She even heard someone mutter under her breath: 'A bit sudden. Is she pregnant?'

On the way home, Arthur told her that it might be Christmas before he was home again. 'If I stick at it, you see, I should be able to leave everything in someone else's hands next year. Then I could be home for good… or at least for quite a while. The more I come home, the longer the job will drag on.'

She sighed. 'It seems such a long time.'

'I've asked George to keep an eye on you during his vacation. He said he'd be happy to play tennis with you… that sort of thing. I promise he won't touch you – he wouldn't dare.'

After all that had happened, she was happy for him to be in charge of her life. 'How lovely – another lieutenant to take Charlie's place.'

He smiled. 'And how would you like to stay in Cambridge for a week or two?'

'Cambridge? Oh, Arthur! I'd love to.'

'I've offered to put George up at the same hotel as you, at least until his term begins. He's more than willing.'

She was overwhelmed with all the good things flooding into her life. She had a fresh start and could forget all about the factory and Robert Watson. Apart from her private work, she was waiting to hear about a college course. Her life had taken on a new direction. She now belonged to Arthur and soon she would be entering his world with his name. Perhaps his parents weren't exactly overjoyed – and they'd be even less so if they knew about Rob – but they seemed to be making the best of it and were by no means hostile.

That Sunday, she lunched at Bloomfield and met people from a wide spectrum of family friends and acquaintances: members of the Colonel's political party and club, Arthur's business colleagues and their wives, affluent neighbours, and others who called in to offer their congratulations. Glasses clinked and biscuits were nibbled. People were interested in her designing career, but she let it be known that she was now concentrating on private work.

At six o'clock they were off to her house. The Armstrongs had decided to have a party of their own and had invited their pub friends and neighbours to celebrate with a glass of off-license Best Bitter.

Leaving the guests to their drinking, she walked with Arthur to a deserted bus shelter not far away. Holding each other close, they kissed passionately. She was close to tears.

'What shall I do without you?'

'You'll soon find yourself very busy. Just keep away from the factory. I don't trust that Robert Watson – he's been too quiet for my liking. You must ignore any plans or schemes to try and get you back. Write to me often and keep nothing from me. If there's an emergency, phone me from Bloomfield and I'll come straight home to deal with it, no matter what's happening over there.'

'Yes, Arthur. I love you. I'll do anything you ask.'

'I love you too, my dearest little girl. Love is all that really matters.'

He walked her home and gave her a final kiss. She stood at the door watching him walk away, tears flowing down her face. At the corner, he turned and waved. Then he was gone.

Chapter Twenty-Three

George was a good tennis player and gave June a hard game, much to her delight. But knowing that he was attracted to her made her feel a little self-conscious. Was he deliberately missing the occasional ball so that it wasn't a complete whitewash?

The atmosphere at the tennis club livened up when his friends came to join them for a game of mixed doubles. After working long hours without a break for eight months, followed by a rather emotional fortnight with Arthur, she found the wholesome activity with people of her own age rather refreshing. Polly was a bouncy, rosy-cheeked blonde who appeared to fancy George rather than the boy she was with – a beanpole called Lee. She was most intrigued to learn that June would be getting engaged to 'old Arthur', as she insisted on calling him.

'Golly, June, why choose tough meat when gorgeous Georgie likes you? Arthur looks as if he took on the whole German army by himself. Nice guy and all that, but so… well, sort of battle-worn. He must be well over forty.'

'Thirty-eight, actually. And he's rather wonderful when you get to know him.'

Lee butted in. 'My uncle fought with him in North Africa and Italy. He says Major Rogers was a popular officer. He was always in the lead, and his men would follow him anywhere.' He combed his hair back with his long thin fingers, and grinned at his girlfriend. 'Experience counts more than looks. You should know that, Polly, we've been going out together for long enough.'

Polly's cheeks grew even pinker. 'Maybe *too* long,' she said crossly.

'Anyway,' said George, 'it's time Arthur married. I couldn't lose June to a better person.'

'I was never yours to lose, George. But I'm pleased we can still be friends,' June told him sincerely.

'And so say all of us,' said Polly, bouncing up and down on her toes and swinging her racquet. 'Now can we get on? We only have this court for another thirty minutes.'

The following morning, just as June was leaving her house to post a letter to Arthur, the postman arrived with a typewritten envelope addressed to her. The letter inside was from John Watson. He said it was imperative that she arranged to see him at once, and would she please telephone for an appointment immediately. She was dismayed at the thought of seeing any of the management. Why did he want to see her anyway? What would she say? Would Rob be there? She just couldn't bear it. She decided to consult Mary Rogers.

She thought it best not to let her future mother-in-law know that she was no longer a virgin. So, without going into details, and playing the incident down somewhat, she told her why she had resigned from Watson and Sons. Mrs Rogers listened in shocked silence.

'I had to resign. I can't go back to work out my notice – it was quite a serious sexual assault. But no one was around to see or hear it as the factory was closing for the holiday and just about everyone had left. If I'd gone to the police it would have been my word against his. If I complain to Mr Watson, he surely won't believe me. And why should he? My attacker is one of the managers and Mr Watson will think I'm trying to cause trouble. I don't want to talk to him... it's too embarrassing. And it would soon get around the factory; it's a breeding ground for gossip.'

Mary Rogers was outraged. 'I thought you had left your job rather suddenly. But this! You poor child. Does Arthur know?'

'Yes. He's been very understanding,' said June, unable to keep a tremor from her voice. 'He wanted to do something about it but I begged him not to.'

'Thank God it went no further. That sort of scandal is bad for everyone, especially the victim.'

June wondered if it was Colonel Rogers who was uppermost in her mind. She couldn't blame her.

'You do nothing,' said Mrs Rogers decisively. 'I shall ring Watson myself. It is quite impossible for you to work at that factory. You are going to marry my son: that is reason enough.'

She indicated that June should follow her to the study. 'We can be more private there,' she told her, her eyes quickly sweeping the hall as if on the lookout for eavesdroppers.

As soon as Mrs Rogers was put through, she asked to speak to John Watson himself, stating her name in such a manner as to demand, and expect, an immediate response. Within seconds she was telling him that June would not be working for them again.

Suddenly, her expression changed from a mask of benign confidence to a grimace of haughty contempt.

'Utterly ridiculous!' she barked.

The knot in June's stomach tightened with anxiety as Mrs Rogers gripped the receiver in anger. What was Mr Watson saying about her?

'There's no need to raise your voice, I hear you quite clearly. But you are wrong – completely wrong!' Mary Rogers said imperiously. 'I know June Armstrong very well indeed, and what you say is impossible – utterly impossible!'

June couldn't understand what was happening. Was she being accused of doing something dreadful or wicked? She watched in bewilderment as Mrs Rogers became more and more angry.

'Ridiculous,' she kept saying. Finally, Mrs Rogers said impatiently, 'I'll bring her along myself this morning and we'll get this matter cleared up straight away. Goodbye!'

She looked at June sympathetically. 'I'm afraid we have to go, my dear, there's been some terrible mistake but it has to be cleared up. You are being accused of theft.'

June's mind was in a whirl. How could this be? 'I don't understand,' she mumbled.

'Neither do I. The fool of a man refused to go into details. Don't worry, we'll get it sorted.'

Within the hour, June, feeling sick with apprehension, was being driven to Watson and Sons in the Colonel's cherished old Rover. She couldn't understand what was happening. Retribution by Rob was always on the cards, but this?

They arrived at the factory and were told to wait a few minutes at the gatehouse. Mrs Rogers was furious.

'This is ridiculous! We are expected. Does Watson know I'm being kept waiting?'

Five minutes later an office girl arrived to escort them to John Watson's office.

Walking up the worn stone steps, the sound of machinery resonating in her ears, June reflected on how things had changed since that first day when she had been led to the design offices. As doors were opened, familiar smells greeted her and she was seized with a longing to be back in the excitement, the cut and thrust, of garment design and manufacture. Why did Rob have to ruin things? Her thoughts were interrupted by Mary Rogers's voice.

'You poor child, having to work in this dreadful atmosphere. But not any longer, I shall see to that.'

John Watson met them at his door. Greeting Mrs Rogers with a polite shake of her hand, he asked her to wait in his office while he took June to the showroom.

'I really think it best if Miss Armstrong hears what we have to say, and be allowed to give an explanation in private. If she feels in need of a character witness, she may wish to call you in later.'

June silently nodded at Mary Rogers, and, filled with trepidation, accompanied John Watson to the showroom. The room was rich with memories of that first exciting interview which launched her career. Rob and Bill Potter occupied two of the four small armchairs placed around the low table.

'Bill asked to come in. He thought you would like his support,' John Watson said, offering her a seat opposite himself.

Bill gave her a friendly smile. 'Good morning, June.'

Watson nodded towards his son, who was studying her through half-closed eyes, his legs casually outstretched and his thumb slowly massaging the cleft of his chin. 'It will become obvious why Robert is here, but likely you already know the reason.'

Ignoring Rob sitting next to her, June sat erect and faced John Watson defiantly. Since it had taken a trumped-up charge to get her there, she now had every intention of exposing Rob for what he was. 'Because he raped me,' she blurted out, her voice too high and strangely unfamiliar to her ears. She swallowed hard to gain control over her emotions. 'I'm surprised he admits it,' she said more calmly. 'You can't blame me for wanting to leave. I should have gone to the police. But I just couldn't do it.' She bit her lip, and fought back the tears that threatened to envelop her. 'Other people had to be considered.'

Watson merely raised his eyebrows and said, somewhat patronisingly, 'You are rather young for the responsibility Robert has given you, and we will take that into consideration, but I will not have my son slandered, Miss Armstrong. I think perhaps you should reconsider your wild accusation.'

'Perhaps we should tell June what she is accused of and start from there,' Bill Potter interceded.

'Very well.' Watson sat back in his chair, hands clasped together with forefingers forming a steeple, which he suddenly pointed menacingly at June. 'Robert informs me that you have been selling our designs as though they were your own, rather than the property of the firm. That you actually get the samples made up on these premises. And you took home – that is, stole – at least one of our latest models from your own sample rail. You conveniently resigned when Rob caught you in the act.' He retracted the bullying steeple and folded his arms.

June was aghast. 'I haven't done anything wrong. Rob raped me! That's why I resigned,' she said shakily, as flashbacks of the event put paid to any attempt to remain in control.

'Since you've raised the subject of sexual activity yourself, Robert also informs me that, in spite of his warnings, you practically prostituted yourself to get a contractor to work for us at discounted rates,' Watson said, raising his voice and shaking his head in disbelief. 'Robert asked me not to mention that you've also used your charms on him to get what you wanted. Since you insist on accusing my son of a serious crime, such wanton behaviour cannot be disregarded.'

June couldn't believe what she was hearing. She looked at Rob, but he was looking at his father and nodding in agreement with him!

'I'm sorry to have to say these things to you,' Watson continued, in the manner of a schoolmaster caning a miscreant. 'The rag trade is highly competitive and it can be cut-throat, but Watson and Sons have a reputation to consider. We will not tolerate licentious, unethical and criminal behaviour!'

He rested from his verbal whacking. 'However, Robert finds you an invaluable assistant – vital to his plans so he tells me – and would prefer that we keep you on. If, that is, you are prepared to accept his guidance. You are very young – only eighteen? And ambitious young people can be very foolhardy.'

Bill Potter chimed in. 'That was rather a lot for June to take in, John. Perhaps she should be allowed to answer one accusation at a time. If you would permit me?'

'Go ahead, Bill,' said John Watson, splaying his hands in acquiescence and leaning back in his chair.

'Just answer simply, June, and we can go over details later. First, have you been selling on our designs?'

'No.'

'Did you get garments made up on our premises?'

'Yes, but they were not the firm's designs, and I personally paid the girls to make them up in their own time. I have a few private clients, friends of Mrs Rogers. Rob knows the truth.' She turned to Rob and pleaded, 'You tell them, Rob. You knew all about–'

'Just simple answers please, June,' Bill interjected. 'To continue. Did you take a new model home the day you left?'

'Yes. Rob gave it to me to wear. Mine was badly torn when he held me down and–'

'Oh really, Miss Armstrong!' John Watson intervened angrily, his face flaring red with indignation. 'You are not doing yourself any favours. My son is here to help you, but you insist on using him as your scapegoat! I can't allow this to go on.'

'But it's true. He pulled me down and raped me on the floor.' Tears of anger and shame filled her eyes. Frustrated, she turned again to Rob. 'Tell them the truth, Rob. You know I didn't steal anything. You gave me that dress. You threw it at me. Told me to wear it.'

Rob shrugged his shoulders and smiled. 'June, my dear, I admit we've had sex on a number of occasions. But how can a mere male resist such a charming temptress? Especially one who enters his hotel bedroom wearing flimsy underwear and invites him to bed her? And the supposed rape you speak of? What do you expect when you strip off your clothes in front of me, begging me to…' He looked at her with a puzzled expression. 'Do you really want me to repeat your four-letter word?'

'Rob! How can you sit there telling such lies?'

'Lies? June, my dear, I'm a big boy, I can take anything you throw at me. Only you know why you want to discredit me. I can live with your voracious appetite, if only you'll come back and get on with what we started. We make a good team. I want to help you. Be honest, haven't I helped you get on here?'

'Yes, but–'

'You found out that I knew what you were up to. That's why you resigned. But stop your double-dealing, put full effort into your job here, and you're off the hook. I need you, June. And accept it – you need me.'

June fought back her tears and sat tight-lipped, shaking her head. This was an unbelievable nightmare.

'I can see that you're embarrassed by this exposure; you like everyone to think you're sweet and innocent.' Rob continued. 'But that's part of your charm. If only you would follow my advice instead of going your own way. I have the experience. Come back and let's get on with the job. I mean, what's the alternative? We can't allow you to profit from theft. You may well have harmed our business already. We would have no alternative but to take the substantial evidence we have to the police.'

'Evidence? What evidence?' she almost shrieked.

'The dress you took, your sample hands' overtime... need I go on?'

'I've already explained–'

'That I raped you? Phil Jones would back me up about your enticement. Then of course there's the waiter at the London hotel, the one who brought champagne to my room. Do you remember him, June? Gosh, you should – he certainly remembers you!'

'But I was wearing my dressing gown when he came into your bedroom.'

The men stared at her. She realised what she had just admitted and shook her head. 'It wasn't like that,' she protested, tears streaming down her face.

Bill Potter looked at Rob and then at her, as though trying to make up his mind who was telling the truth. He told her gently, 'When you applied for a job here, I rang your previous manager. He told me that you were about to be sacked anyway. He claimed you were trying to advance your career through sexual favours. Frankly, at the time, we found it hard to believe.'

'It was lies, all lies. I admit I kneed Mr Brown in the groin, but I had good reason to. He–'

'No need to say any more, June. I understand. Things do get around, you know. But I think perhaps for your own benefit you should listen to Rob. You've done so well here. I've watched you make headway far beyond what most young designers achieve. Don't throw it all away. Whatever the rights and wrongs of this situation, you will be the loser.'

'Bill is quite right,' said John Watson abruptly, clearly wanting to get the matter over and done with. 'You have a great deal to lose, young lady.' He turned to his son. 'Miss

Armstrong has accused you of rape. Do you really want her back?'

'I'm sure June was just being defensive,' Rob said casually. He turned to face her squarely, eyebrows raised and lips curled into a mocking smile. 'Would you like Mrs Rogers to come in now? After what has been said, perhaps she could help you come to a decision.'

How could he be so cruel? He was hitting her where it really hurt. She had no evidence to prove her innocence, the cunning rotter had seen to that. He had taken her home afterwards as if nothing had happened – he must have known she would keep her mouth shut. He had gathered false and misleading evidence to blacken her reputation. He'd even got rid of her torn dress and replaced it with the latest design on the sample rail. Who but Arthur, Charlie and her own family would believe her now? Would Mrs Rogers and the Colonel give her the benefit of the doubt? Maybe. But now that she was engaged to Arthur, what happened to her reflected on all the Rogers family. Should the whole business go to court, mud would stick to the family name. It would be in the papers and Arthur would have to bear it all. But how could she possibly work with Robert Watson again? She broke down in tears, her whole body shaking with emotion.

'No, no. Please don't ask Mrs Rogers to come in.'

Rob came over and put his arm around her shoulders.

'It's okay, June. I'm not cross with you,' he said like a father to a frightened child who had just broken a window. 'All true artists have their little quirks. I don't mind yours, but we have to work together and not be pulling apart. You understand me, don't you?'

June choked back her tears. She pushed his arm away. 'I understand you very well, Rob.'

He sat down again. 'So, back tomorrow, and we'll get on with the job?'

Back to work? Back on the ladder of success? She looked around the showroom and saw framed pictures of her latest designs. They looked fantastic on a professional model. Rob must have had them done recently. Bait? She looked at him. Could she trust him? 'I don't know. I–'

John Watson cut in impatiently. 'Miss Armstrong, we are all busy people. I think perhaps you should have Mrs Rogers to advise you. I'll get back to my office and call her in.' He stood up. 'Robert can inform me of your decision.'

'No! Please, Mr Watson. I have already decided. I will come back. But I have a holiday booked for two weeks in September.' She turned to Rob defiantly. 'I am not prepared to cancel it.'

John Watson frowned. He sat down again and turned to his son. 'Will that suit you, Robert?'

Rob smiled. Obviously, having won the war, he was prepared to lose an insignificant battle. 'As long as June works to make up the time, I can live with that.'

John Watson turned to Bill Potter and gave him a nod. 'Go ahead.'

'We prepared this in case you decided to make a new start,' Potter said, giving June a beaming smile. 'If you would just sign on the dotted line. It confirms that while you work for us, you do so exclusively. No other paid employment and no private clients. It also states that you will be given a share of the profits in Rob's new enterprise. The details have yet to be worked out. You must admit, my dear, it's a generous offer.'

'Yes. Thank you.'

June signed the contract. The whole business was a complete turnaround from what Arthur had planned for her. What on earth was she going to tell him? She was determined to make Robert Watson regret ever wanting her back. And yet… a new enterprise with a share in the profits? Well, she would take her share, make a name for herself, and then…

John Watson rose from his chair. 'I must go now. I'm pleased you've accepted Robert's generous offer, Miss Armstrong. I must admit I would be sorry to lose you… you are quite an asset to the firm. But I expect you to conform to the rules of good professional practice from now on. Learn from my son and you won't go wrong.'

June nearly burst out laughing. Surely she was going quite mad!

Bill shook her hand, muttered something about being glad she was staying with the firm, and followed John Watson out of the room.

Only Rob was left to see her out. He waited for her to rise from her chair and then led her towards the door.

'I'm going to be away for a few weeks. Make me happy, June. Get those designs ready for when I get back and you won't be sorry.' Standing by the door, he turned to face her, his eyes once more piercing into her thoughts. 'Relax, we're on the road to success. Business is booming… we might have to open our own factory soon.' He put a hand on her shoulder. 'You know I can be very generous.'

She shrugged off the hand and took a step backwards. He ignored the snub. 'And you'd better get some stuff done for the old man to keep him happy. Welcome back. I knew you couldn't stay away.'

June met Mary Rogers in the corridor. 'I have received a personal apology,' she lied. 'My attacker is being dismissed and I'm going back. The theft business was just a misunderstanding. But I have a new contract and I have to work exclusively for Watson's. I'm afraid that means no more private clients. I hope you understand. It's part of the deal. I'm really sorry but there's nothing I can do about it. They made me an offer I couldn't refuse. I promise it will only be until I marry Arthur.'

June arrived at work promptly on Wednesday. Rob wasn't around, and it didn't look as if she would be seeing much of him for a while. With no interruptions, she worked hard throughout the day, stopping only for coffee and a sandwich. Each day she would finish at about six o'clock, and George would pick her up. She wrote to Arthur every evening, telling him about all the activities she and George had been engaged in. But in none of her letters, or in her telephone conversations, did she say anything about going back to work with Rob.

George agreed not to say anything. He knew nothing of what had happened and couldn't understand the secrecy, but he said he would do anything to please her.

During the following two weeks, Rob only popped in a few times. He would check her work and go away happy. On one occasion, he asked if he could take her out to dinner one night, but she refused. He didn't make an issue of it.

By the end of her third week back at the factory, she was really enjoying her work once again. Sales were booming and her designs were creating new business. One of the buyers had casually mentioned that his wife was pregnant and having difficulty finding attractive outfits. Surely this was an opening for something completely different: fashionable clothes for the young mother-to-be!

Although she wanted to see Cambridge, she was almost reluctant to leave work for two weeks of fun and games with George. During Thursday evening, she quickly sketched out some ideas for maternity wear, and on Friday left them for John Watson to discuss with Rob while she was away.

Chapter Twenty-Four

June loved Cambridge and revelled in the atmosphere of the place. George took her to the many places he wanted her to see, including St John's College, which particularly impressed her. They were blessed with an Indian summer, and the mellow buildings and bright flowers glowed in golden sunlight. The river and its banks were alive with the activities of young people. Trees, touched with autumn colour, cast dappled reflections on rippling water, and it was glorious to glide silently on the Cam in a punt. June relaxed on cushions and soaked in the ambience of her surroundings, while George revealed his prowess with the pole… until he started showing off and nearly ended up in the river. Sometimes they joined a few of his fellow students in friendly pubs: eating, drinking, chatting, and putting the world to rights. It was a different world; soaked in history and learning, yet vibrant with life and youthful expectations and ideologies.

At the end of the two weeks, George took her to the station, helped her into a first-class carriage, and lifted her case onto the luggage rack. Having said his farewells, he stood awkwardly, looking at her in a state of indecision.

'Was there something else, George?'

He opened his mouth as if to speak, but nothing came out. She gave him a big heartfelt smile. 'Thanks again for everything, I've had a wonderful time. The train will be off in a minute, hadn't you better go?'

He suddenly pulled her to him, kissing her hard and long. It took her by surprise, although she knew he'd been holding back throughout the holiday – in fact, throughout all the weeks since Arthur had left.

'I love you, June,' he panted breathlessly, his eyes pleading for a response.

'I'm really flattered, George. It's a wonderful thing to be loved. But as you know, I've given my heart to Arthur.' She squeezed his arm encouragingly. 'With all the pretty women here, you'll soon forget me.'

'I'll never do that, June. Never!' He turned and quickly left the train as the door was about to be slammed shut.

Just as her train was leaving the station, she saw a young woman arrive on the platform, drop her bags and throw her arms around George's neck. She smiled; a handsome student like George wouldn't be lonely for long.

As she relaxed on the train, she began thinking about the work she would be doing on Monday. New ideas were needed: designs out of the ordinary. Thoughts of the last fortnight's experiences in Cambridge surfaced in her mind and she was suddenly filled with a burst of inspiration. Colours, textures, shapes and images came flowing together, soon to emerge from her mind as concrete ideas in tune with the latest fashion trends. She took a small sketchbook – her constant companion – from her bag. Ideas flowed quicker than she could sketch them.

By the time she reached her destination her sketchbook was full, with drawings and notes on both sides of every page. Adrenaline pumped through her veins. She couldn't wait to get to work on Monday morning and start turning her ideas into solid form. At that moment, nothing else mattered. These were her children: labour had begun and her designs were waiting to be born!

By Sunday evening she had turned many of the sketches into working drawings. She had worked out in her mind how she would cut the patterns, and she could see each of the garments finished and there in front of her.

She was inspired as she had never been before. This was no following of fashion remoulded by her own artistic taste, but original creativity in line with the explosion of new trends flowing out of Paris. It was pouring out of her, and there was no stopping it.

Eager to get started on her new designs, June was at work well before eight on Monday morning. She had already cut out a pattern and was laying it on the fabric when John Watson walked into her room.

'Good morning, June. Glad to see you back.'

She noted that he seemed more relaxed and friendly, actually calling her by her first name.

'Good morning, Mr Watson,' she said, giving him a broad smile. 'I enjoyed my holiday. It was actually quite inspiring.'

'Robert is quite excited about your ideas for maternity wear. He would like you to try and fit in one or two samples while he's away this week. He's promoting the idea amongst a few of our customers, and contacting specialist stores. But we must keep our eye on the ball. Just do one or two to keep him happy, but concentrate on our usual lines.'

June had a much bigger plan in mind. She organised the people who had previously worked for her in their own time, asking them to come in and work on this special project, and promising them big financial rewards. She was totally confident in what she was doing and, if it became necessary, she would willingly pay their bonuses herself. She put in fourteen hours a day, dividing the time between her usual work and the maternity range. Her dynamic personality and capacity for hard work inspired her helpers to even greater effort. She realised that she was like a woman possessed, but she refused to be distracted from her creative endeavours: she had rarely been happier.

Realising how hard she was working, Bill Potter gave her his full support in getting her samples through the various processes. By mid-afternoon on Friday, she sat back and viewed the garments on her rails. It was a good start. Another couple of weeks and they would have a substantial range with which to tempt new customers.

She decided to put the maternity garments on a separate rail and cover it with a dustsheet. Rob was coming in later and she didn't want him to see them straight away. Tired but content, she sent to the canteen for a pot of tea, took out her sandwiches, and ate a very late lunch, savouring the sweetness of success rather than the staleness of her bread and cheese.

Her pot of tea soon arrived and she was just pouring herself a cup when Rob entered through her open door.

'You look happy and pleased with yourself,' he said cheerfully.

At the sound of his voice, an electrifying spasm of excitement took her by surprise. Animosity had been overridden by joyous expectation of what must surely come: his approbation and delight at what she had achieved. He alone understood her deep passion for her work, for he was the one who had generated and sustained it within her. Robert Watson knew the market they were aiming for; his praise would mean success. But she wanted to surprise him, like setting off the finest firework at the end of a display. She wanted to see his reaction and revel in his growing need for her talents.

'I guess I am happy.' She nodded towards her sample rails. 'Some good stuff there, Rob.'

'That's what I like to hear: a real note of confidence. Let's see what I think.'

He walked over and slowly looked at the new dresses in admiration.

'You've really got something different here. These are great. In fact, they're excellent!'

'I'm pleased you like them.'

He thumbed the hollow in his chin. 'I guess you haven't had time to do anything about your maternity wear idea. Pity, I've got people already interested.'

'Rob, you're a *slave driver.*'

'Well you know me… I'm a slave to the business too.'

He silently cast his eyes over the dresses, then looked at her closely. She turned her eyes away, fearful of the emotions his penetrating gaze might stir up within her.

'Seriously, June, I can see you've worked really hard since your holiday. I appreciate it. How about dinner tonight?'

She stood up, walked over to the other dress rail, and threw aside the dustsheet. 'You should look at these first… I think you might be interested.'

Rob looked along the rail, examining each garment in utter amazement.

'I knew you had it in you. You've got the bug, just like me. There's no stopping you now.'

'I take it you like them?'

'*Like* them? Dear girl, you've excelled yourself. This is the foundation for an excellent range. We have a product that opens up all sorts of possibilities. I've found there's a real need in this niche of the market. And you and I are going to fill it… June, you are fantastic!'

He grabbed her arms and was about to kiss her, but he quickly drew back.

'I'm sorry,' he said. 'Bad habit.'

In spite of the panic that had seized her, she smiled. He had actually apologised. Things were going her way. 'I take it you're pleased.'

'Of course I'm pleased. You knew I would be.' With arms akimbo, he shook his head and said with humour, 'Deliberately hiding your talents under a dustsheet.'

'Just like to keep something in reserve.'

He roared with laughter. 'You're in love with your work, all right. Whatever you may say or do, you'll never escape it. Design is in your blood.'

'Maybe. But don't take me for granted, Rob. I love my work, *not* my boss. Understand that and we'll get along fine.'

'You really are a new June! Poised and in control... I like that. And now that you've thoroughly impressed me, can we dine together?'

June felt exhilarated. She was fully in charge of herself and the situation. 'Why not? I deserve a bit of relaxation.'

It turned out to be just what she wanted: a good working dinner. Discussing fashion and future plans gave her fresh verve, and she enjoyed every minute of it. She realised, more than ever, how indispensable she was becoming to Rob's plans – and that gave her a wonderful feeling of power over him.

That night, she wrote to Arthur to tell him that she was back at the factory. She said she was sorry for not telling him sooner, but she hadn't wanted to worry him. She hinted at the difficult choice that had been forced upon her, and said she would explain everything when he was back home. She begged him to trust her and understand her need to stand on her own two feet. Rob had not bothered her and she had seen very little of him. She ended by saying how much she loved him and hoped it wouldn't be too long before they were *carried away with the angels* in their marital bed.

Although June no longer worked fourteen-hour days, the next few weeks were very intense at Watson's. Her creative energy continued to flow, and success fuelled her enthusiasm to succeed even more. Occasionally, she dined with Rob and they would discuss their objectives with buoyant enthusiasm. But she made it clear that she had not forgotten, nor forgiven, what he'd done, and he was careful not to upset her in any way.

Late in November, after viewing her latest designs, Rob asked her if she would like to go to London with him. The maternity range was enormously popular, and their customers would love to meet her.

Buried emotions welled up and seized her. She leapt to her feet and rounded on him. 'Do you really expect me to go to London with *you*? Stay in the *same* hotel? Meet your *London pals* again? Never! I would have to be *insane* after all your lies and scheming. Don't you think it's bad enough for *you* to be in *my* room, standing where you caused me so much pain and humiliation? Where you *raped* me!' Surprised by the strength of her outburst, she started trembling and leaned against her desk for support.

Rob stood back and lifted his hands in an attitude of surrender. 'I'm sorry, June. I make no excuses. I'm guilty as charged. There's no reason for you to trust me. I hurt you badly.'

Emotionally exhausted, June sat down. Rob strolled over to her desk and poured out the coffee brought in minutes earlier by one of the clerks. He sat down and pushed one of the cups towards her. 'Will you join me?'

She took the cup in both hands and sipped the strong brown liquid, more to steady her nerves than to enjoy its bitter flavour. She knew he was looking at her, but she kept her eyes on the gold rim of the china cup.

Everything in her life was now edged with gold. What a change in less than a year: heavy white canteen pots to fine gold-rimmed china. She allowed herself an inner smile of satisfaction. Rob's voice broke into her thoughts.

'You know, if you would like to go to London, we could stay at different hotels. And if it would make you feel any easier, bring someone with you. Your mother maybe. All expenses paid.'

Her *mother*? That did make her smile. She glanced at Rob sitting relaxed in the chair opposite her, coffee cup in hand. He was confusing her, just as he'd done after the rape. But there was something different this time, and she couldn't make out what was going on. Was he truly accepting his guilt? She knew that at the time of the rape he'd believed that she wanted him. Such *arrogance*! No meant no. Her fighting and screaming should have stopped him, not urged him on. He'd refused to accept that she had a private life, and he seemed to think he was merely initiating her into womanhood and sealing their partnership.

But now? Could he really have changed? Perhaps it was time to put him to the test. Forcing herself to keep calm, she put down her cup and sat back in her chair. She looked him straight in the eye.

'Yes, I will go to London. And I don't need my mother to hold my hand, thank you. But first you must admit to your father, in front of Bill Potter, that you *raped* me. And then you must tell them the truth about what happened on the London trip.'

She fully expected him to laugh and then deny her accusation. But he didn't. He put down his cup and thumbed the hollow of his chin, quietly mulling over her demand. After a few moments, he nodded his head.

'That's only fair. I only said those things to make you come back. I need you here… I would have done anything to get you back where you belong.'

June was taken aback. Rob talking about fairness? He was actually going to face his father and confess to lying?

'You must admit, June, here you shine like a star in the sky. I've brought out the best in you. You've had a free hand to prove and develop your talent.'

She could only agree with him. Her success was entirely due to his faith in her creative gifts.

'Yes, Rob. But that doesn't mean you *own* me.'

He nodded. 'Quite right. I'll go now and tell my father the truth. He'll be absolutely furious, but he'll get over it. Bill suspects I'm a liar anyway.'

Without waiting for her to comment, he left the room, leaving her rather dazed by his intended action. After a minute or so, she heard raised voices – one of them sounding exceedingly angry. She suddenly felt a kind of warmth towards Rob, and it disturbed her. But she reminded herself of what he'd done and the warmth turned rapidly to coldness.

A few minutes later, John Watson came into her room and made a profound apology. With Rob standing just behind him, he tried to justify his son's actions.

'I understand Robert thought he was acting in your best interests, and those of the firm.' He cleared his throat. 'I do not believe in dirty tactics and I am ashamed of my own son.'

June glanced at Rob. He was standing with his hands on his hips, but his head was down and she couldn't see the expression on his face.

'I'm sorry, June,' he muttered without looking at her.

John Watson nodded his head and gave a grimace of a smile, presumably satisfied that his son had apologised in his presence. 'As to the...' he cleared his throat again, 'rape. Or rather, to the accusation of rape. I honestly think it would be most unwise to make a formal complaint now. It would only cause a stink. If it came to court, Robert would be advised to say that he misread the signs. The publicity would not help any of us.' He cleared his throat even more loudly. 'The question might well be asked as to why you did not complain to anyone at the time. Let alone be working so damned hard for him now.'

Mr Watson would not stand by and see his son go to prison, she could see that. Whatever the outcome, no one would benefit. She nodded her head. 'I understand.'

'Good. Then we will put this unhappy affair behind us and allow you to continue with your excellent work. I understand a substantial bonus is due. You deserve every penny.' He gave her a brisk nod of his head and left the room.

Still with his head down, Rob came over and sat on the corner of her desk. He picked up a pencil and twiddled it in his fingers. After a moment or two he looked up and gazed into her eyes.

'You have a dignity, June, that is far beyond your years. Your forgiving nature puts me to shame.'

'I didn't say that I'd forgiven you,' she told him frankly. 'That is another question altogether. But I will go to London with you. I want to meet our new customers.'

'Good,' he said smiling. 'I'll get back and do some organising.'

Left alone, June put her head in her hands and did some thinking. Rob puzzled her. Was all this contrite behaviour a sham? Having been cleared of all charges, they had no hold over her and she could now resign. But he must have known that when he confessed to his father. Clearly, he'd had complete confidence that things would go his way. She couldn't resign. Not yet. They were on the brink of expansion. Rob had been talking of getting their own label and their own outlets, and she, June Armstrong, was an essential part of this exciting venture. The more effort she put in now, she reminded herself, the harder it would be for Rob to lose her when the time came to hand in her resignation.

Yes, that was going to be the real payback for robbing her dear Arthur of what was his alone. But now was not the time to dwell on such things, there was work to be done. The London visit was going to take time out of her planned schedule, but it was something she was looking forward to. Perhaps she could fit in a visit to the theatre. A bit of culture would be quite relaxing.

Back in his office, Robert Watson began planning the London visit. Now that June was going with him he thought it best to cancel dinner with Phil Jones. What about Trudy? Better play it safe. No women this time. Keep it strictly business and give June his full attention. Yes, take her to the theatre, she'd like that.

He gave a little laugh – one of relief rather than hilarity. Confessing his guilt to the old man had been a bit of a charade. He knew he'd blow his top. But what else could he do – sack him? And poor old Bill Potter. What an embarrassing situation for him. But then, he'd known the truth all along; he just liked to play politics and still be the good guy.

He had to admit he'd made a serious blunder pressuring June into having sex with him. But only because Arthur had been too much on her mind. Damn it! She'd been deceiving him all along over that man. Even if she refused to admit it, there was no doubting what she'd wanted at the time. The signs had all been there: hard nipples, flushing, panting, gasping, trembling, enticing body odour, moist membranes – her knickers were soaked with the stuff, for goodness sake! Yes, he certainly excited her. In spite of her yelling and fighting, she wanted it all right.

Was the resistance all part of her little game, or did she really fear losing Arthur? She would never admit succumbing to the pleasure, of course. It had to be total rape or goodbye fiancé. Pity; it had been great. Having partially freed her arms, the feel of her fingernails gripping his buttocks still lingered fondly in his memory. So too did her gasps of surprise. That was sexual pleasure all right; no use her saying otherwise. Yes, they made a good team. He might have had a minor setback, but the game went on.

Chapter Twenty-Five

It was the end of another busy week and June was waiting for Rob to take her home. She sat in her chair, relaxing and meditating on the past year.

It was amazing what had happened in those twelve months. She was a different person. What seemed like many years of experience had been condensed into an incredibly short time. She had overcome her feelings of inadequacy, and handled considerable responsibility. She had developed her artistic potential to peaks of success and seen her ambitions take on new forms – pushing her forward to much higher objectives. And she had accepted her sexuality, finding joy and pleasure in demonstrations of shared love.

Thinking of Charles, she realised that she had been given grace to forgive him and that he was now a special person in her life. But what about Rob? He had violated her far beyond what Charlie had done. Could he be forgiven too? Without him she would still only be Miss M's assistant, waiting for some kind of recognition, her creative genius squashed until she conformed to a more staid image. Had the time perhaps come to forgive him too? Was forgiveness possible, at least on an intellectual level?

Rob had behaved far more considerately towards her during the last few months. He'd allowed her to follow her natural flow of energy and had refrained from pushing her. He hadn't needed to. Ever since her holiday in Cambridge she had entered a new phase of creativity. Yes, sometimes she would flag, but he appeared content to go along with her moods. In spite of what had happened, they worked exceedingly well together. Rob was treating her with respect – both as a designer and as a woman. She had found a new confidence and felt in control of her life. Power over weakness? He was right there. Ironically, his own act of physically overpowering her had eventually given her a moral power over him. As she thought things over, she realised that vengeance was no longer on her agenda. But marrying Arthur certainly was. How could Arthur possibly understand her new relationship with Rob?

Her door opened. The man responsible for fulfilling her burning ambitions walked into her room. She smiled and rose from her chair.

'I'm ready,' she told him.

He looked at her with admiration in his eyes. For a moment their eyes met and a warm glow spread through her. Unable to cope with her feelings, she quickly turned away and reached for her coat. Rob opened the door for her and they left the building.

Two days before Christmas, Charles picked June up in Arthur's car and drove her to the station. He gave her a friendly grin. 'I'll walk back,' he said and left her with the keys.

With an aching heart, she watched him walk away. Charlie still loved her, she could see it in his eyes and hear it in his voice. Angela was a bitch! He deserved better. But Charlie had known what he was doing when he married her. Maybe they did love each other. After all, who was she to sit in judgement of other people's relationships?

She sighed, and turned her thoughts to Arthur's homecoming. Her being there to greet him was to be a surprise. There were things she had to tell him, but they could wait: they had a lot of loving to do. A whistle sounded down the line. Excitement welled up within her. Soon she would be in his arms.

The engine steamed into the station and slowed to a stop. There were many people crowding to get on the train and Arthur didn't see her straight away. Suddenly their eyes met. He walked quickly over, dropped his cases, and took her in his arms.

'My darling, God alone knows how I've missed you. How are you, my treasure?'

'I've missed you too... I love you so very much.'

Chatting light-heartedly, she led the way to Arthur's car. He threw in his cases and they were soon on their way to Bloomfield.

The house was resplendent with huge decorated tree, swathes of evergreen and glittering trimmings. As they entered, Arthur's nephews and nieces ran to them with excited voices. A baby was heard crying in the background. Greetings and happy chatter filled the air as the news spread that Arthur was home and that his fiancée was with him. Soon she would be part of Arthur's big family, and the prospect delighted her.

Angela, looking slinky in a close-fitting dress, came over to say hello. She was sweetly polite to Arthur, but sickly sweet to June. 'Still busy sewing, dear?' She didn't wait for an answer; handsome young George had just entered the room.

Charlie's voice sounded above the laughter and gossiping. 'Hello, you two.'

He came over and slapped his brother on the back. While the men were talking, June took Arthur's coat from him and went to hang it up along with hers. She returned to see Charlie whispering something in his brother's ear. Arthur smiled and looked towards her. A few minutes later, he was leading her out into the hall and up the stairs to Charlie and Angela's bedroom.

'Charles is keeping Angela out of the room for a couple of hours so we can be alone – with the door locked, of course.'

'Oh Arthur, dare we?'

He laughed. 'Would you rather go downstairs and play tiddlywinks with the children?'

With excitement tingling her nerves, they entered the bedroom. It reeked of Angela's perfume, and her clothes were strewn around the floor and furniture, but she refused to let that put her off. Charlie's toiletries were set out neatly on a chest of drawers and his uniform hung from a wardrobe knob. They somehow neutralised the signs of Angela's presence.

But Arthur looked pale and exhausted. She knew he'd spent the previous week working many hours, followed by his long and tiring journey home, so she insisted that he take a relaxing bath while they talked together. He didn't need much persuading.

The bathroom was en-suite. It had been converted from a dressing room and was quite large and luxurious: a turquoise and black colour scheme, gleaming chrome, large bevelled mirrors, and hidden lighting – a world away from what she was used to. It gave her considerable pleasure to lovingly smooth the bubbles over Arthur's tired muscles and think of their future together.

While she was admiring his mature manliness, smiling and making little appreciative noises, he suddenly gripped her arm. 'Take that lot off and come and join me,' he said masterfully.

Giggling like a schoolgirl, she slipped off her clothes and joined him in the water.

They towelled each other dry in the bedroom, where shafts of pale winter sun shed light on the highly-polished rosewood furniture, and brought to life the intricate details of the luxurious pink carpet. Soon they were kissing and cuddling on the warm-quilted bed, the touch of Arthur's sensitive hands releasing months of pent up sexual energy. He was an ardent lover and she willingly stretched herself out to welcome his passionate, moist lips caressing her naked body. She sighed with pleasure.

'Will it always be like this?'

'We've only just started on our love life, my darling. The main event may be reserved for our wedding day but then there's a whole manual of serious lovemaking to get through… and it's quite a volume!'

'Arthur, I don't know if–'

'I know, my love. It's no use pretending it didn't happen… we both know it did. But our coming together will be a totally different experience. I can wait until you're ready for marriage.'

'But Arthur, I *am* ready. I don't want us to wait. I love you and want to be with you.'

'I don't want us to rush into anything, my love. I know how much you enjoy your work. We'll have to make compromises and that won't be easy for you. You work all hours and it consumes your time and energy. I don't want you to be torn between your job and me. Our relationship has to be more than good sex… we have to find time for companionship. Marriage is total commitment and I don't want you to feel stifled.'

'But I wouldn't.'

'For these last few months, you've been like a woman possessed. Yes, you were deeply involved before then, but now you're obsessed with your design work. I could tell from your letters and from what others have told me.'

'I'm giving it up, Arthur.'

'June, you gave it up last August. But in spite of the terrible thing that happened, you still went back. Then after Cambridge, you became so involved you hardly slept. It's there in your letters, my darling, you can't deny it.'

She sighed at the truth of his remarks. 'I know. It just happened.'

The muscles in his face tightened. 'How you were able to go back to that factory is hard enough for me to grasp… your love for your career must run deeper than I ever imagined. But to actually work for your *rapist* is beyond belief. I want you to carry on designing, of course I do… it's as important to you as my work is to me. But there has to be another way. There isn't room for Robert Watson in our marriage. He'll be with us in our bed – he's made sure of that already.'

June shrunk back at those dreadful words.

Regret etched deep furrows into Arthur's grey face. He pulled her to him and stroked her hair with his cheek. 'I'm so sorry, my darling. I guess I'm jealous… I love you *so* much and I'm afraid of losing you.'

But his words had brought a chill to her heart, just as surely as a passing cloud had taken heat from the room. She snuggled into his arms, desperate for the warmth of his love to return. 'I love you, Arthur, only you. You don't have to be jealous of anyone… you will never lose me.'

He brought his lips down on hers and ran his fingers through her hair. His naked body was hard against her and she felt the tremor of his earthy desire. But all too soon he groaned and pulled away. He lay back on the pillows, his hands under his head and his eyes closed. 'I have to take a breather… sorry.'

She smiled her understanding. It never ceased to thrill her, the way he was affected by her closeness and touch. She lay back on the pillows too and wallowed in her power over his body, refusing to consider it a mutual thing. Before long, she rolled over on top of him. 'Oh Arthur, you feel so good. Do it all again.'

Ten minutes later, she watched him as he was forced to trip off to the bathroom. She called after him, 'I want us to marry, Arthur. Let's name the day.'

He came back wrapped in Charlie's bathrobe and sat on the edge of the bed.

'Not yet, June. Have your fling with success first. We can go on as we are. You're young; you have plenty of time to settle down and have babies. And you know how hard it is for me to accept what you're doing now – working with *that* man!'

'I can understand that. But let me tell you exactly what happened.'

She gave him a full account of how she was bullied back to her job. His face twitched with anger, but he allowed her to finish.

'So you see, I had to go back. It would have been awful if those wild stories had got around. Mud sticks. It could have harmed you and your family. If they'd called in the police, I could never have proved my innocence, and Rob's guilt. And who would have risked employing me again?'

'Why didn't you tell me? You poor girl. I'm so sorry.' His gentle voice suddenly turned to an angry growl. 'Watson won't get away with this. I'll make him pay for what he's done.'

'That's why I said nothing at the time. I didn't want you rushing back. I couldn't prove my innocence anyway. I felt bad about lying to your mother, but–'

'I know. If you'd told her everything, I'm not sure myself how she'd have taken it. But I already knew you were working again before you wrote to me. I received an anonymous letter. I didn't say anything to you because I wanted you to tell me yourself. *Blackmailed into serving that fiend!* I should have known.'

'I've planned my revenge, Arthur. You don't have to do anything.' She told him of her decision to be Miss

Perfect, and then leave when she was most needed. 'But the odd thing is, when things got that far, Rob confessed to his father what he'd done. John Watson was absolutely furious and apologised to me.'

'So why stay then? You're free to leave now. How can you work with that man?' His concerned expression deepened into a worried frown. 'Are you in love with him, June?'

She sat up stiffly. 'Oh Arthur, no! It's not like that. Rob has changed. He's been really considerate, and he's given me so much freedom in what I do. He's followed up my ideas and things have gone brilliantly. We have new sections set up, ready to service a string of outlets selling our own labels. The market's wide open, ready for us to step right into. The business is really taking off. It's just incredible, *unbelievable,* the way things are going, and–'

He stopped her mid-sentence. 'Can you hear yourself? Are you telling me you can give all that up? No. Never! It's where your heart is.'

'No, Arthur. Don't you see? Rob needs me more than ever. He's really going to miss me when I leave him in the lurch.'

He shook his head. 'You're just kidding yourself. You need Rob to fulfil your dreams, just as much as he needs you to service his plans. Otherwise, he would never have risked confessing. He knew exactly what he was doing.'

There was a knock at the door and Charlie called: 'Lunch is ready… if you two can *spare* the time.'

The house was packed with relatives. Kate had returned to her flat for a few days in an effort to be reconciled with her parents, and Angela and Charles were staying for the period of his leave. Arthur's bedroom had been taken over, so he was using the servant's sitting room. He was delighted with the arrangement: it was cosy and convenient for private moments with June. Having been invited to spend Christmas Day at Bloomfield, June was over early on Christmas morning. Arthur led her to his room, where they were to exchange gifts.

With her eyes closed, he put a necklace of rubies and diamonds around her neck and led her to the mirror over the mantelpiece. She opened her eyes and stared wide-eyed at the expensive gift.

'Arthur, it's *beautiful!* A perfect match for my ring and earrings. Thank you.' She kissed him long and hungrily. Eventually she pulled away. 'I have something for you too.'

He opened the prettily boxed present. Inside was a pair of solid gold cufflinks, finely engraved with his initials. His mind went back to the previous year when she had given him the lighter, still his most treasured possession. How things had changed for her over that one year.

'These are wonderful,' he said. He gazed into the depths of her gold-flecked hazel eyes. 'But not as beautiful as the giver. You are even lovelier than you were a year ago. A poised, elegant and beautiful woman. No longer that shy innocent child I fell in love with. You are everything to me, my darling, and I want so much for you to be happy.'

'*You* make me happy, Arthur.'

But he knew it could only be true when they were together and her mind was not on her work. Once she was back at the factory, a different person would take over – a person in love with his rival – and he couldn't compete with an obsession. But he loved her, and was prepared to accept whatever she was able to give him.

He took her in his arms and they kissed and expressed their love in gentle ways, restricted as they were by time and place. But there would be other places and other times and Arthur was already making plans. They both had until the beginning of January to spend in each other's company. For over a week, they enjoyed close intimacy and freely walked out together. Unashamed of their love and happiness, they held hands, kissed in public and ignored smiles and nods in their direction.

Arthur was aware of the whispered comments about the difference in their ages. The tinge of grey in his hair had increased. June told him it made him look handsomely distinguished, but he knew it also aged him considerably. The grey somehow brought out the lines of stress imprinted on his face during his wartime years. But at least, when he smiled – revealing white, even teeth – his face became more attractive and youthful. With June by his side, he had a lot to smile about. But the last thing he wanted was for people to think she was marrying an older man for his money.

Once she was back at the factory, June became immersed in her design work. As she was so busy, she started going in on Saturday mornings, and occasionally worked late into the evening. Nevertheless, she managed not to cancel any of her dates with Arthur – until late in February, that is…

Arthur was parked in the factory yard waiting to pick her up. They'd agreed to have dinner and go on to the theatre. For a treat, he had bought tickets for the best seats in the house. He waited for nearly an hour, spending the time looking over some notes for an important meeting the next day. Intuitively, he had come prepared to wait… but not *that* long.

Eventually June appeared, looking elegant in a full-skirted red coat with dark fur trim. Robert Watson was with her, his arm around her shoulders. Arthur groaned. He could hear them laughing and talking together and, despite the dim light, could see that Rob was about to help her into his Daimler. Arthur quickly opened his door; Watson turned and saw him. He bent over to say something to June and she looked up in surprise.

'Arthur!' she cried, running over to him. 'I'm so sorry, I completely forgot. It's been a heck of a day.'

Arthur looked across at Rob, who smiled, gave him a cheery wave and slipped into his car. Arthur could hardly control his anger, but when he saw June's anxious face he smiled reassuringly and gave her a hug.

'It's all right, darling, I managed to get some work done while I was waiting. But it'll have to be a quick snack instead of dinner or we'll miss the performance.'

He took her bags from her and put them on the back seat of his spacious new Jaguar while June slipped into the passenger seat. As he was about to start the engine, she said, 'Would you mind terribly if we just had a quick meal and missed the theatre? I'm really tired, and I have a few sketches to do for tomorrow morning.'

'If that's what you want. Or would you rather skip the meal as well and I'll take you straight home?'

'Oh, would you? Then I can grab a sandwich and get on. You really are wonderful; you always know what I want.'

Although heavy-hearted, Arthur managed to force a smile. He drove her home in near silence. When she stopped answering his occasional questions, he glanced over in her direction: the Jaguar's purring engine and smooth ride had sent her to sleep.

After dropping June off, Arthur couldn't decide whether to go out for a meal, or go to the theatre alone. He went home instead, and almost bumped into Betty Butler coming out of the study with a pile of envelopes.

'Hello, Betty, what are you doing here? Has my father got you slaving for him?'

'It's nice to see you again, Arthur. Actually I've been doing a bit of secretarial work for him. Working with the

Conservatives, he really does need the help.' She glanced at him appreciatively. 'You're looking smart... going somewhere nice?'

He threw his hat and coat over a chair. 'I *was*. I bought tickets for that new play at the Little Theatre, but June can't make it. I think I'll get some work done instead.'

'What a shame, I've heard the play is jolly good.'

'Yes, so I believe. Would you like the tickets? If you get a move on you'll still get there in time.'

Her blue eyes twinkled at him over wire-rimmed reading glasses perched on the end of her snub nose. Her thick lips curled into a smile of regret. 'I don't have the car tonight. Anyway, I'm like you, I prefer to go with a companion. And I do have these envelopes to finish. But thanks for the offer.'

He was full of admiration for her. His father could be very demanding and wasn't an easy man to work for. Betty had been a WAAF officer during the war and was an accomplished secretary, but she gave her services free for the benefit of the Conservative Party. Arthur came to a decision: 'Get your coat on, Betty. We might as well go together. You deserve a treat, working for the old man is tough going.'

'But I'm not dressed for going out, Arthur. My hair needs doing too. I must look an awful mess.'

He looked at her more closely. She was a handsome, rather than pretty, woman; not as slim or as shapely as June, but nicely proportioned. Her face was devoid of make-up and her mousy hair was drawn back from her face and rolled neatly above her neck. He knew that she'd lost her RAF fiancé in the Battle of Britain and, according to his mother, hadn't been out with another man since then. Judging from her appearance, he could well believe it; although she looked smart in her navy dress with matching jacket, she was hardly dressed to attract men.

'Not at all,' he told her, taking the envelopes from her. 'Go and freshen up, put on your coat and we'll be off. I won't take no for an answer.'

When she returned from the cloaks, he noticed that she had removed her glasses, combed her hair into loose curls and put on a little make-up. Whether it was her efforts at making herself more attractive, or the excitement of an evening out, Arthur couldn't say, but she now had a bloom and sparkle to her features, and was looking a very desirable woman.

'You look lovely,' he told her, as she turned up the collar of her fur coat, framing the lower half of her face. 'It has to be supper after the play. You look too good to go straight home.'

She blushed like a young girl. 'Thank you, Arthur,' she said demurely. 'I'm not sure about your flattering remarks, but I'd love to eat with you. Apart from tea and biscuits, I haven't had anything since lunch.'

She was about to step into the Jaguar when his father's Rover pulled into the drive. His mother gave him a puzzled look. 'Taking Betty home?' she asked, walking up to them.

'That was going to be my pleasure,' said his father. 'Thank you, Miss Butler, for working over. I'm sorry we're late back.' He looked at her more closely. 'I say, you look quite splendid. Are you going on somewhere? I hope I haven't made you late.'

'No, Colonel, you haven't, so don't worry. Goodnight, sir. I'll be back tomorrow.'

In case they were seen together that evening, Arthur thought an explanation was necessary. 'We're going to the theatre,' he told them. 'I bought two tickets but June couldn't make it. I came home to do some work instead, but Betty was here and she kindly agreed to accompany me.'

Both of his parents raised their eyebrows, but smiled their approval. No prizes for guessing what they were thinking… and hoping!

They said very little on the way to Nottingham. Arthur was having second thoughts about the two of them being alone together. But by the time they arrived at the theatre and settled into their seats, he began to relax. The play took his mind off both work and relationships, and when they left the theatre he was in an ebullient mood.

During supper, he found it pleasantly relaxing to talk to a woman closer to his own age, especially as they had many interests in common. After discussing various cultural topics, they inevitably drifted on to politics. Colonel Rogers had been nominated to fight the next General Election and that put Betty in the thick of things too.

Arthur told her that he intended to assist his father later on, but he was presently involved with his own election. He was to be the chairman of a new company being set up to handle the European end of the business. It was a big challenge. He wasn't worried about the responsibility, but he *was* worried about how it would affect his relationship with June. He didn't need to tell Betty this; she could clearly see it for herself.

'I hope all goes well for you, Arthur,' she said, picking up her glass of wine. 'I'm sure June will be delighted for you. Have you told her yet?'

'Actually, no. I was going to tell her tonight. No doubt she'll be pleased.' He topped up her glass. 'I must admit though, we don't see enough of each other as it is. I'll be expected to attend quite a few functions and such like, and it would be good if she could come to some of them. She's managed to attend a couple of dinner parties with me. She's been great; people are interested in what she does. And she shakes them a bit with her politics. Nothing like a bit of opposition to get folk talking!'

Betty pushed a piece of plaice onto her fork. 'She really is a lovely girl. You're both lucky to have each other,' she said. 'Mmm, this fish is delicious.'

'Yes, isn't it,' he acknowledged, before quickly returning to the subject closest to his heart. 'I know I'm lucky, but I'm not so sure about June. I'm so old compared with my lovely young fiancée.'

'Really, Arthur! You'd better be careful about the old bit – I'm almost the same age as you.'

'Oops! Sorry,' he muttered, and she laughed.

She looked at him thoughtfully and gave him a wistful smile. 'In your case, Arthur, maturity has given you much to offer. But I have a rich, full life too, so I can't complain.'

'And you'll never be old,' Arthur told her gallantly. 'You're one of those refreshingly elegant women who look forever young.'

Betty put down her knife and fork. 'Very tasty.' She looked at him and grinned. 'You know, Arthur, your brother has the reputation for being a bit of a charmer. But, clearly, he has an expert to learn from.'

At half-past midnight, Arthur drove Betty home. He felt relaxed and ready for bed. But having enjoyed being with another woman, he was also feeling just a little guilty.

Chapter Twenty-Six

June had an article written about her in the May edition of *Top Style*, a glossy magazine. She was heralded as a new young designer making her mark in popular fashion. The article also mentioned the proposed new chain of Mothering-Mother shops – the outlets for the June Armstrong exclusive maternity wear.

Arthur read the article and was impressed. His mind went back to the young girl in the white ballet dress; she bore no resemblance to the photos of June in the magazine. She had lost that childlike innocence. The glossy pictures made her look exquisitely beautiful but somehow harder – not the girl he knew and loved. Even so, it was what women were looking for – the Hollywood image – and was a great boost to the sale of her designs.

Shortly after the article appeared, he accompanied her to a function and found it rather novel to be introduced to everyone as 'Miss Armstrong's future husband'. He hung around on the periphery of the party watching her being celebrated. Robert Watson was by her side, vociferously singing her praises and promoting their latest product. But Arthur knew June was flagging and badly needed a break. She was due for a holiday anyway; even Rob acknowledged that when Arthur approached him out of June's hearing.

'Of course she can have time off,' he said grandly. 'Time she did. But don't you think the woman is capable of asking for herself?' He raised a questioning eyebrow. 'Perhaps June prefers her work to what else is on offer?' He turned his back on Arthur to speak to a curvaceous young woman who had sidled up to him. She had a large mouth with pouting shocking-pink lips, and she was flashing her heavy-lashed eyes in a most seductive manner. He noticed Rob's hand on her tight-skirted bottom as they left the room.

After another thirty minutes had passed by – time he resented wasting on meaningless chit-chat and standing around – Arthur collected June's coat ready to take her home. He went looking for her and found her arguing with Rob in an adjoining room. He pushed aside his scruples and listened at the half-open door.

'I can't stop now, there's too much to do.'

'Take the bloody time off, or King Arthur will be dragging you off permanently! Anyway, you're no good to me worn out and weary. You need to recharge your batteries. You might not be able to see it, but others can.'

'But–'

'Don't argue, woman!' he snapped. 'I'll get the essentials done. The rest can wait.'

Arthur felt sick. Of course he was pleased that June would be going on holiday with him, but what he had just overheard alarmed him considerably. He had seen little of her for the last few months. Naturally, he had blamed Robert Watson for driving her so hard. And Rob was indeed at the root of her obsession. But it seemed that June was just as much her own taskmaster. He could only hope that a complete break would help her see reason, otherwise their happy future together was in serious doubt.

Arthur moved some of his work over to a deputy and took June off for two weeks touring Cornwall. As soon as they came within sight of the rugged coastline, with its white rolling surf and brilliant blue sea, June was enraptured.

‘Arthur, this is magic – another world. You know, apart from odd day-trips, this is my first real holiday by the sea. I’m so glad you’ve brought me here.’

He smiled at her enthusiasm. He had always taken things like this for granted and tended to forget that she has missed out. While he had often spent several weeks by the sea, sailing and messing about on beaches, June’s annual holiday had always been a week at home with the pleasures of Wakes Week.

The sun shone for the whole of their holiday. They visited the little harbours, strolled hand-in-hand through quaint winding streets, and watched fishing boats coming in to unload. Sometimes they ate fresh lobsters for lunch, sitting at tables overlooking the busy quayside. They walked the cliff footpaths to admire the magnificent views over the craggy headlands, stopping occasionally to kiss. Finding a small garden café along the route was an unexpected pleasure, and they enjoyed cream tea specials with sweet early strawberries.

Cornwall’s magnificent sandy beaches were a special delight for June. Sharing them with a few other early visitors, they lay sunbathing with the muffled rhythmic roar of the waves sounding in their ears. Occasionally, in the cool shadows of the cliffs, he sat reading while June was sketching.

Sometimes, like a child, June would dabble her feet in little pools left by the tide and warmed by the sun. Arthur loved her for her unsophisticated enthusiasm. ‘Come and look!’ she would squeal when little crabs and tiny glistening fish caught her eye.

Suddenly, June yelled out in panic: ‘Arthur, Arthur, there’s a bomb!’

Alarmed, he ran to look at what she had found. Between the rocks there was indeed what looked like a small bomb.

'Just a practice shell,' he assured her. 'Probably been here for years. Nothing dangerous.' But even so, he experienced a brief flashback to when a shell no bigger than this one had torn apart human flesh – including his own. Freedom had come at a price. Life was precious. He wrapped his arms around her. 'God, how I love you.'

With June giggling like a schoolgirl, he took her hand and dragged her into a cool, dark cave where he stripped off her costume and thrilled her with his touch. All sophistication had finally, and completely, been thrown aside. She was once more the young girl he had fallen in love with – for the rest of the holiday at least.

With the beaches empty, they were able to swim naked in the sea at the end of day. Afterwards, they made passionate love in the bedroom they shared as man and wife. Arthur had never been so happy and June was with him every step of the way, her whole being glowing with joy and love. Robert Watson had been left behind and her career forgotten. She was his, body and soul.

While they were driving home, June sketched busily in a little notebook. He glanced at her occasionally as she handled pebbles, shells, and flotsam she had picked up on the beaches. The sketches she had done during the holiday – of sea and rocks, coast and cliffs, cottages and flowers, boats and harbours – were spread over the back seat, while she pencilled ideas for dresses, fabrics and trimmings. He could see movement and colours flowing from her fingers as she worked with alacrity and deep passion for her craft. She had been inspired, and Arthur knew he would see little of her for quite a while.

While June worked, Arthur made his own plans. He would see about moving her into a room of her own at Bloomfield. It was the only way they'd be able to have any time together.

Their lovemaking was becoming stronger and even more enjoyable; June's surge of creativity was fuelling her libido. But she was engaged on a new project at work that was taking up all of her time and energy, so it was happening less and less often. To compensate, she sometimes crept into Arthur's room and spent the night in his bed. This did not go unnoticed.

The Colonel called Arthur into his study.

'I don't want to interfere in your lives, Arthur, but isn't what you're doing rather risky? Shouldn't you be thinking of marriage by now – make it legal and all that – before it becomes a necessity?'

Arthur wasn't in the least offended by his father's anxiety.

'You don't have to worry, Father,' he said, 'we haven't got that far, and neither will we until we're married. I made that promise when you and Mother agreed that June could have a room here.'

His father cleared his throat noisily. 'Well, I have to say I admire your restraint. But please think it over – appearances you know. I'm not accusing family members of gossip, but you know how people sit in judgement about moral issues. If it got around that you were sleeping together in this house…'

'I understand your concern, sir,' Arthur told him, knowing his father's delicate position. 'We'll try to be more discreet. I'd rather not rush into anything.'

Arthur had to admit that June wanting to sleep with him was quite wonderful, but doing so made it even more difficult to keep control over their sexual appetites. He didn't want to push her into marriage; her mind was very much on her career – hardly surprising, the way it was going.

Another article had appeared in a magazine. A new star had risen in the world of fashion and June was being lauded as an inspired fabric designer. Rob had channelled her new wave of creativity into designing fabrics for their exclusive use, with a small range for general sale. With June so busy, the London holiday they had planned for late November had to be cancelled.

As the end of the year approached, Arthur was fully engaged in his own work. He had been given directorships on other boards, and his requirement to attend functions had increased in line with his responsibilities. June had only managed to accompany him on one of the more important ones. Since Betty Butler was now working for his father more frequently, it seemed natural to ask her to join him at political gatherings and minor social events. Betty liked going and Arthur enjoyed her company. It was also small reward for the extra work she was doing, not only for his father, but also for him.

June raised no objection to the arrangement. 'Don't worry, Arthur,' she said, apparently surprised that he was concerned, 'I don't see Betty as a rival. I'm only too glad that she can help you out.'

A few days before Christmas, family members began to arrive at Bloomfield for their annual get-together. This was something June had been looking forward to – when she had time to think of anything not connected with work. It was going to be an even greater assembly this year. Kate arrived with her partner – Mrs Rogers confided to June that she hoped visitors would think they were just good friends. Clare had invited a boyfriend whom she'd met at Cambridge. George was also home. Without prior permission, he had brought with him a strange-looking girl who spoke little but flashed a lot – especially legs and cleavage. Angela and Charles were staying for a week, and the two families from London, now increased by another child, would be staying for four days.

With considerable difficulty, paid help had been found for Mrs Craven. June had offered to assist her future mother-in-law with domestic chores and social arrangements, but was told politely that everything was now arranged. Christmas seemed to go well in the Rogers household this year. All the guests appeared to get on together, at least in company, although there were sometimes rows in the bedrooms – with Angela out-yelling all of them. All the usual Christmas traditions were followed, and June felt completely at home and very much part of Arthur's family.

But much to her dismay, on the Saturday after Christmas, Mary Rogers enlisted Betty Butler as hostess at a cocktail party for the Colonel's growing band of Conservative Party workers. June had noticed that Betty always seemed to be around Bloomfield these days, and despite what she'd told Arthur, she had a growing uneasiness at the way Mrs Rogers treated her – almost like a future daughter-in-law.

At the cocktail party, June became fully aware that Betty Butler wasn't the neutral woman she had thought her to be. She had taken on a glow of youth that had eluded her... until she had started assisting Arthur. Everything about her was different: clothes, hair and make-up. Her cheeks flushed and her eyes sparkled whenever Arthur entered the room. Anyone could see that this was a woman in love. But there was more: she was well educated in social graces, able to hold a conversation with complete ease and confidence, and well versed in political debate. Men listened to her. It was obvious that Betty would make an ideal marriage partner for Arthur.

Even though they spent a lot of time with each other and appeared comfortable together, Arthur showed no sign of wanting Betty for his wife. Nevertheless, June was determined not to lose him and tried to make herself available more often when he needed her. But with so many commitments of her own, this wasn't easy.

In early March, Arthur sat at his large, orderly desk in his spacious refurbished office, and thought over his situation. He would soon need to make frequent stays in Paris while the new branch was being opened. Ideally he needed his secretary to travel with him, but her husband objected. He also needed June to be with him, but she would be tied up with her own work. That was a pity, because it would have been good for her to experience Paris in the spring. He wondered whether he should ask Betty to go with him.

His mind went back to the last time Betty had helped him out. It had been an evening function, bringing together the Conservative Party and supporters from the business world. As usual, he had driven Betty home afterwards, and she had invited him in for a drink as she always did. Normally he refused, but that evening June was away and he felt like talking to a receptive ear.

Betty had just moved into a flat in the Park area of Nottingham. It was roomy and furnished for comfortable living. The lounge floor was covered with a deep-pile red floral carpet. The feather cushioning of the two gold plush sofas beckoned tired bodies to seek rest in their embracing softness. The pale gold-tinted walls sported finely-framed Impressionist prints, and Arthur suspected one or two of them might even be originals by lesser-known artists. A walnut cabinet displayed a collection of red Venetian glassware, and a matching bookcase was filled with a variety of old and new books. A walnut coffee table topped with a large crystal ashtray invited visitors to smoke. The lighting was subtle, provided by shaded lamps. Red and gold brocade curtains hung full length at the tall Georgian windows, and a log-effect electric fire glowed in the grate. The room felt warm and cosy. The beautifully ornate French clock on the marble mantelpiece told him it was half an hour to midnight.

'Let me take your coat,' said Betty, holding out a hand. 'Please make yourself at home. There are cigars and cigarettes in the boxes on the coffee table.'

Arthur handed over his coat. 'I'll not smoke, thanks. I gave up cigarettes some time ago and I rarely smoke cigars.'

'Well, help yourself to a drink – bottom right-hand cupboard of the cabinet. Or would you prefer coffee?'

'I'll have coffee please, Betty.'

'It won't take long,' she said, and left the room.

He sank into one of the sofas, leaned back his head and closed his eyes. Bliss! He felt himself drifting into drowsiness…

Something soft and moist brushed against his lips. He opened his eyes and pulled himself together. Betty was standing over him, her full lips curled into a gentle smile. She had changed out of her black evening dress into a blue loose-fitting house dress. Its silky softness and plunging neckline made her look exceedingly alluring. She had placed a cup of coffee on the table in front of him.

'Thank you, Betty. I must have dropped off. Rude of me. I do apologise.'

'You're very tired, Arthur,' she said, sitting herself at the other end of the sofa. 'Would you like to stay the night? I have a spare bedroom and you're most welcome to use it.'

He observed her more closely. She looked soft and warm, and most inviting to a man that was hungry for love – even a tired one. Had it been those delightful lips that had awakened him from sleep? Surely he had been dreaming? Betty was far too circumspect to compromise a situation.

He felt a great desire to nuzzle those soft full breasts and sink himself into her inviting body. He looked up and found her watching him closely. Embarrassed, he quickly turned to pick up his coffee. She wasn't exactly beautiful, but Arthur thought her to be a very sexy lady – dangerously so in his current state of mind.

'Kind of you, Betty, but this should wake me up,' he said, sipping his coffee and forcing his eyes to steer away from her seductive breasts.

She bent to pick up her own cup from the coffee table and the neck of her dress fell forward, delightfully revealing two magnificent unrestrained orbs with just a hint of their nipples. They drew his eyes like magnets and began waking up areas of his body better left undisturbed. He forced himself to look at the clock.

'Gosh, nearly midnight. I must be off in a minute.'

'Are you sure I can't put you up for the night? It's bad weather to be driving, especially when you're tired.'

'Very inviting, but I really must be off,' he said, putting down his empty cup and standing up.

She stood up with him. 'If I can ever help you in any way at all, you have only to ask.'

He caught the look of hope in her eyes. 'I most certainly will.' He kissed her cheek. 'You're a lovely lady, Betty. Thanks for everything.'

She left the room to get his coat and he followed behind. She handed it over. 'I've really enjoyed this evening. Thank you, Arthur.'

'No need to thank me. What would Father and I do without you?'

She smiled. 'Manage, I'm sure. But I would be the loser.'

Standing there in her loose flowing gown, her full breasts exposed by the deep neckline, large moist lips slightly parted inviting his kisses, and her eyes pleading him to stay, it was hard to leave. Stirrings within his groin made him hesitate; his mind struggled with his masculine needs.

'Goodnight then, Betty,' he said, opening the door. 'No doubt I'll see you at Bloomfield tomorrow.'

'Goodnight, Arthur.' Her voice sounded a little sad. It wounded him.

He was about to go outside when he suddenly turned, took her in his arms and kissed her full on the mouth. She responded just as he'd hoped she would, and he was powerfully moved by her roused sexuality. But he quickly realised that it had been a dangerous gesture. He wanted to go back inside and...

Pulling away, he said, 'I can never give you more than a kiss, but I really do appreciate your friendship.'

She nodded in understanding, and closed the door behind him.

Returning his mind to the present, Arthur considered the propriety and fairness of asking Betty, a woman clearly in love with him, to accompany him on business trips and social functions. Could he trust himself not to make advances? Knowing she was available and willing was more than enough to excite him.

He longed for June when they were apart. He wanted to be near her, to touch her, to make love to her. They had gone little further than they had a year ago. He knew she was ready and willing for anything, but he couldn't trust himself not to go all the way. If he wanted to stick to his moral and religious beliefs, marriage was the only answer.

Even so, if he didn't want Robert Watson looming over their marriage like a beguiling spectre, June must be free of his power over her. And that surely meant her leaving the firm. But she needed to make the move herself, trusting that there would be alternative outlets for her talent. He sighed; he didn't want a wife who would always be hankering for what she had lost. The last thing he wanted was for her to walk out of his life. He decided to ask her that evening about going to Paris with him, and try to get her to discuss their future together. After all, Paris would be an opportunity for her to combine her obsession with fashion with the pleasure of their being together. Maybe it would even prompt her to look at alternatives to her present work.

He was picking her up from work in the late afternoon so as to have plenty of time to get ready for the evening's event. It was to be an important social gathering of top management and their wives, with the aim of cementing relationships within a constantly expanding international corporation. It was important for June to be there, and she had promised not to be late.

Arthur drew up outside the factory, ready to go straight off. After ten minutes, he began to wonder if June had forgotten. After another ten minutes, he got out of the car and asked the man in the gatehouse to give her a ring. There was no answer from her office phone. Having been told the way to her room, he ran up the stairs to find her.

As he passed an office with Robert Watson's name on the door, he heard June's laughter. He opened the door and there she was, sitting on the edge of his desk, looking through a pile of sketches. Rob was standing over her, an arm over her shoulders.

'Hello,' Arthur said pleasantly, forcing a smile so as not to give Rob the satisfaction of knowing his true feelings. Anger, frustration and jealousy were eating at his soul.

June looked up. Judging by her shocked expression, she had only just realised where she was supposed to be.

'I'm so sorry, Arthur, I completely forgot,' she said anxiously. 'I'll get my coat.'

Rob looked at Arthur and smiled. 'Going somewhere nice?' he asked, folding his arms and casually sitting on the corner of his desk. 'Don't keep her out too late – early start tomorrow.'

Arthur felt like knocking the supercilious grin from his handsome rugged face, but that, of course, would be playing straight into his hands. Instead, he glared at him menacingly. 'June is the one who decides when she goes home – or what she does with her life, for that matter.'

Rob raised his heavy brows. 'Really? Since she's engaged to you, that does surprise me.'

June appeared at the door, putting her arms through her coat sleeves. She glanced at each of them and an anxious look spread across her face. 'Come on, Arthur, I haven't long to change,' she said, catching hold of his arm and dragging him off.

As they were driving home, Arthur released a deep sigh of frustration. 'Just occasionally, do you think you could make an effort to be on time?'

'I said I was sorry, Arthur. I hope you won't start being difficult.'

'Betty would have come with me, but I want you there: my future wife. Tonight is really important, a question of building up relationships within the group. You knew I'd be waiting for you. Surely, whatever you were planning with your precious Rob could have been done in the morning?'

'Rob's away tomorrow. We're both going to London soon and we have to get things ready.'

'June, I'm also going away soon. I hope the dates don't clash. I want you to come to Paris with me. I'll be away early next month, and a few more times during the year.'

She sighed. 'Do you have to? Can't someone else go? I don't want you to leave me.'

'I don't have to leave you – you can come with me.'

'Not now, Arthur. I told you what I'm doing. It's the new fabric range. I have to be there. Rob needs me with him.'

'I need you with me.'

'But, Arthur, I'm designing the prints, you know that.'

Frustration finally got the better of him. 'I don't think it's possible to forget what you do,' he said heatedly. 'Right! Carry on with your work. I'll ask Betty to come with me. I can get her to do my secretarial work.'

June's face flushed with pique. 'And share your bed, Arthur?'

'I'll ignore that remark,' he said angrily.

He stopped the car and turned to her.

'It's not working. Do you want to break off the engagement?'

June shook her head vigorously. 'No! Never! I love you!'

'I need a wife, June. I want *you* to be my wife. But you're in love with your job. Robert Watson means more to you than I do.' Jealousy was tearing him apart.

'That's not true, Arthur. Please don't think that.'

'What am I to think then? I'm kept waiting while you're laughing with your rapist! He even had his arm around you. God, woman!' he raged, 'Do you know what that does to me?'

'It's not what you're thinking. I really *do* love you,' she said, her eyes filling with tears. 'It's just that I get caught up in things and get carried away.'

Arthur smiled wryly as he thought about what he so longed for. 'Carried away by ecstasy? Isn't that what we both want – in our marital bed?' He turned his head away and stared through the car's windscreen. He sighed deeply. 'At least, that's what *I'm* longing for.'

She touched his arm. 'I'm sorry, Arthur,' she said softly. 'I'm really sorry.'

His anger vented, he took her hand and squeezed it in acknowledgement. 'Better get you home.'

Arthur waited for June in the study. He took out his pipe and lit it – something he hadn't done for quite a while. It had come as a shock to him when he realised just how much resentment he had been harbouring. It would not do. In future they must be more honest with each other.

He heard June calling to him and joined her in the hall.

'Will I do for you, Arthur?' she asked, putting out her arms and twirling around.

She was wearing one of his favourite dresses of red moiré silk. It had an off-the-shoulder neckline, figure-hugging bodice, and a wide flared skirt. Her rubies enhanced her natural beauty. Her make-up was delicately, but effectively applied: darkened lashes and eye shadow emphasising her sparkling hazel eyes, a little rouge heightening her perfectly smooth and youthful cheeks, and a touch of lipstick accentuating her white, even teeth. Her rich dark hair, recently swept back, had been allowed to fall loosely about her shoulders in glossy curls. She looked absolutely stunning. And he knew, beyond doubt, that she had done it all for him.

'My darling, you have never looked lovelier.' He took her in his arms and held her close. 'Thank you. I'm a lucky man to have you love me. I'm so sorry I upset you. Forgive me?'

For the rest of the evening she was his perfect companion. People there were interested in her, not just as Arthur's future wife but also for herself. The attention brought out her innate charm. She sparkled, and Arthur felt proud that she would soon be his wife. Why be jealous of Robert Watson? He was merely the catalyst that brought her talents to life. Despite being so much older, and not in the least good looking, *he* was the one June loved. Yes, he was indeed a very lucky man.

On the way home, Arthur desperately wanted to make things right between them.

'I'm so sorry, my love. You have as much right to get on with your job as I have with mine. Seeing you with Watson, well, I suppose I was jealous again. He sees so much of you, and does so much for you. He gets you excited, makes you elated and fulfils your dreams. I can give you so little in comparison.'

'That's not true, Arthur; you give me all your love. It's my fault. I've been selfish and I've taken your love for granted. I've hurt you badly. Please forgive me.'

'You must do what you have to do, my dearest. I'd rather have you with me just occasionally than not at all.'

They were late getting home, but Arthur found June just as restless as himself. They needed to let each other know that their love hadn't changed.

'I know it's late, Arthur,' June whispered, as she helped remove his jacket, 'but please come with me to take a shower. I feel dirty and I want you to make me clean again.'

They made love until the early hours of the morning. June wasn't just a passive partner; she played an active part, delighting in feeling his reactions to her touch. He sensed that she was in the mood for new experiences, and he enjoyed catering to her ravenous appetite. He joined her in rapturous delight as she groaned with pleasure and pleaded for more. Suddenly she pulled him hard against her.

'Now! Now! Please, oh, please… make me yours for ever.'

How could he say no to her pleading, when he himself had brought her to this point. He had his own hunger too. He wrestled with himself. As much as his body was crying out for satisfaction, he resisted the temptation to break his resolve.

So he used all his knowledge and practised skills to bring her to an ecstatic orgasm. She relaxed in his arms, happy and exhausted. Completely in tune with June's orgasmic rhythm, Arthur had gained intense pleasure himself. But he was not content; things had gone far, but not far enough. There was only one thing he could do about it.

'Marry me, my dearest love. I'll accept any conditions. I'll take second place to your work. I need you so badly... I'm constantly burning up. I can't wait any longer.'

'Arthur, darling, I want to marry you... more than anything else in the whole world.'

'My love, we'll make it soon. We'll plan our marriage to fit in with your commitments, but we must make it *soon*. I need you so very much.'

'Whatever happens, I'm coming to Paris with you. Nothing will stop me.'

'Then we'll get married before we go. My love, my darling, darling June, you've made me so happy.'

Arthur was dropping off to sleep when he felt June moving out of his bed. She bent over him, kissed him, and whispered, 'Go to sleep, my love, I'm going to my own room now. I'm staying home tomorrow. Sleep well, darling.'

June returned to her own room. She looked around at the expensive rosebud wallpaper, pink and cream striped curtains, pink quilt, thick cream carpet, and rich mahogany furniture. She thought about her bedroom in her parents' house: rich by poor people's standards, but poverty compared with how she was living now. But she wasn't marrying Arthur for richer living. The salary she expected to receive in the future promised her independent means of a very high standard. No, she was marrying for love alone.

Although she liked, and indeed loved, some of Arthur's family, she hated the snobbishness that went with their superior status. Somehow she was going to have to bridge the Armstrong and Rogers households, and that wouldn't be easy. But life with Arthur was what she wanted, and to make it work would mean making sacrifices.

She sat down at her desk, pushing aside the sketches and jottings, took out a sheet of writing paper from a drawer, and carefully wrote out a letter of resignation. The Friday before leaving for Paris with Arthur would be the day she would say goodbye to Rob. The Saturday, she decided, would be her wedding day – divorced from the firm and married to her dearest Arthur.

She was already up and dressed when Arthur popped in to see her, just before he left for a business appointment at eleven o'clock.

'Why aren't you still in bed? You need your beauty sleep.'

She looked up from her desk and grinned. 'I have a wedding to plan.'

Arthur came over and kissed her. He glanced at her sketches of wedding gowns. 'All these? How long have you been up?'

'Hey, you mustn't see them,' she told him, gathering them quickly together. 'But you can look at this.'

She handed him her letter of resignation. Arthur read its contents and frowned.

'Are you sure you want to do this, June?'

'Absolutely. I don't want to lose you any more than you want to lose me, so I have to do this. It's the only way.' She saw a look of concern spread across his face. 'Something else will turn up,' she told him cheerfully.

Arthur kissed her, and said he had to go. 'I'll see you this evening. I'll put this letter in the post for you.' He turned at the bedroom door. 'Take Monday off as well as today. It'll give them time to digest what you're doing. I'll ring in for you and say you won't be in. If they ring, don't answer the phone. Promise me, June. I don't want any of them upsetting you.'

She realised that Arthur was taking over her life, but somehow it felt good. Arthur was her lover, her guru, her prop, and her comforter. 'I promise,' she said. 'And I won't go in until Tuesday. Anyway, I have something very special to do.'

Chapter Twenty-Seven

Arthur was shown into Robert Watson's office. Rob rose to meet him, his face impassive.

'If you've come to knock me down, I won't resist,' he said, splaying his hands in open surrender. 'You have that right, and no one is going to stop you.'

Arthur controlled such desires. He had killed and maimed during his military service, and he had seen his own comrades killed. It had turned him against physical violence of any sort. Anyway, he needed the man's co-operation.

'You have acted despicably towards my fiancée… something of which you are only too aware. And no doubt you have continually taken advantage of June's forgiving nature. But I don't think violence would solve anything, except to make you feel better about yourself, and I'm not here to ease your conscience.'

'Well in that case, perhaps you'd better sit down and tell me why you have come.'

They both sat, with Rob's desk between them. Arthur placed an envelope in front of Rob and looked him in the eye.

'Perhaps you'd better read that.'

Rob opened the envelope and casually read the letter of resignation as though he already knew what was in it. He put the letter aside and slowly rubbed at the cleft in his chin with his right thumb, remaining silent for a few moments before commenting.

'I must put you right about something,' he said casually. 'June was free to go her own way from the day I confessed to my father that I had cheated and lied. She has not forgiven me for what I did to her. Forgiveness is not in the scheme of things. But she stayed, as I knew she would, because she couldn't leave… didn't want to leave. I have made her what she is and given her full scope to fulfil her growing ambitions. No one could have done more for her.'

Arthur knew only too well the truth of what he was saying. He listened impassively, trying not to give away his thoughts and feelings and – he had to admit – his admiration for the man he so much detested.

Rob leaned back in his chair and put his hands flat on the table, clearly at ease with himself. 'June is no youngster, Arthur,' he said, his heavy brows rising slightly. 'She's a mature woman with a mind of her own. Her gift is far greater than that of any other designer I've worked with. Her designs are the basis of several new and very successful ventures. This energises her… she's driven from within and there's no stopping her.'

Arthur said nothing. All that Rob was saying was true.

'June may think she loves you. No doubt you make her feel secure, loved and highly desirable. But all you do is make her dependent on you. If you really loved her, you would set her free to be the woman she is, not the child you once knew.'

'Do you think I don't know that?' Arthur retorted. 'I've seen the changes and I know about her consuming passions. And that's exactly what it's doing to her – eating her up,' he said vehemently. He took a deep breath to calm his anger. 'There are other ways to fulfil her potential. That is what I want to discuss with you.'

'We can discuss what you like, but you must realise that as long as I leave a door open for her, she'll come back to me. I will not destroy June's ambitions, or my own plans, by closing that door.'

Arthur nodded his head. 'There may be something in what you say, but there is an alternative.' He produced another envelope and put it in front of Rob. 'This is a specimen contract that I would like you to look at. You see, I think it is possible for June to carry on working for you after we marry. But not as she's doing now. I will not have my wife at your beck and call, nor will I stand by and see her ruin her youth and health.'

Rob sat forward and rubbed at the cleft in his chin. 'Go on.'

'As you may recall, it was after a visit to Cambridge, relaxing in magnificent surroundings, that June became so revitalised. Cornwall also inspired her.'

Rob interjected, 'That may be true, but I wouldn't stop her from going any place she wants to.'

'I'm sure you wouldn't; it's in your own interests. But I'm going to need my wife with me... Paris to start with. I need her support, just as much as she's going to need mine. June cannot work to her present contract. She knows it, and that's why she wrote her letter of resignation. If you look at that piece of paper before you, you'll see what I'm proposing.'

Rob looked at the document while Arthur explained.

'June can continue to design for you, but will only visit the factory to see her finished designs. She may also visit to confer with you as to how things are going generally. There will be times when my work will take me to Europe, and as I said, Paris in particular. That will be good for her... she'll be stimulated by the place. And if June is creatively challenged, it'll be good for you too.'

'I must admit the idea has possibilities. I'll put it to my father. But I want June here with me, Arthur. Permanently. And that door will remain open.'

Arthur was profoundly irritated by Rob's reply. He breathed in deeply through his nostrils and calmed himself. He leaned back in his chair.

'June will not return on a permanent basis. She made that choice herself. No one forced it on her. She doesn't know I'm here this morning… nor is she aware of what I've proposed.'

Rob raised an eyebrow. 'Really? Well, the way you treat her, I suppose that's not so surprising.'

Arthur's stomach muscles tightened. 'I didn't want to put it before her unless I knew there were possibilities for its acceptance,' he explained. 'Personally, I'd prefer that my wife had no contact whatsoever with a despicable rapist, and downright liar. But if she wants to stay loyal to you, that's her affair. I won't prevent her.'

Arthur rose from his chair. 'I expect to hear from you within a week. Or I shall be looking elsewhere for alternatives.'

When June returned to work on Tuesday, she was nervously anticipating an unpleasant scene with Rob. So she was surprised when he greeted her with a smile and wished her happiness in her coming marriage. Even then she half-expected a storm of rebuke, but none came. He didn't even mention the fact that she'd let him down by not coming in on Friday and Monday.

Did he already have someone in mind to replace her? No, she would surely have heard. He was expecting her to change her mind, that must be it. Too bad. He was going to have to get used to the idea and find another designer to work with him. That thought suddenly cast a shadow of jealousy over her, but she shrugged it off. She was about to have a new beginning. Her gifts would flow in another direction. It was going to be a wonderful, exciting future, shared with the man she loved.

After bringing her up-to-date with the work in hand, Rob suddenly asked her about the wedding.

'I suppose it's going to be a splendid affair. You'll be designing your own dress, of course. Any ideas yet?'

She was touched by his interest. As she started telling him about the various designs she'd been sketching, her excitement began to surface. Snatching up a pencil, she sat down and began drawing on the pad she always kept handy. Rob perched himself on the corner of her desk, his eyes following her scribbling hand.

'Excellent. That one is particularly good,' he said pleasantly, placing his hand over hers.

She felt a thrill shoot up her arm. Confused, she pulled her hand away.

'Yes, I think that's the one,' she said, pleased that he was taking an interest. Yet part of her was still expecting a sudden outburst, a cruel remark or a sardonic comment.

But overjoyed by his apparent attempt to be friendly, she began sketching other ideas, including dresses for the bridesmaids: Pat, Rose and Clare. He was clearly impressed, and asked her to go into details of fabrics and trimmings.

'I must admit, I'm rather hazy about what's available,' she told him, 'I must do a tour of the department stores.'

'Certainly not! I'll give a few reps a ring… get them to show you their bridal fabric ranges. I'll arrange it for this week.' He gave her a warm smile. 'I could also get you visits to the local lace manufacturers and wholesalers. You can see what's available and order a few samples. Having the fabrics in front of you might help you decide which of your designs to choose.'

June was quite overcome. She looked at him with warmth in her heart. 'You're really going to all that trouble just for me?'

'Not really,' he said, giving a little laugh. 'I'm thinking bridal wear could be a new line for us. Might as well cash in on your enthusiasm.'

June thought he was joking and happily laughed with him.

'It's no joke, June. I really mean it.'

Knowing Rob as she did, she wondered how she could possibly have thought otherwise.

Rob had already taken on a first-class pattern-cutter and an extra sample-hand to assist June. For the next two or three weeks, they all worked hard to get a small range together. Because of her impending wedding, June had considerable enthusiasm for the project. John Watson himself had insisted that the firm pay for her dress and complete trousseau. Although Rob had always insisted on her getting her due rewards, such largess was an unusual sign of his father's gratitude.

Less than a week before she was due to leave, John Watson called her to his office. Smiling benignly, he motioned her to sit at his desk in front of him.

'We would like to keep you on–'

'I won't be withdrawing my resignation, Mr Watson,' she said, sharply interrupting him. 'I'm getting married and it's quite impossible to continue working here as well. Don't think you can bully me with dirty tactics again. It won't work.'

Although Watson visibly cringed, he made it obvious that he intended to be heard by loudly clearing his throat.

'You have every right to take that attitude after the unfortunate incident,' he said, clearly trying to cover his embarrassment with gruffness. 'However, you must admit that coming back has given you opportunities that very few designers, young or old, can ever realise.'

'I can't deny that. But you also have benefited,' she responded with a proud lift of her head.

In deep thought, Watson sat back and rubbed both forefingers into the cleft of his chin.

'That's quite true, my dear,' he said after a few moments. 'But what we are planning could suit both of us.' He leaned forward and pressed both hands on his desk. 'The scheme is this: you carry on designing for us, but from home. You will submit your ideas to Robert, who will deal with them to the final stage. We will require you to come in occasionally, to view the finished products, and to co-ordinate and discuss present and future ranges. In other words, you will act as a designer-consultant in the areas you are presently working in.'

June was taken completely by surprise. It was surely the perfect solution.

'That would be marvellous,' she said eagerly. 'I'll have to discuss it with Arthur of course, but I'm sure he'll agree.'

'I'm sure he will, my dear. Let me know by tomorrow and I will get the contract finalised.'

On the day that June was due to leave, Rob walked into her office and sat on the edge of her desk. She had been expecting him to drop in, and an intense nervous excitement had built up within her. She felt his eyes watching her as she cleared away a few papers and binned others.

'Hello, Rob,' she said casually, refusing to look up, knowing full well that he would mesmerise her with his charm. As it was, his very presence was causing her heart to beat faster and her hands to shake. 'I'm just clearing my desk.'

'So I see.'

She gathered the few remaining sketches together and slipped them into a folder. Her desk was now tidy, with just one or two folders ready for filing.

Well then,' he said, picking up a pencil and twiddling it in his fingers, 'tomorrow, you'll be Mrs Arthur Rogers.'

'Yes. And I'll no longer be married to this place,' she said, rising from her chair – his proximity was far too disturbing for her to remain seated. 'But I recognise that you put me on the road to success. I guess I have to thank you for your encouragement.'

'I knew you'd thank me one day.' He came over to the dress rail where she was standing. 'But we both know you'll always be married to this place. You'll never be able to divorce yourself from Watson's... and certainly not from me.'

She stopped fiddling with the dresses. With considerable effort, she controlled her taut nerves and turned to face him.

'No, Rob, you're wrong. I love Arthur.'

He gave a half laugh. 'You're in love with your career, woman! Arthur is just someone to lean on... and for respectable sex. We both know that. Even Arthur knows it. You're still working for us because you need me to fulfil your dreams. You'll only achieve fulfilment from doing what you love, and I'm the only one who can guarantee to give it to you.'

'You don't know Arthur. He awakened me to love. You don't know what real love is, or you wouldn't say that.'

'Don't I?'

She looked up at him and felt the intensity of his gaze. Suddenly, she saw him in a new light. Apart from lust, there was pain and longing in that look. At last she truly understood, and a thrill, a chilling mixture of sexual excitement and awe, ran down her spine.

As he drew closer, they continued to communicate eye-to-eye. He put his arms around her and slowly their lips came together. She felt the power of his earthy love, and she was afraid. Not that he might rape her again, but that she would put up no resistance if he tried.

She pressed her hands against his chest. 'No, Rob. I love Arthur, and tomorrow we marry. Let me go,' she pleaded. 'Please let me go.'

But he pulled her closer to him. She felt his heart thundering in his breast, no less than the beating of her own.

'See what you do to me,' he whispered, his voice shaking a little.

Her mind was yelling at her to push him away again, but she refused to obey. Her body was on fire with lust for him. She stopped struggling and parted her lips in open surrender to his kisses. She found herself flowing into him, deeper and deeper...

He suddenly released her and stepped back with his arms open. His dark eyes glinted beneath their heavy brows.

'You see, June, I'm not holding you here. You've been free to leave for ages but you can't bear to go. You belong here with me... you know you do. I'm the only one who can give you what you really want... what you crave: recognition, success, fame – the thrill of flying high. I set free your creative genius and without me it will die. Our souls are united, and so are our bodies. You may not love me, but you want me... you need me. You may be going through that door today, but you'll be back. The door will always be open for you and you'll walk straight in... and straight back to me!'

'Am I interrupting something?'

It was Rob's father, in an obvious hurry. He handed her a document.

'This is your new contract, June. It's just as we agreed. Perhaps you would like to sign it before you go?'

Trying to control her shaking, she looked at the document being placed in her hand. John Watson's sudden arrival may have restored her reasoning, but her emotions were still raw. Everything Rob had faced her with was true, and that made her fear for her future with Arthur. She came to a quick decision.

'Thank you for the offer, Mr Watson, but tomorrow I'll be making a different kind of contract, and will be unable to honour this one.'

While the men stood in shocked silence, she tore the contract in half and threw the pieces in the wastebasket. Then she snatched up her bag and coat and hurriedly left the office. With determination, she closed her ears to all sounds. She did not look back.

Arthur was waiting to take her home in his shiny black Jaguar. He stepped out and helped her into the passenger seat. She told him about tearing up the new contract and what she had said to Mr Watson.

Arthur touched her eager face and kissed her tenderly. 'It took a lot of courage to do that, my darling. I'm really proud of you.'

They set off home. Arthur smiled to himself. Their love had stood many a test. He could be certain, beyond all doubt, that June truly loved him and that she was the woman he'd waited for all his life. But he was also certain that he knew more about his wife-to-be than she did about herself, and he was already planning for her future.

Epilogue

June sat at the huge desk in the study and looked at the calendar. It would have been their eighteenth anniversary tomorrow. Sounds of laughter came from the garden and she looked out of the window to see her four children playing tennis. It pleased her to know that joy could live with pain.

She rocked back in her chair and let her mind return to those early days when she had first met Arthur. She quickly traced the exquisite moment of that first kiss. Then she delved into her memories to recall how Arthur had cast out shame and fear and awakened her to love. She sighed; such golden treasure untarnished by time.

She looked around the room and thought of the house as it had been before they – the second Mr and Mrs Arthur Rogers – had taken it over. On the whole, not much had changed to the family home.

She smiled as she remembered the cosy room at the back of the kitchen where Arthur had made tender love to her. That room was now a bedsit for Nanny Joyce, her housekeeper.

And there was Kate's flat where her sister-in-law had entertained her lover. That had now become the workrooms where her skilled staff interpreted and produced her personally designed garments for a discerning clientele.

The room at the back of the house where she had once stitched for Mary Rogers had been extended and altered several times, and was now her studio where she designed fabrics, dresses and lingerie. She recalled how, fifteen years earlier, Arthur had negotiated with Robert Watson for her to have her own label – 'June Rogers Originals' – with the garments being sold exclusively in his growing fashion empire. Dear Arthur, he always knew her needs.

She looked with sadness at the pile of condolence letters still waiting for her to read. She wanted to personally acknowledge each one, but it was so difficult. There were letters from people in all walks of life: fellow officers and men who had served with Arthur throughout the bloody campaigns; European diplomats and men of high rank in Parliament and Ministry; senior staff from a number of companies; friends, neighbours, and people he'd faithfully served in his Parliamentary Constituency.

How her dear Arthur was loved and admired. Friends and opponents alike spoke of his brilliance in diplomacy. Many people wrote of his financial acumen, and of his ability to organise down to the finest detail. They all said he was a born leader, and a man of high moral character, always indefatigable and courageous in battle, especially in his long fight against his final illness.

June turned to the card that lay apart from the rest. Once more she picked it up to read the simple message written below the formal printed one.

'The door is still open. Start to live again.'

'The door is still open…' She had a flashback to a single night of passionate madness ten years earlier, and the memory brought her body alive. It was an instinctive response over which she had no control, flowing as it did from the depths of her creative being. Even in her sorrow, her over-excited nerves rippled as she fought to control her thoughts and emotions.

She looked at her children in the garden. Young James was playing the fool. James… Every day he grew more like his true father. One day he would have to be told the truth.

'But not yet, Arthur. I can't. It's too soon,' she whispered aloud.

A feeling of weariness swept over her. She put her head in her hands and let the tears flow.

After she had recovered, she picked up her pen ready to write. But the words would not come. She looked at the photograph before her.

'My darling Arthur, what am I to do?'

Too engrossed in her thoughts, she didn't hear the footsteps until her visitor had entered the room. She sensed his presence behind her back just before he placed his comforting hands on her shoulders.

His voice was gentle. 'Hello, June.'

She stood up and turned to face him.

'Charlie, how lovely to see you.'

His eyes searched her face, as though fearful of deepening her wound. 'Before he died, Arthur asked me to come to you,' he said tenderly.

'Oh Charlie, my dearest Charlie. My Arthur's faithful lieutenant.'

'Not any more, June. I'm just someone who loves you – who's always loved you.'

He enclosed her troubled face in his sensitive hands and kissed away her tears.

Gladys Hobson was born and bred within five miles of Nottingham. Without qualifications, she trained as a dress designer. After the birth of her three children she gained an interest in education and was accepted for training at Loughborough College of Education. Interested in spirituality and pastoral care, she took early retirement and trained for church ministry. Now living in Cumbria with her husband, she spends most of her time writing.

Gladys Hobson is the author of When Phones Were Immobile and Lived in RED BOXES.
An illustrated book of childhood memories 1939-1953
ISBN 978-0-9548885-0-3

Her novels include:

Blazing Embers (Angela Ashley)
ISBN 978-0-9548885-2-7

When Angels Lie, all hell is let loose and demons fly! (Richard L Gray)
ISBN 978-0-9548885-1-0

In partnership with Yorkshire poet, Bob Taylor, she has edited and contributed to Northern Lights, an illustrated anthology of poems and short stories.
ISBN 978-0-9548885-5-8

Magpies Nest Publishing:
www.magpiesnestpublishing.co.uk